the
SOLDIER'S
LADY

4 Historical Stories

SUSANNE DIETZE, JANETTE FOREMAN,
GABRIELLE MEYER, LORNA SEILSTAD

BARBOUR BOOKS
An Imprint of Barbour Publishing, Inc.

THE COLONEL'S DAUGHTER

by Gabrielle Meyer

Dedication

To my dear friend and fellow museum addict, Erica Vetsch.
I'm so thankful we discovered one another on this writing journey.
You're one of the greatest gifts God has given me as a writer.

Historical Note

When doing research on Fort Snelling in modern-day St. Paul in my home state of Minnesota, I discovered that Zachary Taylor (future twelfth president of the United States) was the commanding officer there between 1828 and 1829. When he left, he went to Fort Crawford in Prairie du Chien, Michigan Territory. There, he met his second-in-command, Jefferson Davis (who would later become the president of the Confederate States of America). Jefferson Davis was described as a "handsome, witty, sportful, and altogether captivating" graduate of West Point Academy, and Taylor liked him immensely. At Fort Crawford, Davis met and fell in love with Taylor's daughter, Sarah Knox Taylor, who was a well-known beauty. They wished to be married and sought her father's permission, but Taylor refused. He did not want his daughter to live the difficult life of a military wife on the frontier. Davis loved Sarah (also known as Knoxie) so much, he chose to resign from the military, and he and Sarah were married on June 17, 1835 (six years after they met). They moved to a farm near Vicksburg, Mississippi, on land Davis's brother gave him.

I wish they'd lived happily ever after, but just two days short of their three-month anniversary, Sarah died from malaria while on their wedding trip. Davis was devastated and deeply mourned her death for eight years, to the dismay of his family and friends. Eventually, he married Varina Howell in 1845, and together they had six children. Davis rejoined the military, and in 1847 he served as a colonel under the command of Zachary Taylor in the Battle of Buena Vista during the Mexican-American War. He became a senator from Mississippi in 1848, secretary of war under President Franklin Pierce in 1853, and finally president of the Confederate States of America in 1861.

It was this true-life story that inspired Nathaniel and Ally's journey in *The Colonel's Daughter*. When I read sad stories, such as this one, there's a part of me that wants to rewrite the ending, and so I have.

Chapter One

Fort Snelling, Michigan Territory
June 1828

A light knock was the only warning Major Nathaniel Ward had before Lieutenant Dunn entered his office and upended his life. "The steamboat *Clarion* has just arrived, sir."

Nathaniel capped the inkwell and set his pen down beside the report he'd been working on. He stood from his desk and stretched his lower back, thankful for the chance to take a break. "I knew it would arrive today or tomorrow." The boat would be full of supplies and a dozen new soldiers from Jefferson Barracks in St. Louis. Supplies were in desperate need after the long winter and would be welcomed. "I'll be along presently to oversee the unloading."

The lieutenant's lean face was filled with apprehension. "They've brought passengers, four to be precise, and of a very *delicate* nature."

It wasn't unusual for the steamboats to bring passengers. Settlers, tourists, and speculators often came to Fort Snelling by way of steamboat up the Mississippi River. Some just passed through on their journey further north, while others stayed outside the fort in one of the few boardinghouses available.

"Are they ill?" Nathaniel asked. The last thing they needed was an epidemic. With the recent unrest between the Dakota and Chippewa Indians, the post's commander, Colonel Benson, had more than his share of trouble. Even now, he was meeting with a Chippewa chief at a lodge near St. Anthony Falls, seven miles up the Mississippi River from the fort. Nathaniel had stayed behind to await the new soldiers and supplies.

"No, sir, quite the opposite. They're disembarking now and will need to be escorted here straightaway."

Nathaniel was growing tired of the lieutenant's evasive responses. "Who are they? Dignitaries of some kind? They didn't send word of their imminent arrival. We are not prepared." He reached for his black shako and set it atop his head as he started for the door, a list of orders already formulating in his mind.

Lieutenant Dunn shook his head, sweat beading his brow. The man was usually easygoing and unruffled, even in battle. But something had shaken him. "It's the colonel's wife and daughters, sir."

A gust of wind pushed against Nathaniel from the open door at the same moment the lieutenant blurted out the news. "The colonel's family?"

"Yes, sir." Dunn stood at attention, his eyes betraying his disquiet. "And they've already caused quite a stir, if I may say so. The entire wharf is in chaos."

And the fort would be too, if the colonel's stories about his daughters were true.

In battle, quick decisions were the responsibility of the commanding officer. Since the colonel was absent from the fort, the task lay on Nathaniel's shoulders. "We must take the situation under control." He slipped his sword into the scabbard on his left hip and stepped out of his quarters, speaking to the lieutenant as he walked.

"Make haste to the colonel's home and let his staff know Mrs. Benson has arrived. They will not have much time to prepare, but there's little we can do about that now. I will go to the wharf and welcome them."

"Yes, sir." The lieutenant nodded, relief on his face. No doubt the man was eager to hand the responsibility to Nathaniel. He saluted and rushed off to warn the colonel's staff.

The fort had been built to help control the fur trade in the area and was quite large for a frontier post. Built on a high bluff at the confluence of the Minnesota and Mississippi Rivers, the fort was shaped like a diamond with the tip of one point looking over the high bluff and the rivers. At that tip was the commanding officer's elegant quarters. At the outer tips were batteries, and along the four sides were officers' quarters, several barracks, the commissary, a hospital, and more. In the center of it all was the green parade ground. Everything ran in perfect order under the command of Colonel Edward Benson, whose family was suddenly descending upon the fort.

For early June, the sun was remarkably warm as Nathaniel left the gatehouse, calling for a wagon to be deployed. No doubt four women would need the assistance of a vehicle, not only to make the trek up the steep hill, but for their luggage. Nathaniel didn't have sisters, and his mother had died when he was born, but he'd seen enough officers' wives to know they came with more gewgaws and trinkets than they could ever use. Trunks and trunks full of them. It was enough to make a man squirm—even a seasoned soldier like himself.

Women, in general, were a mystery to Nathaniel. With no females in his household growing up, he'd only observed them from afar in school, at church, and in the community—and what he'd observed usually left him confused and befuddled. Emotions seemed to rule the day where females were concerned. A more disconcerting thing he could not imagine. As soon as Nathaniel turned eighteen, he'd left for West Point where he'd been surrounded by order, discipline, and reason.

Emotions were never taken into consideration on a military post, and he liked it that way.

As he walked down the steep embankment to the wharf far below the fort, Nathaniel looked for signs of the impending group. The fort was not without women. On the contrary, there were always a few milling about at any given moment. Wives and daughters of officers and enlisted men, as well as washerwomen and servants. There were also Indian women and fur traders' wives who came and went. But Nathaniel usually kept his distance from all of them, save the officers' wives who occasionally invited him to dine with them and to attend the weekly entertainments they hosted. They felt a keen responsibility to pair Nathaniel with a wife, but he had yet to meet someone he wanted to pursue.

He'd determined that women were fine—at a distance, but they rarely fit the mold of his orderly and disciplined life.

The *Clarion* was docked, and Captain Tonder stood overseeing the new troops. Several noticed Nathaniel's approach and saluted him. He nodded acknowledgment as he moved toward the clutch of females standing just beyond the gangplank on dry ground. From his vantage point, all he could see was a mass of colorful gowns, large hats, and piles of luggage.

The oldest woman, and the only plump one among them, was ordering several privates about, pointing at the trunks and bags, her commanding voice high above the other sounds on the wharf. "I want everything brought to the colonel's quarters, posthaste, and do be careful with the trunks. The last time they were manhandled at Jefferson Barracks, one of the trunks was dropped and it cracked. You can imagine my dismay, so do not disappointment me, young man."

Bright pink, purple, green, and blue gowns stood out in stark contrast to the browns and yellows of the landscape all around them. Flowers, feathers, and other plumage swayed in the breeze above their hats, and frilly parasols popped up, like gunshots. *Bang, bang, bang.*

Nathaniel almost flinched.

"Ally, your parasol." The older woman tsked at the one not holding a parasol. "Do you want to be freckled by mid-July? The sun is our bitter foe. I will not have you throwing away everything you've learned at finishing school, just because we're on the frontier."

The woman in question—the one without the parasol—turned and sighed. She pulled a parasol out of nowhere and popped it up, setting the handle on her shoulder.

Nathaniel had heard rumors of Colonel Benson's daughters and their great beauty, but he'd only thought them to be tall tales, repeated by lonely soldiers. One glimpse of them now told Nathaniel otherwise.

"Ah, Major." The older woman caught his eye and marched toward him, more formidable than any enemy Nathaniel had ever encountered. He had an overwhelming desire to call out to his men to retreat. Instead, he held his ground. "Has my husband sent you to retrieve us?" she asked.

All three of the younger women turned to look at him then, each one as beautiful as the next, and each shockingly different from the other. One had blond ringlets and stunning blue eyes, the second had thick auburn hair and chocolate-brown eyes, and the third had hair as black as a raven and dark brown eyes to match. It was hard to ascertain which one was the oldest or the youngest, but it was clear the rumors were true.

Nathaniel bowed before Mrs. Benson, finding it difficult to

formulate words as all four ladies stared at him. "Major Nathaniel Ward, at your service, ma'am. I've taken the liberty of ordering a wagon for your use. The colonel is currently away from the fort, but he should arrive back within the day."

"Very good." Mrs. Benson had the same brown eyes as two of the daughters. "He will no doubt be surprised to see us. It would be nice to settle in before he returns." She motioned toward the young ladies. "May I present the colonel's daughters? Miss Jeanne, Miss Constance, and Miss Allyson."

The blond bobbed a curtsy first, the raven haired second, and the auburn one third.

"Ally," the auburn-haired creature corrected her mother as she met Nathaniel's gaze, her clear brown eyes smiling. "You may call me Ally."

"*Miss* Ally," her mother said with authority.

Thankfully, the wagon stopped nearby after their brief introductions, and Nathaniel made himself busy ordering some privates to load the luggage. He then helped the women to climb up into the conveyance.

As each one passed him, he was overwhelmed with scents foreign to the rough outpost. Rose, lavender, vanilla, and other feminine aromas he couldn't begin to discern. Their flounces and ribbons fluttered, and their wide skirts needed to be artfully managed as they maneuvered around. Everything about them seemed superfluous and exhausting.

When everyone was settled, including Nathaniel, who decided to accompany them, he finally had his wits properly under control again. And that's when he noticed the upheaval brought upon by the Bensons' arrival. Soldiers, hungry for female companionship, gawked at them. Fur traders, with few manners and less formality, called out to them. And Indians, familiar with the less colorful fort women, stared in open curiosity.

Mrs. Benson turned her nose up at the lot of them. Miss Jeanne and Miss Constance preened under the attention. But Miss Ally did neither. Her gaze roamed over the fort, the river, the landscape, and the ramshackle buildings as if she were taking a drink after being in a parched land.

She took it all in, and then her eyes landed on Nathaniel—and she smiled.

It nearly unseated him.

Ally Benson was starved for the frontier. It was home to her and always would be. St. Louis, though it wasn't as large as Philadelphia or New York, was much too crowded for her taste. A person couldn't breathe in the city. But here, on the edge of civilization, there was room to let her imagination soar.

A bright blue sky domed overheard with a few wispy white clouds spread out like a brush of paint against a vivid canvas. The bluff jutted up at her right, where the rivers joined. The Mississippi bent out of sight around the opposite side of the bluff, but the Minnesota River continued on as far as she could see like a brown, silken ribbon. The ramshackle buildings outside the fort were much like the ones she was accustomed to as a child growing up in one fort after the other. It wasn't until she turned eight that her mother had removed them to St. Louis permanently. And though they'd been living in the growing city for ten years, it had never felt like home—not like life at a fort.

"I hope you'll find Fort Snelling to your liking." Major Ward spoke to Mama, though his gaze traveled over Ally and her sisters. As the youngest of the three, Ally often felt overshadowed by her older sisters, but he let his eyes rest on her for a moment longer than necessary. Not Jeanne. Not Constance. Her.

She felt the first hint of a blush warm her cheeks at the attention.

"I imagine it's much like all the others," Mama said with pursed lips. "Dirty, uncivilized, and dangerous." She rarely let an opportunity pass without airing her strong opinions, especially to a new audience. "I loathe and abhor fort life. It's not meant for delicate constitutions." Which is why Mama had given up following Papa from fort to fort ten years ago. She'd done so for the first twelve years of their marriage, giving Papa four daughters, one year after the other, but could not continue. She had wanted to return to her home in Boston but had settled on St. Louis, being close enough to visit Papa from time to time.

"My eldest daughter, Laura, married a fort doctor two years ago," Mama continued, assuming that Major Ward was interested. He gave her his undivided attention, suggesting he was a gentleman, but she doubted he cared about Laura or her abysmal life. "Her husband is stationed in Texas. She writes to me often, and her letters are so forlorn and melancholy, I have a mind to march to Texas and bring her home." Mama's greatest fault was being too candid with people, especially strangers. Ally would have moaned if she weren't used to her mother. "But I won't." Mama shook her head. "Because I warned Laura about being married to a military man." She cast a look at her three unmarried daughters. "And now she must live with the dire consequences."

Jeanne and Constance rolled their eyes, and Ally did her best to ignore her mother. They were all painfully aware of her opinions about marrying into the military. She had forbidden each of them, in no uncertain terms, which had prompted Laura's scandalous elopement with Dr. Sandford. Now, two years later, with one baby born and another on the way, Mama was almost gloating at Laura's remorse.

Major Ward opened his mouth, as if he was going to offer his condolences, but he snapped his mouth shut instead.

Smart man.

"Major Ward," Constance said as she twirled her parasol, "have you been at Fort Snelling long?"

"I arrived soon after your father a year ago." He sat with perfect posture, his back straight and tight, his uniform spotless. "Before Fort Snelling, I was at Fort Crawford near Prairie du Chien." His blue eyes were restless as they scanned the area, a habit she'd witnessed in other military men over the years. Always searching, watching, waiting.

Constance continued to ramble on as the mules pulled the loaded wagon up the hill to the fort gates. Within minutes, her sister had already set her eyes on her next conquest: Major Nathaniel Ward. The poor man. He looked completely out of his realm of experience where her sister was concerned, but once Constance or Jeanne had their sights set, their prey was as good as caught.

Ally couldn't blame Constance. The major was a very handsome man, but looks weren't everything, as Ally had learned with some of the men who had called on her. The officers and enlisted men would keep Constance and Jeanne busy all summer, and her mother would stay occupied trying to dissuade them, but Ally had much bigger plans.

She'd come to Fort Snelling for one reason, and one reason only. She planned to talk her father into letting her stay. Permanently. She had no wish to return to St. Louis and face the husband-hunting season her mother had planned. She was now eighteen, which meant she was of marriageable age. If she had been born a male, she would have already been sent to West Point, or some other military school, and would be preparing for a life of adventure. But she'd been born a girl, much to her and her father's dismay, and had no say in what her life might look like.

Unless her father sided with her. Then Mama couldn't say no. But when had Papa ever gone against Mama's wishes?

They passed through the gates and entered the parade grounds. Ally inhaled a deep breath, the scent of gunpowder, boiling laundry, and woodsmoke filling her lungs. At the apex of the fort stood a beautiful one-story limestone house with quoins at the corners. The hipped roof boasted four chimneys, two on either side, and a stepped stone parapet rose from the lower edges of the roof directly over the front door where a semicircular fanlight window gave relief to the limestone. Three windows flanked the door on either side. It was at once charming and elegant.

"I'm happy to see the house is acceptable," Mama said to no one in particular. "Just as the colonel said in his letters."

"I believe you'll find it to your liking," Major Ward said. "The kitchen and cellar are in the basement, with a walkout, allowing proper ventilation for the staff."

Mama crossed her arms and lifted her chin as they came to a stop at the house. "It hardly matters how lovely or properly ventilated the home when it's surrounded by the frontier."

Poor Major Ward. If Ally was correct, the man was very good at his job. He wouldn't be a major at such a young age if he wasn't. But the look of complete and utter mystification on his face was almost comical. She pressed her lips together in case a giggle tried to escape. She'd seen it a dozen times. Staid and stoic military men coming apart in Harriet Benson's presence.

The wagon had not even stopped before Major Ward disembarked, as if he couldn't wait to be done with his task. Several enlisted men were summoned to help unload the luggage, while the major assisted the ladies from the wagon. Ally was the last to get out, and the major looked up at her for a split second before he offered his hand. They were both wearing gloves, but at his touch, a pleasant shiver ran up the length of her arm. His gaze snapped to hers, and she wondered if he'd felt it too.

She pulled away, a bit shaken, and whispered her thank-you.

The front door opened, and an older woman and man stepped out to greet the new arrivals.

"I'm Mr. Delany and this is my wife, Mrs. Delany," the man said with a bow. "It is our pleasure to serve Colonel Benson, as well as his family."

Mrs. Delany offered a tight curtsy, and Mama acknowledged them with a simple nod of her head.

"We're sorry we didn't have more time to prepare," Mrs. Delany said, her eyes filled with displeasure. "The colonel didn't tell us you'd be coming."

"He didn't know," Mama said. "I made the decision very last minute. There wasn't time to alert him."

"Then you'll have to excuse us if things aren't as you'd like."

"There will be time enough to make things right." Mama made introductions, and then Mr. and Mrs. Delany led them into the house.

The large central hall had a room on either side. To the left was the dining room and to the right a parlor. Directly ahead was a handsome staircase that led to storage under the attic, and behind the public rooms were two bedrooms and Papa's office. Mama's things were brought to Papa's room, and the other would be shared by the sisters.

Major Ward stood in the hall while everything was unloaded and put in its proper place and while Mama made an inspection of the home. Jeanne and Constance followed Mama about, commenting on the house as she did, making their opinions known. The three of them sounded like hens clucking in a roost.

Ally stayed in the hall with Major Ward, as uninterested in her mother's and sisters' opinions as he appeared.

"May I ask where my father has gone?" she finally ventured to say to the tall officer.

"He has gone to St. Anthony Falls to speak to Chief Eshke-bugecoshe. I expect him back soon."

The sooner the better, Ally decided, for both the major and herself.

Chapter Two

As soon as propriety allowed, Nathaniel had excused himself to allow the Bensons to settle into their new home. He'd gone back to his quarters and stood guard at the window the rest of the afternoon, one eye on the commandant's home, the other on the fort gate, praying the colonel would soon return.

He didn't have to wait long before the colonel appeared with the retinue of soldiers he'd taken to the falls. Nathaniel quickly donned his shako and put his sword back in its scabbard before exiting his quarters to meet with his commander.

"I've been informed," Colonel Benson said as he met up with Nathaniel, a gleam of pleasure in his blue eyes. He walked quickly across the parade grounds, no doubt in a hurry to see his wife and daughters. "It's been two years since I saw them last." A cloud shifted over his clear gaze. "A calamitous time for them to come, I'll grant, with the recent unrest, but a welcome surprise." His face cleared again as he looked over at Nathaniel. "You've met them?"

"I have, sir." Nathaniel could not hide the horror from his voice. Mrs. Benson and the young Miss Bensons—at least the two older Miss Bensons—were sentimental, emotional, and erratic. And he'd only spent thirty minutes in their presence.

Thankfully, Miss Ally didn't seem to fit with the others, a fact that he'd thought about all afternoon. If he had to guess, he'd say Miss Ally took after her father in that regard, though he hadn't spent enough time with her to know for certain.

Colonel Benson laughed. "Mrs. Benson is a woman who knows her own mind. Don't let her frighten you. She uses her tongue to control a world she doesn't always understand. You'll grow used to it."

Nathaniel wasn't sure he wanted to. As the colonel's second-in-command, he spent a great deal of time with his commanding officer—which meant he'd probably spend time with his family as well. Nathaniel's relationship with his father had been cold and distant. His birth had been the cause of his mother's death, and his father had never forgiven him. Through the years, Nathaniel had been blessed with several mentors and friends in the army, but none who had taken him under his wing like Colonel Benson. The man took his job very seriously and demanded utmost respect and discipline, but he was also kind and thoughtful. The closest thing Nathaniel had ever had to a loving father.

"Is there anything I can do for you?" Nathaniel asked just before they arrived at the colonel's house.

"Come to dine with us and then we'll speak further." Colonel Benson stopped. "There's much to discuss about my meeting with the chief—and about my family's arrival." He glanced at the house briefly before looking back at Nathaniel. "I have a feeling my wife will have a few orders to give as well."

Nathaniel couldn't help but smile as he saluted the colonel.

For two hours, Nathaniel tried to keep busy, waiting for the appointed supper hour. When the bugle finally blew, he was prepared to see the colonel's family. He had shaved, washed, and put on a fresh uniform. His white wool pants and dark blue wool coatee were brushed, and his tall black boots were polished. His baldric, the leather belt he wore over his shoulder to hold his scabbard at his side, had been oiled. But it wasn't only his uniform that was prepared. This time he felt mentally ready to face the flush of females.

At least, he hoped he was ready.

It was only a few long strides from the three rooms Nathaniel lived in on the officers' row to the colonel's front door. The sun was still hanging in the sky, the summer solstice not far off. They would enjoy light until close to ten. Nathaniel much preferred the long days of summer over the short, cold days of winter.

"Welcome, Major Ward," Mr. Delany said when he answered the door. "The colonel is waiting for you in his office."

The colonel's wife and daughters could be heard in their bedrooms preparing for supper, so Nathaniel bypassed them and knocked on the door leading to the colonel's office at the back corner of the house, behind the dining room.

"Come in, Major." The colonel motioned to a chair in front of his desk. "My wife never did follow the sound of the bugle, but I'm happy the ladies are running late. I need to speak to you before we join them."

Nathaniel took the chair offered to him and removed his hat. He set it in his lap and waited.

Colonel Benson was a fit man, with graying hair at his temples and the constitution of a bull. He was a formidable adversary but a stalwart companion to his friends. When he leveled his gaze on Nathaniel, there was something like an apology in the depths of his eyes.

"I have new orders for you, Major." Colonel Benson closed the book on his desk and clasped his hands. "My wife's arrival has necessitated some changes, and she has made a request I cannot deny."

Unease clawed at Nathaniel's chest as he waited for the colonel to continue.

"Mrs. Benson and my daughters will stay with us for the next six weeks, but at the end of those six weeks, she has every intention of boarding the steamboat and returning to St. Louis, with all three of my daughters in tow."

"A reasonable plan." Nathaniel wouldn't expect anything less.

"Yes, one would think." The colonel rose and walked to the window. He stared outside for a moment. "However, both you and I know the lure of a pretty woman. My daughters are charming and a bit naive, a poor combination at a frontier post." He looked back at Nathaniel. "They are also of a marriageable age. My wife fears they will succumb to romance here at the fort. Our oldest eloped to marry a military surgeon, and my wife does not want any of our other daughters to follow in her footsteps."

Nathaniel wanted to ask why she had bothered to come to the fort if she feared such a fate, but he refrained. It wasn't unusual that she and her daughters would like to see their husband and father.

"When they return to St. Louis, she hopes to marry them off to bankers, merchants, or other businessmen. I daresay she has her mind made up." His smile was rueful and a bit disappointed. "She knows firsthand the danger and depravity of living on the frontier. I do not blame her for her feelings."

Still uncertain how this concerned him, Nathaniel didn't respond.

"With the Indian unrest and the trouble we're having with the fur traders of late, I will not have the time, or ability, to keep my daughters and wife entertained or guarded at all times." Colonel Benson smiled at Nathaniel. "That will be your job."

Nathaniel's pulse accelerated. "Me?"

"Yes. I trust you more than anyone else at the fort. If I cannot be with my family, you're the only man I'd ask." The colonel paced back to the desk, his hands behind his back. "From now, until they depart, I want you to keep an eye on all four. Whenever they leave the house, I would ask that you guard them and keep them safe. If any of my daughters show even the slightest romantic inclinations, it will be your job to snuff them out and report to me. I will do my best when I am with them, but when I cannot be here, it will fall upon your shoulders."

There was nothing Nathaniel could do but acquiesce to his commander's orders, but surely the colonel must know he wasn't the man for the job. "Are you certain you want me to undertake this very delicate and important position?" He clutched his shako. "I have very little experience with women. I wouldn't know what to do with them."

Colonel Benson laughed, the sound ricocheting off the walls. "They'll tell you what they want, have no fear. You won't be left guessing with this lot."

A knock sounded at the door. "Papa?" came a gentle voice.

"Ah, Ally." The colonel's face softened as he opened his office door. His auburn-haired daughter stood just outside with a sweet smile.

"May I come in?" she asked.

"Of course, my dear." He allowed her to step into his embrace. "Have you met Major Ward?"

"Yes, earlier today." She turned her smile on him, and it had the same effect as before.

He quickly rose and gave her a short bow. "It's nice to see you again, Miss Benson."

"Ally, please," she said. "Unless we're with Mama, and then it's Miss Ally, I suppose."

The colonel smiled down at her, his affection for his youngest daughter shining from his eyes. "Or you could call her Pumpkin, as I do."

"Papa." She swatted playfully at his chest. "No one may call me that, except you—and only when I was a child."

"Is supper ready?" he asked.

"Yes. Mama sent me in to tell you she's in the parlor waiting." Ally's brown eyes were filled with curiosity. "But she said to make sure you don't join us unless you've spoken to Major Ward about her request." Ally glanced curiously at Nathaniel.

"We've had an opportunity to speak," Colonel Benson said. "And I believe the major is prepared for his task."

Nathaniel wasn't and didn't think he'd ever be, but what choice did he have? "Of course, sir."

"Good. Shall we join the others?"

"Papa, I have a request to make as well," Ally said before they left the office. "Perhaps you could make a little time to discuss it with me after supper?"

The colonel nodded. "For you, anything."

Nathaniel followed his commanding officer out of the office, both honored and dismayed to be tasked with protecting his most precious possessions.

If anything happened to the Benson women on Nathaniel's watch, he was guaranteed a demotion.

"It has been a most pleasurable evening." Major Ward stood near the open front door, his shako in his hands as the Benson family fanned out around him. He bowed and then made his departure, but not before glancing in Ally's direction one last time and tipping his head in farewell.

Ally stood between her mother and Constance. Her cheeks grew warm at the extra bit of attention. The major's blue eyes were so attractive, a burst of butterflies took flight in her stomach.

Papa closed the door and turned his attention on his wife and daughters. "I think you've scared the poor fellow. I wouldn't be surprised if he snuck off in the middle of the night and deserted the army."

"Really, Edward." Mama smiled, and Ally suspected she knew exactly how she came off to the major. "He looks like he's made of sterner stuff than that. A few females shouldn't concern him."

Constance swept into the drawing room, sending a scathing look toward Ally. "He hardly noticed me."

"And all the better." Mama followed Constance. "I'll not have an officer turning your head this summer."

"But the major is so handsome," Constance said. "How could I not notice?"

"Edward?" Mama sent a beseeching look toward her husband.

"You know how your mother feels," Papa said to Constance. "You must obey her. Major Ward is the finest officer I know, and any of you would be fortunate to find a husband like him, but Mama has other plans for you. Outside the military."

Constance pouted and fell dramatically to the sofa. Jeanne, just ten months younger than Constance, sat gently beside her, an air of indifference about her countenance. "If I were to bother with an officer," she said, "I wouldn't choose Papa's second-in-command, though he is handsome. I would find one of the men whom he *doesn't* approve of. Wouldn't that be more fun?"

"No more of this talk." Mama took a seat in the drawing room and lifted a piece of needlework into her hands. "Even in jest it isn't pleasant."

"Papa." Ally touched her father's sleeve and spoke quietly, hoping to gain his attention before he settled in with Mama. "May I have a word with you now?"

"Of course."

"In your office?"

"What's this?" Mama looked up from her handiwork.

"Ally and I have a few things to discuss." Papa put his hand under Ally's elbow to lead her away.

"Secret tactics, I wonder?" Mama asked.

"Perhaps." Papa smiled and directed Ally to his office, taking up a candle from the dining room as they passed through.

Night had fallen and with it the quiet sounds of wide-open spaces. As far as Ally could see, beyond the windows overlooking the bluff, was darkness. There were no lights, no wagons, no buildings, or people. Just space. Wonderful, breathtaking space.

Papa closed the door behind Ally and set the candle on his desk. The light sent shadows dancing around the edges of the small room. He held a chair for her and then took a seat next to hers. "What is it you want to discuss, my dear?"

For as long as Ally could remember, she and her father had been close. As a little girl, she had followed him wherever she could, went riding, hunting, and fishing with him. She learned all she could about the military to speak to him about the things that interested him—and, in return, he had shown an interest in the books she loved, the games she enjoyed, and the dreams she carried in her heart. When she was younger, she had wished to be a boy, so she could follow in his footsteps and become an officer. But her mother had feared over Ally's interest in the military and had settled them in St. Louis, hoping to rid her youngest daughter of her fascination.

It had done the opposite.

Tears pricked the back of her eyes as she finally faced her father—the one person who understood her above all others. "I've been so miserable."

Concern tightened the corners of Papa's eyes as he took Ally's hands in his own. "What's this?"

"I despise St. Louis and Madame Lansbury's School for Young Women." She refused to let the tears gather and fall. A soldier would never cry. "I loathe the city and long for the open frontier."

"Your letters have said nothing about your unhappiness. Why didn't you say something?"

"What would be the point? Mama wanted me to finish my schooling." She took a deep breath. "But now that I'm done, I know what I want."

"Your mother has plans to find you a good husband. She wants to see you happily settled."

"Happily settled?" Ally tried not to sound cynical. "I could never be happy in St. Louis, or any other city." The ever-present, deep, gnawing feeling in her chest twisted at the thought. "I long for space to stretch out and explore. I miss the frontier with every breath I take. I miss military life."

Papa leaned back in his chair. "I think you've romanticized your childhood, Ally. The frontier is a harsh mistress. Very few women can handle the stark realities accompanied with military life. Your own moth—"

"Mama was raised in Boston with a grand home and a dozen servants. It was a hard transition for her—but I was not raised that way. Living in the city is a hard transition for me. My earliest memories are of frontier life. I've never been happier than at a fort, with you."

A gentle smile tilted Papa's lips, but his eyes were sad. "And I've never been happier than when you and your mother and sisters were with me."

Hope flickered to life, promising to fill the cavernous darkness in her heart. "A commander should have a hostess, should he not? One to entertain fort visitors and keep up the morale among his men?"

A knowing gleam filled her father's face as he removed his hands from Ally's and set them on his lap. "Ah, I think I see where this is going."

"I'm eighteen now," she said quickly. "If I were a boy, I would have a whole host of choices before me. I would not hesitate to follow you into the military."

"As I well know."

"I do not want the life Mama has planned for me." Ally tried not to sound desperate, but she couldn't deny the panic she felt at the idea. "I want to stay here, with you. I want to live on the frontier and do my part."

"Your part is to make your mother happy."

"Nothing makes her happy." A hard edge tinted her voice, and she immediately regretted it.

"Your mother has been greatly disappointed in life." Papa defended his wife, just as he should. "She did not know what she was agreeing to when she married me—and I was too selfish to warn her properly. I wanted to make her my wife, and I believed that our love would sustain her through any hardship or difficulty we might face." He couldn't meet Ally's gaze as he looked down at his hands. "I was wrong, but I vowed to do whatever I could to make her happy. If living in St. Louis, away from the fort, makes her happy, then I will bear the loneliness of having you all live away from me."

"But what about my unhappiness? Doesn't that mean something?"

"If your mother wants you to marry a stable, respectable man in the city, then I will support her choice." Papa finally looked at Ally, sadness in his gaze. "In the long run, you will thank us."

Ally tried not to let her disappointment show. She had known that she wasn't going to win the war with this one battle. There might be dozens more ahead of her, and she wouldn't retreat or give in to defeat now. "If I were to convince Mama to give me a trial run, to stay here with you once she returns to St. Louis, would you allow me to stay?"

"You know there is nothing on this earth that would make me happier." His gaze was so confident and steady, so full of love. "But it would take a miracle for your mother to agree to that plan, as you well know."

"But, if she did?"

"Of course I would allow you to stay."

The hope in her heart continued to sputter. "Then I shall speak to her and ask her for her permission."

"I would caution you." The expression on Papa's face reminded Ally of the look he had moments before he left the fort on a campaign. There was steadfast determination with a hint of concern. "Play your hand well, Ally, for you may only have one hand to play."

A smile tilted Ally's lips. "I am well aware of Mama's moods and her feelings, and I have spent a great deal of my life learning how to maneuver around her."

"Spoken like a true soldier." Pride shone in his voice.

"Who do you think convinced her to come and visit you this summer?" Ally grinned. "It took me weeks to make her think it was her idea."

Papa laughed. "And glad I am that you did." He stood and extended his hand. "Now, shall we rejoin them?"

Ally nodded and rose to follow him. So far, her strategy was working, but the hardest part of her battle was still ahead.

Chapter Three

The day was pleasant enough, though Nathaniel had taken little notice. Earlier that morning, during drill, the colonel's daughters had come outside to watch the men on the parade ground. It wasn't unusual for spectators to watch, but they rarely concerned Nathaniel. Today, however, he'd been so distracted, he'd almost failed to call out a formation. Several of the enlisted men had taken notice, if their raised brows and elbow ribbing was any indication.

It wasn't simply the presence of the Benson ladies that made Nathaniel nervous—it was his responsibilities toward them as well. After drill, the men had been released on fatigue duty, some to the gardens and fields, others to a building project, and still others to the sawmill. There had been rumors of a British fur trader working illegally to the north, and Nathaniel had sent a contingent of soldiers to investigate the report. He would have gone himself if the colonel hadn't needed him at the post.

"Will you wait to be summoned?" Captain Robert Tonder asked

from his seat beside Nathaniel's desk. "Or just show up at their front door to report for duty?"

"The colonel said they will let me know when I'm needed. With his early morning departure to meet with Chief Eshkebugecoshe again, I imagine I'll be summoned at some point." Nathaniel stood in front of his small mirror, wiping a wet towel over his neck and face to remove the dust from the parade ground. He examined his face as he ran his hands over his cheeks. Should he shave again?

Robert laughed. "I didn't think I'd see the day when a woman would capture your attention."

"What are you talking about?"

"Which one is it, then?" Robert leaned forward. "The blond? The raven-haired one?"

Nathaniel looked at the captain with a sharp gaze. "I'm not interested in any of them." His conscience caught on the half-truth. Miss Ally had more than caught his attention. She was so unlike her mother and sisters, he'd lain awake well after the last bugle call, thinking about her. There was something in her faraway gaze and quiet confidence that called to him. More than anything, he wanted to know if she was different from most of the other women he'd met, or if she was just as sensitive and excitable.

Something told him she was not.

"How could you not notice?" Robert asked. "No one can talk of anything else."

Nathaniel set the towel on a drying hook and turned to give the captain his full attention. "The colonel has asked me to keep my eye on them. If you've noticed my interest, it's because I've been commanded to give them my attention."

"Which you're doing quite well. I saw you on the parade ground. You've never been so distracted."

A knock sounded on the door. Nathaniel chose to ignore his

friend as he opened the door and found a private standing outside. "You've been summoned to the commandant's house."

"And so it begins." Robert stood, the red circles on his ruddy cheeks even brighter than usual. "Remember, you are the envy of every officer and enlisted man in this fort. Do not abuse your opportunity. We've all been warned to keep our distance, but you've been given unfettered access."

Nathaniel grabbed his shako and slid his sword into its sheath, his stomach turning a bit at the prospect of spending time in the Benson ladies' company again. What did they have in mind to do today? What, exactly, was his duty?

"If you could put a good word in the ear of the auburn-haired lass, I'd be most appreciative." Robert gazed past Nathaniel out the door toward the commandant's house. "Actually, any of them would do for my purposes."

Nathaniel straightened his back, his eyes narrowing. He and Robert had been good friends for years, having served together at Prairie du Chien, and he'd never demanded respect from the man, because it had never been an issue. For the first time, he spoke down to the captain. "I'll have you remember the colonel's orders. Keep to yourself and we'll have no trouble."

Robert's eyebrows lifted, but he did not respond.

Nathaniel stood by the door, indicating Robert should leave. "Go lend your assistance at the sawmill, Captain."

After a slight pause, Robert saluted Nathaniel and then left his quarters.

It was time to face the firing squad, or at least, that was what it felt like.

Nathaniel stepped out into the blazing sunshine and started toward the commandant's house. It wasn't simply the unpredictability of the women that troubled him. Miss Constance had paid him undue attention the night before during dinner. He'd never been good around flirtatious women. The last thing he wanted was to lead them on, yet he didn't want to be insulting either. He tended toward silence and feigned ignorance in those situations and then was often accused of being aloof.

Miss Ally, on the other hand, had been engaging and charming. If anything, Nathaniel had wanted more of her attention. She and her father had bantered, and though Colonel Benson had been good to draw Nathaniel into the conversation, he'd very much felt like an intruder on a family reunion the night before.

The front door opened before Nathaniel had a chance to knock.

"Major Ward, Mrs. Benson and the young ladies have been awaiting you." Mr. Delany opened the door wider and moved to the side for Nathaniel to enter.

"Ah, Major." Mrs. Benson and her daughters had their bonnets in place and were standing in the entry hall. Their hands were properly covered in gloves, and they held their closed parasols at the ready. "Here you are."

Nathaniel bowed before them. "At your service."

The three young ladies offered curtsies, and then Constance and Jeanne entwined their arms, whispering to each other as they smiled at Nathaniel.

Ally stood on her own, her dark pink gown accentuating her small waist and bringing color to her high cheekbones. She was even more beautiful than he remembered, her dark brown eyes sparkling with life and excitement. She smiled at him, and Nathaniel was afraid his heart might stop. What was the matter with him? He almost forgot the colonel's orders as he stared at her, but Mrs. Benson soon drew his attention away from her youngest daughter.

"We'd like to take a turn about the fort, if you please," the older woman said. "And with my husband gone, we have called upon you to give us a tour."

"I'd be honored." He belatedly realized he'd forgotten to remove his shako when he entered, which he rectified as he pulled it from his head now. "Anything you need."

She nodded. "In that case, there's to be a dance tomorrow night, and we'd like to extend the invitation to the officers and their wives as well."

"I will see that it's done."

"You'll be sure to come to the dance, won't you, Major Ward?" Constance asked.

Nathaniel glanced at their mother. "If I'm invited."

"Of course," she said.

"Then I would be honored." Though the thought of dancing with any of these beautiful women was a bit disconcerting. His dancing was barely passable, and he had a feeling the Benson sisters were properly trained.

"I do hope you'll save a dance or two for me," Constance said, batting her eyelashes.

"And me," Jeanne added.

"One dance each," Mrs. Benson warned. "And not another more."

Nathaniel nodded and couldn't help but glance at Ally. Would she save a dance for him as well?

She just watched him, her quiet confidence more attractive than all her sisters' flattery combined.

"Shall we go?" Mrs. Benson asked.

"I am at your disposal." Nathaniel opened the front door and motioned for them to pass.

"Parasols ready?" Mrs. Benson sent a pointed glance at Ally.

Ally sighed and was the last to pass Nathaniel as they stepped out of the house. She opened her parasol and set the handle upon her slender shoulder.

"I pray you have the patience of a saint, Major," she said under her breath. "You'll be in need of it today, I fear."

The ominous warning was tinted with a bit of humor, and Nathaniel couldn't help but smile.

"I have patience in abundance," he assured her.

She smiled at him. "I'm happy to hear it."

He closed the door and set his hat upon his head. "Where would you like to start?" he asked Mrs. Benson.

"Oh, I don't suppose it matters all that much. One fort is just like another."

"On the contrary, Mama." Ally tilted her parasol so she could see her mother. "Each fort has its own unique personality and attributes. Don't you think this one is quite lovely here on the bluff with the view of the rivers and the prairie lands?"

Mrs. Benson looked out at the view her daughter spoke about and sighed. "I suppose it is very beautiful."

"And safe, is it not, Major?" Ally turned to Nathaniel. "With these thick limestone walls and high vantage point, it's quite protected."

"One of the strongest forts on the frontier."

"My father said you have excellent relations with the Indians here and there's an abundance of food and natural resources for comfort." Ally's smile warmed her whole countenance. "There's not another fort like it."

"I suppose, if one was forced to live at a fort," Mrs. Benson conceded, "this one would be a pleasant place to reside."

"Quite so," Ally said, nodding her head for emphasis, a self-satisfied smile on her face.

"Shall I take you to the round tower?" Nathaniel asked. It was on the very opposite tip of the diamond-shaped fort. "It was the first structure completed on the fort eight years ago."

"Lead the way, Major."

Several officers came out of their quarters onto the long, narrow porch, tipping their hats to the ladies as they passed. A few of their wives also emerged, and Nathaniel was obliged to make introductions. Children played behind the officers' quarters, and a handful of girls sat in the shade of the porch and worked on sewing projects.

Constance and Jeanne used the opportunity to smile and flirt with the officers, while Ally seemed preoccupied with educating her mother about the fort's attributes in between introductions.

"Is that the school?" Ally asked Nathaniel, indicating a one-story limestone building. "Papa told me it has been closed for a year."

"The building serves as the school and the chapel. Unfortunately, the school has closed. Mr. Marsh, our teacher, removed to Prairie du Chien and we have yet to replace him."

"And the children?" she asked. "Do they have lessons?"

"Not formally."

She looked over at two little boys sword-fighting in a dusty yard with sticks. "How very unfortunate."

"Do you have a mind to teach?" Constance asked Ally.

"I've always thought it would be exciting to shape and form the minds of children."

"I can see you now, a dour schoolmistress in a severe gray gown and no curls."

Jeanne laughed with Constance, but Ally seemed not to pay attention, her gaze still on the school. "Perhaps I will be a teacher, after all."

"Hush now," Mrs. Benson said as they left the officers' quarters on their way to the round tower. "I'll not hear such talk. You've been trained to be the wife of a fine gentleman, and I'll not settle for anything less."

Something twisted in Nathaniel's gut at Mrs. Benson's words. Even if he could attract Ally's attention, which he doubted, he would never be good enough for a woman such as her. It was best to put her, and any romantic notions he was developing, far from his mind. Not only because she'd never return them, but because he could not defy his commanding officer.

They passed the long, narrow hospital and approached the two-story round tower. It stood twenty-five feet tall and sixteen feet wide. Nathaniel opened the heavy wooden door and motioned for them to enter.

A rush of cool air chilled Nathaniel's skin as they entered the darkened interior. Long, narrow musket slits faced both outside the fort and toward the parade ground, letting in little light. It stood empty and was built as a last defense for the soldiers, should they need it. Thankfully, in the eight years since it had been built, they'd never had an occasion to fight.

"Would you care to go to the top?" he asked. "There is a commanding view of the fort and the surrounding country from there."

"That would be lovely." Mrs. Benson nodded.

They climbed the stairs to a second floor that mirrored the one below and then climbed another set to the flat roof. The year before, the army had placed a twelve-pound cannon there, in case they needed to defend the fort during the Ho-Chunk War of 1827. It sat unused in the heat of the sun.

Nathaniel squinted as they stood at the top, looking out over the parade grounds and the buildings comprising the fort. They had a wonderful view of the rivers and the prairie land beyond the bluff. On the north side of the fort were large stands of trees interspersed with more prairie land.

"I've heard the Falls of St. Anthony are quite lovely," Ally said, coming to stand beside Nathaniel. "Some call it the Niagara of the Mississippi."

"I've never seen Niagara, but the Falls of St. Anthony are very impressive." Nathaniel looked down at her, and she moved aside her parasol to meet his gaze. He was arrested with her beauty once again. It made his heart pound hard and his thoughts go muddled. There had never been a woman before her who had so captured his attention.

"Do you suppose we could arrange a visit to the falls?" she asked.

He would have said yes to anything at that moment. "Of course."

"And may we invite some others?" Constance asked.

"Perhaps some officers?" Jeanne asked.

"Only if we also invite their families." Mrs. Benson gave her daughters a cautionary look. "I'll not have any single officers accompany us."

"But Major Ward is single, are you not?" Constance asked, feigning ignorance, since she had asked him the night before if he was married.

"I am," he said, to be polite.

"Major Ward is different," Mrs. Benson insisted. "Your father has assured me he is the most trustworthy man at the fort. I shall have no fear that he'll run away with one of your hearts."

Heat gathered under Nathaniel's collar, and he could feel a flush creeping up his neck. He couldn't stop himself from seeking Ally's gaze and found she was watching him with a keen look on her face.

After their tour, Ally was more energized than she'd felt in years. The sights and sounds of the fort left her yearning for more. She couldn't explain the sensation, nor did she care to explore the facets of her longing. Only her father could understand, so she didn't bother to share her feelings with her mother or sisters.

"I believe we're in need of a nap," Mama said to no one in particular as they approached the commanding officer's home. "Thank you for your time, Major Ward. You are quite knowledgeable about Fort Snelling."

The last thing Ally wanted to do was nap. On the contrary, she'd rather return to the schoolhouse to have a look at the space. An idea had formed while they'd been on their tour, one that might help in her argument to stay at Fort Snelling.

"It has been my pleasure," Nathaniel said. "If there's something you'd like to see in more detail, please let me know."

"I would love to see inside the schoolhouse," Ally said.

"Whatever for?" Mama asked.

"I've had an idea to open the school for a few weeks while we're here."

A quiet hush fell over the group as Mama studied Ally—and everyone waited for Mama's response. It was no secret that Ally had been restless in St. Louis. It was one of the reasons Mama had finally acquiesced to visiting Papa at Fort Snelling.

As Ally looked at her now, she knew her mother was gauging whether this was a battle she wanted to wage. Ally was not content to sip tea and stitch all day. She needed activities and goals, something to fill her days with purpose. If not, she quickly became wearisome to her mother.

"I'll speak to your father about your idea and see what he thinks," Mama finally said. "We might all benefit from a pet project this summer."

Excitement filled Ally's stomach, and she found herself looking toward Major Ward. The respect and admiration in his eyes were unmistakable.

"I will need to take an inventory of the supplies available and how I might operate the school before we speak to Papa." Ally tried not to reveal her enthusiasm, knowing Mama would find it most unladylike. "Perhaps Major Ward could take me there now so I can be prepared with my ideas when Papa returns."

Mama squinted as she looked toward the sun, as if ascertaining the time. "I suppose it will be acceptable. The school is in the middle of the fort, and there's still plenty of daylight left." She glanced at the major. "Do you mind terribly?"

"Of course not." Major Ward made a small bow. "As I said, I am at your disposal."

"I want to be a teacher," Constance whined. "May I go as well?"

"No." Mama shook her head. "You and Jeanne wilt in the sun like garden roses and need your rest or you will be unbearable by evening."

Accompanied by much complaining, Mama ushered Constance and Jeanne into the house and then turned and speared Ally with a look. "No more than thirty minutes, mind you, or I'll send out the army to find you."

Ally didn't doubt her.

The door closed, and Ally let out a weary breath, her shoulders relaxing. She looked toward the major and found his own shoulders loosening. "You did admirably, Major Ward. I commend you for your long-suffering patience."

His smile was quick and complete, and it took Ally's breath away. She'd not seen it since her arrival and wondered how often he let it shine. It made his blue eyes sparkle and revealed matching creases on either side of his generous mouth. The smile was more than charming—almost dashing, in a way—and made him unbearably handsome.

"I've never met your mother's equal," he confided, his cheeks filling with color. "Excuse me for saying such a thing."

"Please, I admire your candor. I love and adore my mother and sisters, but I sometimes wonder if God made a mistake when He placed me in this family. If it weren't for my father, I would have run away in search of my real family by now."

"You are much like your father."

"Am I?" She lifted her shoulders a bit, pleasure warming her chest at his praise. "I consider that a great compliment, Major Ward. I daresay you could not have pleased me more, even if you'd said I was the most beautiful woman you've ever met."

"That is also very true."

Ally paused to study Major Ward's face and found no guile or pretense there.

"If you don't mind me saying so," he added quickly, embarrassment coloring his words.

She'd grown accustomed to the praise of gentlemen and often found it tedious and annoying. But when she faced Major Ward, she sensed he was not one to lavish compliments or say things he did not mean, which made his words hold more importance.

"I do not mind," she said gently. "And I thank you."

They stood for a moment, neither one speaking, and then he offered his elbow. "Shall we go to the school?"

Ally wrapped her hand around his arm, thrilling at the sensation that filled her at his touch. She'd taken the arms of countless men, but never had she wanted to draw closer to them. She inhaled the scent of soap and a subtle cologne. Something deep and inexplicable drew her to the major, and she suddenly wanted to know everything there was to know about the man. Yet she had a feeling that he did not share easily. He was strong and solid, a man her father had grown to love and trust like a son. Though her father was a good man, he did not lavish his respect on just anyone. In a little under a year, Major Nathaniel Ward had somehow made his way into her father's confidences, further intriguing her.

Instead of asking him about his past, she decided to open up about hers and hoped he'd feel comfortable to share with her as well.

"If you hadn't guessed, I'm desperately lonely for the frontier." She couldn't hide the yearning in her voice.

"I had noticed your enthusiasm." He smiled, steering her away from the officers' quarters, along the path leading by the enlisted men's barracks. There was not as much activity on that side of the fort, and she appreciated the uninterrupted time with him.

"I have asked my father if I may stay."

Major Ward turned his gaze to her. "Permanently?"

"That is my wish. Though my mother will be hard to convince. She has a mind to marry me off to a wealthy gentleman."

"Yes, I couldn't help but overhear."

"Oh, Mama has no compunction about being overheard. She's intentional about what she says, even if it's inappropriate or indelicate." Ally felt at ease speaking to Major Ward, especially about matters her mother had openly shared. "She fully intended for you to hear her. She wants you and everyone else at the fort to know her daughters are not to marry military men."

"Even though you wish to stay at the fort?"

"Especially because I want to stay." Ally was not ignorant of her mother's fears. "Do you enjoy the frontier, Major?"

"I do. This is the northernmost fort on the western frontier, and though it can be lonely and monotonous at times, I cannot imagine any other life. I was the youngest of six boys raised in a small home in New York, so I very much enjoy the space and privacy afforded to an officer on the frontier."

"Did you always want to be a military man?"

He stared straight ahead, and she wondered if she'd pushed him too far. Many men entered the army to run away from their pasts, and not all of them liked to discuss it.

"My mother died bringing me into the world. I always believed that my father blamed me for her death." He finally looked at her, and she couldn't pull her gaze off his. "My oldest brother inherited my father's farm, and the others chose various jobs within the village. My father was eager to be rid of me, so after I went to West Point, I never returned home. It's been years since I've heard from any of them."

"I'm very sorry to hear that." For as much as her mother and sisters frustrated or annoyed her, she'd never questioned their love. If anything, her mother's devotion to her family was a bit suffocating.

"Do not trouble yourself on my account. The army has become my family."

"Truly?"

"I have found my place in the world. It gives me purpose and is very rewarding."

"You must work very hard. You're one of the youngest majors I've ever met."

He shrugged. "I do my duty and do not question my superiors. When there is work to be done, or a battle to face, I trust everything I've been taught and lean on God for the rest."

"You've earned deep respect and admiration from my father." She watched his face as she spoke to him. "Not many men can say the same."

"Your father is the finest commander I've ever served. He makes it very easy to respect him."

Hearing him praise her father was almost as rewarding as hearing him praise her.

They crossed the parade grounds to the schoolhouse, and Major Ward opened the door.

"I fear you will be disappointed." He stood back so she could enter. "Mr. Marsh brought most of the books with him when he came, and he took them when he left. There are only a few primers and a map or two left."

Ally's eyes adjusted to the darkened room, which was both a school and a chapel. A small teacher's desk sat at the front with several rows of benches facing it. A blackboard hung on the wall, along with two maps. One of the United States of America and another of the world. They were both over a decade old and did not accurately represent the territories, which were frequently changing.

"I could use some of the books in my father's library," Ally said, not discouraged by the lack of supplies. She'd never been afraid of a challenge. "And I could ask the families if they have things to donate, like slates and such."

Major Ward stood near the door, watching her. "Would you truly like to teach, Miss Benson?"

"Ally, please," she said.

"Then, if you'd like, you may call me Nathaniel."

It was very familiar, but given his relationship with her father, it didn't feel wrong to address him by his given name. "I would like it. But only when we're alone."

He smiled again, and her heart did a little flip. "I don't know how often we'll be alone."

She dropped her gaze and pretended to look through one of the primers on a shelf. "The answer is yes, Nathaniel, I would like to teach." She put an emphasis on his name, loving the sound of it on her lips. "I detest being unproductive." Even admitting it made her shiver. "Do you not feel the fleeting passage of time? The sense that life is slipping by at an alarming rate? I cannot be idle when there are so many in need of help."

He nodded. "I feel that way all the time."

"I don't want to waste my time in a stuffy parlor, sipping tea with gossiping women."

"Thankfully, that's rarely something I worry about."

Ally laughed. "You're very fortunate, then."

"You have no idea. The thought of making small talk with women is terrifying at best."

Yet he seemed completely at ease with her. "Then you and I have something else in common." She ran her hand over the surface of the desk and found a layer of dust. "Perhaps you and I can join forces this summer. I will endeavor to steer the conversations toward meaningful topics."

"And what shall I do?" he asked.

"You shall join me in that conversation and be as wonderful and charming as you are now." The words were out before she realized what she was saying, and her cheeks filled with heat.

Nathaniel watched her, a smile forming on his lips. "I shall endeavor to do my part."

Something deep and inexplicable filled her with joy, and she felt even more certain that she was right where she was meant to be.

Chapter Four

"I've had time to think about it, and I believe a school would be a wonderful idea." Papa smiled at Ally. "Several of the officers' wives have expressed such a desire."

"It will give her something to do, if nothing else." Mama pulled on her second glove and stood from the dressing table where she'd been preparing for the dance. Their guests would be arriving soon. Ally had dressed as quickly as possible and come to her parents' room to receive her father's answer.

"Oh, thank you!" Ally stood on tiptoe, the skirts of her gown rustling against her father's legs, and kissed his cheek. "I shall spend tomorrow preparing the schoolroom and start classes on Monday morning."

"You'll be sure to tell everyone it will only be for a month, at most." Mama ran her gloved hand over her coiffure.

"Of course," Ally said obediently. "But four or five weeks is better than nothing."

"I thought you wanted to do some exploring," Papa said. "Major Ward mentioned a trip to the falls."

"I will only have school four days a week. That will leave the other three for a bit of fun and relaxation."

Papa stood in his dress uniform, impeccably groomed. He'd been ready for almost an hour but had sat with Mama to visit while she dressed. When Ally had entered to speak to them and she saw them together, it had reminded her of her childhood. Her parents were deeply in love and thoroughly enjoyed each other's company. They teased and bantered, and Papa always brought his troubles to his wife. Mama's unhappiness with fort life had nothing to do with Papa, but she could not live on the frontier. It was something Ally had always struggled to understand. Wasn't Papa enough? Was her distaste of the frontier more powerful than her love for the man she married?

But it made Ally wonder. If she fell in love with a man in the city, would it take away her desire to live on the frontier? Would it make city life bearable? She wasn't sure. For the first time in her life, she felt a pang of empathy for her mama's plight with marrying a military officer.

"Enough talk about schools," Mama said. "Our guests will arrive any moment, and I want to be in the entry hall to receive them when they do."

Papa opened the bedroom door. "Shall we?"

Ally wanted to discuss her hopes and dreams for staying at the fort with her mother but knew it was not the time, nor the place. Though it would take great patience, Ally would continue to wait for the right opportunity. Perhaps, if the school was a success, and Mama saw how indispensable Ally was to the fort, she might have a fighting chance.

The door to the other bedroom opened, and Constance and

Jeanne stepped out into the hall. They were both dressed in their finest silk gowns, their hair artfully styled in a profusion of curls at the sides of their heads. Their gowns were of the latest fashion, with lower waistlines and large, puffed sleeves.

"Ah, my dears." Papa went to them and placed a kiss on each of their cheeks. "You both look lovely."

"Thank you, Papa." Constance touched a curl close to her ear and looked over Ally's appearance, her disapproval evident. "I warned you not to rush your toilette, Allyson dear."

"One can never take too much time with her appearance," Jeanne added. "Especially before a social engagement."

Ally was very pleased with the way she looked. Her gown was just as fashionable as her sisters', and she'd even curled and styled her hair similar to theirs, though she had not taken the time to create as many curls. Her greater concern had been with talking to her father before their guests arrived.

"Ally looks every bit as lovely as you two," Papa assured them. "I'll not have your petty jealousies interfere with the evening."

"Jealousy?" Constance's eyes opened wide. "Papa!"

"Hush, now." Papa lifted his chin, indicating there would be no more discussion.

Mr. Delany stood at attention near the door, and when a knock sounded, he glanced in Papa's direction. "Are you ready, sir?"

Papa and Mama took their places near the door. Constance, Jeanne, and Ally stood beside them. Constance cast Ally a heated look before smoothing her face and plastering on a delicate little smile.

"You may open the door, Mr. Delany," Papa said.

For almost an hour, Ally stood in the hall, greeting their guests. She'd met several of them already, but there were many more whom she had not had the pleasure of meeting. All the officers had been invited, whether married or single. There were well over thirty men in attendance and around fifteen wives and older daughters. Their gowns were just as beautiful and exquisite as those in St. Louis, creating a bouquet of colors. The furniture in the front hall, dining room, and parlor had been pushed to the edges of the rooms, allowing free space to move and eventually dance. Three soldiers had been brought in to play music in the parlor, their fiddle, flute, and fife making a merry sound.

Ally watched intently for Nathaniel, though she didn't want to look overeager or draw attention from her mother. She was kind and courteous to everyone she met but glanced often toward the door.

She finally caught a glimpse of him walking along the crushed gravel path from the officers' quarters to the commandant's house. He was so tall and so handsome in his uniform, with the red sash tied about his waist and the gold shoulder wings against the dark blue coatee. She couldn't quell the flutter of anticipation in her midsection, nor the flush that crept into her cheeks. The others seemed to fade away as he drew closer, and when he glanced up and caught her eye in the flickering flames of the torches outside the house, her heart beat a quick tempo. He had rarely left her thoughts since he'd taken her to the schoolhouse the day before, and she had spent most of the day hoping he'd come to call. But with her father present, there was no need for him.

"Ah, Major Ward." Papa saluted the major and then shook his hand. "Thank you for coming."

Nathaniel shook Papa's hand and then bowed over Mama's hand. "Thank you for the invitation."

"It is our pleasure," Mama said.

He greeted Ally's sisters, and then he stopped in front of Ally and took her hand. Just like the others, he bowed, but he held her hand for a bit longer than necessary.

"It's nice to see you again, Major Ward," Ally said, wishing she could call him by his given name but knowing her mother would never approve.

"And you, Miss Ally." He let go of her hand and brushed his gloved fingers together. It was such a simple gesture, one that might have gone unnoticed by the others, but she wondered if his hand tingled like hers from their touch.

"I do hope you will save me a dance this evening," he said to her. "I confess, I'm not much of a dancer, but perhaps you'll forgive my poor attempt."

"I'd be delighted." With his powerful, lean body, she would be surprised if he was a poor dancer.

"Welcome, Captain Tonder." Papa greeted the next gentleman to arrive. "May I present my wife, Mrs. Benson, and our daughters, Miss Constance, Miss Jeanne, and Miss Allyson?"

The captain was a handsome man with a ruddy complexion and dark, almost black eyes. He was not overly tall, and his brown hair was thick and curly.

"It's a pleasure to meet you," he said to Constance first.

"The pleasure is entirely mine." Constance fluttered her eyelashes and offered him a coy smile. "Do you dance, Captain Tonder?"

"I do, indeed, Miss Constance. I hope you'll favor me with the honor of a dance later."

"Perhaps I will." Constance's voice and mannerisms were slow and purposeful. Had she turned her attention away from Nathaniel to a new prey?

The captain's eyes darkened, and he nodded at her before moving on to Jeanne and then Ally.

He took Ally's hand in his and pressed it gently before bringing it to his lips. "Miss Allyson, I have been admiring your beauty from afar. I see that up close, you are even more lovely than I imagined."

Constance inhaled a sharp breath, and Nathaniel took a step forward.

"Thank you," Ally said, not wanting to be rude.

"And will you save a dance for me as well?" the captain asked her.

Ally glanced at Nathaniel and found him watching her for her response. Though he had no claim on her, a part of her had no wish to dance with anyone but him. Of course, her mother would never allow it. Only engaged or married couples danced with each other more than once in an evening, and even then, never more than three times. She had no choice but to dance with the captain.

"I'd be happy to save a dance for you, Captain Tonder."

"I'll look forward to it all evening."

The men walked toward the dining room where refreshments were being served.

Constance sent Ally another contemptuous look, but Ally paid her little mind. Her attention was captured by Nathaniel and the fine cut of his shoulders, the way he rested his hand upon the hilt of his sword, and the height that set him apart from all the others.

He glanced back at Ally and tipped his head when he found her watching him. A thrill of excitement raced up her spine at the thought of dancing with such a fine man.

She'd never felt such anticipation in all her life.

As the colonel's second-in-command, Nathaniel had danced first with the colonel's oldest daughter, Constance, and then with Mrs. Benson, and then with Jeanne. They had danced the cotillion, the quadrille, and a schottische. The room had grown warm and the dancers more animated as the punch continued to flow. Laughter and lively conversation made the tight room feel even tighter, though all seemed to fade away as Nathaniel approached Ally, his heart thumping madly.

She stood with a second lieutenant whose red neck and shining eyes suggested he was quite taken with the beautiful young lady. Nathaniel stood just behind Ally and caught the lieutenant's eye, tilting his head to the side, silently indicating his dance was over.

The lieutenant stood at attention and saluted Nathaniel, causing Ally to turn.

"Major Ward." Her smile was bright and lovely, and he hoped she had been looking forward to this moment as much as he had.

"Will you allow me the honor of this dance?" he asked.

"Of course." She turned back to the lieutenant, a smile in her voice. "Thank you. I do hope you hear from your mother soon."

The lieutenant blushed furiously and bowed before her then took his leave.

Soon, the musicians began the next dance. It was a waltz. Nathaniel's pulse picked up speed at the idea of holding Ally so close. Since their time together at the school yesterday, he'd thought of little else. She had proved to be a sensible and levelheaded young lady, and they'd found much in common. She was one of the first women he'd met who did not make him cringe, or muddle his head with confusion and uncertainty. On the contrary. She made him smile and laugh and look forward to what she had to say. He wanted to know her opinions on several topics. Instead of avoiding her, like he had most women in his acquaintance, he'd been hoping for a reason to spend time with her again.

He'd never wanted something more in his life.

He bowed before her, and she curtsied; then she stepped into his arms. His left hand gently folded around her right, and he took a deep breath before slipping his right hand around her small waist, honored for such a privilege. He tried not to let his reaction show on his face but feared he was not successful. How could he not react?

Every muscle in his body tensed in response to holding her so close, and when her hand lifted to his shoulder, and she met his gaze with her own, he forgot to breathe.

"Miss Ally," he said on a rush of air. "You're quite lovely this evening."

She looked up at him through a fringe of long lashes and smiled, her chest rising and falling. "Thank you," she said, just as breathless. Did she feel the way he felt, standing this close? If she did, what did that mean?

They stood that way for a heartbeat before Nathaniel realized the other couples had already begun to waltz. He took the first step, self-conscious of his lack of experience, but found that she and he moved in perfect rhythm. They glided around the room with ease.

She continued to look up at him, and he could not tear his gaze away from hers. He'd never seen such beautiful brown eyes, or such a creamy complexion. All he'd ever known was the hard discipline of military life and the coarse behavior of men. In his arms, Ally was soft and pure and gentle. Until this moment, he had not realized how much he yearned for the tenderness only a woman could provide. For the first time, he understood why men longed for—and pursued—the companionship of a wife. How much sweeter his world would be if Ally was a part of it.

"My mother warned me about waltzing." Her voice was low and warm.

"And what did she say?"

"That I must keep the gentleman at arm's length, and that I must keep my eyes down and never meet his gaze."

Nathaniel swallowed, drawing her a fraction closer in his arms. "Why not?"

"She says the act is too intimate between an unmarried couple."

He was so captivated by her, he hardly noticed anyone else in the room. "And do you agree?"

She studied him and smiled. "It is not often I find my mother's opinions to be true, but at the moment, I believe she's correct."

They were surrounded by dozens of people, yet dancing with her felt like the most intimate thing he'd ever done in his life. "I quite agree."

He returned her smile, suddenly feeling as if he'd known her his whole life. As if his arms had been made to hold her and his heart had been molded to fit beside hers. The sensation was so powerful, it overwhelmed him.

"Nathaniel?" she whispered.

"Yes?"

"Could you take me outside for a breath of fresh air?"

"Of course." He slowed his steps and came to a stop, offering her his elbow.

She wrapped her hand around his arm and allowed him to lead her into the front hall and out the door.

Other couples had taken to the fresh air, and Mr. Delany stood watch near the window, ensuring everyone's reputation remained intact.

The music was muted as they stepped outside. Torches had been lit along the gravel paths leading up to the commandant's house, sending flickering shadows over the parade grounds. Above their heads, a magnificent sky boasted millions of stars, shimmering in all their glory.

"I'm sorry for ending our dance so soon," she said as she came to a halt on the path and turned to face him, her hand sliding away from his arm. "It was growing a bit close in there."

"You're trembling. Are you cold?"

"The very opposite." She struggled to meet his gaze. "I—I don't know what came over me."

If it was anything like what he'd just experienced, he knew exactly how she was feeling. Yet dare he hope she felt as he did? How did a man go about asking such a delicate question? And, even if she did share his affection, what would it matter? He was well aware of her parents' feelings about military men. It was foolish to even consider such a thing.

"Would you care to take a turn about the parade grounds?" she asked.

"I would like that very much."

She took his arm again, still trembling.

"Would you like me to retrieve your shawl?" he asked.

"No, thank you. Despite what you might think, I'm overly warm and appreciate the cooler air."

They began to walk away from the house. "Are you feeling well?" he asked.

"I'm quite well, thank you." When she looked up at him, the torchlight flickered in her eyes. Her smile was tentative, yet full of fond regard, and it almost undid his composure. Would he never be able to see her smile without it affecting him in such a way? "And how are you feeling?" she asked.

"I've never been better." It was completely true—and terrifying at the same time. Now that he knew how she could make him feel, how could his life ever be the same?

In just a few days' time, Nathaniel feared that he had lost his heart to Miss Ally Benson—yet he suspected he was not the first man to fall in love with her so quickly. He had heard the rumors about her and her sisters before they arrived. Was he a fool for feeling this way? He had thought he had stronger willpower and better sense. He had laughed and scoffed at weak men in the past, criticizing them for their lack of self-control. But here he stood, completely besotted. A more frightening or heartbreaking reality he could not imagine, because she could never be his.

A movement caught Nathaniel's eye as two people slipped around the perimeter of torchlight and disappeared behind the barracks.

Nathaniel's entire body became alert.

"What is it?" Ally asked, watching him carefully.

"Please return to the house," he said calmly, though any number of threats could be possible. "I'll join you there shortly."

To her credit, she did not question him but lifted the hem of her gown and retreated in the direction they'd just come. In a moment, she entered the house and did not look back.

Nathaniel put his hand on the hilt of his sword and moved to the barracks, his feet light and silent on the gravel. It might be nothing more than a couple of enlisted men who were curious about the party and had gone to peer through the windows, or it could be as complicated as two Indians coming into the fort to make trouble. He'd only glimpsed the figures' stealth shadows a moment before they disappeared.

There were guards not too far away, but he didn't want to make a scene if it wasn't necessary. He'd call out an alarm, if needed, but for now, he'd simply assess the situation.

When he moved around the corner of the barracks, he found a man and woman embracing in the dark.

"What's the meaning of this?" he asked.

The man pulled away and looked at Nathaniel. His body went rigid as he saluted the major.

Constance stood there, showing no signs of concern at being caught with Captain Tonder.

"Captain, you'll return to your quarters at once, and remain there until further notice," Nathaniel said. "The colonel will deal with you as he sees fit." He then turned to Constance. "And Miss Benson, you'll return to the dance with me."

"Why, Major Ward, I thought you'd never ask."

He frowned at her obvious indifference to the situation, suspecting this was but a game to her.

Captain Tonder saluted Nathaniel again and made haste toward the officers' quarters.

"Now that we're alone." Constance sidled up to Nathaniel, her feline smile illuminated by the moonlight. "I've been wondering what it might be like to kiss you."

She came toward him, and he stepped back, his muscles tight. "You forget yourself, Miss Benson." He began to walk away, putting space between them, hoping she'd follow.

Thankfully, she was not far behind. Her anger and frustration evident in the lines of her face.

Chapter Five

On Monday, Ally opened the school with much anticipation. She had twelve students, and most of them were eager to learn. The two little boys who had been practicing their sword fighting with sticks the week before had more interest in becoming soldiers than in becoming scholars, but she did her best with them.

The first week slipped by quickly, leaving Ally exhausted yet filled with a sense of purpose. She saw Nathaniel on two separate occasions, when he came to dine with her family, but neither occasion had afforded them any time alone. They had enjoyed one another's company, though, especially when Papa brought up subjects that he knew they'd both like discussing. Ally was well versed in Indian affairs and politics in Washington, much to her mother's horror. And she was delighted to learn that Nathaniel was an avid reader, like herself. They spoke about Daniel Defoe, Phillis Wheatley, Benjamin Franklin, Washington Irving, and many others. She, Papa, and Nathaniel stayed up well after Mama and her sisters had retired for the evening, and, if it wasn't for the final bugle call of the night, Ally was certain their conversations could have lasted through until morning.

When Saturday arrived, Ally was eager to spend the day with Nathaniel visiting the Falls of St. Anthony. Papa would remain behind to deal with the British fur trader who had been apprehended and brought to the fort, but there would be others accompanying them. Two officers and their families had been invited, including a few of Ally's students, and there would be a small contingent of enlisted men who would drive the wagons and provide extra protection, should the need arise.

The day was overcast, though warm, and smelled of the potential of rain. Ally sat on a bench in the back of one wagon, Constance and Jeanne beside her. Mama sat in the front with Nathaniel and a private, who manned the horses. Three of Ally's students sat in the wagon bed, their excited chatter almost matching Ally's mood.

The little party of adventurers would not let the slight chance of rain hinder their excursion, nor would Ally let Constance's poor attitude deprive her of enjoying her day.

Though no one had spoken of the situation that had sent Ally back to the house during the dance, she suspected it had something to do with her sister. There had been terse conversations between Constance and Papa in his office, and since that evening, Nathaniel had been especially reserved with the oldest Benson sister.

"It won't be much farther," Nathaniel said to those in his wagon as he turned slightly on the bench. They'd been traveling for almost two hours, and he'd been commenting on the terrain and surrounding countryside as they went. The land was beautiful, with gentle hills, towering trees, and glimpses of the majestic Mississippi River.

"If it weren't for the clouds," Mama said, "the day would be practically perfect."

"The weather is a study in extremes," Nathaniel commented to Mama, though he spoke loud enough to include Ally and her sisters. "In the winter, the temperatures can be as high as forty or fifty degrees, or dip as low as thirty below zero."

"My goodness," Mama said.

"And, in the summer," he continued, "it's not uncommon to enjoy beautiful days like today, at seventy-five degrees, but it's also not unusual to have extreme humidity with temperatures in the upper nineties in July or August."

"It *is* a study in extremes," Mama agreed. "And my husband tells me the snow can be quite deep in the winter, yet the growing season produces an abundant harvest."

"Yes." Nathaniel nodded. "It's a remarkable land. With the wealth of lakes and rivers, and rich soil, I foresee cities and towns here in the future that will rival those in New England."

"That is something I'd have to see to believe." Mama pursed her lips, as if the idea was too farfetched for her to imagine.

Ally only smiled. She loved Nathaniel's optimism and vision, even if her mother was a naysayer. But, if she could have her way, she'd never want this beautiful and untamed land to hold so many people.

The sound of rushing water met Ally's ears before she saw the falls. When they rounded a bend in the wagon road, her eyes opened wide at the sight before her. Stretching across the wide river were a series of breathtaking waterfalls, with lush, green islands separating them. They were not straight, but curved in and out, at varying heights, offering a magnificent view to behold.

The military sawmill, which Papa had told her about, sat quiet on the western banks. It had been built to produce lumber for the fort and the fur traders' and Indian agent's buildings.

When the wagon finally came to a stop, Nathaniel leaped from his seat and reached up to help Mama disembark. After she was on her feet, he did the same for the rest of them, giving Ally a smile as he helped her down. The other wagon also came to a stop, and the second group of passengers joined them.

They stood on the riverbank for a long time, commenting on the strength and importance of the river for their burgeoning nation. Some of the children threw rocks into the water, while the young boys waded about with their pants rolled up to their knees. A picnic lunch had been brought along, and the enlisted men went about setting it up for the officers and their families.

"What do you think?" Nathaniel asked Ally as he stood beside her.

She was at an utter loss to describe the beauty of the falls. "I've never seen anything so grand." The mist from the crashing water settled upon her face, and she closed her eyes, savoring the feel of it. "It makes me even more conscious of the power and majesty of God, to know He carved this creation from nothing and gave us the ability to recognize its splendor."

When she opened her eyes, she found him watching her.

"Somehow," he said quietly, "it's even more magnificent with you standing here."

Ally smiled at his words, knowing he did not say them lightly. He turned back to the river and his hand brushed slightly against hers. He did not move it away but allowed it to linger. Neither one wore gloves, and the sensation it created—the simple pressure of his bare skin against hers—made all else fade away for a moment.

Was he as aware of her as she was of him? She wanted to believe he was, especially because he'd initiated the touch, but she could not be sure.

He began to pull away, but Ally reached out with her pinkie finger and hooked it around his for the briefest moment before letting go.

Nathaniel turned his face to look at her, questions swirling in the depths of his blue eyes.

Without a word, Ally offered the slightest nod and a hint of a smile.

She had spent the last several years discouraging gentlemen, trying so hard not to lead them on. She detested her sisters' flirtatious ways and their deceitful charm and didn't want to give anyone false hope. But Nathaniel was different—far different—and she wanted him to know how he made her feel.

It wasn't much, only a simple acknowledgment, yet it seemed to give him a fresh wind of confidence. His chest expanded and his shoulders lifted. He studied her, as if seeking to confirm what he'd just seen. His earnest face made her smile and caused a flush to rise in her cheeks.

He grinned and brushed his hand against hers again. A thrill raced up her spine and made her pulse thrum in her wrists.

"Oh dear," Mama said, wringing her hands. "I'm afraid Constance and Jeanne have wandered off."

Ally turned to her mother, scanning the small group that had gathered. "Did they tell you they were leaving?"

"No. I noticed they were wandering downriver, but I was so overtaken by the falls, I didn't pay them much attention."

"Have no fear, Mrs. Benson." Nathaniel followed Ally to her mother's side. "I don't think they could have gone far."

"Do you think they've been kidnapped?" Terror made Mama's voice rise high.

"No, I do not," Nathaniel said calmly.

"Will you go look for them?" she asked.

"Of course."

"I'll go along," Ally said to her mother. "Two sets of eyes and ears are better than one, and, like Major Ward has said, they couldn't have gone far. We'll be back very soon."

Under normal circumstances, Mama would not have let Ally

leave with an unmarried man, unescorted, but she was so full of fear, she hardly paid it any mind.

Nathaniel led the way, walking quickly, Ally by his side. The path was well worn as it hugged the riverbank. Trees grew up on either side of the path, soon shielding them from the others.

"Do you think harm has befallen them?" Ally asked.

"I do not." He hesitated and then said, "I took a quick inventory of our party and realized two of the privates are also missing."

"Oh." Of course.

His hand brushed against hers again, and she looked up at him shyly, a smile hugging the edges of her mouth. He returned the smile, his eyes lit with a myriad of emotions. She suspected her own gaze reflected the same.

Through the trees, not too far ahead, Ally glimpsed her sisters sitting on the riverbank, their bare feet dangling in the water. Two enlisted men stood a little farther back, watching her sisters as they giggled and splashed in the water.

Nathaniel's steps slowed, and he finally came to a stop before they were spotted by the others. "It looks like they're safe."

"Yes, but Mama will not be happy."

"Your father might also have something to say to the privates about this."

"I almost feel sorry for them. No doubt they were powerless to resist my sisters' charms."

"I'm beginning to understand how they feel." Nathaniel gazed down at Ally, warmth and affection in his eyes. "Though, if you'll pardon me for saying so, I believe your sisters know exactly what they are doing to those privates—but I do not think you know what you are doing to me."

The breath stilled in Ally's lungs, her lips parting in surprise at his declaration.

"Forgive me, Ally." He shook his head. "I have no experience with these things, and I have no right to say this—but I think you know. You must have guessed, surely, that I've grown to care for you. I know it's too soon, and that your father would never approve—"

"You're wrong," she interrupted. "My father thinks very highly of you, Nathaniel."

"Not if he knew I was saying these things to you. I'm sorry."

She took a step closer to him and touched his hand. "You have nothing to be sorry about." She looked down at his hand, so strong and powerful. "I rather like to hear you say them."

"Ally?" His voice was husky as he reached out and took her other hand in his. "Am I a fool for feeling this way so soon?"

"If you are," she said, "then so am I."

Longing shimmered in his gaze. "I have no right to say these things, let alone feel them. I've spent my entire life believing that love and romance were not meant for me, but here I am, standing alone in the middle of the woods with the colonel's daughter, throwing every bit of caution to the wind to declare myself." He laughed, amazement echoing in the sound. "Yet I cannot imagine not telling you. You've turned my world upside down, Ally Benson."

"And you've done the same to mine, Major Ward." Her heart nearly burst with joy at his speech. "I'm so happy you've told me."

But even as the words left her mouth, cold reality settled over her like a fresh blanket of snow, and she had to struggle to keep the smile on her face.

"What is it?" he asked, concern darkening his eyes.

"My mother."

He looked toward the direction they'd just come and dropped her hands, as if anticipating Mama's arrival.

She shook her head at his assumption. "She has made her position very clear." Disappointment sliced through Ally, replacing the moment of pure joy with the truth of the situation. Her mother would never agree to a courtship between one of her daughters and the good major, and Ally could never go against her parents' wishes as her oldest sister Laura had done. If she was being honest with herself, she knew that the feelings she shared with Nathaniel must come to an end, and the sooner the better, for the both of them.

Nathaniel sighed. "She would never approve of me."

"It's not you," Ally said quickly. "It's the military. I know Papa adores you, and under normal circumstances, he'd be overjoyed." Even saying it brought another flush to her cheeks.

"But these are not normal circumstances." Regret clouded his voice. "And there is little hope for a courtship, is there?"

Ally could not look at his face. Her own pain was compounded by seeing his. The promise of something beautiful had been so fleeting, yet the loss of it felt all-consuming.

The first rumble of thunder reverberated through the heavens, and Ally glanced up toward a menacing cloud.

"Is there any hope?" he asked. "If I should speak to your father?"

"Papa would never go against Mama's wishes, especially where her daughters are concerned." Tears pricked the backs of her eyes, but she refused to cry. She'd only just met Major Ward. Surely she was being overly dramatic about the whole thing. "I'm afraid, if you spoke to him, he'd assign you to a different position."

"I see."

She took a steadying breath. "The most we can hope for is a dear friendship." Even as she spoke the words, they felt flat and unreasonable. "We will have to endeavor to forget our feelings and treat one another with friendly indifference."

His hand came up and rested on her cheek. His touch was painfully gentle as he gazed into her eyes. "I could never treat you with friendly indifference."

Her heart pounded, and she began to tremble, just as she had during their dance together.

"But, if that's all I'm allowed…" He ran his thumb over the curve of her cheekbone and then lowered it once again. "Then I will have to accept my fate."

"Come," she said, her voice catching on the word. "We should get the others, before someone comes looking for us."

It took all of Ally's willpower to step away from Nathaniel, because when she did, she knew she'd never find her way back again.

⤴

For one brief moment, the world had been full of intense possibility and happiness. A life that Nathaniel had never dreamed possible had not only fully formed in his mind but had been dashed like a wave against the cliffs a moment later. To know Ally Benson returned his affection had been almost too good to be true. To hold her hand, and caress her cheek, had been a great privilege. But the moment he saw her emotions shift, and she reminded him that Mrs. Benson would never approve of the match, he'd never felt so bereft.

Yet there was nothing to be done. If he'd been facing an obstacle in his military career, he'd beseech his commanding officer for benevolence. But he knew exactly what he'd receive if he approached Ally's father now. Nathaniel would be reassigned, just as she said, and that was the last thing he wanted. Even if he could not court her, he could at least spend time with her in the few remaining weeks she had at the fort.

They returned to the clearing with Constance and Jeanne in tow. Nathaniel had told the privates, in no uncertain terms, that they would be reported to the colonel. Again, Constance had shown no remorse for getting a soldier in trouble. Jeanne, on the other hand, appeared a little embarrassed and contrite at being caught.

"Thankfully, the rain has held off," Mrs. Benson commented an hour later as the picnic lunch items were being returned to the wagons.

"I hope we can make it back without getting wet," one of the captains said, glancing up at the ominous clouds. "Perhaps we should be off." He looked to Nathaniel for confirmation.

Nathaniel nodded, his heart still heavy from what had transpired in the woods with Ally.

Everyone started back toward the wagons, talking and laughing. An air of gaiety had befallen the group, though Nathaniel struggled to join in.

Suddenly, Mrs. Benson cried out in pain and fell awkwardly to the ground.

"Mama!" Ally reached out to try to stop her fall but could not reach her in time.

"Oh dear." Mrs. Benson moaned as she pulled herself up to a sitting position. Dirt stained her gown and hands. "I'm afraid I've twisted my ankle."

Nathaniel was at her side in a moment, surveying the ground around her. A hole, left by some creature or another, was covered over with tall grass.

"I must have caught my toe." Mrs. Benson's cheeks turned a rosy pink as she glanced about the group. "How clumsy of me."

"May I take a look?" Nathaniel asked.

"Oh dear," the older woman said again. "I think I'll be fine, if you'll just give me a hand up."

"Are you certain?" Nathaniel didn't want her to be in pain.

"I'm certain." She tried to rise on her own, but Nathaniel and Ally reached for her at the same moment. He put his arm around Mrs. Benson's waist, and Ally took her free hand in her own.

When Mrs. Benson was resting on her good foot, she shook out her skirts and pushed their helping hands away. "Stop fussing," she said to Nathaniel and Ally. "I'm fine."

Nathaniel backed off, but Ally stayed by her mother's side, unperturbed by her reprimand.

The colonel's wife tried to take a step, but she gasped and leaned heavily against Ally.

"Oh Mama," Ally said with a frown.

Nathaniel returned to the older woman's side. "I insist on taking a look."

"You'll do no such thing," Mrs. Benson countered, her voice tight with pain. "Help me to the wagon, and I'll have the fort surgeon look at it when we arrive."

Ally glanced up at Nathaniel, a look of frustration in her gaze. "She'll not be dissuaded."

"Then allow me to carry you," Nathaniel said. "It's the least I can do."

"Oh fiddlesticks." Mrs. Benson straightened her back. "Just lend me your arm."

Nathaniel did as she instructed. With Ally's help, they returned Mrs. Benson to the wagon and set off for the fort.

The wind picked up speed, and the sky grew darker. Mrs. Benson moaned with each dip and swell of the land. Nathaniel sat beside her and tried to offer comfort, but there was little to be had in the wagon. He had suggested she lie in the back, but she refused, claiming she wasn't an invalid.

About a mile away from the fort, the rain began to pour in earnest. It quickly drenched the little party and added to Mrs. Benson's discomfort.

Nathaniel tried not to look at Ally on the way back, because every time he caught her eyes, the longing in his heart twisted into grief. She was so close, yet completely out of his reach, and the reality of it was too much to bear. He needed to stay busy, to distract his mind and heart, and the sooner they returned to the fort, the sooner he could accomplish his mission.

When they finally arrived back at Fort Snelling, Nathaniel had the private deliver them to the commandant's front door; this time, he didn't allow Mrs. Benson to protest his help. He lifted her into his arms, which was no small feat given her padded size, and delivered her safely to her parlor settee.

"Really, Major Ward," Mrs. Benson said, her lips puckered up like she'd eaten a sour lemon. "I am capable of walking on my own."

"No, you're not," Ally said, bringing an afghan to cover her mother. "And the major has done nothing more than his duty, per Papa's instructions."

"I'll send for the surgeon," Nathaniel said, water dripping from his shako. "And return later to check on you."

Colonel Benson appeared at the parlor door at that moment, his smile soon turning to concern at seeing the bedraggled group. "What's happened?" He rushed to his wife's side, the look of fear on his face completely out of character for the fort's commander. He knelt beside Mrs. Benson and took her hand, pressing it to his lips. "My dear, are you hurt?"

The scene upended Nathaniel's senses. Even in the harshest of circumstances, he'd never seen Colonel Benson lose his composure. But one look at him now and Nathaniel felt rattled to his core. The colonel was practically distraught at the sight of his wife in pain.

Ally met Nathaniel's gaze, and for the first time, he fully understood what the love of a woman could do to the strongest of men. It was the most unsettling feeling he'd ever had.

"It's nothing, my darling." Mrs. Benson laid her hand upon Colonel Benson's cheek, a soft smile on her lips. "I've merely twisted my ankle. It will mend, in time."

"Are you sure?" he asked, hopeful uncertainty in his voice.

"Of course." Mrs. Benson was like a different person with her husband. Gone was the pride and harsh words, and in their place were tenderness and compassion.

"Major." Colonel Benson turned to Nathaniel, his voice once more in control. "Send for Dr. White immediately."

Nathaniel saluted his commanding officer and turned to leave the house without looking back at Ally or anyone else.

He walked through the pounding rain to the hospital, his heart and mind churning.

Seeing Colonel Benson so weak and vulnerable had done more than unsettle him; it had given him a glimpse of true love and made him wonder if what he felt for Ally really was love, after all. What he saw between the colonel and Mrs. Benson was more than a feeling or a sensation. It was more than a pounding heart or a physical attraction. More than a stolen moment in the woods. It was sacrifice, commitment, and putting one's heart outside oneself to lay in the hands of another. It required trust and hope, and a great deal of faith.

But, more than anything, it required selflessness. And for a man who had spent his entire life looking out for himself, having no one else to see to his wants or needs, Nathaniel wasn't certain he knew how to be selfless.

Chapter Six

Another week passed, and this time, Papa did not leave Mama's side for more than an hour or two at a time. Ally spent her days teaching and her evenings entertaining her mother. Papa had put a strict punishment on Constance and Jeanne, forbidding them to leave the house without his presence, which meant they left very little. Guilt pricked Ally's conscience, knowing she'd also broken his trust by being alone with Nathaniel in the woods. Though she didn't tell her father what had happened, for fear he'd ban Nathaniel, neither did she go out of her way to leave the house, other than to teach.

But none of it mattered, because Nathaniel appeared to have taken Ally's advice that they remain only friends. He was cordial and kind, but gone was the warmth he'd shown her near the falls. He had come to dinner on three separate occasions, at Papa's insistence, but he hadn't remained afterward to play games or visit. When she saw him in the fort, he acknowledged her but did not go out of his way to speak to her. And with Papa's close attention to Mama, and her inability to go anywhere, there was no need for the major to accompany them on excursions.

There had been no time to speak to one another about what had happened, and as the days wore on, she became more and more uncertain that anything *had* transpired between them.

The sun was kissing the horizon on Saturday evening as Ally sat in the dining room, several books spread out before her. On Monday, she planned to teach the children about the Virginia Company, the Great Puritan Migration, and the events leading up to the European expansion into America. She lifted several tomes off the table and looked at their spines, trying to find the book she'd been studying at school on Thursday. It was nowhere to be found.

"Perhaps I left it at the school," she mused to herself.

"What's that?" Mama asked from across the hall in the parlor.

Ally rose from the table and stretched her back. It ached from sitting all afternoon. "I think I left one of my books at the school."

"Oh." Mama bent over a piece of needlework she'd been stitching and didn't bother to look up. "You should clear your books away as it is. Mrs. Delany will want to set the table for supper soon. Major Ward will be joining us again."

A thrill of excitement raced up Ally's spine at the announcement. She hoped he would stay after supper so they could talk. "I would like to read a bit more before supper. I want to have my lesson prepared for Monday and with tomorrow being Sunday, I won't have the luxury to work."

Mama finally looked up and glanced out the window. "There's still enough daylight. Perhaps you should go and get it before it grows dark."

The schoolhouse was visible from the front of the commandant's house, and Mama would have a good view of her on the way there and on the way back.

"I think I will go. It will be good to stretch my legs."

Constance sat on a chair in the corner reading a book, while Jeanne stood near an easel drawing a picture of the falls. Neither one offered to accompany her.

It didn't matter. She'd enjoy a bit of solitude after so much time in the house with them, and it would afford her the opportunity to think about what she might say to Nathaniel.

"I'll be back shortly." She retrieved her hat and pinned it in place before stepping out of the house.

The last vestiges of sunlight streaked across the sky in brilliant bursts of pink, purple, and orange, relieved only by the slashes of gray clouds on the horizon. The grass on the parade ground was a deep green from the earlier rains that week, and birds trilled from the trees on the bluff. Ally filled her lungs with the fresh air, thanking God for every day she had at the fort. She refused to let herself think about the day she'd be forced to leave, praying that God would find a way to let her stay.

The fort was quieter than usual, owing to the supper hour. Mama liked to eat later than was typical, so Ally let her eyes wander over the fort in no fear of encountering an unwanted gentleman.

When she arrived at the schoolhouse, she opened the door and slipped inside. The book she'd been looking for was on her desk, just as she'd suspected. When she'd left on Thursday, she hadn't taken the time to wipe down the chalkboard, so she did that now, wanting the room to look fresh for the chapel service in the morning. She hummed to herself as she worked and didn't realize someone had come into the schoolhouse until he spoke to her.

"I wish my teacher had been as pretty as you."

Ally's heart pounded at the unfamiliar voice, and she turned to find Captain Tonder had entered. She hadn't seen him since the night of the dance over a week ago.

"But I probably wouldn't have had enough focus to learn anything if she had been."

"Captain." Ally set the piece of cloth she'd been using to erase the board on her desk. "I didn't hear you enter."

He smiled, his ruddy complexion giving him a boyish air. "I'm sorry to have frightened you."

"It's quite all right. I was just about to leave." She reached for the book, not wanting to be alone any longer than necessary with the man. Forts were small, and gossip could spread in an instant. If someone saw her walk into the building and then saw him enter a few minutes later, her reputation could be shattered.

"Must you leave so soon?" He walked toward her, putting himself between her and the door. "I've been hoping for a chance to get to know you a little better. We never did get that dance."

"I'm afraid it will have to wait until next time." She tried to maneuver around him, but he stepped in her way. Her pulse picked up speed. "Th—there's to be another dance this Friday."

"I heard." He took another step toward her, forcing her to back up against the dusty chalkboard. "But I've been banned from attending social gatherings while you and your sisters are at the fort."

She had nowhere left to go, and he was standing so close she could smell alcohol on his breath. "Please," she said, trying not to sound desperate. "I would like to return home."

"You will, after we've had a little fun." He put one hand up to her chin as he gazed at her lips. "Are you as friendly as your sister, I wonder?"

Her body began to tremble, and she hugged the history book to her chest, the only defense she had. "Let me go, sir." She tried to push past him again, but this time he put his arms around her and trapped her hands against his chest.

"When I'm ready to let you go. Not only did I miss that dance, but I didn't get to finish my business with your sister. I aim to get what's coming to me now."

The door crashed open, and Nathaniel stood on the threshold, a look of murder in his eyes.

∽

Panic rushed along every nerve in Nathaniel's body as he took in the scene before him. Ally was crushed in Robert Tonder's arms, pure terror on her face. In a split second, Nathaniel was across the room, grabbing the captain by the nape of his neck. With strength born of fear and anger, he pulled the man away from Ally as if he weighed nothing.

"What is the meaning of this?" he demanded of the shorter man, afraid of what he might do to him if he discovered he'd hurt Ally.

"I didn't mean anything by it," Tonder said. "I was just having a little fun. Nothing that the young lady didn't invite."

Ally inhaled a shocked breath, and rage filled Nathaniel's eyesight with spots. His grasp tightened on the man's collar, stretching the material against his bulging neck. Captain Tonder choked and reached for his collar to try to pry it loose.

"You forget yourself, Captain." Nathaniel used every shred of willpower to keep his actions under control. "You are facing a dishonorable discharge, if I have anything to say about the matter." He let the man go.

Captain Tonder stumbled and fell to the ground, hatred seething from his body. He opened his mouth to speak, but Nathaniel took a menacing step toward him.

"I would advise you to keep your mouth closed. If you utter one more slander against this lady, I cannot promise you that you'll see tomorrow." He breathed heavily, willing himself to calm down before he chanced a look at Ally. "Did he hurt you?"

She shook her head, tears glistening in her eyes. "No." She swallowed and lifted her chin. "I am unharmed."

"Thank God for that."

A lieutenant appeared at the door, and seeing Tonder on the ground, he looked to Nathaniel for orders.

"Take him to the guardhouse and see that he's locked inside a cell," Nathaniel said. "The colonel and I will tend to him later."

"Yes, sir." The lieutenant saluted Nathaniel and then bent to take hold of Captain Tonder's arm.

After the two of them left, Nathaniel's anger began to fade, and in its place was intense fear—fear of what could have happened if he hadn't caught a glimpse of the captain walking into the schoolhouse. The sight was so unusual, Nathaniel had left his quarters to check on it himself.

His hands began to shake as he stared at Ally. He wanted to go to her and put his arms around her to convince himself she was safe, but he stayed right where he stood, afraid that if he took her in his arms, he'd never want to let her go again.

"Are you certain you're all right?" he asked, finding his voice just as shaky as his hands.

She lowered the book she'd been clutching and nodded.

"Ally." He took a step toward her, forcing himself not to go any farther. "I've faced death on the battlefield before, but I've never been so frightened in my life as I was just now." Part of him hated to admit he was vulnerable, but the other part needed her to know how much he cared for her, even if he could do nothing about it.

All week, the sight of Colonel Benson, on his knees, weak and defenseless before his wife, had haunted Nathaniel's every move. How could a man as brave and courageous as the colonel be reduced to a puddle of nerves at the sight of his injured wife?

It wasn't until Nathaniel had seen Ally at the mercy of an attacker that he finally realized what had overcome the colonel. Edward Benson loved someone more than himself.

The thought of being wounded or dying was nothing compared to the thought of seeing Ally hurt or injured. Nathaniel could withstand his own pain, but he could not bear to see Ally suffer. He would take on her burdens and troubles a thousand times over if it meant sparing her.

Was that love? Was that the definition of selflessness? Was that what he'd witnessed between the colonel and his wife?

Ally began to tremble, and tears gathered in her eyes.

He could no longer let her suffer alone. He crossed the space and took her into his arms. "Are you certain you're not hurt?" he asked, unable to hide the worry from his voice. He wanted to soothe her, to take away the fear and uncertainty from the moment. He ran his hands along her back, reaching up to cup the back of her head in his hand.

She was pressed against him, the tears falling from her eyes as he cradled her. "I'm fine," she whispered. "Just a little shaken."

"Then that makes two of us." He tried to make his voice sound light and unaffected, but it was useless.

She finally pulled back, and he let her go.

"I've ruined your uniform," she said as she put her hand up to the tearstains on his chest.

He covered her hand with his, certain she could feel the heavy beat of his heart beneath her fingers. "I'm sorry for what he did."

"Don't be," she whispered, looking up into Nathaniel's eyes. "Be thankful you came to me in time."

Her words speared his heart, and he lifted her hand to his lips, pressing a kiss to the back of her fingers.

She closed her eyes at the touch, and his gaze lowered to her soft lips. A longing so deep, and so strong, filled him in that moment; nothing else mattered. But he would not steal a kiss from Ally Benson, or anyone else. He would not take something that was not his, no matter how much he wanted it for himself. If he did, he'd be no better than Captain Tonder.

"Darkness is falling." His voice was husky as he lowered her hand but did not let it go. "I will escort you back to your parents."

She opened her eyes and nodded. "Thank you."

He slipped her hand around his arm and led her out of the schoolhouse.

As they walked across the parade grounds, he stayed close to her side.

"Why have you been so distant this week?" she asked quietly.

Nathaniel sighed and stared out across the expanse of green grass toward the commandant's house. "I have had much to think about."

"Have you come to any conclusions?"

He smiled and placed his free hand over hers. "I have. Just recently."

"Does that mean you'll stay after supper?" She also placed her free hand over his. "I've missed our conversations a great deal. I daresay Papa has missed them too."

Nathaniel wasn't certain how wise it would be to spend so much time with her. It only increased his longing and would make their parting all the harder to bear.

She stopped and looked up at him, her beautiful brown eyes beseeching him. "Please."

He knew that from that moment, until the moment he died, he'd never be able to say no to Ally Benson again. "Of course."

Her smile was slow and sweet, and if they had not been standing in the middle of the parade ground, he could not have stopped himself from kissing her.

Chapter Seven

The parlor window had been cracked open to allow a cool breeze to blow into the room. The lace curtains ruffled on the wind, dancing a gentle waltz to the sound of a song Ally could not hear but could easily imagine. Her own heart played a silent tune, humming with joy as she sat in the parlor with Papa and Nathaniel long after supper was finished.

Mama, Constance, and Jeanne had retired for the evening, claiming boredom from Ally and Nathaniel's talk of Byron and Keats.

Eventually, Papa just sat and listened as he watched the pair exchange thoughts and ideas. Nathaniel's blue eyes lit with passion as they discussed eighteenth-century poetry, and Ally realized there were few men who could express themselves as well as he did. She was both relaxed and fully energized, leaning back in her chair but feeling as though she sat on the edge.

When Ally remembered Papa was still present and thought to look his way, he offered her a smile, seeming to enjoy their conversation as much as she did.

"It is growing late," Papa finally said as he rose from his chair. "As much as I am enjoying this conversation, I fear the bugle will soon be reminding us we should retire."

Nathaniel also rose, turning respectfully to her father. "I'm sorry to have kept you awake this long, sir."

Papa put his hand on Nathaniel's shoulder in a rare show of affection for his second-in-command. "Nonsense. I've enjoyed myself immensely."

Ally stood and clasped her hands in front of her gown, not ready for Nathaniel to leave but knowing she had little choice. It would be hours before her mind could settle and find rest. She would think about their conversation long after he left.

Papa started to walk toward the hall, and Nathaniel turned to Ally, his blue eyes filled with respect and deep affection. "I've had a lovely time tonight, Miss Ally. Thank you for inviting me to stay."

"It's been my pleasure, Major Ward."

"Ally," Papa said, pausing near the door to the hall. "Why don't you see the major out? My head is pounding and I'm more tired than I thought." He smiled at her. "Blow out the lights before you retire." And with that, he walked across the hall and stepped into his bedroom, closing the door softly behind him.

There were only two lamps lit in the parlor; the rest of the house was dark and quiet.

Nathaniel's face was cast in shadows as he looked at her. Neither one spoke or made a move to leave.

A thousand words rushed to Ally's mind and heart, yet she knew not what to say to him. Earlier, after he'd returned her to her house, he and Papa had left to deal with Captain Tonder. The man had been dishonorably discharged from the army and would be jailed until a steamboat arrived to take him away from the fort. Papa had been outraged, just as Nathaniel had been, but he was happy Major Ward had come to her rescue.

All throughout the evening, Ally was afraid someone might notice her feelings for Nathaniel. She tried not to show them, but it was as difficult as if she'd been required to hold her breath that whole time.

She was in love with Major Nathaniel Ward, and no matter how much she tried to convince herself that they could be friends or that she didn't care for him, her feelings continued to grow.

Now, as they stood alone in the darkened room, the remnants of their conversation still enveloping them in their sweet aroma, Ally's heart ached with longing to be in his arms.

"The bugle will blow at any moment," he said quietly.

"Then we should say our goodbyes now," she answered, just as softly.

They started toward the hall, their hands brushing against each other before Nathaniel reached out and took her hand in his.

Butterflies fluttered in her stomach as they stopped in front of the closed door. Here, in the hall, there was no lamp, yet there was enough light from the parlor to mark the outline of Nathaniel's handsome form.

"Do you think your father suspects?" he whispered.

"I'm not certain." Though she doubted her father would have allowed them to be alone if he had.

Nathaniel lifted his free hand to caress the side of her face, as he'd done in the schoolhouse. Only now, Ally leaned into the touch and closed her eyes, loving the feel of his fingers against her skin.

"Do you think there is any hope?" he said.

Her heart squeezed at his words, knowing Papa could not give his blessing without Mama's consent, no matter how much he might like Nathaniel.

"Ally." Nathaniel spoke her name, almost reverently.

She opened her eyes. "Yes?"

"I love you."

Her breath caught and her lips parted as she stared at him.

"I know I do not deserve to say such things—"

She placed her finger on his lips to silence him. "It is I who does not deserve to hear such things."

His hand reached up and captured hers. He pressed it against his lips. "I know it's impossible, but I can no longer deny what's in my heart. I couldn't live with myself if I didn't tell you."

She stepped closer to him and reached up to place her other hand on the side of his face. "My dear Nathaniel," she breathed. "I love you too."

His hands slipped around her waist, and he pulled her closer. "My heart is yours alone." He lowered his head until his lips were a breath away from hers.

She knew he would not kiss her without her permission, so she raised up on her toes and pressed her lips against his.

Her arms went around the back of his neck, drawing him closer as his arms wrapped around her, pressing her against his chest. His lips were soft, yet eager.

She'd never been kissed before and had not anticipated such sweetness. Their bodies molded together as one, making her feel whole for the first time in her life.

The kiss was brief—much shorter than she would have liked—but Nathaniel pulled away, breathing heavily, his heartbeat pounding so hard she could feel it against her chest.

"I fear I've only lit a fire I cannot possibly quench," he said.

Ally smiled, amazed at the wonder of attraction and desire. "What a gift God has given us to enjoy."

"I fear I could spend hours exploring such a gift." He rested his forehead against hers. "But if I do not stop now, I'm certain I would abuse your father's trust."

The bugle called in the parade grounds, signaling an end to their night.

Nathaniel pulled away from Ally, as if it was the hardest thing he'd ever been forced to do.

"Good night," he whispered. "I shall relive that sweet kiss for days to come."

And, with that, Nathaniel left the house.

Ally closed the door and leaned against it for several heartbeats, listening to the sounds of his footsteps on the gravel as they faded into the night, knowing her life—and her heart—would never be the same again.

⟡

Life had never looked as bright as it did that following week. Nathaniel couldn't wipe the smile from his face or hide the joy radiating from his heart. The sky was bluer, the grass was greener, and his work held more purpose than it had ever held before. Each morning, he was awake before the first bugle call, and each evening, he laid his head upon his pillow thinking about the woman he'd grown to love.

He crossed paths with her several times, when she was coming and going from the school, walking to the sutler's store with her sisters, or visiting some of the wives on the front porch of the officers' quarters. He went out of his way to see her, stopping by the school to inquire if she needed assistance, making frequent calls to the commandant's home on errands, both real and imagined. When he was invited to supper, he often stayed after to talk with Ally and her father, though they hadn't been given another opportunity to be alone.

With each passing day, Nathaniel became more and more

convinced he wanted to marry Ally. Her visit to Fort Snelling was already half over, and the thought of her leaving was too painful to even consider. If Ally said yes, and they could somehow get the blessing of her father, he knew she'd want her mother and sisters to be there for the ceremony. He didn't want to wait to propose until right before they were slated to leave. He'd need to give them time to prepare for a wedding.

But each time Nathaniel thought about facing Colonel Benson to ask for Ally's hand in marriage, his courage faltered and he put it off for one more day. If the colonel said no, things would become very awkward between him and his commanding officer—not to mention the real possibility that Colonel Benson would forbid Nathaniel from seeing Ally again.

That thought alone made him hold his tongue. But the longer he waited, the more he yearned to make Ally his wife.

On Thursday evening, Nathaniel knocked on Colonel Benson's office door, well before the appointed supper hour. His hands shook as he held his shako under his arm and waited for the colonel to invite him inside.

"Major Ward, come in." The colonel held the door for him and then closed it when Nathaniel entered. "Have a seat."

Nathaniel had seen the colonel several times that day already. They'd been together during drill, during inspections, and at a meeting of the officers.

"What can I do for you?" the colonel asked as he took his own seat.

The room was hot, even with a window open. Nathaniel had already begun to sweat before he'd entered, but now, with the added warmth and the uncertain nerves, he felt like he was suffocating.

There was no point in drawing out the conversation or taking up more of the colonel's time than necessary. Surely he wouldn't be surprised when Nathaniel told him the reason for his visit. He was Ally's father and knew her better than most.

But this wasn't simply Ally's father Nathaniel was speaking to. He was also Nathaniel's commanding officer, a colonel in the United States Army, a man who had the power to not only control Nathaniel's future but determine the state of his heart as well.

"I've come to speak to you about your daughter, sir." Nathaniel's voice was tighter than he'd ever heard it before. It was almost embarrassing. "Ally."

Colonel Benson sighed. "I was afraid you might come to me about her."

Nathaniel would not back down now. "Permission to speak to you as her father, sir."

It took a moment for him to answer, but he eventually nodded. "Permission granted."

Nathaniel leaned forward, trying desperately not to sound like a fool. "I love her, with all of my heart. I'd like to ask her to marry me."

The colonel studied Nathaniel for several heartbeats.

"I know I am not worthy of her, and my love has grown quickly." Nathaniel almost laughed. "I didn't see this coming, please believe me. I know you put your trust in me, and I've lost that trust."

"You have not lost that trust, Nathaniel." Colonel Benson leaned forward and put his clasped hands on his desk. "I knew the moment I asked you to watch out for my wife and daughters that I was risking this very thing." He offered a sad smile. "Do you know why I've grown so fond of you? Why you've become like a son to me?"

Nathaniel shook his head.

"Because there's a part of you that reminds me of Ally. As I grew to know you, I realized you and she have much in common. It was only a matter of time before you two discovered it for yourselves."

"Then you approve?" Nathaniel's heart beat steady with hope.

"I could not think of a more worthy or deserving man for my Ally." His smile fell, and he shook his head. "But I cannot give you my blessing, Nathaniel, as much as it would please me to do so."

Dread washed over Nathaniel like a tidal wave. "Sir?"

"Ally and her mother and sisters are the most precious things on this earth. I would live and die for them. I would do anything in my power to make them happy."

Nathaniel knew that full well.

"Which means"—he let out a weary breath—"I cannot give you my blessing, because Mrs. Benson would never agree." He rose from his desk and placed his hands behind his back as he walked to the window. "Ally was too little to remember, and we did our best to hide the truth from our daughters." He looked back at Nathaniel, his countenance heavy. "I only tell you this now so you can understand. Mrs. Benson was accosted by a well-respected visiting officer in our home at Fort Knox, and I was not there to protect her. When I took the matter to my superiors, I was warned to keep the incident to myself or lose my position. I told Harriet I would fight for justice, but she refused to let me throw away everything I'd worked to achieve. We had four young daughters, and the thought of starting over was too daunting for either of us to consider. She'd never been fond of military life and had withstood Indian attacks, starvation, and deprivations no well-bred lady should have to endure. The incident was enough to convince her the frontier was no place for a woman and children. She took the girls to St. Louis and has lived there ever since."

Nathaniel swallowed, horrified to know the truth. Just thinking about what might have happened to Ally with Captain Tonder, had Nathaniel not intervened, sent ice through his veins. He couldn't imagine what the colonel and Mrs. Benson had endured.

"The military failed my wife, and there isn't a day that goes by that I don't consider resigning to be with Harriet and my daughters." The colonel returned to his desk, though he didn't sit. "But the army is in my blood. This is what I was born to do, and Harriet knows that even better than I know it myself. I was married to the military years before I met Harriet. When I told her I would give it all up for her, she knew I would only be a shell of my former self. I love her all the more for her selfless sacrifice to encourage me to stay."

"I'm sorry." It was all Nathaniel could think to say, though he knew it was a weak platitude.

"When our oldest daughter eloped," the colonel continued, "Harriet cried for months. I believe a part of her relived that horrible day she'd endured over ten years ago. Daily, she fears for Laura. The only thing that gives her hope and relieves her dismay is the knowledge that her other daughters will not suffer the same horror."

Nathaniel sat on his chair, his heart feeling deflated and hollow. He couldn't even look at the colonel, let alone speak. Empathy for Mrs. Benson gave him a new understanding and respect for the woman.

Yet with that understanding came the deep realization that she would never give her permission for Ally to marry a military man, no matter how much hope he possessed. And Ally would never go against her mother's wishes. He wouldn't dream of asking it of her, no matter how his heart would break.

"So you see," Colonel Benson said gently, his words heavy with regret, "no matter how perfect you and Ally might be for one another, and no matter how much I would enjoy having you as my son, I cannot give you my blessing without my wife's consent."

Nathaniel held his hat in his hands, studying the plume protruding from the top. It shifted and moved with each breath he took.

"I'm sorry, Nathaniel." Colonel Benson stood for a moment and then returned to his chair. "But now I must speak to you as your commanding officer."

Nathaniel knew what was coming, and he steeled his heart as best as he could.

"I should have never allowed you to spend so many evenings at our home. That is my fault. I saw your growing friendship, but I hadn't realized it had progressed this far. The only way I can think to prevent this from going further is to ask you to refrain from seeing Ally. I know it will be impossible to avoid her altogether, since this fort is so small, but you must not go out of your way to see her. It will be for both your good." His words sounded as painful to speak as they were to hear.

"And what of the dance tomorrow night?" Nathaniel hated to ask, knowing the answer before it was given.

"I don't think it would be a good idea for you to attend." The colonel paused and shook his head, his voice filled with regret. "It would only prolong the inevitable. Ally will be leaving very soon, and there is nothing either of us can do to prevent her from going."

Everything in Nathaniel wanted to protest, to fight until he had what he wanted. But, above all else, Nathaniel respected Colonel Benson. It took a moment, but he was able to gather the strength to stand and salute his commanding officer. "Yes, sir."

The colonel's eyes were sad, but in that moment, even though it hurt, Nathaniel knew the love of a father and a husband. He was truly doing what he felt was best for his family.

Colonel Benson returned the salute and nodded at Nathaniel. "Thank you, son."

Nathaniel turned on his heels, fighting the urge to shout in anger or bash his fist against a wall. But he'd been trained to follow orders, regardless of the cost, and that was what he would do.

He walked through the dining room and met Ally coming out of the parlor. Her eyes revealed her surprise at seeing him. She smiled, her dear, beautiful lips rising in pleasure at the sight of him.

Nathaniel came to a stop, the longing and love he felt for her making it feel as if his heart might burst from the force of it. But with that longing came the fiercest heartbreak he'd ever experienced. She stood just five feet away from him, yet she could not be his.

Ally's smile fell and she swallowed, her gaze briefly drifting to her father's office door and then back to Nathaniel. And that was when he knew that she knew what had just transpired.

"I'm sorry," was all he could muster before he left her standing in her father's hall.

Chapter Eight

Melancholy hovered over Ally that evening and all the next day as her sisters and mother prepared for another dance. Ally could not bring herself to speak to her father about what had happened in his office before she met Nathaniel in the hall. Part of her wanted to pretend they had not spoken, as if putting off the inevitable made it not so. She wanted to hold on to hope that it was not as she feared, but the quiet sadness around her father's eyes when he looked at her told her all she needed to know.

"Your mother and I have come to a decision," Papa said as they ate supper before the dance that evening.

Ally glanced up from the baked chicken she was pushing around her plate.

Papa looked right at her, though he addressed everyone. "There is a steamship scheduled to arrive on Monday, and we've decided you will all be on the boat when it returns to St. Louis that evening."

It was as if time stood still as they looked at one another.

Mama did not meet Ally's gaze as she moved her own food about her plate.

"But why?" Jeanne asked.

"We think it's best," Mama said as she finally met Ally's gaze. "For everyone."

They believed that somehow, putting space between her and Nathaniel would make them forget. The very idea of never seeing him again made her feel like she was drowning. The future in St. Louis, married to a stuffy banker or merchant as Mama had hoped, looked more daunting and bleaker than ever before.

Ally did not respond to her parents. How could she? What could she say to convince them to change their minds? She had listened to her sister Laura cry and plead for days on end to give their blessing for her marriage, but they had not given in. If anything, they'd only become more stubborn and determined to save her from herself. Ally would not follow in her sister's footsteps, though it made her heart weep to think about leaving Nathaniel behind.

They did not speak of the departure again but began to prepare for the dance as soon as the meal ended. Ally had no wish to attend the festive event, but she longed to see Nathaniel again, and even though it would be a miserable evening saying goodbye to him, she would handle it like a seasoned soldier and not retreat.

"You look as if you're attending a funeral and not a dance," Constance said to Ally moments before their first guest arrived. "Either you need to put a smile on your face, or you should excuse yourself so the rest of us can enjoy the evening."

Papa glanced at Ally, the sadness in his eyes deeper than she'd ever seen it. She could not look at him again, afraid she'd lose her composure.

They greeted their guests much like they had done before. Ally watched for the familiar figure of the man she loved, but when the door was shut after the final guest arrived, he was not in her father's house.

Mama, Constance, and Jeanne walked toward the parlor, but Ally stood where she'd been for the past hour. Papa walked up to her and put his hand on her forearm. "He won't be here tonight, Ally."

She didn't look at him but stared ahead. "Did you forbid him?"

"I told him it wasn't a good idea." His voice was heavy with heartache. "It's for the best."

"You keep saying that." She shook her head, fighting tears, her voice low so their guests would not hear her. "But whose 'best' are you referring to? Mama's? Because she's the only one who wins in this situation."

"I only have your best in mind, Ally." He spoke just as quietly.

"No." She finally looked at him, a tear slipping down her cheek. "You love the military. You've put your life on the line countless times for its sake. Nathaniel and I love it as you do. It's Mama and her fear that you have in mind." She wiped impatiently at the tear, hating her weakness. "And I understand why you are on her side; I truly do. But this is not Mama's life you are dealing with. It is mine and Nathaniel's. Countless women thrive on the frontier with their husbands. Just because Mama could not tolerate this life does not mean I cannot. I longed to stay on the frontier even before I met Nathaniel. Now I'm more certain than ever that this is where I belong." She pressed her lips together to try to compose her emotions. "You and Mama lived your life, and now it is time I live mine. I love Nathaniel, and I want to be his wife." She met her papa's gaze and had to steel herself from the sorrow she saw there. "But you know I will not defy you. I would die before I hurt you or Mama."

She was afraid if she stayed in the hall and continued to speak to her father she would say something she'd regret and draw unwanted attention. But she couldn't remain in the stuffy house either. She needed air, space to breathe and to grieve.

Without asking permission, she opened the front door and stepped out into the torchlit night. A gentle breeze ruffled the hem of her gown, and the full moon shined bright, casting shadows on the parade grounds.

Ally refused to cry until she had a place to do so in privacy. She walked around the side of the house toward the hill that sloped away from the basement kitchens. Here, there was nothing to hinder her view of the moon-soaked countryside at the foot of the bluff. The rivers sparkled, and the shadow of a cloud floated gently over the land.

An outcropping of rocks beckoned her to come and rest and to find a place to pour out her tears.

Never in her life had she felt so heartbroken or full of sorrow. She sat on the hard rock and stared up at the expanse of sky overhead, tears streaming freely down her cheeks. Despite the pain, she felt the arms of God enfolding her in a loving embrace, offering her a safe space to grieve. She had to believe this was God's will, if He had allowed it to happen. She couldn't imagine why, or what it all meant, but her faith told her there was a purpose and plan, even if it made no sense to her.

She didn't know how long she sat there crying before a gentle presence made her turn.

Nathaniel stood near the house, quietly watching her. He wore his uniform but did not have his hat or sword with him.

She rose from the rock, and he walked toward her, his arms outstretched to welcome her into his embrace.

"I'm sorry, Ally." He held her close, as if protecting her from everything that wanted to hurt her in the world. "I spoke to your father, but—"

"I know." She didn't want to hear the truth all over again.

"I tried, my love, but he will not be persuaded."

Ally nodded, knowing her father far better than Nathaniel knew him. "He will not be moved on this, for my mother's sake."

He released her from the embrace and took her hand in his, leading her to the rock she'd recently occupied. He sat, drawing her with him, so they were pressed against each other. He put his arm around her and kissed the top of her head.

"Your father will not give his blessing, because I'm an officer in the United States Army."

"I know," she whispered.

"So I've made a decision."

Ally looked up at him sharply, afraid of what he was about to say. "Nathaniel—don't—"

"I have already drafted my letter of resignation."

Ally shook her head as she looked up at Nathaniel. "I can't let you resign."

He had thought of little else since he'd spoken to Colonel Benson the day before, but he knew he would need to make Ally understand. He pulled back and took her hands in his so he could look into her beautiful eyes. "When I was a boy, my father saw to my physical needs, but he did not fill the emotional void left from the death of my mother. I was surrounded by a large family, yet I lacked the love that my heart desired." He moved a curl off her forehead, allowing his finger to graze over her silky skin. "I joined the army because I was searching for a purpose and a place to belong. The military fed my need for acceptance and approval. There were a series of expectations and rewards, and with each accomplishment, I was given respect and admiration. For the first time in my life, I felt like I fit somewhere."

She studied him in the moonlight as he spoke, listening intently.

"But my heart was still searching until it found you." He smiled, the love he felt for her permeating each word he spoke. "In the military,

I found a place to belong, but I hadn't found a home or a family. The army offered me discipline and purpose, but it didn't offer me love. And love is what my heart has been seeking my whole life." He caressed her cheek with his thumb, wiping away a lingering tear. "Now that I have found what I've been searching for, nothing else matters. If I lost you now, I would never find a home for my heart again, and I would miss the greatest opportunity of my life. The military means nothing to me without you. There is no doubt in my mind that this is the right thing to do. I've never been more certain than I am right now."

Ally tilted her head, her eyes sad, yet filled with hope. "I love you, Nathaniel. But I do not want you to give this up, unless it's what you truly want."

He kissed her then. She came to him willingly, melting into his embrace. Her lips were soft and pliable, full of a tender sweetness he wanted to spend the rest of his life tasting. To think that she could be his, for as long as they both should live, seemed almost too good to be true. He would spend the rest of his days thanking God for Ally's love.

When she finally pulled away, they were both breathless.

"Where will we go?" she asked.

"Wherever you'd like."

"I do not want to return to St. Louis." She clung to him and he to her. "I want to stay on the frontier for as long as possible."

"Then we shall turn to ranching, or farming, anything that will keep us on the edge of civilization." He smiled, loving that they were both in agreement about how they would live. "I don't care where we go, or what we do, as long as we do it together."

"And will you be sad that you gave up the army?" She watched him closely, and he knew he could not lie to her. She would see it in his eyes if he did.

"There will be a part of me that will miss all of this. It's all I've known for almost half my life." He kissed her again, trying to banish her uncertainty and misgivings. "But I will gladly give it up for something that is infinitely better."

She nuzzled into his embrace and rested her cheek against his chest. He set his chin gently on the top of her head, knowing he would never want to be apart from her again, no matter what it cost him.

"My mother would not let my father leave the army," Ally said quietly, as if she was having second thoughts. "She loved him too much to let him give it up for her."

"We are not your mother and father. You and I are charting a new course."

Ally looked up at him again, searching his face for the truth. "I could not bear for you to resent me later because of this."

"Oh, my dear, sweet girl." He kissed her again. "The military is not the beginning and the end of all things. It is simply one choice, out of a thousand or more, that I could choose from. But today, and every day forward, I will choose you, above anything else on this earth. I promise you that with all my heart."

A smile, unlike any other, graced Ally's face, weakening Nathaniel's knees and overpowering his senses. "I would caution you to use that smile sparingly, my love."

"Oh?" she whispered, not letting it falter.

"It may tempt me to do things we might both regret. . .at least, until we're married." He was only half teasing, a smile on his face as he warned her.

"I see." She tilted her chin down, so he could not see her lips, and when she looked up at him again, the smile was only slightly dimmer. "Then I shall reserve it until after we've said our vows—but not a moment longer."

He wrapped her in his arms again, and this time he kissed her until they were both breathless and a bit senseless as well.

Chapter Nine

A lly and Nathaniel agreed that it would be best to speak to Colonel Benson in the morning and not bother him during the dance. Nathaniel had left Ally near the front door and returned to his quarters, where he'd finished the final draft of his resignation letter.

But he'd been unable to sleep. The reality of his decision to leave the army, coupled with the sweet knowledge of marrying Ally, kept him awake through the long hours of the night. If he could choose, he would have both the military and his bride, but he could not start his married life off on the wrong foot with his commanding officer—especially if he was to be Nathaniel's father-in-law as well. He could not elope with her and keep his position as an officer, but neither could he let her slip away either.

That left only one choice, which he would choose a thousand times over if it meant Ally could be his.

The first bugle cry of the morning found Nathaniel on his feet, preparing to face the day. He dressed quickly, taking great pains to look as presentable as possible. Not long after reveille, he assembled on the parade ground with the officers and enlisted men, including Colonel Benson, for roll call. After he and the colonel did their morning inspections, the mess call sounded and Nathaniel chose to join the others for breakfast at the commissary. It wasn't until after fatigue duty was assigned that Nathaniel found a spare moment to speak to his commanding officer.

As was his usual practice, the colonel returned to his home to work in his office. Nathaniel went to his own office in his quarters and picked up his resignation letter, saying a prayer for courage as he closed the door and walked the short distance to the commandant's house.

The sky was overcast and threatening rain as he knocked on the front door. He was nervous to face the colonel yet as confident as he'd ever been, knowing he was doing the right thing.

It wasn't Mr. Delany who opened the door, but Ally, dressed in the same gown she'd worn the first time he'd seen her on the wharf. Her brown eyes were filled with the same bittersweet emotions he felt churning in his heart. Her lips were smiling with tender hope while her face had a sadness he could not deny. She was mourning the loss of his military career, just as he was mourning it, and he loved her for it all the more.

"Good morning," she said as she took in the sight of him, her gaze landing on the letter he held in his hand. "Did you sleep at all last night?"

He shook his head. "And you?"

"Not even for a moment." She opened the door wider, inviting him in. "Papa's in his office."

He removed his shako, suddenly feeling like a schoolboy again, uncertain and nervous.

"Don't be afraid," she whispered to him as she put her hands on his arm. "He will understand."

"Ally?" Mrs. Benson called to her from the parlor. "Who's here, dear?"

"Nathaniel."

Her mother's sudden intake of breath was audible, even from where they stood in the next room.

"He's come to speak to Papa." Ally smiled up at him. "Do you mind if I come with you?"

He'd thought to discuss this with her father alone, but he would not deny her request. If they were to be partners in life, he would not have them start their journey apart. "No. I do not mind."

Mrs. Benson appeared in the hall, limping on her bad ankle. "Major Ward, we didn't expect to see you again."

Nathaniel took a deep breath. "I've come to speak to your husband on a very important matter."

Her eyes were large as she nodded. "Yes, of course."

Ally wrapped her hand around Nathaniel's elbow and led him through the dining room.

"You're not going to join them, are you?" Mrs. Benson asked Ally, hobbling along close behind.

"I am," Ally said.

Nathaniel knocked on the colonel's door, feeling much more confident than he had the last time, now that Ally was beside him.

"Come in."

Ally turned the knob and pushed the door open.

Colonel Benson looked up, his eyes betraying his surprise at seeing all three of them outside his office. He quickly rose and indicated that they should enter.

Mrs. Benson hovered by the door for a moment, clearly uncertain about what she should do. He doubted that she was in her husband's office very often, if at all.

"Come in, Mama," Ally said, extending her hand to her mother. "This concerns you as well."

The invitation seemed to cause her mother even more distress, but she entered the room and closed the door behind her.

"Please have a seat," Nathaniel said to Mrs. Benson, holding the chair for her.

She watched him closely as she lowered herself into the chair, and then she cast a petrified look at her husband.

Ally stood beside Nathaniel and removed her hands from his arm.

"What is this about, Major Ward?" the colonel asked, standing behind his massive desk.

Nathaniel stood as straight as a rod, addressing his commanding officer as he'd been taught. "I've come to hand in my resignation, sir."

Colonel Benson's mouth slipped open in utter shock. He stared at Nathaniel for an unreasonably long time before he shook his head. "Did I hear you correctly, Major?"

"It has come to my attention that the woman I love has been forbidden to marry a military man. Because I love her more than life itself, I have decided that being with her is far more important than my career in the army." He stepped forward and extended his letter to the colonel. "As soon as my resignation is accepted, I request permission to marry your daughter, Colonel Benson."

"At ease, Nathaniel." Colonel Benson did not take the letter Nathaniel extended to him. Instead, he walked around his desk and held out his arms to his daughter.

Ally went to him, and he held her tight, kissing the top of her head. "My dear girl," he whispered. "I'm sorry we've put you through such heartache." The colonel looked up at Nathaniel, regret in his eyes. "And I must apologize to you too, Nathaniel. The last thing I wanted was to force your resignation."

"You did not force anything. I am giving it freely." Nathaniel went to Ally's side and faced her father. "I have never been so sure of anything in my life. I want to marry Ally, and, more than anything, we want your blessing on our union, even if that means giving up my commission."

Mrs. Benson reached up her sleeve to pull out a handkerchief. "Oh my," she said as she patted her wet cheeks. "I had no idea it had come to this."

"I told you he asked for her hand in marriage," Colonel Benson said to his wife.

"Yes, but I didn't realize, until this moment, how much they loved one another." She swallowed and clutched her handkerchief in her lap.

The colonel went to his wife. "Do they remind you of anyone?"

She pursed her lips and shook her head. "A pair of naive lovers, much like we were."

He smiled down at his wife and put his hand on her shoulder. "And would we have let anything stand in our way?"

"We would not." Mrs. Benson sighed. "Not even two meddling parents who thought they knew what was best for us."

"And how did we turn out?" Colonel Benson asked his wife.

"Fair to middling, if I do say so myself." She dipped her head. "I concede, we could have made better choices along the way, but I think we've done our best with what we've been given."

"I daresay they will as well," the colonel said as he smiled at Nathaniel and Ally.

"Then you'll give your blessing?" Ally asked.

"I could not think of anything I'd like better," Colonel Benson said to his daughter. "What do you think, Mrs. Benson?"

"I think we have a wedding to plan," Mrs. Benson said to her husband just before turning her smile on Ally.

"Oh, thank you." Ally left Nathaniel's side and hugged her father and then her mother, tears of happiness slipping down her cheeks.

"Congratulations, Nathaniel," Colonel Benson said, extending his hand. "You've made me very happy."

Nathaniel couldn't find the words to express his own happiness. Instead, he shook the colonel's hand, squeezing it tight within his own.

"I suppose we'll have to postpone our return to St. Louis until after the wedding," Mrs. Benson said to Ally. "You'll want to be married with both your mother and father present."

Ally nodded.

"And then there will be the matter of setting up your house," Mrs. Benson continued. "It will be difficult to get all the things we'll need for your trousseau, but I don't think it will be impossible. Military wives learn to make do with what they have. You'll be no different."

Ally wiped her tears away as she blinked at her mother. "What do you mean?"

"Major Ward, do you truly wish to resign your commission?" Mrs. Benson asked him.

"If it's the only way I can marry Ally, then I will give it up in a heartbeat." Ally joined him again, wrapping her hands around his arm.

"And, if you could have both Ally and your career, what then?" She watched him carefully.

Nathaniel looked from Mrs. Benson to the colonel, and finally to Ally.

She nodded and gave him an encouraging smile.

"If I could have both, I'd consider myself blessed beyond measure."

"What are you getting at?" Colonel Benson asked his wife.

Ally's mother slowly stood, using the desk to support herself. When she finally met Nathaniel's eyes, she didn't purse her lips or scowl at him, as she was wont to do. Instead, she rested her gentle gaze on his. "My greatest fear for my daughters is that they would marry a military man who would put his career above them, at any cost."

"Harriet," Colonel Benson said.

She lifted her hand to him and shook her head. "I was tempted to make my husband choose between me and his career, and because of my own fear that he would choose the army over me, I forced him to stay. I know what sacrifices are required for life on the frontier, and for a long time, I was willing to make them. But I let fear win and it made me very unhappy, even in St. Louis. I thought if I was stubborn enough, I could bend Ally to my will, and she would find happiness living in the city. It wasn't until this moment that I realized I could never change Ally, and nor do I want to anymore. I cannot continue to rob her, or you, of the happiness you so clearly find in each other."

"Oh Mama." Ally's tears started up again.

"And, the truth is," Mrs. Benson continued, "no matter where you live, you will not be immune to sacrifices or trouble. If this is where God has called you, then this is where you should stay."

Colonel Benson smiled at his wife, pride shining from his eyes.

"Does this mean you will not accept my resignation?" Nathaniel asked the colonel with a smile of his own.

"I have no intention of accepting it now, or in the future."

"Good." Ally leaned into Nathaniel and laid her head against his shoulder. "Because I have no desire to leave anytime soon."

Colonel Benson took his wife's hand, a bit of hope in his raised brows. "Does this mean you're ready to rejoin me, love?"

Mrs. Benson's lips pursed, and she looked at her husband out of the side of her eyes. "I may be persuaded, after a fashion. But let us get through Ally's wedding first, and then we shall discuss it at length, and in private."

The colonel nodded and grinned, looking for all the world as if he'd just won a battle.

And perhaps he had.

~C~

Ally Benson left the bedroom she'd been sharing with her sisters in the commandant's home on the first Sunday in August wearing a pale blue gown and holding a colorful bouquet of wildflowers. Nathaniel had picked the blossoms on the prairie beyond the bluff that she loved so well and presented them to her the night before.

She lifted the flowers to her nose and took a sniff a moment before her father stepped forward to offer his elbow. "Are you ready, my dear?" he asked.

With a nod, she wrapped her free hand around her father's arm and allowed him to lead her into the parlor.

The chapel, also used as the school building, held unpleasant memories for Ally, so she had decided to marry Nathaniel in the parlor of her father and mother's home.

Papa patted Ally's hand as they turned in the hall to face the room of well-wishers—and the man waiting to become her husband.

Nathaniel stood near the cold fireplace in his dress uniform, looking more dashing and handsome than ever. His blue eyes were filled with awe as he gazed at her, and the look on his face made all else fade away. She was reminded of the evening, several weeks ago, when they stood in this very room, all alone. He had kissed her for the first time that night and declared his love. Her stomach filled with butterflies at the thought of the next time they would be alone, when they would finally have the freedom and privilege to live together as man and wife. She wondered, once again, what she had done to deserve his affection and admiration.

The chaplain stood next to Nathaniel, a Bible in his hands as he waited for Ally to join them.

"Who gives this woman away?" he asked the room.

"Her mother and I," Papa said, and then he kissed Ally's cheek and joined his wife.

Mama smiled at Ally and nodded once. In the three weeks since she'd given Ally and Nathaniel her blessing, a change had come over her, in bits and pieces. The bitterness and fear that had dictated so much of her life had begun to fade away, and as her ankle healed, so too did her heart. She'd announced to all of them yesterday, in no uncertain terms, that she would not be returning to St. Louis after all, and that they would simply have to put up with her at the fort.

Papa took Mama's hand and slipped it through the crook of his elbow. He looked just as handsome as Nathaniel, in his dress uniform, his back straight and proud, his eyes full of joy as he looked upon his daughter and her soon-to-be husband.

Ally returned her gaze to Nathaniel and offered him the smile she'd given him the night he'd proposed to her on the rock overlooking the bluff. She had waited these many weeks, reserving it for this moment.

His hands tightened around hers, the look in his eyes deepening with desire, while he pledged his life to hers for better or worse, in sickness and in health, until death should part them.

The ceremony was over within minutes, and then Mama hosted a wedding breakfast to mark the occasion. Fifty people were in attendance, forcing everyone to remain standing while they held their plates of food. It was not how Mama had wished to host the event, but she made do with little complaints, saying it was one of many sacrifices she was willing to make for the army.

Not long after the meal was over, but not soon enough for Ally and Nathaniel, they were excused from the festivities and left the house, walking hand in hand toward Nathaniel's quarters.

"Do you know, Mrs. Ward," Nathaniel said as he lifted her

hand to his lips, their feet crunching on the gravel path, "I do not believe there is a man, living or dead, who has ever been as happy as I am in this moment."

A sound behind them made Ally turn, and she found her parents, their arms around one another, standing at the door of the commandant's house. They lifted their hands and waved.

Ally smiled and waved back, shaking her head at their sentimentality, before they slipped back into the house and closed the door.

"My father might disagree with you," Ally said with a smile. "Though I will not."

It only took a moment before they were standing on the porch outside Nathaniel's rooms. He turned the knob, pushed open the door, and then, without warning, scooped her into his arms and carried her across the threshold.

She caught her breath as she wrapped her arms around his neck, laughing at the weightless sensation.

"And what about you?" he asked on a whisper, his lips an inch away from hers. "Are you happy, Ally?"

She touched his dear face with the backs of her fingertips and looked into his beautiful eyes before she kissed his lips. "Completely," she whispered.

He returned her kiss, deepening it with each passing moment.

"Perhaps we should shut the door," she said when she pulled away to catch her breath.

He grinned and used his foot to shut the door behind him. "I almost forgot."

Ally tilted her head back and laughed, completely and irrevocably happy. Not only was she on the frontier, with space and room to breathe, but she was in Nathaniel's safe and loving arms, exactly where she was always meant to belong.

Gabrielle Meyer lives in central Minnesota on the banks of the Mississippi River with her husband and four young children. As an employee of the Minnesota Historical Society, she fell in love with the rich history of her state and enjoys writing fictional stories inspired by real people and events. Gabrielle can be found at www.gabriellemeyer.com where she writes about her passion for history, Minnesota, and her faith.

FRONTIER OF HER HEART

by Susanne Dietze

Dedication

To Matthew, my favorite font of knowledge on American history, U. S. Grant, and the Civil War. I am so proud of you!

A merry heart doeth good like a medicine:
but a broken spirit drieth the bones.

PROVERBS 17:22

Chapter One

Fort Humboldt, California
Late February 1854

Emily Sweet puffed her breath through her lips, directed upward to blow her hair from her eyes. She was only halfway through chopping onions, and her hands were slick with juice so she didn't dare touch her face. Unfortunately, a lank tendril of pale yellow hair fell over her right eye, driving her to distraction.

Didn't seem to matter how many pins she used. The neat bun she twisted her hair into each morning was always untidy by lunchtime.

So was the rest of her, perspiring from her proximity to the stove, smelling like grease and onions, but that was the life of a cook, wasn't it? And Emily was glad for it. She'd thanked God every day since she'd been hired by the fort commander, Colonel Robert Buchanan, to cook for the forty-odd members of Company B, Fourth Infantry. She and her twelve-year-old brother, Harry, were even given a tiny redwood house to live in, across the parade grounds from the kitchen.

Harry was happy and thriving here but perhaps getting too

comfortable, making friends with a few of the soldiers. Especially the new doctor, Boyd Braxton, who'd come to relieve the assistant surgeon who was on some sort of assignment with the inspector general. That was the thing with soldiers. They didn't stay anywhere long, and the last thing Harry needed was to grow close to someone who would leave. He needed permanence and stability.

So did she, for that matter.

Behind her, the sound of the door pushing open alerted her to someone's presence. It was about time Harry returned. "Did you find a good cabbage for me?"

"I did not," said a voice that was not Harry's.

Emily turned around. Molly Luther, the apple-shaped wife of the fort baker, Percy, lingered in the threshold, chuckling. A streak of flour lightened her iron-gray hair, and more speckled her purple skirt, evidence of her hard work at her husband's side. She and Molly often shared a cup of tea and conversation during afternoon lulls—a welcome respite, since they were currently the only two females at the fort. But it was a little early in the day for a visit.

"Sorry, Molly. I sent Harry to the garden, but clearly he's having a hard time finding a good cabbage. Or something else has distracted him." She was ten years older than Harry and sometimes had to remind herself what it was like to be a child. She tried to ensure he had enough time to play, explore the stables, and watch the blacksmith, but this was a fort, and everyone had a job to do. Even Harry.

Molly tipped her head back toward the door. "Harry's playing ball with Dr. Braxton. Or he was before the hunter arrived. That's what I came to tell you. There's game for you."

The news of fresh meat was welcome. The quartermaster, Captain Grant, had hired a colorful local by the name of Seth Kinman to provide game for the fort, supplementing the occasional beef and the standard rations of salt pork for Emily to cook.

But the other bit of information Molly offered? Emily wasn't as pleased that Dr. Braxton invited Harry to play catch again. "You'd think the doctor would have better things to do than toss a ball around." There were over forty people living in this fort. Surely one of them needed his services. Instead it seemed the dark-haired newcomer was always grinning or joking about something. . .sometimes at Emily's expense. He said she didn't smile enough. Why did he tease her so?

Molly did a terrible job of biting back her amusement. "That charming new doctor's hard to resist, you know."

Even Molly thought him amiable? Well, it wasn't as if Emily hadn't noticed his finer qualities. He bowed his head in prayer before he ate, and he thanked her after meals. He was handsome too, tall and broad, with straight brown hair that fell over his brow and a lopsided smile that she might have found attractive if, and only if, she weren't immune to the doctor's charms, as surely as if she'd been inoculated.

She had plans, and they did not involve following an army man hither and yon for the rest of her life. Or any man, for that matter.

But for the time being, she had a job, and the hunter had brought her game, so she might as well see what he'd brought. Using the knife, Emily pushed the pile of chopped onions into the large pot on the stove. Then she dunked her hands in a basin of soapy water and dried them on her apron.

"Do you know what the meat is?"

Molly shook her head. "My guess would be elk."

It was almost always elk.

"Let's go, then."

Emily and Molly strode outside over damp tufts of wild grass. The winter temperatures might be milder than back in Iowa, where she was raised, but that didn't mean the breeze didn't sting her ears and make her wish she'd brought a shawl. Here on a bluff overlooking Humboldt Bay, cool breezes sometimes swept over the water, and fog clung too long on many a morning at the fort, but the strategic location allowed an excellent vantage, as well as proximity to a handful of settlements in the region, should a need arise.

The fort was a year or so old, composed of fourteen redwood buildings set in a U shape around a central area where the soldiers drilled and gathered, as they did now. A dozen or more men dressed in blue French frock coats surrounded Kinman, a scruffy-bearded fellow of indeterminate age dressed in buckskins and a bushy fur cap that added a few inches to his six-foot-something height.

But Dr. Braxton's gaze wasn't fixed on Kinman. It landed on Emily, accompanied by that charmingly lopsided grin of his. "Look what Kinman's brought for you, ma'am."

The hunter's smile was only just visible in the cleft between his mustache and his white-striped beard as he held up a brace of pheasants. "Howdy do, Miss Sweet."

"Good day, Mr. Kinman." She took the birds from his callused hand. They were heavier than she expected. "Thank you. We'll have quite a supper out of them."

"Sorry no elk, but I was in a hurry. Managed to get you some rabbit alongside these, though." He gestured at a greasy-looking sack at his feet.

"You snare 'em?" Harry's voice rose in excitement. "I've been working on snares with the doctor here. Just the tyin'. We haven't tried to catch anything 'cause nothin' comes around the fort but mice."

"Something to catch the mice would be helpful, actually," Emily muttered. Like a cat. She'd enjoy a good mouser on the premises.

Kinman eyed the doctor. "You're the new doc, eh?"

"Boyd Braxton." The doctor shifted the leather ball he held so they could shake hands.

Emily leveled her brother with a meaningful look. She knew Harry liked the doctor and that they'd tossed the ball around, but she hadn't heard a peep about them tying snares. Had they gone outside the fort? The idea of Harry wandering off with a veritable stranger sat on her stomach about as well as curdled milk. "When were you tying snares? And where?"

Realizing he'd been caught withholding information from his sister, Harry's mouth formed an O. "We were on the doc's stoop, honest."

"Day before yesterday when you were seeing to your laundry, ma'am." The doctor shoved a section of hair back from his smooth forehead. "I learned how to tie snares when I was Harry's age. I was determined to catch my own supper in the woods, but all I managed to catch was poison ivy."

Everyone but Emily laughed.

Kinman fisted his hands on his hips. "Well, I did not snare these black-tailed hare." His booming voice drew the attention back to himself, which was where he seemed to like it best. "I lured the critters close with my fiddling, and then?" He mimicked grabbing one.

"Faugh." Molly snorted. "You're not fooling anyone, Mr. Kinman."

"I reckon you're right, ma'am, but did I ever tell you about the time I fought a grizzly with my bare hands?"

"Land sakes!" Molly's hands went to her round cheeks.

The hunter's tall tales made Boyd Braxton's sound tame by comparison. Mr. Kinman continued on with some nonsense about him wrestling a full-grown bear, his audience enraptured. Emily, however, didn't have time for this foolishness. The birds were getting heavier by the moment. "Help me take these to the kitchen, Harry."

Her brother's mouth turned down in disappointment, but he grabbed the birds and sack of rabbits like they weighed no more than goose down pillows and ran for the kitchen. Emily brushed off her hands and intended to thank the hunter, but he was still engaged in his story, his hands curled like bear claws. If she left now, no one would miss her.

Dr. Braxton disproved that thought by appearing at her shoulder in an instant, matching her shorter stride as she walked toward the kitchen. She could feel the weight of his gaze before she glanced up at him.

For once he didn't look to be teasing her. Quite the opposite, in fact, with his eyes creased in concern. "I didn't mean to offend, showing your brother how to snare."

"It's not the snaring I object to. It's him wandering off without my permission. The fort may lack a fence, but that doesn't mean it's safe for a boy to roam about the area."

"Duly noted. I assure you I'd never wish to see Harry come to any harm."

"For that I am grateful."

That should have proven a satisfactory end to the conversation, but Harry burst from the kitchen. "Finished, Doc. You still got the ball?"

"I do, if it's well with your sister."

Much as she loved her brother and was glad to be his guardian, she did not enjoy the discipline part of things. It was necessary, though. "Play is for when the work is done."

"Just five minutes more, Em." Harry took the ball out of the doctor's hand and tossed it in the air to himself. "Then I'll help you and finish my lessons, I promise, but I need to stretch my legs."

"Which is why I sent you out for cabbage."

"I'll get that too." He grinned. "Come on, play with us, Em."

"Fresh air does a body good," the doctor said. "And exercise is as vital as book learning. Helps clear the head too, which is what I needed."

"You're saying you're a better doctor for tossing a ball?"

At Harry's toss, Boyd caught the ball one handed. "I believe so, yes. Join us."

The doctor's smile widened, as if he actually did want her to frolic on the parade ground like a hoyden. And mercy, if she were the woman she'd been two years ago, carefree with a world of possibilities ahead of her, she would have been eager to participate. But she was no longer that person, so she remained steadfast. "I don't have even five minutes to spare, Doctor."

"Come on, Emily." Harry's playful tone was a perfect imitation of the doctor's.

A knot of tension developed at the base of her skull. "You have five minutes, Harry, and bring the cabbage with you when you come in."

"I need more time than that. Please?" he begged.

She shook her head, and maybe that was why she didn't see the ball Harry threw until it was about to strike her. All she could do was shriek before the ball smacked her in the nose.

Hard.

Boyd had only wanted to see the cook smile. But that wouldn't be happening anytime soon now that she'd been hit in the face with his stitched leather ball.

He rushed to Emily. Her hands were over her face in a protective gesture, but they prevented him from seeing what damage had been done. Gently, he touched her wrists. "May I take a look?"

"I'm fine." The words came out stuffy, like she was ill with catarrh, but she removed her hands. Blood dribbled from one nostril and slicked her palms.

"Aww, Emily, I'm so sorry!" Harry gripped his sister by the

shoulders. "I didn't mean to break your nose!"

"It's broken?" Her jaw fell.

"Not necessarily." Boyd had reset a few noses in his time, and while the pain involved was short, it was intense. Grown men wept like babies. Therefore, he was relieved when he could offer a better diagnosis. "Not broken, but it is bleeding from the impact."

He tugged a handkerchief from his pocket and pushed it against Emily's nose.

She recoiled at the pressure. "Is that much force really necessary?"

"To stanch the flow, yes. Why don't you come to the hospital and lie down?"

"The hospital?" Harry's voice rose to a nervous screech.

Emily took the handkerchief from Boyd. "It's fine, Harry. It's just a bloody nose. A minute and it'll stop. I don't need to lie down in the hospital."

Boyd understood she didn't want to scare the boy, but he nevertheless needed to tend the wound. "At least come sit down for a few minutes."

"If sitting is all that's required, I'll do it in the kitchen so I can attend my stew." With a swish of her brown skirt, she turned around and marched toward the kitchen.

Obstinate female. He caught up to her, aware of Harry and a handful of soldiers following in his peripheral vision. "You need a clean compress on it, and you should rest. Are you dazed or feeling faint?"

"I am nothing of the sort. Continued pressure stops the flow quite well, and if it doesn't, a few drops of cider vinegar will do the trick. Thank you anyway."

One would have thought the hospital was full of rattlesnakes, the way she was avoiding it. Or maybe it was just him she wanted to elude. What did he do to make this woman dislike him so?

He felt quite the opposite about her. He hadn't been at the fort a quarter hour before he noticed her. How could he not, with her golden hair, large brown eyes, and willowy figure? She had a becoming smile too, which she shared with the other soldiers. She wasn't too friendly, of course, but polite and pleasant. And she was downright familiar with the baker and his wife, so it wasn't like she had a disagreeable disposition in general.

No, it was just Boyd who made her cantankerous as a ready-to-hibernate bear. And he was doing everything he could to make her smile.

"Never heard of using cider vinegar. You're going to put me out of a job."

She stopped walking just outside of the kitchen, removed the handkerchief, and twitched her nose, as if satisfied the bleeding had stopped. Sure enough, it seemed it had. "Unlikely, but just as you can boil beans and make yourself a supper, I can see to basics myself."

"You're suggesting I can't cook beyond boiled beans?"

He hadn't realized the group of soldiers he'd seen had followed them all the way to the kitchen until they oohed in chorus at his remark.

Her brown eyes widened. "Can *you* cook beyond boiled beans?"

"Not really, no." He laughed.

Her eyes narrowed in a disapproving look. "Everything is a joke to you, isn't it?"

"Not everything, but life's meant to have a heap of fun in it."

She snorted in disagreement and then winced, as if the act hurt her nose. "If one has a heap of time left over for fun, Doctor, then fine, but most of us do not have that luxury."

"Luxury's not the word I'd use. A life without joy in it sounds pretty gray indeed."

She crumpled his bloody hanky in her fist. "There's joy to be had in a job well done."

"I agree, ma'am, but that still leaves out sunsets and music and laughter."

"Some of us are working when the sun sets, Doctor."

Private Hank Philpott lifted a thick finger in the air. "Maybe being a cook is harder than being a doctor," he offered helpfully.

Boyd felt his brows lift. "Clearly you haven't spent much time in the hospital, Philpott."

"I have been in a kitchen, though." Philpott flushed scarlet. "Sir."

"Kitchen work is tough sometimes. Maybe you two should switch jobs for a day," Harry suggested. "See how hard the other works."

Everyone was silent a full five seconds before one of the men rubbed his stomach. "Please don't. I like a good meal."

So did Boyd. Not to mention, he'd be derelict in his duty if he let the cook—or anyone, for that matter—take over as fort doctor.

Time to stop whatever this was. . .his attempt to make the cook smile. He'd failed at that, and he was taking men from their duties. "I'll leave you to your tasks, ma'am."

Emily twitched her nose again. "And you to yours. I'll wash and return your handkerchief shortly. Come on, Harry. You can fetch the cabbage later." She marched to the kitchen.

Harry didn't follow at once. He sidled up to Boyd, his narrow shoulders slumped. "She must be really upset if she doesn't want the cabbage anymore. How bad did I hurt her?"

"She'll be fine, and don't worry about her being upset. She knows it was an accident. Just gotta be careful when you're throwing a ball that the recipient's looking." Boyd thumped Harry's shoulder.

The lad nodded, but his lower lip stuck out in a defeated gesture. "See you at supper, Doc."

"See you, Harry."

Boyd juggled the ball between his hands. Good thing it hadn't caused more damage, but he didn't regret taking a few minutes to play with Harry. He'd meant what he said about fun. The Bible was full of references to joy, and none of them were condemning.

Emily Sweet was far too young to be this world-weary. Such a shame. Life was too short to be spent in gloomy seriousness. Boyd had experienced enough difficulty to make him determined to enjoy life as much as he could.

Much as he enjoyed his fun, though, it was time to return to work. He tossed the ball in the air and caught it one-handed as he walked toward the hospital.

The hair on his nape prickled, as if he was being watched. He looked to the left, and sure enough, Colonel Buchanan stood watching him, his mustache unable to hide the down-set turn of his mouth. Did the colonel think Boyd was the one who threw the ball and hurt Emily? He'd happily explain that he wasn't, but he would take responsibility.

Boyd braced for the reprimand, but the captain's attention was caught by something behind Boyd. Boyd turned to get a gander. The quartermaster, Captain Ulysses Grant, entered the fort, stroking his shaggy brown beard, riding an equally shaggy mule. The quartermaster was excellent at his job, securing the usual rations and supplies while also supplementing them, depending on availability. In fact, he had been the one to arrange for Seth Kinman to obtain game for the fort. However, Grant had one particular vice. His uncertain posture told Boyd he'd been at that tavern in Eureka again. By the way Colonel Buchanan marched over to meet the quartermaster, it was clear he wasn't pleased with him.

Someone was in deeper trouble than Boyd for a change.

Chapter Two

After serving the soldiers their supper of beef and bean stew, pickled chowchow, and Percy Luther's fluffy biscuits, Emily filled a dishpan with soapy water so she could scrub the handkerchief Boyd Braxton loaned to her. When it was clean, she hung the square of white linen on a small rack near the stove to dry. She could iron it tomorrow and return it to him, fresh as a spring morning.

The stack of things to do was never ending around here, but the work kept Emily from dwelling on unpleasant things, like how she and Harry had ended up in the fort in the first place. No, it was far preferable to focus on the tasks at hand—and she had several chores to see to in the little dwelling she shared with Harry. Her brother sat near the stove with a book in hand.

"That *Count of Monte Cristo* a good story so far?"

He made an affirmative humming sound.

"And glad I am to hear it." Emily had traded an older, less enjoyed book for this one with the barber in Bucksport. Pity there wasn't a more reliable way to obtain books. There wasn't much around these parts, and Harry was such a quick reader he'd require new material within the week.

The outer door opened, and Molly strode in with an expectant look in her eyes. "Percy had some extra sugar and made cry baby cookies, if you'd like to come to our place and share them with us."

"Really?" The cookies were Harry's favorite. "May we, Em? Huh?"

Emily relished the company more than the cookies. "We'd be delighted, thank you. I'm finished here—"

The door opened again, admitting Colonel Buchanan, who to her knowledge had never stepped into the kitchen before. "Miss Sweet? Have you a moment?"

"Of course, Colonel." Why was he here? Had there been something wrong with the food? Her stomach tightened. "I hope supper was satisfactory."

"Quite." The graying fort commander patted his flat stomach. "Your skills are a blessing."

What a relief. Her hand went to her throat as the colonel exchanged greetings with Molly and Harry. "How can I help you?"

Before he could answer, the door swung open yet again and Dr. Braxton entered the kitchen, his brow scrunched with curiosity. "You asked for me, Colonel?"

"I did. You know everyone, of course."

He greeted the room. Harry's and Molly's hellos were far more enthusiastic than Emily's. Before she could blink, though, he'd moved to stand over her, his gaze fixed on her nose.

"Glad to see you looking better. Your nose, I mean."

His proximity made the hairs on her arms stand at attention, so she stepped away. "Thank you for offering your handkerchief. And your opinion, unnecessary though it was."

He laughed and then gestured at the fort commander. "Colonel, the patient is hale, if that's what you were concerned about."

"I'm relieved to hear it, but no, I have something else in mind. A favor to ask both of you."

"Certainly, sir." Emily would agree to whatever Colonel Buchanan asked of her, so grateful was she that he'd given her this job last year. Taken her and Harry in, as it were. Without him, who knew where they'd be? Serving mush to gold miners at a so-called restaurant that was little more than a saloon, probably.

The doctor's eyes narrowed. "How can we be of help, sir?"

The colonel cocked his head to the side. "I overheard something about you two switching jobs?"

Oh dear. "Harry was just making a joke—"

"I'd never abandon my post, sir—"

"Of course not." The colonel lifted his hands in a calming gesture. "But the men are gossiping like biddies about it, and it gave me a thought. Fort life can be monotonous, as you know, and while the men are free to do what they wish on their own time, I disapprove when they return to the fort inebriated. Pardon my saying so, ladies."

His concern for her sensibilities was touching, but Emily had seen far worse than tipsy Captain Grant when she lived in the mining camp. "I'm not sure how to help with that particular issue, sir."

She was naught but a cook, and she already cooked three meals a day for them. A glance at the doctor told her he was as confused as she.

Colonel Buchanan's gaze flickered between them. "I'd like to offer a more wholesome diversion here inside the fort, and since you two are so entertaining, why not make you the focus? I'm thinking of a competition of skills, all in good fun, of course. I won't condone the men placing bets on it. This is for amusement only."

Emily's mouth dried like she'd eaten a plate of crackers. "I don't know what you mean."

"A competition?" Molly repeated.

"A competition!" Harry's tone was altogether more admiring. "Between Em and the doc. What's harder, doctoring or feeding the fort? When can we start?"

"Wait just a minute." Boyd scratched the shadow of stubble on his cleft chin. "Sir, are you suggesting a contest to find out if kitchen work is harder than doctoring? Because Miss Sweet's work is hard. Never said it wasn't, and I don't wish to propagate any ill will that way."

For once, Emily agreed with Boyd. "And doctoring takes a lot of knowledge and skill. I'd never say otherwise."

"Glad to hear you acknowledge one another's efforts, but that wasn't quite what I meant." The colonel's lips twitched, as if he was thoroughly enjoying this. "I was thinking there could be two challenges, a healing challenge and a cooking challenge, with a third competition to break a tie if necessary. Not all on the same day, but as opportunities arise."

A cooking challenge was self-explanatory. But the other? "What do you mean by a healing challenge?"

"Can you, Miss Sweet, heal a minor condition as well as our doctor? And in the same way, can you, Dr. Braxton, cook something tasty?"

"The answer to both of those is no." Boyd folded his arms. "I can't cook, and with all due respect, I will not deny medical attention to anyone simply to entertain the soldiers, sir."

"I didn't mean she'd do an amputation, Doctor." The colonel held up his hands. "I meant something simple that doesn't necessarily need a physician, like Miss Sweet did today with her nose. She had a homemade remedy, didn't she? Something about vinegar, I hear?"

"Yep, but she didn't need it, sir." Harry elbowed Emily in the ribs. "She's good at makin' remedies."

Emily shook her head. "That doesn't mean anyone should be

entrusted to me for care. I am no doctor."

"I promise if there's blood or a serious illness, I won't set it to a challenge. Only a minor ailment shared by two of the men who volunteer to be treated by either of you, and we'll see whose patient heals faster or better."

Two identical ailments presenting at the same time could seem farfetched, but Emily had lived in the fort for almost a year. The soldiers always seemed to come down with catarrh, nausea, or bellyaches at the same time. But that didn't mean one of them would agree to let her attend to him, and Emily's shoulders relaxed. "Could be awhile for two men with a similar problem to agree to this."

Maybe forever, which would be fine by Emily.

"I'm guessing the men will be happy to wait." Colonel Buchanan smiled. "The cooking challenge may well come first. We'll just have to see what happens, but don't fret, Doctor. I won't set out anything I think beyond either of your ken."

"Emily would love to do it." Harry was practically bouncing on his toes, the traitor. Emily had no desire for such a competition, much less the time. Didn't she have enough work to do?

She hated to say no to the colonel, but this was ridiculous. "I'm not sure, sir."

"Aw, Em." Harry's jaw set.

"Why not, Emily?" Molly looked disappointed too, with her lips all pouted up. "It sounds like a pleasant change from the tedium around here."

Boyd chuckled. "Fun for you all watching, maybe. For us? Success will go to the one with the expertise in that area, and each competition will put the loser in his or her place. I don't mind that much but—well, all right. I don't mind at all, I guess. I'm all for diversions here and there, if you're certain none of my patients will come to harm, sir."

"I don't intend to be put in my place," Emily blurted without thinking.

"You don't, eh?" Boyd's eyes sparkled. "Does that mean you're willing to do it?"

Earlier today, she'd only wanted to see to her simple nosebleed herself, away from the smiling-eyed doctor. Now look what had come of it. Harry and the colonel were looking at her with such expectation, and she owed the colonel a great deal, so...

She took a long breath. "I suppose."

Harry whooped. The colonel nodded and Molly clapped. Emily wanted to shoo them all out of her kitchen with a tea towel, but it would be rude to the colonel.

"What prize to the winner, sir? Bragging rights?" Boyd's eyes gleamed with a competitive spark.

"Sure, bragging rights." The colonel rubbed his cheek. "And five dollars coin, from me."

Five whole dollars. Well, that changed things. Emily could use that money.

She didn't realize she was smiling until she met the doctor's gaze. He was smiling back, that lopsided grin that most women would probably grow weak-kneed over. But Emily was not most women. She turned back to the colonel, who was starting to speak again.

"I'll set the competitions when I see an opportunity," he said. "If two of the enlisted men have a shared health problem and don't mind you tending them for the competition, Miss Sweet, we'll go from there."

"Sounds fair, sir."

"This will be fun." Boyd extended his hand to her.

Fun had nothing to do with it. She shook his hand, surprised by his gentle but firm grip. "To a fair competition."

"All's fair in love and war, you know."

She snatched her hand back. This was neither love nor war. It was a silly contest to bring a little levity to the fort.

Well, maybe it was war after all. Because she'd been fighting to provide for her brother and maybe even put enough money away to take Harry someplace with a real school and young'uns his age. If this competition could earn her five dollars, so be it.

On with the war.

 ᦉ

The next afternoon, a tentative knock sounded on the door of Boyd's office at the small hospital just off the parade ground. He looked up from his inventory of supplies. "Enter."

A freckle-faced young private, Burton Tripp, stuck his head in the door. "Busy, Doc?"

"Only with minutiae. You ailing, soldier?"

"No, sir. But I have a question."

Ah. Boyd was accustomed to men dropping by for the sole purpose of asking a question. In his experience, however, either something serious afflicted them and they were too embarrassed to admit it, or they had vague complaints as an excuse for seeking his advice or company. They were homesick or lonely, and he could understand that himself. Some of the soldiers here were seasoned veterans of the war against Mexico, like Captain Grant and Sergeant Waldo, but others, like Tripp, weren't much older than Harry, away from home for the first time.

Boyd was glad to help. And to make them laugh, if he could. Show them life might be uncertain, but that didn't mean a body couldn't have a good time and enjoy God's good gifts. Boyd's early life had been far too dour, and he never wanted to live like that again—or see anyone else live that way.

"So what's your question, Tripp?"

The pale-haired lad looked around. "I noticed you don't have a steward."

Now this was a change of Boyd's routine. "You volunteering?"

"If the opportunity presented, yes, sir."

Tripp had a wide-eyed eagerness about him. He also looked all of nineteen. "Any experience?"

"My pa's an apothecary. He taught me to measure and mix powders and such, but I'd like to learn other things too."

"I admire a man who's willing to learn. If it's all right with Colonel Buchanan, it's fine with me."

Tripp beamed a smile. "Thank you. I won't let you down."

"I'm sure you won't." The fort was quiet anyway, without much need for Boyd's surgery skills. Tripp would probably do little more for him than organize tools and distribute headache powders.

Tripp tapped a short finger on Boyd's desk. "I'm grateful, sir, because you see, I'm curious about being a doctor myself."

"Really?" Boyd had never mentored anyone before. Officially, anyway. But he was always glad to teach those in the field who weren't as far along as he was. It was how one learned. "I'm happy to loan you some of my books, then."

"Thank you, sir. If it's not too late for me to go through the schooling. My birthday's in two days and I'll be twenty-two." Tripp shrugged.

Tripp was a little older than he looked. "It's never too late to try something new, private, but you're plenty young. Maybe helping me might give you clarification."

"I hope so. How'd you know you wanted to be a doctor?"

At once, Boyd's memory took him back to when he was Harry's age, tasked with his first job. He was supposed to sweep and dust the medical office for Dr. Munn to earn a little money. He'd had nothing of his own and was as eager for the pennies he'd earn as he was for the escape from the dour children's asylum where he lived. But it hadn't taken long for Dr. Munn to ask Boyd for his help wrapping a splint, and that was the moment Boyd knew. Medicine was where he belonged.

"I was twelve years old when the local doctor took me under his wing."

A good man. Even if—

Never mind. "Let me know what the colonel says about you being my steward."

A rap on the office door sounded, and then Sergeant George Waldo, a Missouri man past thirty with a fair beard, poked his head in the door. "Busy, Doctor?"

"Come on in."

"Actually, sir, you're to come out to the parade ground, if you ain't occupied with a sick body, that is. Colonel Buchanan has the first task for the competition betwixt you and Miz Sweet."

The contest already? That was faster than expected. "Healing or cooking?"

"I reckon I don't know." Waldo's eyes flashed. "But Miz Sweet's not lookin' the least bit cowardly at the prospect of either challenge, sir."

"I imagine she isn't." Boyd rubbed his hands together. "Let's see what the colonel has for us, then."

Tripp and Waldo thumped each other's backs in excitement. Buchanan had been right about the men being eager for diversions. If Boyd made an utter fool of himself at the cooking challenge, he'd be glad to have provided a bit of levity to the fort.

Colonel Buchanan and Emily stood in the center of the parade grounds, surrounded by a dozen or more men, while more soldiers poured from the barracks and offices. The baker Percy Luther and his wife, Molly, came too, wiping their hands on their aprons. Wide eyed, Harry talked to his sister, who nodded, jaw set.

Buchanan grinned at him. "Glad you're free, Doctor. Ready for the challenge?"

"I am, sir. Ma'am." He tipped his hat at Emily.

"Doctor." She didn't smile.

Buchanan held up his hands, calling for attention. At once the crowd fell silent. "You all have heard about our friendly competition, and I'm happy to announce it's time to begin. Both Dr. Braxton and Miss Sweet have agreed to participate in a cooking challenge and a healing challenge, with a tiebreaker challenge if required. I'll remind you all this is all in fun, even for our two patients today. That's right, we're starting with the healing challenge. I've got two volunteers with similar symptoms who've agreed to be treated by either the doc or the cook."

Harry tipped up his chin. "Sir? What if the volunteers ain't sick with the same thing? Or heal on account of a good nap?"

Buchanan shook his head. "Can't control that, son. This is as fair as I can make it."

Boyd required clarification for his peace of mind. "I assume their symptoms are minor, of course." He couldn't allow anyone with a serious injury or illness to suffer on account of a silly challenge.

"They're not life threatening, as I promised you earlier. And both patients are game to volunteer. In fact, it was their idea."

Then Boyd was ready to start. "What's the ailment, sir?" Ankle sprains? Dyspepsia?

Buchanan gestured to the slender fort bugler and squat drummer standing in back of the group. It wasn't hard to miss the fatigued set of their shoulders and red eyes. "Privates Coe and Kittredge, you both volunteered for this, and a coin toss determined which of you will be treated by which competitor, correct?"

"Yes, sir."

Coe's scratchy voice and Kittredge's subsequent coughing fit said it all. The fort bugler and drummer both suffered congestion of the lungs, which seemed a far more serious ailment than Boyd was comfortable denying treatment. "I'm not sure this one's a good idea, Colonel."

"I'm fine with it," Kittredge said. "I got Miss Sweet, and I say she can heal me up good."

"And I say you'll know what's best, Doc," Coe said. "Right now I can't get a big enough breath to blow the horn."

"Fine." Boyd met Kittredge's watery gaze. "But if you worsen or don't improve in a day, you come see me, hear? Any sign of fever—"

"I'm not so heartless that I'll let a man suffer just to best you." Emily took Kittredge's arm. "Colonel, may I help this man now?"

"By all means."

The gathered men cheered. Emily led Kittredge to the kitchen, followed by Harry and the Luthers. Boyd tipped his head at the hospital to indicate he and Coe should walk over. "How long you felt poorly, Coe?"

"Not long, Doc. Both Kittredge and I woke up like this." He coughed again. "You can help, can't you?"

"I'll do my absolute best." Boyd led the bugler into the hospital, followed by Tripp, and set Coe on a chair near the stove. "Sit on down for a spell."

Boyd gathered his stethoscope and a few other implements. A thorough examination assured him that his patient did not suffer a fever, accelerated pulse, putrid throat, or pneumonia. Coe and Kittredge most likely suffered a catarrh, or cold, or had encountered some sort of miasma from the atmosphere. Either way, he could help. "My guess is Miss Sweet will be making up a mustard poultice for Kittredge. I'll do the same for you, but I'll also add a tonic."

"What if she has a tonic too? Will we lose?"

"I'm more concerned about you feeling better than winning or losing, but as far as I know, I'm the only one with tonics in the fort. Why don't you select a cot, make yourself comfortable, and rest while Tripp and I mix the poultice? Actually, Tripp, I seem to be low on ground mustard. Dash over to Captain Grant and get some, will you? Tell him it's for the hospital."

"Yes, sir."

Thank the Lord that Grant kept more varied supplies than the average quartermaster, and would no doubt have some mustard on hand. In the meantime, Boyd administered a dose of his preferred tonic, a concoction formulated back east that eased symptoms and helped patients sleep. Coe was propped up in the cot washing the tonic down with a swig of hot coffee when Tripp returned, packet in hand and his freckled features lit with surprise. "You won't believe this, Doc."

"Grant inebriated again?" The quartermaster was a pleasure to be around except when he got lonesome for his family in Missouri and turned to drink.

"No, sir. It's Miss Sweet. She's leaving the fort."

"What do you mean leaving?" Forever?

"She walked out, wearing her go-to-town bonnet and carrying a basket. Maybe she's going to buy tonic in Bucksport. Poor Kittredge. He's going to be waiting a while, no matter what she's doing."

Boyd whistled. What was Emily doing? It hadn't even been ten minutes since the competition started. Whatever she was doing outside the fort wasn't helping Kittredge right now.

Poor Kittredge, indeed.

Chapter Three

The next morning while it was still dark, Emily made the short trek from the quarters she shared with her brother across the parade ground to the kitchen, as she did every day. Drawing her shawl closer about her shoulders against the chill, she lit the stove and started a pot of porridge. She was adding a spoonful of salt to it as the first full rays of dawn peeked beneath the wooden slats of the kitchen door, accompanied by the *rat-a-tat-tat* of drums sounding out reveille. Soon, soldiers would be gathering for their morning drills, and then they'd be hungry afterward. Before she fried salt pork, however, she mustn't forget to put on the coffee.

The kitchen door opened, admitting a rush of chill air. "Morning." Harry's greeting was muffled by his yawn.

"Good morning, love." She reached for him and kissed his mussed blond hair. She didn't have to bend at all anymore to do that. Soon she'd have to stretch on tiptoe to kiss him on the cheek. "Help with the porridge?"

"Sure. May I have coffee today?"

"Make sure half is milk." It was hard to get milk into him otherwise.

They tended to their chores in the silence typical of early mornings, and it wasn't long before breakfast was ready. Emily ladled bowls of porridge for herself and Harry, setting out a common plate for their pork, leaving room for the biscuits Percy and Molly would deliver any minute now. At a scratch on the door, she turned. There they were now. "Come in."

Instead of Percy and Molly, Boyd entered, rubbing his hands together against the cold. "Good morning."

"Good morning. Coffee's in the next room."

"I'm not here for coffee. Well, I am—I do want some coffee. Tripp brewed a pot for us this morning, and it can't touch yours, I'll tell you that."

"Tripp?"

"He's my steward now. Good fellow, eager to learn, and most helpful with tending Coe through the night, right into morning." His gaze leveled with hers. "We were awake when we heard the drums sound out a wake-up call. Sounded a lot like Kittredge."

"Who else would it be? He's the lone drummer in the fort."

"Who else indeed. I rushed out to see how he fared, and you know what I found?"

"A healthy man?" Wrapping the pan handle in a towel, she moved it off the stove to cool.

"A healthy man." Boyd shook his head. "Although Kittredge's recovery was so swift, Tripp wondered if Kittredge was actually sick in the first place."

Harry's brows met. "You heard him cough, Doc. He was sick all right."

"I agree, he was. And Coe is still ill, sorry to say."

"Poor man." Emily would continue to pray for him, then.

"Want some redwood tips? We've got more," Harry offered.

The doctor tipped his head as if he couldn't hear well. "More *what?*"

"Redwood tips," Harry enunciated. "The tips of redwood needles. Emily had to go get more from the woods yesterday."

"So I did." She forked the last of the salt pork onto a fresh platter and, with a nod, indicated Harry should carry it into the adjacent mess hall.

Boyd stepped closer. "That's why you left the fort yesterday? You went foraging for pine needles?"

"Tea brewed from the tips is beneficial for lung inflammations. Oh, and I made up a mustard-and-onion poultice, of course. I admit Private Kittredge is not at peak health, but he claimed he was improved enough to go about his regular duties today. I sent some tips with him and showed him how to make more tea."

At Harry's return, Boyd shook his head. "Never heard of it, but maybe I should take you up on that offer, Harry, and try the tips."

Emily met her brother's gaze. "There's a sachet in the cupboard."

Harry dashed to fetch it then handed the cheesecloth packet to Boyd. "It's one of the remedies Emily learned when our pap was dying."

Boyd's eyes dulled. "I'm sorry for your loss."

Before Emily could thank him and change the subject, Harry continued on, clearly needing to talk about it. "We'd hardly been in California long enough for Pap to find more than a few specks of gold when he got sick. We were hungry afore coming to the fort. Emily didn't think I saw her, but she mixed dirt in her food to make it stretch—"

"That's enough, Harry." She softened her words with a smile. She didn't want the doctor to hear any more, but she shouldn't have used such a sharp tone. "Come eat. I don't want your food to get cold."

It was obvious from the deep wrinkle in Boyd's brow that he didn't require any more information to understand, anyway. He could guess that when the fort opened, they'd come desperate for shelter and work. The colonel hired Emily out of pity. She'd never cooked for ten people before, much less forty.

But her arms had grown strong, and so had her heart. She and Harry were safe, they ate well, *and* she was paid. The work wasn't even that hard. Rations of pork and salt beef, flour, coffee, tea, beans, vinegar, and sugar were provided in abundance, but the soldiers' diets were supplemented by fresh meat and vegetables, thanks to the garden, local beef and poultry, and Seth Kinman's game. She could also often get more luxurious items, like dried fruit, spices, and more, due to their proximity to San Francisco. This job had been a tremendous blessing.

And she made enough to squirrel away much of her earnings for better things for Harry. She wouldn't be eating dirt again, God willing.

Molly poking her head into the kitchen doorway from the adjacent mess hall put an end to her bad memories. Emily rushed to meet Molly and Percy, the short, balding baker, catching a whiff of the fresh biscuits steaming in the large bowls they held.

"Good morning." Molly's singsong voice was especially chipper. "Everyone's talking about how well Private Kittredge is doing. I think you may have won the first challenge."

"We'll see what Colonel Buchanan says." Emily looked back to the door between the kitchen and the mess hall, where Boyd now lingered.

Molly's cheeks flushed. "Oh, hello, Doctor. Sorry, I didn't see you there."

Boyd laughed. "It's all right. I think Emily won too."

He didn't look the least bit pained by the loss as he took a seat in the mess hall. Surely it had to bother him some, since the second challenge was a cooking contest and she was undoubtedly going to win that too.

Meanwhile Emily's porridge was probably cold as creek pebbles. She waved to Molly and Percy and joined Harry in the kitchen, not paying any attention to the temperature or taste of the food. By the time she scooped the last spoonful of porridge, the colonel was asking for her to join the assembled men in the yard in ten minutes.

"The competition," Harry said around bites of his third biscuit.

"Probably. Remember not to talk with your mouth full."

Emily used the time to tidy up and set aside the small amount of leftover salt pork for later use. She set out onions for chopping after the colonel's announcement, and then Harry called for her. She smoothed her apron as she went out, Harry at her side.

She wasn't ten feet from the kitchen when the applause began. Even poor Private Coe, the still-sick bugler, was clapping. So was Private Kittredge, who should probably be in bed resting today. The most enthusiastic applause, however, came from Boyd.

Goodness, he really wasn't upset. He seemed downright happy for her.

She shook her head at the men as she passed to join the colonel, her face heating in a flush. She'd never endured such attentions before.

"Order." The colonel's call for quiet was not military standard, but then again, neither was this competition. "I think we've all heard Private Kittredge was improved enough to drum for us this morning. Therefore the winner of the first competition is Miss Sweet."

After the subsequent round of applause quieted, Emily rubbed her temple. "Sir, this one instance was hardly indicative of our healing skills. This wasn't real doctoring and everyone knows it. It's not like someone broke a bone."

"Don't you dare belittle your skills, Emily." Boyd's voice was kind but firm. "Your knowledge helped ease a man's symptoms. I'm glad to have learned this redwood tea remedy from you."

Some men would have sulked at having lost a challenge, or grown angry. A few would have been embarrassed to have lost to a woman, and surely, as a doctor, Boyd's pride must prickle at losing this particular competition. Boyd was clearly not *some men*, however. Indeed, no man had ever talked to her this way, like her accomplishments and thoughts were of value. Like that was more important to him than being the best at something, especially in his field.

Well, he *was* the best in his field here at the fort, and he should know it. "Nevertheless, I'm no doctor, nor do I want to be. Your job is safe, Boyd."

She'd never called him by his first name before. It had always been *Doctor* or nothing, except in her thoughts. Why had it slipped out now?

It didn't go unnoticed either. Boyd's grin showed all of his teeth. Molly's brows went up to her cap line, and Percy pressed his lips together as if holding back a smile.

The colonel's hands rose again, thankfully diverting attention away from Emily. "I have yet to decide the nature of the second competition, but I'll remind you all, it involves cookery. If Miss Sweet wins, then she will be named the victor, but if Dr. Braxton wins, we'll be forced to break the tie with a third contest."

"Don't see how that'll happen." Harry rubbed his hands together.

"Us neither, boy," said a soldier. Sergeant Waldo, a veteran of the war in Mexico, if Emily wasn't mistaken. She'd heard him speak of his military engagements as well as his young family back home in Missouri. Two little girls with red curls.

The colonel indicated it was time to return to work, and the group scattered to their various assignments. At once Emily started mulling over her day's tasks, including Harry's schooling. If she won that five dollars from this competition, she'd be much, much closer to taking Harry somewhere with a real school.

"Emily?"

Boyd had used her first name now too. Did that mean they were more than competitors?

Ridiculous. They could never be friends. Could they?

They weren't exactly rivals, though. She held out her hand for shaking. "Thanks for being so gracious."

This handshake lasted longer than the previous one. "It's all in good fun, even the losing."

"Ah, yes. This is all about fun for you." She'd almost forgotten, so impressed was she by his cordiality.

"Private Coe will have more fun too, once he finishes that tea of yours."

"He might have been sicker than Kittredge, you know."

"Maybe. But the contest is what it is. May I walk you back to the kitchen?"

She nodded, although she was not even thirty feet away from the kitchen, so there wasn't a need for an escort. What did he want from her? "Do you need onions for a poultice?"

"No thanks, but I do have a favor to ask of you. It involves Tripp. His birthday's tomorrow, and I thought he should have a cake."

She hadn't expected that at all. She'd expected—what, more teasing? "That's a thoughtful gesture."

"It's his first birthday away from home. I remember mine. Long time ago, though."

Her first birthday after Pap died was difficult but made easier to bear by Harry's hug and the small nut cake Percy and Molly had baked for her. "I can speak to the Luthers about baking a cake for him."

"Actually I want to be the one to do it. It's part of the gift."

How kind of him. Boyd was full of surprises, and his graciousness for his steward was the greatest one yet. "I'm sure Percy and Molly will be happy to help you, then."

"I'd rather you taught me."

It took a moment for Emily to find her tongue. "Me?"

"If you don't mind, sure. I know you're busy."

She was. There were meals to prepare and Harry's lessons. Then she realized why he was asking her. "This isn't about Tripp, is it? You want instruction in the kitchen before the cooking challenge."

"You and I both know I have no chance of beating you at the cooking challenge." His head tipped to one side. "Honest, it's for Tripp. Can you show me how to bake him a cake? Maybe that apple cake you made that time the Luthers were ill?"

So that explained why he wanted her help and not the Luthers'. She'd taken on their baking duties one day when they were both ill and had made cakes with surplus dried apples. This wasn't personal at all. But, like Private Tripp, she knew what it was like to be lonely on one's birthday, so she nodded.

"I have time tomorrow morning. We'll need a few things that aren't regular rations, but Captain Grant might have them in the commissary. Dried apples—which have to soak overnight, so I'll get that started now—raisins, sugar, flour, eggs, and the like. I'll send Harry to ask."

"I'll drop in later to pay for it. Thank you. Now, I suppose I'd best see to my patient."

She didn't watch him go but shut the kitchen door behind her and stood there, back pressed against it, for the span of several erratic breaths. Boyd drove her mad, with his ready smile and determination to enjoy everything. Even losing to her in the challenge.

So why was she looking forward to spending time with him

tomorrow? It should be a burden, a chore, not. . .this. Whatever it was. This sense of expectancy.

Oh no.

Emily pushed away from the door and wiped her sweat-damp hands on her apron. Enough of this nonsense. She'd agreed to help him because he was doing something kind for Tripp, and that was that. It would model generosity and kindness to Harry, and God would be pleased with her for helping too. Yes, this was definitely the right thing to do.

As long as she didn't get carried away. She mustn't lose focus on what was most important: being prepared for the future. The Lord had put her here, now, and her job was to ensure Harry was secure if something happened to her.

Maybe that's why Boyd's cheerfulness bothered her so much, because to be so jovial, he had to have had an easy life. He wouldn't be so quick to tease and grin if he knew life was an uncertain journey fraught with dangers. Like she did. And maybe she resented him for it.

That's not Christian-like of me, is it, Lord? Comparing myself and my road to others. Well, God had used Boyd to teach her a lesson, hadn't He? And for that she was grateful. She should probably pray about it more. . .and think about basting the pheasants, roasting in the oven.

But she caught herself basting the pan, not the bird. And when she did it, she wasn't praying. She was thinking of Boyd Braxton's lopsided smile again.

Oh dear, she had better get ahold of herself. And fast.

The next morning after Boyd sent an improved Private Coe back to the barracks, he rapped his knuckles on the cold kitchen door. At Emily's call to enter, he stepped inside the warm, homey space, which today smelled of game grease and wood smoke. Harry sat at the worktable with a book and slate, and Boyd greeted him with a few words and a shake of his shoulder.

Emily turned from the stove. "Ready to make Tripp's cake?"

"If you aren't too busy."

"Not at all. Last night's pheasant is minced for hash, and the boiled hare has to cool, so this is a perfect time."

He sniffed again. "Glad it's not the dried apples I smell," he teased.

"I should hope not."

He'd only wanted to see one of her rare but lovely grins turned his way. "What does it take to make you smile, Emily?"

She made a noise like a sneezing cat. "I'm smiling."

"No, you're not, Em," Harry said. "You're doing this." He stretched his lips into a grimace.

"You. Book." She pointed. Then she smiled at Boyd. "See? I'm smiling."

She was, but Boyd hadn't been the one to put it there, so it didn't make him as happy as it should've. "So, Emily, why don't you tell me what to do here."

"Now *that* prospect makes me smile." And she did, a pretty smile that made Boyd's shoulders relax. "I soaked the apples overnight, there in that bowl. Fetch a knife and chop them on that board, and then put them in this pot."

He stared at the block of knives. One would think he'd know which to use, since he had his share of blades back at the hospital, but scalpels and bone saws were far different than these. Thankfully she pointed at one, and he set to chopping the water-plumped apple slices. They were a little slimy and he had to hold on to them. "How big should they be?"

"Bite sized."

"Sized for your bite or mine? Or a bear's?"

Harry laughed even if Emily didn't. "Half an inch, I should think, so they stew well in the molasses."

Harry looked up. "May I lick the spoon?"

"You may." She nudged Boyd's elbow. "That's good. Now put them into the pot and stir."

While Harry hopped up to take the brown-coated spoon from his sister, Boyd mixed the apples-and-molasses mixture. The feel of the sanded wood in his hand and the circular motion of the spoon reminded him of something. "This is sort of like laundering clothes, isn't it?"

Then he splattered himself with the molasses mixture.

"Aside from the size difference between a laundry paddle and a mixing spoon, the intent of laundry is to get things clean. And look at you. What would the colonel say?" Emily offered him a damp towel to blot his coat, and there it was.

A small smile.

Harry dropped his spoon into the washtub with a splash. "You should be wearing an apron, Doc."

He wore one in surgery, didn't he? "I guess so, although it's too late to keep this coat fresh looking."

"I'll spot-clean it for you, but put this on anyway." Emily opened a drawer in the oak cabinet and tugged out a folded white bundle.

The apron was a little tight, but no matter. "Mighty kind of you, ma'am."

"Just don't burn those apples." Firm words, but her tone was soft.

When Emily decreed the apple mixture ready, she instructed him to measure a cupful of raisins and then, once stirred into the mixture, a cup of butter. Three cups of flour, though he spilled some on the stove. "Now I know why Molly is always wearing this stuff."

"Here." She added a spoonful of extra flour to make up for the lack and swiped the mess. "Flour gets into everything. Do you know how to crack an egg?"

"That I can do." Phew.

"We need three, and then a teaspoon of this."

This looked like some sort of medicinal powder, white and fine. Definitely not salt. "What is it?"

"Soda. Then add some of this."

He recognized the delectable smell of the reddish-brown cinnamon she measured out for him. His mouth practically watered. "Tripp's going to like this."

"I'm sure he will. Now mix it all up and bring it over here to pour evenly between these two pans. I've already greased and floured them for you." She gestured to the worktable.

He mixed the concoction until it looked uniform. Since his dominant right hand was coated in slimy egg white, he gripped the pot's handle with his left hand. His *bare* left hand.

Scorching pain radiated from his palm as he yelped.

"Oh! Not without a towel. I'm sorry." Emily took his hand and flipped it over, palm side up. "I should've given you better instructions."

Boyd analyzed the bright pink color and the sensation in his hand. A day or two and it'd be fine, and thankfully it wasn't his right hand. "It's minor, but if you have some milk to dunk it in, that'd be most appreciated."

"Of course. Yes." She released him to rush to the icebox. "I'd have thought you'd use some fancy ointment."

"I just might, later, but milk draws out the burn as good as anything."

Harry chuckled. "You two agree on something."

Boyd smiled, but Emily didn't find any humor in the situation. Her cheeks were bright, her eyes crinkled in concern. "I'm sorry. It's my fault."

"No it's not. Just an accident on account of me being ignorant in the kitchen."

She poured milk into a bowl and set it on the table, pulling out the chair beside Harry's for him. "I should have been more mindful. I am so sorry, truly."

He plunked his hand into the bowl. The cold milk was blissful on his palm. "No need to apologize anymore, please."

"I'll finish the cakes." Harry hopped up and, smartly gripping the pan handle with a tea towel wrapped around his hand, poured out the contents into the pans. Then he swiped a blob that had dribbled down the side and tasted it. "Pretty good, I'd say."

"That's a relief." The chill temperature of the milk numbed Boyd's hand.

Harry slid the cakes into the oven and shut the door with a smack. "I finished my sums, Em. May I go to the smithy now? You said I could watch them shoe the horses."

"So I did. Go on, but stay out of the way and come back by lunch."

"Yes, ma'am." Harry dashed from the kitchen so fast it was impossible not to laugh.

Emily gave Boyd the side eye as she took Harry's seat. "His life isn't entirely made up of chores and schoolwork, you know. He gets fresh air and exercise."

"I wasn't trying to goad you when I said all that, Emily." When her brow arched, he laughed. "Well, maybe I was a little. I just wanted to make you smile."

"I smile plenty."

"Do you now? What makes you smile?"

"Harry. Thinking about what it'll be like for him to live in a big enough town that he can attend a real school. I know most boys don't go past eighth grade, but he's smart. He reads books as if words were food and air to him. I want him to have every opportunity."

Opportunities that didn't exist at the fort.

Boyd scanned Harry's assignments spread over the table. He'd finished a composition on Napoleon—neat penmanship too—and two pages of mathematics. "Looks like you do an excellent job teaching him."

"I'm about at the limit of my knowledge, however, and I struggle to find resources for him. On occasion I can buy a text or piece of fiction in one of the settlements, and I often trade books with the barber in Bucksport, like I did for this one." She tapped a brown volume on the table.

The Count of Monte Cristo by Alexandre Dumas. "An engaging story."

"He's certainly enjoying it. I just wish he had access to more books and an experienced teacher." She looked up. "Did you have a formal education?"

"Medical school, yes, but the orphanage was fairly simple when it came to instruction. Not many books lying around."

Her face utterly transformed. Gone was the mask she usually wore—he hadn't even known until now it was a mask, but now, her eyes and cheeks went soft, and her lips parted. "I didn't realize you grew up in an orphanage. I'm sorry."

Pain throbbed in his palm. The milk no longer numbed it, so he removed his hand from the bowl and wiped it off on the dishtowel Emily had brought over. He hadn't planned on telling anyone at the fort his story, but things were different with Emily, so he met her gaze. "I don't remember my mother. She died giving birth to my sister Annabeth when I was two."

"And your father?"

"He had a beard and dark eyes. He died when I was four, maybe from an infection. We had no people to care for us, so my sister and

I were placed in the orphanage. Then within the year, I lost my sister to influenza. I was well and truly alone in the world then."

Tears beaded on her lower lashes. "That must have been terribly difficult."

"I don't remember anything different." Just memories of being loved once, and a whole heap of hurt after that.

"It's wonderful that you became a doctor."

"I had help, of course. When I was Harry's age, I was sent to work with a local doctor. Munn by name." Seth focused on the pain in his hand so he wouldn't think about the pain in his heart stirred up by all of these memories.

"That's when you found your purpose."

"Not initially. I wanted something else when I met Dr. Munn, but yes, I realized if I became a doctor, maybe I could save someone from being an orphan like I was."

She leaned forward, so close he could see green flecks in her brown eyes. So close he could sense the change between them, as charged as a lightning strike. They were the real Emily and the real Boyd right now. No competition between them, no teasing, no vexation. Just two people who—

Weren't even friends, were they? She bristled like a pinecone when he came around. Usually. But right now, she stared at him like she wanted to see into him, and he. . .well, he cared for her. Plenty. Not in a way he wanted to scrutinize. Just appreciate.

It was hard to *just appreciate*, though, when his heart was pounding in his chest at her nearness.

Her lips parted. "What was it you wanted when you met that doctor, Boyd?"

He'd wanted a lot of things, living in the austere orphanage. Toys. Books. Thicker socks. But there was one thing every orphan wanted—

Harry burst into the kitchen, startling them both. "The colonel's decided on the next competition."

The charge in the air vanished. Emily stood and gathered the milk bowl, not looking at Boyd. "Already?"

Boyd's heart was still thunking from his close encounter with Emily. How could she sound so calm? She must not have been as affected as he.

Harry took her vacated spot at the table. "When Seth Kinman comes back, you two have to cook whatever he brings in next."

"All right, then." Emily returned to the stove.

"Huh." Boyd was glad to hear his voice didn't sound as shaky as he felt inside.

"You don't look too upset, Doc." Harry neatened his work area.

"I reckon I'm not too worried about it." Maybe he should be, since Kinman could bring in quail or wild hog as easily as deer, and Boyd didn't know how to prepare a single one of them fit for eating. However, he couldn't wave a white flag of surrender. Sure, he'd lose the competition, but he had to give the soldiers something edible. The true purpose for this contest was bringing levity to the fort, and Boyd was determined to do his part.

What he would have given for something fun like this when he was at the orphanage.

"Why don't we ask to postpone this one? It's a tough challenge, and you're all burned up." Emily came back and inspected his hand as if she were the doctor, not him. She didn't touch him, probably not to cause him pain, but he wouldn't have minded the brush of her fingers on his palm.

"I'll heal by the time Kinman returns." The hunter was as unpredictable as he was unforgettable. "Maybe he'll bring in dried apples and I'll make this cake, and won't that beat all?"

Even Emily laughed a little at that. "Everything's funny to you."

"If a man doesn't laugh, he'll spend his days crying."

"Or working." There was the old Emily again, her jaw set in a serious expression. "Let's see if those cakes are done, and then you should go put some fancy ointment on that burn."

At least he knew how to tease the old Emily. "Are you saying you see the merit of fancy ointment?"

"Don't tell anyone." She grinned.

Maybe she wasn't quite the old Emily again, after all.

And right there, burned hand, doomed competition looming over him, aching orphaned heart and all, he felt as if he'd won.

Chapter Four

E*lk.*

For a week now, Emily had waited for Seth Kinman's return, preparing herself to receive game from possum to snake. Instead, today he'd brought in the meat he'd been hired to hunt in the first place. Every once in a while the hirsute hunter surprised them with pheasant or hare, but elk was the most abundant quarry.

It was also boring. She prepared elk so often she could do it in her sleep.

"An easy win for you," Molly said over tea while Emily took a break from peeling potatoes. Outside, the men were doing some sort of drill. Harry loved to watch those, so she sent him outside with instructions to stay out of the men's way. When Harry returned soon, they'd have schoolwork to do, so she had better hurry and find a recipe so she could seek Molly's opinion on it.

"I expected something else, something more gamey, so I thought I might need to mask the taste. I've been looking into recipes with robust flavors, and I've decided I'd like to do something different. Something special." Emily had but one cookery book, and she opened it to the meats section. "I have one day to finalize my plans while the elk is butchered. We're cooking it tomorrow."

"The doc has a day to plan too."

"At least Boyd's hand is better." He'd shown her his healed-up palm and fingers after supper last night. "I wouldn't have wanted to compete if he'd still been injured. I already have an advantage as it is."

"How thoughtful of you to consider *Boyd* like that." Molly's tea sipping didn't hide her sly smile.

"I call you and Percy by your Christian names. It doesn't mean anything."

"But we aren't eligible bachelors."

"Really, Molly. You know I'm not interested in that at all."

"No, you want that five dollars from the colonel so you can break my heart and leave the fort."

Emily couldn't deny it. "Come with us."

"To where?"

"Somewhere with schools for Harry and cooking jobs for me. San Francisco, maybe?"

Molly fiddled with her cup. "We can't stay at the fort forever, we know that. It's been a good job, though, and we like it. It's like a little town here."

"A little town full of men." Emily rolled her eyes.

"Men who'd marry you if you'd look twice at them." Molly illustrated the speed with a snap of her fingers.

"Ridiculous. They're not interested in wives, or they wouldn't have joined the army."

Molly laughed so hard tears streamed down her rosy cheeks. Emily ignored her friend and thumbed through her cookery book, past the usual poaching, roasting, and frying recipes.

At last Molly sighed, signaling an end to her laughter. "Darlin', you're as pretty as a daffodil and smart about most things, but you don't know a thing about romance."

"That's how I intend to keep it. I have to take care of Harry."

"What will you do in a few years when he's grown?" Molly almost looked pitying. "You need to think about that sooner or later."

"Later, then. For now I must be prepared so he'll have what he needs in the way of education and money should something happen to me."

"Nothing's going to happen to you."

A kind sentiment, but not a realistic one. "Bad things happen, Molly. Pap died and left us with nothing. Did you know Boyd grew up in an orphanage? Parents die sometimes."

"So do children." Molly stared down at her hands, flat on the table. "Percy and I had two, you know. Both died at birth. We never did have any more either."

"Oh Molly. I'm sorry. That's horrible." Emily gripped her friend's hands. "I didn't mean to suggest you hadn't gone through something difficult. I shouldn't have spoken to you that way."

Molly pulled her hands from Emily's to pat them. "Life is never without hurt, but you can't spend your life worrying. The Bible warns us against it."

"It's not worry. It's preparation. Squirrels store up for winter, and I can too. For Harry. I think it wise."

"I understand preparation, Emily. I do." Molly fidgeted with her saucer. "But I agree with the doc about needing some fun in our lives."

Not this again. "Harry has plenty of fun. He's outside watching the soldiers drill right now."

"Not Harry. You."

As if on cue, the sounds of Private Coe's bugle and Private

Kittredge's drum sounded from the parade ground, rhythms Emily recognized as signifying the end of drills, and a clear reminder of the purpose of the fort where she and Molly dwelled. "It's not like we have a ladies' society here. Actually, you and I *are* the ladies' society, and look, here we are, having a meeting. I'd say that's fun."

Molly snorted into her tea. "Much as I don't want you to leave the fort, maybe it'll do you good to go to San Francisco. You'll meet people. Maybe attend parties and do interesting things."

"I'm participating in the challenge. That's interesting, isn't it?"

"I suppose it is." Molly didn't look convinced. "What do you suppose the doctor's going to do with his elk?"

"I have no idea. The man wasn't exaggerating when he said he couldn't cook, although he can crack an egg just fine."

"So show me your cookery book again."

The two women pored over the recipes for a quarter hour before Emily settled on her choice. "I need to visit the quartermaster for a few ingredients. Hopefully he has these two."

"I'll let you see to that, then." Molly pushed back her chair and rose. "You'll make a wonderful supper for us, I'm sure of it."

"Thank you." Impulsively, Emily kissed her friend's soft cheek. "I am grateful for our society of two here at the fort."

"As am I." Molly's cheeks colored at Emily's affectionate display.

Once Molly left the kitchen, Emily gathered a basket for the short trip to the commissary. Hopefully Captain Grant was on duty—and sober—and she could get what she needed. The recipe she'd chosen would take extra time, and she'd best get started.

Captain Grant was indeed on duty in the commissary, but he wasn't alone. A tall, dark figure traded a handful of coins for a paper-wrapped bundle.

She'd recognize Boyd's broad shoulders anywhere. He was speaking too. Something about "doing her best in a difficult situation."

Her? As in Emily? She hadn't taken Boyd for a gossip, and the idea didn't sit well on her stomach. "Good afternoon, gentlemen."

Boyd turned to face her and tucked the bundle behind his back. "Hello."

"Ma'am." Captain Grant's eyes twinkled. "How can I be of assistance?"

If they'd been caught discussing Emily, neither of them showed the least sign of guilt over it. That was the thing with eavesdropping. One always assumed the topic was oneself, to vexing results. Emily shook off her suspicion and focused on the task at hand. "I am content to wait until you and the doctor are finished with your transaction. Medical supplies?" She craned her neck to attempt a glimpse at the bundle.

"It's personal." Boyd's grin indicated he was enjoying himself.

"Personal, as in the competition?"

"Maybe, but I've sworn Captain Grant to secrecy. You'll just have to wait until the contest."

Grant's eyes reflected his smile. "Who's judging this cooking contest anyway?"

"The men." Boyd winked at Emily. "They have to eat it, so they should get the say."

Emily never had complaints about her cooking. Then again, without her, the soldiers could be eating stale biscuits and beans cooked over an open flame, so she mustn't get too full of herself. "They're in for a treat tomorrow."

"Oh?" Boyd's dark eyes twinkled. "A new recipe, then?"

She'd given too much away. "Maybe, but I've sworn Molly to secrecy." She adapted his statement about Captain Grant.

He laughed. "I'll leave you and the captain to your business. Good day."

Once he left, Emily withdrew a short list from her pocket.

"Captain, have you any of these ingredients?"

"This and this." He poked the paper with his forefinger. "But the rest of these? I don't even know how to say that one."

"No matter. It will work without them." It just wouldn't taste as interesting.

As Captain Grant gathered the items for her, he chuckled. "This competition betwixt the two of you has been great fun for the fort, ma'am. Gives us something to think about other than how far we are from home and family."

"You're married, Captain?" She'd heard he was, but never from him.

"Yes, with two small boys. Just babes, really." His smile fell. "My Julia is a sight to behold, raising those young'uns alone right now. Just got a letter from her today."

Ah, so that was probably the woman he and Boyd had been discussing. "She sounds like a woman of amazing fortitude."

"She's far stronger in our time apart than I am. I don't do so well, ma'am, but everybody knows that."

Things made a little more sense now, when it came to Grant's visits to the tavern in Eureka. Everyone knew he had a problem indulging in spirits. Emily didn't condone his choice, but she now understood the man a little better. Clearly, he was desperately lonely without his family. "I shall pray for you, sir."

"That's right kind of you, Miss Sweet." He offered her the items. "It would give me great pleasure to pay for these myself."

"Oh, I couldn't allow that. This spice is dear in price." But the cost was worth it if she won the five dollars tomorrow after the competition's end.

"Please, ma'am. You do so much for us, and you've got a brother to provide for."

She tucked the items into her basket. "It's not necessary, but, thank you, Captain Grant."

Wishing him well, she returned to the kitchen, determined to pray for the captain as she went. She hadn't done much in the way of praying for the men, unless they were ill, but after her talk with Captain Grant, she realized each man here was in need in one way or another. Folks struggled with wounds no one could see. She was a prime example of that.

She nodded at several men as she passed. Sergeant Waldo, Colonel Buchanan, Privates Coe and Kittredge, who were both hale and hearty after their lung issues. And then Private Tripp, Boyd's freckled new steward, who'd thanked her for helping with his birthday cake at least three times a day since Boyd presented it to him.

Boyd. How was he in need? There was more to him than met the eye, and she'd misjudged him. Perhaps he joked so often, not because his childhood was bright, as she'd first thought, but because it had been so lacking in mirth, in that orphan asylum. Perhaps he sought cheer because he'd lost so much. He became a doctor to save others from similar losses. Did his attempts work? Did he have peace?

Emily wasn't sure she had peace. Not in sufficiency. She prayed for it, even as she strove to provide for Harry.

The doctor himself stepped out of one of the offices, whistling. When he saw her, he flashed his lopsided grin, and something fluttered in Emily's midsection.

Land sakes. She was feeling something. . .romantic in nature, and of all the men in the entire world, it was for Boyd Braxton.

This would not do. She double-timed her steps to the kitchen. Feelings would pass. Had to pass. And quickly.

Right now, she had a contest to win.

◯

Before the sun rose the next morning, Boyd and Tripp went to work. Not in the hospital, but near his quarters, away from the parade grounds. With the elk.

It didn't take long for men to exit the barracks, pointing at the spit he and Tripp had set up. A few men whooped, despite the early hour.

Tripp rubbed his flat stomach. "I'm ready for breakfast. Going to the mess hall?"

"Nah, I'd better tend this." He'd never roasted meat before, much less an entire side of elk, and he was afraid to leave it alone. "I've got coffee and hardtack." And a little jerky in his pocket.

Tripp grimaced. "If you say so."

Hardtack was no substitute for Emily's breakfast beans, salt pork, or chipped beef and biscuits, but Boyd was determined. Not to win, of course. He was no cook. But to make an effort. The competition was all about bringing cheer to the fort, and he'd do his best, but he wouldn't dare waste food by leaving this all alone for who knew what to happen to it.

Lord, let it be tolerable on everyone's bellies. That was the hope.

Except within the hour, it started to smell. . .good.

Not long after, a figure in a full skirt of pine-green calico marched over the grass, her face as resolute as any soldier's. Emily stopped six feet away and stared at the meat on the spit. "What is that?"

"Elk."

She rolled her eyes. "Of course it's the elk. But I smell hog meat. That's what you bought from Captain Grant yesterday, isn't it?"

"It is. Thought it'd be a nice addition to the elk, and a tasty change from the usual salt pork." The aroma was still faint, but it was becoming more mouthwatering by the minute.

"I'm impressed, Doctor."

His jaw dropped in an exaggerated display. "Well, I'll be. You like something I do?"

She rolled her eyes. "It's called being cordial."

"You like my bacon idea."

"I'm starting to regret telling you so." She stared at the elk, and the morning breeze stirred tendrils of her golden hair onto her cheeks. She looked up at him then, as if she felt his stare.

"What?"

"Green is a pretty color on you, with your brown eyes."

Those brown eyes flashed. "Don't tell me you're trying to flatter me into sharing how I'm preparing my elk."

That wasn't it at all. But it was a safer answer than the truth that he found her lovely. "Caught me."

Shaking her head, she took a step back. "One word of advice, Boyd. Ensure that elk gets thoroughly cooked. Wouldn't want the hospital full of folks with upset bellies, now would we?"

"Thanks for the warning. And the compliment."

She waved his comment away as she left, but she was smiling.

Throughout the day, he and Tripp took turns tending the roast and seeing to their duties. Boyd gulped down a dry biscuit at lunchtime in his quarters, sitting at his rolltop desk so he could attend to correspondence. His rooms here were far too ample for a bachelor, but the usual occupant was a family man. Soon enough the regular assistant surgeon would return and Boyd's duties here would be complete.

Where would he go next? Another fort? These postings were few and far between, but something would come up. God always provided a way. Even if, like the orphanage, it wasn't quite what Boyd wanted. Sometimes God's gifts were like that, weren't they? Not what he'd choose, but God brought good out of difficulty.

God had shown good by giving Boyd Dr. Munn as a mentor. And bringing him here, a pleasant place. California's land was fruitful, and the people kind.

And look at how God had provided for Emily and Harry. Boyd's gut wrenched at the thought of Emily supplementing her food with soil in order to feel full. But they were no longer in such dire straits, thanks to God's help.

Even in the toughest of times, God's children needed to look to Him in hope and trust. Not always easy, but it was the only way to live. Boyd didn't fear the future anymore, knowing God held it in His hands, and he determined to enjoy every moment of the life God had given him.

Speaking of enjoyment, he needed to inspect that elk to ensure it was neither underdone nor overdone. He took one of the scalpels from his medical bag and strode outside.

The knife was small, but sharp, and he carved off a tiny bite. Thankfully it didn't appear to be raw. He dropped it onto his tongue.

And savored it.

"Tripp, tell me what you think." He nicked off another fragment.

After tasting it, Tripp's eyes grew big.

Meanwhile, a host of men gathered around. "Smells ready," Kittredge said with a pointed tone.

"Where's the colonel? We wanna eat."

"This reminds me of the town festival at home," Tripp said. "Roasted venison for the feast, cooked on a spit right in the square."

"We do something like that too, with extended family." Private Philpott looked wistful at the memory. "But for us it's pork, slathered in my mama's tomato and vinegar sauce."

"Aw, no. You can't use tomato. It's gotta be mustard." Coe playfully wagged his head.

A lively discussion ensued about the proper way to roast pig, and Boyd felt a smile stretch his lips. Seemed like the fellas enjoyed watching the elk on the spit, talking about things, as much as they anticipated eating it. There was something about cooking outdoors, wasn't there? As long as the meal wasn't hardtack boiled in coffee, of course.

At last Colonel Buchanan approached with Emily and Harry, whose eyes were large at the sight of the elk—or maybe it was the delicious aroma that caused his excitement. In any case, the colonel called for order.

"By the smell of things, both cooks are ready for their dishes to be sampled for supper. Come on in the mess hall and get a spoonful of Miss Sweet's offering, but don't eat it until you come out and get a hunk of Doc Braxton's. Then eat them side by side and cast your votes."

Had he said *spoonful*? Boyd had expected Emily to prepare steaks, but it sounded like she'd made a stew. Whatever it was, it was sure to be filling and delicious.

He tipped his hat at her. "Ma'am."

"Doctor. See you after supper."

"Tripp, we need a better knife for serving." Boyd had a board set up to carve the elk, but no decent kitchen utensils. "Go ask Miss Sweet. Oh, and a big fork too."

Tripp dashed after her as she strode back to the mess hall, the men at his heels. By the time Boyd had finished wrangling the roast to the board, Tripp returned, implements in hand. Men followed with their plates, lining up for his elk.

The first in line was Private Coe. Boyd set a chunk of his roast beside hunks of meat covered in a vibrant yellowish-orange sauce. A beguiling but unfamiliar aroma met his nostrils. "What is that?"

"I have no idea." Coe shoved a hunk of Boyd's elk in his mouth.

Rather than return to the mess hall, the men sat in groups on the grass. It might be late winter, but here on Humboldt Bay they lacked the snow and freezing temperatures they might be experiencing in other parts of the nation. The men were as animated and relaxed on the ground as if it were a summer picnic.

Once the men were fed, Emily approached, carrying two plates.

"One's for you and one's for Private Tripp."

"At last." Tripp took his plate and speared a large piece of meat, disappearing into the crowd with it.

"Thanks, Emily." Boyd took a chunk of meat and a fork. "What did you make?"

"A dish called curry. This recipe is at least fifty years old." Her chin lifted in pride. "Captain Grant didn't have all the required ingredients like coriander or cloves, but I did have clove oil for toothaches and turmeric on hand."

"Tumer-what?"

"Something I got awhile ago from the shopkeeper in Eureka. His wife said brewing it in tea helps with her digestion, so I thought I'd try it. Can't say I noticed any changes, but I found another use for it at last. Regardless, I think the curry turned out well enough. Certainly a change from the usual fare around here."

It was different, that was for sure. And while Boyd liked garlic as much as the next fella, what on earth did turmeric taste like?

He dipped his fork into the sauce.

Spice sparked on his tongue, tempered by a sweetness that was like nothing he'd eaten before.

"Tasty." It was the truth.

But not as tasty to the men as his roast elk. When the colonel called for a show of hands, even Harry raised his arm in the air to be counted among those who preferred Boyd's offering. Then the lad blushed in guilt when his sister gaped at him.

Boyd won the challenge. Forks down.

"Congratulations." Emily thrust out her hand. To her credit, she didn't look upset. A tad bewildered, maybe. He couldn't blame her. He'd felt similarly when she won the healing challenge.

"You're still the better cook."

"I know."

Laughing, he released her hand. "You're something, aren't you, Emily?"

"If 'something' means I'm going to beat you at the tiebreaker challenge, then yes."

"Then I'd better keep my eye on you."

He'd meant in the upcoming challenge, but his eyes must've misunderstood his words, because his gaze stayed fixed on her as she strode across the parade ground, all the way until she disappeared from view.

Chapter Five

I still can't believe you lost." Molly's plump lips pursed the next afternoon when she bustled into the kitchen, a basket of hot rolls in hand. "You're taking it well."

Emily measured tea for the pot. "I can't say it didn't sting my pride, losing at my own area of expertise. I admit to feeling envious, though. Not so much that Boyd won, but that he gave the men an experience they enjoyed. His barbecue allowed them to socialize and eat in the fresh air and talk in a way they don't usually get to. It was a gift to them."

"I didn't think of it that way. Nevertheless, you did a wonderful job with the task."

"Thanks, Molly." She poured boiling water into her teapot, atop the tea leaves. "Honestly, I'd forgotten men just like *meat* sometimes. My pap was that way. Give him a campfire-roasted joint of venison and he was a happy man."

Molly chuckled and took a seat at the table. "What are we eating tonight?"

"Elk stew, what else?" They still had enough elk for days. "Anyway, lately I've come to a realization."

Molly set a roll on her saucer. "What's that?"

"I don't think about the soldiers very often."

"That's obvious," Molly muttered.

"I don't mean as suitors, Molly. I mean as people. To pray for them." Emily sat down beside her. "My head's always known everyone in the world has sorrows, but the truth is, I generally only pray for myself and Harry, and you and Percy. Not for any of them, not unless they're sick or something."

"That's a thing that can be changed at any moment."

"You're right, Molly. Thank you."

"Let's start now." Molly extended her hand across the table, and Emily took it. Together, they thanked God for their blessings, praised Him, and then prayed for the soldiers at the fort, the settlers in Bucksport and Eureka, the local Wiyot, and even President Franklin Pierce. It felt quite good when they finished, and Emily didn't miss her usual prayer of beseeching the Almighty for provision so she could leave Fort Humboldt. Not at all.

Their tea and the rolls were lukewarm after praying, but neither of them seemed to mind. They enjoyed a comfortable chat for several minutes, until Harry burst into the kitchen. "Em, Mr. Kinman's here."

"Manners, Harry."

Her brother looked at Molly. "Pardon me, Mrs. Luther. Good afternoon."

"Good afternoon to you as well, Harry." She grinned. "So what's this about our favorite game hunter?"

"He's here," Harry repeated.

"More elk already?" Usually Seth spread out his visits more than that. If he'd brought more meat, Emily would have to turn it into jerky.

"Didn't see any, ma'am. But word is he brought a fiddle and he wants to play for us tonight."

"A musical evening. How marvelous." Molly clapped with delight. "I'll welcome any music that isn't a bugle and drum, no offense to Privates Coe and Kittredge."

"So will I." Anticipation flooded Emily's veins. "It sounds wonderful."

The rest of the afternoon her mind was on the upcoming evening's entertainments. Was this how the soldiers had felt on the days when there was a competition between her and Boyd? If so, she could better understand why Colonel Buchanan had conceived of the idea, and why Boyd agreed to it so readily. Knowing something different and fun lay on the horizon, Emily had a smile on her lips. It was like being a child on Christmas Eve, knowing that soon, Santa Claus would visit and bring her a piece of fruit and penny candy.

Once supper was finished, Harry rushed to the kitchen door and shot a pleading gaze at Emily. "Come on, Em. He's gonna start without us."

She untied her apron strings. "You aren't going anywhere without your coat."

"Aw, Em. It's practically spring."

"I don't care what season it is, it's chilly tonight." She had no thermometer, but a cold breeze carried in from the bracing Pacific. "Take your hat as well."

"It's back in our quarters. Come on, Em, it's not that bad. I don't need it, see?" He pushed open the door to the night.

She tied her own bonnet on. "Fine, but if it gets colder, go get it, all right?"

"Yes, now come on. I hear him tuning." His tone grew pleading.

With half a smile, Emily shoved her arms into her coat and followed him outside. As she'd expected, the damp air snuck under her collar and beneath her hem, chilling her exposed skin. It was easy to ignore the nip biting her nose and cheeks, though, with the strains of a stringed instrument coming from the torchlit parade grounds.

Seth Kinman stood a full head taller than the other men on a regular day, but some of the soldiers must have rigged up a small stage for him, because she could see him in his entire buckskin-and-fur-clad glory, bow in hand, instrument tucked beneath his bearded chin.

There was a place beside Boyd at the side of the crowd, near a flickering torch. With Harry having run somewhere else, she claimed her spot there—because it was a good place to see Seth Kinman, of course. It had nothing to do with being near the doctor.

But she smiled up at Boyd anyway.

"I'm glad you came." His grin warmed her cold toes.

"I wouldn't miss an evening of music." It took effort, but she broke her gaze from his to look at Seth. Hmm. "Something's not right with that violin."

"That's because he crafted that fiddle himself." Boyd's grin stretched to his cheeks. "It's fashioned from a mule jaw."

What a tease. "Very amusing, Doctor."

"What?"

It had been awhile since she'd heard a joke or tall tale from him, but here he went again. "A mule jaw. Ha, ha."

"From his favorite mule, Dave."

Her lips curled. "Now that's downright distasteful, even for you."

"I'm distasteful?" He adopted a wounded expression. "When?"

"Oh, stop. You'll do anything for a laugh."

He couldn't respond, because Seth raised the bow and, with a flourish, drew it down. A familiar tune came forth from the odd-looking fiddle. " 'The Arkansas Traveler.' I love this song."

Boyd grinned down at her. "It's one of my favorites too."

The others clapped to the beat and tapped their boots, and some sang along. Emily swayed to and fro enough to make her crinoline and skirt swish. She wished the song would never end.

After a while, though, she wondered if her wish had come true. How many verses did this song have? It had been ten minutes or more since Seth began.

At a pause, everyone applauded and whistled, only to be cut short by the song starting up again.

Emily felt her brows scrunch. Then Boyd leaned down to whisper in her ear. "Don't you like the song anymore?"

His words were meant to tease, but his warm breath on her cheek and earlobe sent shivers down her spine.

The only thing to do was tease him back. She stood on her tiptoes to speak in his ear. "Of course I do. I hope it lasts all evening." She almost said it with a straight face.

Boyd pointed to a patch of earth where Percy and Molly danced to the music. Emily was a terrible dancer herself, having had little opportunity to practice. There had been a few nights of celebration at the mining camps with Pap, but since he'd been gone, she had no time for frivolities like that. The fort had been good for her that way, allowing her to focus on work instead of yearning for fun.

Until she'd met Boyd, of course. Since then, she'd been warring with herself over allowing herself a little fun. And look at her now, tapping her feet to the music instead of sitting in her quarters darning socks—

Someone gripped her elbow and tugged.

"Come on, Em, let's dance." Harry's eager face glowed in the torchlight.

How could she say no to that? With a quick smile to Boyd, Emily took her brother's hand and hurried to join the Luthers on the improvised dance floor. Following Molly's example, she shed her coat and her bonnet in expectation of growing warm from the exercise. She and Harry probably made an amusing sight, bouncing like popcorn and stepping on one another's feet, but he seemed happy, and that made her happy.

After Private Tripp cut in, however, followed by a handful of other soldiers, she realized no one cared about her dancing skill. They just wanted to have fun.

She told Colonel Buchanan as much when he took her arm.

"Everyone needs to be at ease once in a while," he agreed.

Was fun part of rest, or being at ease? Emily had never given the matter thought, but right now, smiling and laughing and enjoying a festive evening, she felt more relaxed and yes, rested, than she had in weeks. Months, perhaps.

"This was a lovely idea." She tipped her head at Seth Kinman on the stage. "He's certainly accomplished with this song."

"Hard to believe that's a mule jaw fiddle he's playing, but it sounds fine by me. Kinman makes all sorts of things out of bones and horns and pelts, you know."

Emily stumbled. "You mean it *is* a mule jaw? I thought Boyd was teasing me."

"Not about that." The colonel's eyes twinkled.

"There's a first time for everything, I suppose. Even a novice like him winning a cooking contest." She peered up at the colonel. "Have you decided what the next contest will be?"

"Is that a request for a hint?"

"Of course not, sir."

He chuckled. "I see I'm not as good at joshing as the doctor."

"There's no one quite like him, that's true."

"He's a good fellow. Speaking of, I think you're about to be claimed by another partner."

Who would dare cut in on the colonel?

Boyd would, it seemed. And he didn't seem the least bit sorry about it.

After she curtsied to the colonel, she lifted her eyes to Boyd's. His dark eyes narrowed, as if he inspected her in a professional capacity. "Do you have need of a doctor, Emily?"

Despite his inspection, she knew better than to take him seriously when his eyes sparkled like that. "Why, do I look flushed?"

"As a matter of fact, you do. But I'm more concerned with your feet."

What was wrong with her feet? "They're fine. A little sore."

"Precisely. Dancing with every able-bodied fella at the fort will do that to a young lady."

"I have *not* danced with everyone." Did he comprehend her pointed glare? She hadn't danced with *him*.

"Then if your feet aren't too achy, perhaps you could tolerate one more dance."

When he smiled that lopsided grin of his, she couldn't help but smile back. "I could tolerate it, I suppose, if someone were to ask me."

But he didn't. He just stared at her.

❧

Emily was a lovely woman anywhere, anytime. Her propriety and ladylike manner complemented her large eyes and sweet features. Here in the torchlight, however, with her cheeks flushed and her blond hair loosening from its coil at her nape, she was breathtaking.

Perhaps that's why it took him so long to ask her. He couldn't find words.

"Doctor?" she asked. "Are *you* unwell?"

Yes, he was. He'd never felt like this before. Since he was fourteen or so, he'd been wary of attaching to anyone. Before that, a few friends in the orphanage who'd been like brothers had found homes with distant relatives, and his favorite matron had married and moved across town. He'd missed them terribly, and once he realized he'd never be adopted, he decided not to care about anyone else so much that it would hurt when they left, as everyone eventually did.

But he couldn't help it now. He'd developed feelings of a disquieting nature for Emily Sweet. He had no idea what to do with them, but he couldn't let the evening pass without grasping the opportunity to hold her in his arms.

"Will you dance with yet one more man, then?" he managed to ask.

"Whom do you mean?" She smiled up at him in feigned innocence.

"Minx. Are you teasing me?"

"If anyone here deserves to be teased, Boyd, it's you, don't you think?"

"Will you dance with *me*, Emily?"

"I would be delighted."

As a doctor, he was accustomed to touching others, but holding her hand like this sent a weakening wave up his arm. "I don't really dance," he blurted.

"Me neither."

But they were moving, maintaining eye contact, and he didn't care anymore how his feet moved or what he looked like. Only that this was an exhilarating moment, being with her, enveloped by music, her eyes sparkling in the flickering light, while she smiled at him.

He was sunk. Doomed. Destined for a broken heart, if he allowed himself to fall all the way in love with her, which he was definitely in danger of doing. *Lord, I'm not a marrying man. I'm not. . .*

It didn't have to matter, did it? It was just a dance, and there was nothing wrong with enjoying the moment with a beautiful woman who made his pulse gallop. Experience the moment. He could do that.

The moment didn't last long enough; Kinman stopped the never-ending song. Boyd let Emily go, and the world felt a little colder.

"Thank you, sir." She made a little curtsy, as if she met royalty.

"It is I who am humbled, ma'am." He bowed at the waist. The song might be over, but he didn't quite want the evening to be. Not just yet. "Since it appears Kinman is finished, may I escort you back to your quarters?"

"That would be kind, thank you. First I must retrieve my bonnet and coat. Oh." She stopped when Private Tripp approached, her coat and bonnet in hand.

"Ma'am. Didn't want these to get stomped on by the other fellas."

"Thoughtful of you, Tripp." Boyd was curt enough that he hoped Tripp would get the hint and go away.

He didn't. "Mighty kind of you and Mrs. Luther to dance with so many of us, ma'am."

Had the baker's wife danced with the fellows too? Boyd hadn't noticed. His eyes had been only for Emily all evening.

"It was a pleasure." Emily glanced up at Boyd.

When Tripp still didn't leave, Boyd's stomach sank. "Someone ill?"

"I'm afraid so. Something ain't right with Waldo."

Private Coe escorted the sergeant toward Boyd, holding him by the arm. "He's woozy and aches all over, Doc."

"Poor man." Emily tutted.

He touched her arm above the elbow, lightly, but hopefully enough that she'd understand his regret. "I'm sorry."

"Go on. I hope it's nothing serious, but I'll send Harry over with some broth." And with that, she nodded and slipped away.

Boyd fixed his attentions on Sergeant Waldo. The fellow's red-rimmed eyes and vacant gaze gave Boyd pause. He placed the back of his hand against Waldo's hot forehead.

Hmm.

After a few questions, Boyd could rule out several causes. Waldo lacked lesions, so it wasn't eruptive fever. Nor was it typhoid, scarlet fever, mumps, or milk sickness, but it was more severe than the runny nose that accompanied catarrh. "Come on to the hospital. Seems like a probable case of influenza."

"I've got the grippe?"

Grippe, ague, influenza. Whatever one called it, it was miserable. "Sorry, but yes."

"Gonna bleed me?" It was an attempt at a joke, but Waldo looked as if he wasn't in favor of the idea.

"Never been much for bleedings. Or purgatives, for that matter."

"Won't argue with you there, sir." Waldo's voice was raspy. "I'm cold."

Boyd put his arm around the fellow. "I'll fix you a hot water bottle, then, and give you a spoonful of tonic and a glass of medicine." Dr. Munn had taught him to combine twenty grains quinine with a pint of diluted wine, but lacking the wine, he'd use water or broth. It was the quinine that did the work, in Boyd's opinion. "A few days' rest and you'll feel much better."

Provided the influenza didn't cause pneumonia, but Boyd wouldn't think of worst-case circumstances right now. Waldo was a healthy young man. Nevertheless, Boyd had better bunk in the hospital tonight, rather than his quarters.

He wouldn't get much sleep, but those long, quiet hours of darkness were conducive to prayer, and he had a lot to bring to the Lord right now. Waldo, for instance. And Emily. Boyd needed God's help cutting down his feelings for her where they stood.

He wanted to value their time together, but a short time was all it could be. No matter how he was starting to feel, there was no such thing as forever. Not where he was concerned.

Chapter Six

Despite the full light of the sun the next morning, the parade ground wasn't much warmer than it had been last night for Seth Kinman's fiddle concert, not with the breeze nipping Emily's fingers and nose. Hopefully Colonel Buchanan's third competition, which he was announcing now, would take place indoors.

She hadn't expected the competition so soon, but the colonel had summoned everyone shortly after breakfast. Fortunately, the noonday meal of beans supplemented with salt pork—and a little elk, truth be told—already simmered on the stove. Emily was not otherwise occupied.

But Boyd must be, for he hadn't come to breakfast, nor was he on the parade ground yet. Ah, there he was, exiting the hospital, his pace slower than usual as he strode toward her. His welcoming smile wasn't quite bright enough to hide the dark pouches beneath his eyes, and now that she was closer to him, she could see how wrinkled his coat was. "You slept at the hospital?"

"All part of the job." His half grin didn't quite comfort her.

"I'd hoped Sergeant Waldo would feel better today, but he must be feeling poorly still for you to have been up all night."

His smile fell. "Influenza, I fear."

Emily's pulse ratcheted. Influenza could mean anything from a day of discomfort to a week of misery. Or worse. Clearly, Boyd had better things to occupy his time than a silly contest. "We mustn't compete today, then."

"Waldo's sleeping, and Tripp's with him. I can step away for a short time, if the contest won't take too long. I'd hate to disappoint the fort. Excuse me while I inform the colonel, and we'll see what he says on the matter." His hand landed on her sleeve, a light touch, but one that seared her to her shoulder. "Don't fret, Emily. It'll all be well."

As he walked away, Emily drew her crocheted shawl tighter about her shoulders. "I hope so," she said to the air.

"Emily?" Molly came up behind her. "What's the competition?"

"I don't know yet, but we might postpone. Sergeant Waldo is down with influenza."

Molly's features tightened. "Percy went back to bed with a headache. I hope it's not a sign of worse to come."

"I pray not." She reached for her friend's warm hand.

Boyd returned, stifling a yawn even as he greeted Molly. "The colonel says it's a quick competition. I'm game to go ahead if you are."

"Are you certain?"

He yawned again but nodded when he was done.

Poor Boyd. She'd take breakfast to him and Private Tripp as soon as this was over. "All right, then."

The appearance of two chairs from the mess hall, placed atop the makeshift stage used by Seth Kinman last night, told Emily the contest would take place right here. What on earth would they be doing?

Colonel Buchanan held a bulky, folded gray blanket—no, maybe two blankets, with that bulk. Over his arm, he carried a basket with something black and limp hanging over the edge, almost like an old sock. "Time to break the tie between our assistant surgeon, Dr. Braxton, and our cook, Miss Sweet. I'm assigning them a quarter hour to complete a task."

"What's he gonna have you do with blankets? Pitch a tent?" Molly scratched her chin.

Emily looked up at Boyd. "Well, you've won that. I haven't made a hideaway out of pillows and blankets since I was younger than Harry."

"I can't imagine you doing that."

"Pap used to help." He'd loved those rainy afternoons, spending time on play forts and games. He'd always been more dreamer than farmer and was quick to abandon their Iowa crops to chase gold dust in California. She and Harry were still paying the price for Pap's thirst for adventure.

It was a good reminder that while they'd had fun and made memories to cherish, she mustn't allow herself to follow in her father's footsteps. She must be responsible. Someone had to be.

"Thinking about your father?" Boyd nudged her shoulder with his. "You must miss him something awful."

"Every day."

"Maybe it'll feel like he's here with you, making a tent—"

"It isn't a tent." Molly shushed them. "Listen, you two. He's talking."

Biting her lip, Emily looked to the colonel.

". . .then at the end of fifteen minutes, the hole that has been patched the best will be declared the winner."

A sewing contest! Emily then understood the black fabric poking out of the basket. It was patching material of some sort. Presumably, the basket also held needle, thread, and scissors. She had an advantage here, and in all fairness, she should make it known to both Boyd and the colonel.

"I make all my own clothes." It wasn't a boast but a statement of fact.

She shouldn't have been surprised that Boyd simply shrugged. "I've sewed up my share of lacerations. I think I have a fair chance."

Sewing skin was not the same as hemming an apron, but if he was willing, she was too. She blew on her cold fingers to warm them for the task.

At once a shiver went through her, and not because of the cool breeze. This was the final task. If she won, she could realize her dream of settling in a town with a good school for Harry. She would have everything she'd worked for this past year.

Half of her quaked at the thrill of it. The other half felt more like grief. When she and Harry left, they'd be leaving everyone here at the fort too. Her gaze flicked to Boyd.

Oh dear, she would miss him. The realization kicked her in the chest, and before she could analyze what that meant, the colonel had bundled a needle, thread, scissors, and patching material atop each of the blankets and laid them on the chairs. He pulled out his pocket watch.

The task was at hand.

Emily dashed past Boyd in a blue gingham whirlwind, leaving him flat footed. Grinning, he rushed after her and scooped up the blanket and other materials. Emily had already dropped into her seat and unfolded the blanket. Mercy, if he was going to finish, he'd better stop watching her.

Trying to concentrate over the soldiers' hoots, Boyd sat and examined his supplies. A sturdy needle, which he placed between his lips for safekeeping. Ancient-looking scissors and heavy black thread, far coarser than the silk stuff he used in the hospital. A scrap of black wool for the patch, and at last the gray blanket with a hole the size of a playing card near the hem, like someone had tried to poke their foot through it.

Since the colonel hadn't seen fit to provide a ruler, Boyd measured the hole with his hand. Out of the corner of his eye, he could see Emily's arms moving.

"Stitching already, Cook?" he teased.

"Aren't you, Doc?" she teased back.

One of the men thumped his palm on the makeshift stage. "Less jaw jackin' and more sewin', if you mean to win this, Doc."

"Oh, I mean to win."

"How interesting. So do I." Emily squinted her left eye and focused on the patch.

"Go, Em, go!" Harry yelled. Several of the men echoed in chorus.

Boyd needed to ignore them and focus, although it wasn't easy to sew in this position. He was more accustomed to sewing while standing, so he pushed his knees up to give himself a higher workstation, as it were.

Boyd cut a patch bigger than the hole, threaded the needle, and set to work. The needle plunked in a soothing rhythm, up and down to the beat of the crowd's chants.

"One minute!" The colonel shouted.

Boyd tied off his stitches in a sturdy knot. A snip of the scissors and he was done. His hands raised in the air. Had he been faster than Emily?

Her hands lifted at the same time.

"A tie?" Harry's mouth was agape. The soldiers howled.

"Guess I'll have to judge the handiwork to select a winner." The colonel lifted Emily's blanket for inspection. "Mrs. Luther, your opinion please?"

The baker's wife joined him on the stage, whispering and nodding. She pointed out a few areas, and then it was time to examine Boyd's blanket. While they scrutinized his sewing, he looked to Emily and winked.

Did her cheeks flush on account of his wink or the chilly wind?

"It's a tie," Colonel Buchanan announced.

"A tie?" Harry gaped.

"A tie!" Boyd laughed. "Wonders never cease."

"Sorry, Emily, but his stitches are as tidy and tiny as yours." Mrs. Luther patted her friend's shoulder. "See for yourself."

Emily blinked at the blanket thrust in front of her eyes. "You're right. Well done, Boyd."

"Thanks, Emily."

Harry folded his arms. "So what do we do now? Another contest?"

"Maybe a tiebreaker for the tie," Molly suggested.

"I'll give the matter some thought. Hadn't expected to come up with a fourth competition." The colonel gathered the blankets. "Thanks for your sportsmanship, Miss Sweet, Doctor," he said quietly. "You've brought some enjoyment to the men."

"You're welcome, sir." Emily stood. "I'd better return to the kitchen."

"And I'd best get back to the hospital." Boyd met Emily's gaze. "Could I trouble you for more broth today?"

"Of course. I have some simmering. Harry can bring it over in a minute."

Harry was tossing the ball with two of the soldiers who were off duty, judging by their regular clothes. Boyd didn't want to take the boy from his fun. "I'll come for it myself." Fetching the broth would give him an extra minute with her too.

"All right." Emily tugged her shawl around her shoulders and led the way to the kitchen.

"Cold?"

"A little."

"I'd give you my coat, but I don't think the colonel would approve of me being out and about in my shirtsleeves."

"I'll be in the warm kitchen soon enough. I just wish I'd worn a bonnet." She tucked a loose tendril of hair behind her ear.

He stifled the urge to adjust it when it whipped free again in the next gust of breeze and tickled her nose. So much for nipping his feelings for her in the bud. They were as strong as they'd been last night when they danced and didn't seem likely to fade anytime soon.

Maybe that explained why his tongue was tied. He grappled for something to say. "That was fun, wasn't it? Not the sewing, necessarily, but the whole competition."

"More than I expected, yes. I know I said I didn't have time for fun, but I was wrong. There are enough hours in the day to finish my work and be a little spontaneous too."

He pushed open the kitchen door for her and followed her inside. Ah, it felt good to be out of the wind. It felt good being with her too. "There's more fun to be had, outside of the contest, you know."

"True. Last night was a rare occurrence, wasn't it?"

"You mean listening to 'The Arkansas Traveler' for three quarters of an hour? I'd say so."

Smiling, she took a jar and ladled a rich brown broth into it. "Mr. Kinman's repertoire is rather limited, it seems."

There was nothing wrong with this conversation, but Boyd crawled out of his skin with wanting to engage in a different one. One where he told her how he felt. It was foolish, but he couldn't stop himself. *Lord, have mercy.*

"You know, Emily, we have a lot of fun together. Not just the contest, but other things. Like baking the cake for Tripp. That was enjoyable, wasn't it?"

"A little, I suppose." Her cheeky reply told him she was teasing. But for the first time, he wasn't in the mood for it.

"I like to talk to you. To be with you."

Her hand stilled on the jar lid. "You do?"

"I think you like to be with me too. Like you don't dislike me so much anymore."

Her breath hitched. "Maybe."

He moved closer. So close he could kiss her if he wanted to. And he wanted to, but not yet. Not before he said what he needed to say. "Maybe then I could take you on a walk tonight around the fort. Before it gets dark. I thought it might be nice to look at the bay. Watch the waves and talk."

Her eyes were soft, and her pretty lips smiled. A genuine, sweet smile he'd never forget. "That would be. . .pleasant."

Sweet relief flooded his veins. "I'm glad."

"I am too."

He gave in to his impulse and tucked the wayward strand of blond hair behind her ear. "I figure Assistant Surgeon Simpson won't be back for a few more weeks, at least. That means, if you're amenable, we can take a dozen walks together. Enjoy what time we have."

She blinked. "What do you mean, enjoy what time we have?"

"When Dr. Simpson returns, I'll have to go elsewhere." He shrugged. "I'd like to spend as much time with you as possible before I leave. Or you leave. You're planning to take Harry away one of these days, right?"

That wasn't the right answer. He could tell immediately by the unhappy twist of her lips. "So you're suggesting exercise. Not anything more than that."

Exercise? "I've made a blunder of making myself clear, then, because I was thinking we could court for the time being."

She slunk out of his reach. "Courting implies a lasting arrangement, Boyd. Not one to two weeks of watching waves before you leave."

She wanted an arrangement? A relationship like *that*? That meant she had feelings for him, didn't it? A good thing, a wonderful thing, but Boyd's throat tightened. "I can't do *lasting* anything. Life's too uncertain to plan that far ahead."

"Life's too uncertain *not* to plan." She stared at the far corner of the room. "I should have known."

"Known what? That I'm not worth your friendship?"

She looked at him as if exasperated. "To listen to my head instead of my heart. You and I value different things, Boyd."

"We care for one another. Isn't that a good place to start? Besides, I think we do value the same things. God. Doing our work to the best of our abilities."

"Harry and I need permanence. A home. We have slept in tents, shanties, rented rooms, and on kitchen floors for the last two years. It's been awful. Don't you want a home, Boyd?"

"I haven't had a home since I was four years old."

"All the more reason to want one, I'd think."

"Hard to say when I don't know what life in a home is like, Emily. Since the flu took my sister, not a single person on earth has cared for me enough to put me first, the way you put Harry. I don't begrudge you wanting a place to call your own, but I'm not sure I know how to be part of a family anymore or how to. . .to love, even. Not right, anyway. I used to want a family so badly, Emily, but no one who came to the orphanage wanted me. Not the fancy couples who took the babies, not the farmers who wanted strong boys to work their fields. Not even Dr. Munn."

"The physician who took you in?"

"He didn't take me in. He paid me to sweep his office. Then he offered to train me, and I was so eager for his attention I agreed to it. Later on, when I decided to be a doctor, he even paid for my education. But the one thing he couldn't bring himself to do was adopt me."

Emily blinked. Licked her lips. "Maybe—"

She broke off, probably realizing how feeble any excuse would be. Dr. Munn had the means to educate Boyd, so surely he could have sheltered, fed, and clothed him. Dr. Munn just hadn't loved him. There was a difference.

"Family's as foreign to me as Mandarin. But friendship, I know. And that's what I can offer you. My hand of friendship. If you're wanting more than that, then I'm sorry. I'd like to spend time with you, enjoy your company, until you or I leave the fort. That's all."

She handed him the jar of broth, her face that mask she'd worn the first few weeks of their acquaintance. "I see."

He'd hurt her, splashed his own pain onto her. But he couldn't give her what she wanted. He tucked the jar into the crook of his arm. "Be careful, thinking your security is in a place or people. God's the only sure thing there is in life, but He does give good gifts. I'll pray you and Harry find a good home, whenever you leave."

"Thank you." She turned away, lifting the lid off a pot on the stove. The aroma of meat and beans hit him. "I'd best get back to work."

"Goodbye, Emily."

"Goodbye." It sounded like a permanent farewell, not just the sort of goodbye that meant they'd see one another at supper.

So that was that, then.

Boyd turned to go. His hand was on the latch, but he hadn't turned it before the door flung open, almost smacking him in the face. Private Coe panted in the threshold.

"Coe?"

"It's Harry, Doc. You and Miss Sweet better come. Fast."

"What's happened?" Emily's voice rose in a panicked pitch. "He was just tossing a ball around—oh no, did it hit him in the head?"

"No, ma'am, but he's not quite right. Like he's sleepwalking. He stumbled a few steps before sitting himself on the ground."

Boyd raced to the parade grounds. What if Sergeant Waldo wasn't the only one in the fort to fall sick?

Chapter Seven

Harry was sick. And she was helpless to do anything but watch as Boyd carried the lad to the hospital and settled him onto a cot, muttering words like *febrile* and *insensible*.

How could this have happened? Minutes ago, Harry had been laughing, enjoying the sewing challenge, tossing a ball with some of the soldiers. Now, he was feverish and lethargic.

Within the hour, Emily had Harry changed into his nightshirt and perched on the side of his narrow cot, attempting to spoon broth into his mouth. "Please, Harry? Just a sip."

"Not hungry." His voice was a rough whisper.

"You need liquid."

His dry lips parted enough for her to slip the spoon into his mouth. He managed a swallow, but some of the pale liquid dripped down his chin.

"Let him rest for now." Boyd's voice behind her was comforting, but surely he knew the boy needed to drink. It wasn't worth arguing;

Harry needed sleep too, and that seemed to be all he wanted to do. Setting down the bowl and spoon, she blotted perspiration from Harry's hot forehead and pulled his covers up higher over his chest.

She craned her head to look back at Boyd. "How did it come upon him so fast?"

"Influenza can be like that. One minute, a body feels a little strange. And the next? Only place for you is bed."

She'd experienced that before but not to this extent. Usually it started with a headache.

But as she looked around at the other occupied cots, she understood this was no ordinary influenza.

Sergeant Waldo lay in his cot, curled on his side. Two other soldiers had walked into the hospital after Harry was brought in, complaining of body aches and sore throats. One slept, but the other stared vacantly at the ceiling with glassy, red-rimmed eyes.

She glanced at the full bowl beside her. "Perhaps that fellow should have some broth."

"Tripp and I will see to it."

"I'm not going to leave now anyway."

"All right, then. Thank you." Boyd stepped away, rubbing the back of his neck. It was the act of a tired man. Or a worried one.

When Boyd knelt over the resting soldier, she took the broth to the wide-awake one. "Try a little?"

He was her age, maybe, with round cheeks and pale eyes. He obediently took the soup for a short time before he shook his head. Finished.

"Try to rest now."

He blinked. "I was up all night, ma'am. When I shut my eyes I see things. Bad things. Like there are monsters in my head."

He'd succumbed to the influenza yesterday, then, poor fellow. "Those are fever dreams."

He sighed, as if too weary to speak.

"What's your name?"

"Philpott." He squeezed his eyes shut. "Ever'thing aches so bad."

"I'll see if the doctor has something to help." As she rose, two newcomers entered the room. Kittredge rubbed his forehead, and the other, a man whose name she thought was Jones, leaned against the wall. Boyd and Tripp each took one in hand, led them to empty cots, and asked questions.

Six patients now. Her brain calculated how many quarts of broth she'd need to prepare along with today's meals for the healthy men. If only there were someone else to cook so she needn't leave Harry. Her darling boy. She checked in on him, noted his fitful sleep. "I love you," she whispered over him.

Lord, he's all I have. I love him more than my own life. Please heal him. Heal all of these men, please.

But her selfish heart didn't want to pray for those men as much as she wanted to pray for Harry. *If Harry doesn't get better—*

She halted the horrible thought where it was. Thinking such things did no good.

Her hand was trembling when she removed it from Harry's cot.

"Boyd?" She kept her voice low.

He looked up. "Something changed?"

Yes, everything had changed now that Harry was ill. She'd known nothing in life was certain and she had to be equipped for the worst, but losing him was the one thing she hadn't prepared for. She'd wanted to give him his best life, but now?

"I don't want to leave him, but I have to return to the kitchen for a while."

"He'll rest. Try not to fret."

Easier said than done. "Private Philpott is achy and having fever dreams. He needs something to help with the pain."

"You probably want to use willow bark rather than a proven tonic, don't you?"

His tone wasn't sharp, but she couldn't help but feel it was a reference to the sorts of discussions they had that led to the competition between them in the first place. Those conversations in the first days of their acquaintance riled her up like a cat caught in a downpour. Well, she was riled all over again.

"What I want is to ease these men's suffering. And seeing as I lack yarrow or willow bark to help with the fevers, please give them whatever tonic or remedy is available. Pardon me, but I have work to do."

He didn't stop her, although she half expected him to. Maybe he was angry with her, as upset by their conversation in the kitchen as she was.

But how couldn't she be upset? He'd wanted to court her for what, five minutes? Break the barriers around her guarded heart and then leave? Pah.

The noonday meal was a rushed affair, fried pork and the slabs of bread the Luthers provided. The men could do as much themselves with their regulation frying pans, but it was the best she could do today.

Fortunately, she'd left a pan of beans soaking, and while she'd intended to ladle them alongside chunks of meat tonight, she'd make soup instead. That way she could start it simmering now and leave it unattended to look in on Harry. Oh—and she mustn't forget the broth. She worked on both simultaneously, boiling hambones and chopping onions.

Tears slipped from her eyes, but she couldn't blame the onions this time. Did Harry need her? Was he resting, or fitful? She swiped her eyes with the back of her hand. Instead of worrying, she should pray, so she did while she finished preparing the soup.

At last she was at a good place to leave the kitchen and return to the hospital. Before she left, she washed her hands and face and gathered the book Harry was reading. He'd need something to occupy him when he woke up.

When she returned, yet another patient had come in, so now all but one cot was filled. This patient sat up, looking weary as he answered Private Tripp's questions about aches and chills.

"What's causing this to happen to all of us?" the man asked, his voice anxious.

Tripp shrugged. "Something in the fog, maybe."

Private Philpott appeared to be more comfortable now, but Waldo writhed as if in quiet agony. He must ache something fierce. Boyd bent over him, a bottle in hand. *Dear God, let whatever that tonic is ease Waldo's suffering.*

Emily knelt on the ground beside Harry's cot. Hearing her, Harry's lids cracked open. "Em? I'm thirsty."

"I can help with that." She forced her voice to sound cheery as she lifted the small pitcher of water at his bedside table and filled the glass that had been resting upside down beside it. "Can you sit up?"

He managed to prop up but flopped back on his pillow once he'd swallowed a few sips.

"I brought you a book."

"Hurts to move my eyes."

Oh. "It'll be here when you're ready. Do you need anything else? I can help you get to the outhouse."

"Doc helped me with the pan."

She swung to look at Boyd, gratitude swelling in her chest. She'd expected him to help Harry, of course, but for some reason, this particular act—when Emily was away to spare Harry's dignity—touched her heart.

Boyd held Waldo's wrist, counting the beats of his heart. Then he looked up at her, unsmiling. Lowering Waldo's arm, he jerked his head as if to ask her to come closer.

She brushed Harry's hair from his face. "Be right back, my love."

"Don't want to talk no more anyway. Hurts."

"Rest, then." She rose and met Boyd at the far end of the room, away from the two rows of cots. Whatever unpleasantness had passed between them, she appreciated his care for her brother. "Thank you for helping Harry."

His brows lifted as if surprised. "Why wouldn't I help him?"

"I know it's your job, but—"

"I care about him, Emily. Even if you and I aren't friends, I still care about you both. I hope you know that. And I'm sorry I goaded you earlier." He looked down. "The words slipped out about the willow bark. I guess it was easier to bicker with you over something stupid than speak plain like this. This isn't the time for it, but we're both hurting over what happened in the kitchen earlier, and I didn't help matters."

He was hurting too? Because she'd rejected his so-called offer? It didn't make much sense, truthfully. He'd only wanted to spend time with her while they were both at the fort. That meant parting soon enough, so why did it cause him pain that she cut it off a few days or weeks earlier?

Didn't he understand she'd done it to protect her heart?

She rubbed her forehead, as if the act could order her thoughts. Regardless of how she felt, Boyd was correct and this was no time to wallow over feelings. "This situation certainly calls for civility. I'll do my best to keep things courteous."

He looked as if he wanted to say more, but he didn't, so she did the only thing she could think of. She changed the subject.

"That tonic seems to have made the men feel more comfortable. What is it?"

He showed her the bottle then set it down on the worktable.

"It's not a cure, but it does relieve some of the pain. I'm afraid it doesn't help with fevers, though, and Waldo's is higher than I'd like. I'll have Tripp sponge him with cool water when he's done with Kittredge."

Emily glanced back at the steward, who dabbed a damp rag over Private Kittredge's brow and neck. "I'm not needed in the kitchen for a while, and Harry's resting. Why don't I tend Kittredge for a spell?"

"You'd do that?"

"Of course." Tripp looked tired anyway. Poor fellow must not have slept any more than Boyd last night. His eyes had a glassed-over look to them, and his jaw was slack, as if he breathed through his mouth. "This influenza is worse than any I've seen."

Boyd rubbed his neck again. "It's torture watching your sibling suffer. My sister died from influenza. I'll do all I can to prevent it from taking your brother too."

She recalled the information the moment he said it. She also remembered other things he'd said, about trying to save people so their families wouldn't be torn apart. "I remember now. You became a doctor to keep families together."

"Families like Waldo's." He turned his head to look at the sergeant, curled on his cot. "I don't want his girls to lose their father."

"The way you lost yours."

He looked away, and at once she saw him differently. Not as a teasing man who wanted everything to be fun, not as a man whose grin made her legs weak, but as a frightened boy suddenly alone in the world. No wonder he didn't want to forge a permanent attachment to her, to anyone. He feared losing all over again.

Emily let out a slow breath. "I understand now why you only wanted our time together to be temporary. You're afraid."

His gaze met hers. "I'm not afraid."

"Of caring for someone and losing them? Yes, I think you are. I am too."

His eyes argued with her, but he didn't speak, so she licked her lips and reached out. It was folly, madness, but she couldn't stop herself from taking his hand and placing it at the base of her throat, where her pulse pounded hard and fast through her veins. "See how afraid I am?"

He stared at his hand on her neck. "Why are you afraid?"

"Because life holds no guarantees, Boyd. I still think it's important to do all I can to prepare for the worst, but despite the risks inherent in this life, I wouldn't trade loving Harry for anything in the world. Or Molly and Percy. Or even someone like—"

Someone like you.

She couldn't say it. She had her pride, and he'd made it clear he only liked her enough for a brief period of. . .whatever it could be called. Certainly not courting, which as she'd told him, implied a long-lasting relationship. Perhaps leading to marriage.

She would leave it unsaid, then. Let him decide what she meant.

"Emily." Her name was quiet on his lips. Almost sweet.

She looked up, but his gaze caught on something over her shoulder. His hand fell from her throat. "Tripp?"

"Doc." Tripp stumbled toward them. "I'm sorry."

Lord, have mercy. Tripp was ill too.

The moment Boyd took Tripp in his arms, he was transported to a different time and place. Instead of Tripp, it was Annabeth under his arm, his baby sister, two years old, teeth chattering from feverish chills.

He'd forgotten until this moment how he'd clutched Annabeth's hand through the slats of her crib while she lay ill. Only now did he realize the matron knew Annabeth was dying and that was why he'd been allowed to stay with her.

Annabeth's loss changed him forever, and since then he'd worked, in one way or another, to protect his heart from that feeling of loss again.

Oh, he'd lost patients, of course. But no one he loved.

He scarcely knew Tripp, but these past several days, they'd grown somewhat close. Close enough for Boyd to grieve what was happening.

As he laid his steward on the cot by Harry's, long-dormant emotions rushed through him. Losing his parents. Losing his sister. Losing his identity as part of a family, part of a community, even part of a church. When he and Annabeth moved to the orphanage, everything had changed. It was as if he'd been ripped away from what it was to be a Braxton. To be himself.

That ripping sensation was happening again inside of him. Not that he'd lose his identity. Or his livelihood. He was a man now, equipped to care for himself and make his own choices.

But emotionally? He was back at the root of where he'd been when he was four years old and Annabeth died. This was—

This was his heart opening to feelings he'd closed off for a long, long time. Feelings of caring for someone and fearing the loss of them.

This isn't Annabeth. "Tripp is young, healthy." Not as young as Annabeth had been. She'd practically been a baby.

"He is," Emily said. He hadn't realized until then that he'd spoken aloud.

"He's got a home to return to. Folks."

"They'll be so glad to get his next letter, once this is over. Here." Emily unbuttoned Tripp's frock coat. "Private Tripp, can you lift your arm for me?"

"I'm sorry, Doc. I fought it." He allowed Emily to remove his coat.

"Enough of that nonsense, Tripp." Boyd eased off his friend's boots. "You should've told me earlier."

Tripp started to answer but coughed instead.

Boyd covered Tripp with the blanket and met Emily's gaze. "Even his elbows are hot, but his fever isn't as high as some of the others. Looks like I'm going to need more quinine mixture."

"Tell me what to do. I'll do it."

For a moment, he considered telling her how to prepare the mixture. Without Tripp to help, caring for eight patients—and maybe more coming—would be difficult, and her assistance would be a blessing. More than that, he wanted her to stay because her presence made things better. They'd hurt each other, yes, but Boyd would take the pain if it meant being with her a little longer.

But she had her own tasks to see to. She was a cook, not a nurse.

"It would be of great help if you could see Captain Grant and ask for quinine. If he's out of it, tell him to send someone to Eureka for it. Ask him to inform Colonel Buchanan the hospital's full of grippe patients, and then when it is convenient, bring me any broth you have in the kitchen. I shouldn't be asking that much of you, but with Tripp ill—"

"It's the least I can do." She touched him on the shoulder before she left.

The touch burned him like a brand, throbbing with each pulse while he measured quinine into cups, prayed, and tended to each patient. He still hadn't recovered from touching her throat. He'd felt the rapid, firm rhythm of her pulse there, a testimony to her fear, she'd said. Fear of what? Her feelings for him?

It didn't matter. If she didn't want to court during their last few days or weeks here at the fort, where did that leave them?

At an impasse, Lord. So why talk about it anymore? Just help me forget her. Except. . .I don't want to forget her. Ever. What's a man to do, God?

Meanwhile, he was surrounded by men in need. To a number, they were miserable as only the grippe could make a person, achy, chilled or sweating, coughing, exhausted but unable to fully rest. Boyd had endured influenza a few times himself, and he treated it often. But this rush of patients with this severity of symptoms was unusual.

Lord, we need Your healing presence here.

Late afternoon swallowed the sun, and Boyd lit the lamps, glancing with envy at the patients' water glasses. He hadn't taken a drink in hours, had he? In a minute, he'd grab one. First, he needed his stethoscope to listen to Philpott's chest. Where had he placed it? Ah, hanging over Harry's cot. As Boyd placed it around his neck, the door opened. Draped in a shawl, Emily held a large basket. "Supper."

"Thank you. I'll feed the men in a moment."

"Actually, I'll feed them while you eat." Her tone brooked no argument.

Boyd felt a smile pull at his dry lips. "How about we both feed them?"

"You can help once you're finished eating." It was her bossy voice, the one she used for Harry when he needed to study. She strode past him to the desk and set down the basket, removing a tin bowl, spoon, and jar, which she opened. The aroma of meat and spices made his mouth water. "Come while it's hot."

"Yes, ma'am. Once I wash up?"

"That goes without saying."

It was almost flirting.

Once he devoured the bean soup and thick bread Emily had brought, he helped the remaining patients swallow down some broth and new doses of quinine or tonic, whichever was required at the moment. Sergeant Waldo, however, seemed to worsen despite the medicines.

"Time to ice him."

Emily rolled up her sleeves.

They lacked enough ice to create a bath for the sergeant, but they could wrap large chips of it in rags and place them strategically about his body. While Boyd set the ice under Waldo's neck and knees, Emily pressed cold compresses to the sergeant's head, cringing at his shivering but holding fast.

Boyd didn't look up at the soft knock, but he recognized the sound of Colonel Buchanan clearing his throat. "Doctor? When you're able, I'd like to hear your thoughts."

"Of course." There wasn't much he could do at the moment, anyway. Adding another small bundle of ice onto Waldo's torso, Boyd rose to explain the situation to the fort commander. "There could be more sickened. If there are any spare cots in the barracks, I could use them."

"Consider it done. Miss Sweet?"

She looked up, eyes wide in surprise. "Sir?"

"With Private Tripp down, will you stay and help Dr. Braxton? I know you're not a nurse, but you're needed here. Don't worry about meals. The men can fend for themselves."

"I will stay." She said it as firmly and clearly as any soldier would have. Boyd's heart swelled in his chest.

Another knock sounded. This time it was Captain Grant, leading one of the soldiers who tended the stables, the redhead with a new bride back home. "Oh no, not Gibbs too?"

Grant nodded as Boyd led the ailing fellow to the vacant chair at his desk. As he settled the man down, feeling his forehead and looking for signs of rash, he could hear the conversation behind him.

"Fetch more cots for the doctor, Captain," the colonel was saying to Grant.

"Yes, sir. Before I go, though, there's no one left to care for the animals. The other men are resigned to languish in the barracks until they're on duty, but I reckon they won't feel up to it tomorrow. Request permission to tend the horses myself."

"Granted."

It seemed a wise fit. Grant was good with horses, and he could tend his quartermaster duties as well.

Boyd smiled at the redheaded private. "We'll have you in a cot soon, Private Gibbs."

"Thank you, Doctor."

Boyd looked up. Emily ministered to Waldo, but her gaze fixed on Harry. She'd been brave, but surely she feared losing him the way he'd lost his sister after his parents. He well-recalled that particular anguish, but what was it Emily had said?

"Despite the risks, I wouldn't trade loving Harry for anything in the world. Or even someone like..."

Someone like whom? Clearly, someone she might love differently than the way she loved her brother.

Someone more like a husband?

Boyd's blood ran hot, and it wasn't from influenza.

Chapter Eight

Over the grueling three days and nights that followed, Emily and Boyd were too busy and weary to talk about anything beyond quinine, fevers, and whose turn it was to eat and doze. Two more patients joined the nine they had when Private Gibbs came in, but no one else had become sick, thank the Lord. Nevertheless, eleven people comprised a quarter of the fort inhabitants—a terrifying thought.

Never before had Emily seen febrile convulsions, much less nursed a man through them, but praise God, this morning, the patients who'd suffered them two nights ago—Sergeant Waldo and Private Tripp—sat up, feeding themselves bread sops soaked in milk. Judging by the grimaces they bore, neither cared for the slimy meal, but they swallowed it down.

Thank You that everyone lived through this, Lord. Emily's gaze took in the other patients, some of whom seemed better than others, but all of them had passed through the worst.

Harry was propped up also, his empty bowl beside him on the bed and a book in hand. Emily tapped the book's spine. "Still a good story?"

"I'll say. Edmond Dantès just learned about the treasure of Monte Cristo. I reckon he's gonna go find it."

"What makes you think that?"

"The book's called *The Count of Monte Cristo*, Em. Why else would it be called that if Edmond wasn't going to have something to do with Monte Cristo?"

"I guess you're right." Emily's heart almost burst, seeing him back to his normal self. Almost normal, anyway. He was still weak, but at least he had the wherewithal to sit and read. Emily smoothed his blanket over him. "You'll be finished with this book in no time. I'll have to see if the general store in Eureka has any new volumes."

Then again, it might not be long before they left the fort for San Francisco or Sacramento. Accessing reading material for Harry's voracious appetite wouldn't be quite so challenging in one of those towns.

Everything would be easier, in fact. Oh, she wasn't so naive as to think the grass was greener in another pasture. Anywhere she took Harry would be an adjustment. She would have to find a job, and no matter how hard she worked, they would never be able to afford luxuries. She didn't care, as long as there was enough to give Harry an education.

And after that? Molly's words about what Emily would do after Harry was grown rang in her ears. Emily had never given the matter any thought, but now that she sat still, the thought niggled at her. If she had the means to do anything in the world, beyond ensuring Harry was educated, what would it be? If God gave her extra financial means, how would she spend it?

A fanciful question, perhaps. But then her gaze fell to Harry's book, and something took root in her brain.

"Emily?" Boyd's gentle tone called her from across the room. "Have a minute?"

"Sure." She ambled to meet him, hand going to her aching lower back.

Boyd's forehead furrowed. "You in pain?"

"Just from bending over so much. I'm sure you feel the same."

"It's a good ache." His gaze fixed on Waldo.

"You've given his girls their father back."

"The Lord did that." He grinned.

"Seemed to me like He used your hands to help. At any rate, I'm glad he and all the others are on the mend. Oh, but you needed something from me, didn't you?" Most of the men had either eaten or would do so, once they awakened, but she could take dirty dishes and linens out, or fetch more water.

"I don't need anything, no, but I was thinking you should return to your quarters. Get some rest."

She could stand freshening. She hadn't changed her dress in two days. But rest? "You haven't slept much either."

"I can run for miles on catnaps."

"Your teasing nature isn't dampened by fatigue, I see."

"Our patients are much improved. How can I not feel happy?" She stifled a yawn, which made him laugh.

This was their first real conversation since the first night when Harry had fallen ill. Not that she'd wanted to talk about anything beyond patient care, especially considering she'd behaved brazenly that night. Why, she'd taken Boyd's hand! Not just taken it, but placed it *on her throat*. Heat suffused her face, embarrassment, pure and simple.

Embarrassment, but not regret. At that moment, she'd seen Boyd in a new way and wanted him to know he wasn't alone. But while she shared his fear, she had chosen a different path. She had determined to love despite the risk of loss.

She'd prove it too. "Come outside for a moment?"

Boyd followed her outside, shutting the door behind them. He lifted his face to the pale sunlight breaking through the morning fog. "I can actually smell the brine of the ocean in the air today. Marvelous. I'll open some windows."

Emily took a deep breath of that salty air. "Since our patients are improved, I'm going to speak to Colonel Buchanan today. I think it's time Harry and I left Fort Humboldt."

"What do you mean, leave?" Boyd couldn't control the tense pitch of his voice, not at a time like this. "Find work in a city? Now?"

She lacked the funds, and as far as Boyd knew, the colonel hadn't settled the matter of the competition prize. He'd said goodbye to her the other day and meant it, but his foolish heart still ached at the thought of her leaving.

"I'm not certain I have enough money, that's true, but it's time. I trust God will provide." Her chapped hand brushed a wayward blond strand from her cheek and tucked it behind her ear. "It won't be imminent. Harry's weak, and I owe Colonel Buchanan ample notice."

Arguments tumbled one over the other on his tongue, but at last all he could utter was a question. "Why now?"

"You know why. Harry and a home. It's been my plan all along, but you were right when you said my security shouldn't be in people or family. My security should be in the Lord. Nevertheless, He put us in families, didn't He? It's His way of seeing us care for and be cared for by people. And I'd like to spend what I can of my life in a home filled with love. With people I love."

"I knew, that night when you took my hand." He swallowed

hard. "I knew you were telling me you cared, but at the same time, you were saying goodbye to me."

She blushed pink as a rosebud. "I don't want to say goodbye, Boyd."

"I don't either, but I understand." He'd made his choice, and it didn't involve romance or family. He cared enough for her, though, to want her to have the best life possible. The life she wanted and deserved. Even if the thought of never seeing her again sliced him to the bone. "Where will you go?"

"San Francisco. I have enough money saved for a few nights at a boardinghouse or modest inn before I find work. I figure someone in a city that large can use a cook. There has to be a good school there too, I'm sure of it." She shrugged. "As well as books."

"Books? Oh, for Harry. He's a voracious reader."

"I'm sure there are others out there just as hungry to read. Other children. It struck me just now how God has used others to bless me and Harry. I want to be a blessing too, and I think one way He wants me to do that is to put books into children's hands. I'm not sure how yet, but there has to be a better way than trading or waiting for shipments. It's just a matter of finding them and making them available to others."

He'd heard of places where folks could borrow books. "You want to work in one of those social lending libraries?"

"Social libraries charge a fee, but I'd like to find some way to collect and share books without charging money. Maybe it's foolish, but since I think God's put it on my heart, I'd like to try."

"Doesn't sound foolish at all. Sounds rather kind of you, Emily."

"It feels good to want to do something like this."

"I'll pray for you, Emily."

"And I'll do the same for you."

If he offered his hand for shaking, he'd pull her in for an embrace, so he kept his hands at his sides when she paused a moment before leaving for her quarters.

The following week was morose, knowing she was here but leaving. He cleaned the hospital, ordered new supplies, returned the extra cots to the barracks, wrote reports, and instructed the improving Tripp on various aspects of modern medicine. He had few patients, and the most excitement he had was the fracture sustained by one of the privates falling off his horse.

Until the colonel summoned him, that is.

"Good work with the influenza."

"The Lord spared the men, sir, but I did my best."

"It'll be a shame to lose you, but orders are orders."

"Sir?"

"Assistant Surgeon Simpson and his family are returning. His tour's finished, but the orders don't say a thing about another assignment for you. I'm sure you'll have a new spot shortly, somewhere interesting. You're a man of adventure, aren't you?"

"I do try to experience life at its fullest, sir." Except right now, he felt empty to his bones.

"Maybe we can finish the competition before you and Miss Sweet leave. You heard she's departing, didn't you?"

It was the talk of the fort. "I did, sir."

"Well, I need to give out that five-dollar prize I offered."

"I'd be obliged if you gave it to Miss Sweet, to help her land more solidly on her feet. In fact, add this to it, but don't tell her it's from me." He dug a large coin from his pocket and placed it on the colonel's desk with a soft clink.

At least the coin would help her pay for safe, comfortable lodging for a few days. The thought of her and Harry in a hovel made his stomach turn.

By Friday he was desperate for distraction from his gloomy

thoughts. One of the fellows returned from time off with a short stack of reading material, and Boyd was glad for a turn to peruse the local newspapers. He brought the copy of the *San Francisco Daily Herald* back to his office and sat behind his desk with a cup of strong coffee.

He scalded his tongue on the first sip, but he didn't care. Not after he read a headline that sent his heart pounding out of his chest.

"I hate to see the back of you, dearie." Molly blotted her eyes. "But Percy and I will visit you and Harry in San Francisco, someday. Write when you're settled so I know where to reach you."

"I shall."

"Be sure to tell me what happens with your book idea. How do you even know where to start?"

She'd given the matter some thought. "I'm going to ask the local clergy for advice. Perhaps there are members of their congregations who would be willing to part with books they're no longer reading, since I'll be donating the books to a good cause. There's at least one orphan asylum in town, and I suspect they'll be glad for the reading materials."

Boyd had said he didn't have many books growing up. Maybe she could ensure some other children didn't experience the same lack.

"No better cause than orphans, I'd say." Molly patted the table for emphasis. "But I'll miss you something fierce when you and Harry leave tomorrow."

Harry looked up from his history assignment. "I'll miss you too, Mrs. Luther. And your biscuits."

"You won't find a lighter biscuit in San Francisco, I assure you." Molly's chest puffed out. "Speaking of baking, though, I'd better help Percy."

Emily rose to hug her friend. "Thank you for everything, Molly."

"Ah, dearie. You've been a true friend."

Once Molly left the kitchen, Emily moved to stand over Harry. "Your work looks good."

"Thanks." He still looked a little thin nearly a week after leaving the hospital, but there was a rosy quality to his cheeks that relieved her.

"Would you mind if I took a short walk? I'd like to look around once more, and this seems as good a time as any."

"Sure. I'd go with you, but I told a few of the fellas we could toss a ball later, and I know you'll be mad if I don't finish my work first."

"Not mad, but yes, I'm grateful you're seeing to your assignments. Have fun, but don't overdo."

"I won't."

Since she wouldn't be out long, she didn't bother donning a bonnet, but she did grab a shawl. The early March sun might be warm, but the wind could be cool. San Francisco had chill and wind too, or so she'd heard. Tomorrow she'd find out.

But for now, she took in the moment, paying note to the odor of the damp grass underfoot, the peeling paint on the bake house, the clanking of the blacksmith at work, the bustle of dozens of men in uniform, the horsey smell of the stable. And at the far end of the fort was the cliff, overlooking the bay. She paused there, drawing her shawl around her shoulders, watching two small boats out on the gray water.

Lord, You hold our futures. Thank You for giving me confidence and strength to go, even though my heart aches over Boyd. My heart is in Your hands, just as my future is. I hope someday it won't hurt quite like this anymore, but thank You for showing me what love feels like.

She brushed a strand of hair back from her cheek.

"Emily?"

She spun around. Boyd marched toward her as if he was under orders, his mouth a grim line. He held a grayish paper in his hand. For her?

"Boyd, is something amiss?"

"Sure is." He halted one foot from her, so she had to crane her head to look in his eyes. "You can't leave yet."

"Whyever not?" Was there danger outside the fort?

"Because you need this." He thrust the paper in her face. A newspaper. What was she supposed to look at? Headlines announced the price of gold, coal gas lamps dazzling theatergoers, an orphan asylum seeking educational materials, a bank robbery...

Then it hit her between the eyes. "The orphanage?"

"They want books. I was thinking maybe when you collect some, you might be interested in sharing them with the children there."

Perhaps this was confirmation of the Lord's intention for her. "I was just telling Molly something similar. I've been thinking folks might be more willing to part with their old books if they know they're going to a good cause, such as an orphanage. I had no idea where one might be, but now I do."

It was thoughtful of him to share this with her, even though they'd been avoiding one another since she left the hospital last week. She offered the page back to him. "Thank you for directing me to a place to start."

"You can keep the article. I don't need it."

"True." She tucked the paper into her sleeve for now.

"I've memorized the name and location. So I can find it easily."

"The orphanage?"

The grim set of his lips softened into a smile. "I seem to be in need of a new job. Assistant Surgeon Simpson's coming back."

"You're being sent to San Francisco?" Was there a fort there?

"I haven't the faintest idea, but you, Emily Sweet, have made me start ruminating on things I didn't like thinking about. One of those things is my work. It's been beneficial, giving me new experiences. But I've been rather aimless."

"I thought you wanted to be aimless."

"I wanted to be free of attachments. But then you walked away from me."

With good reason. "You didn't follow me."

"I couldn't, because I'd made my choice to never be vulnerable to pain again, but you know what? It didn't work. I've never known pain quite like I've suffered since you told me goodbye at the hospital, Emily. I used to think I stopped wanting a family when I realized Dr. Munn didn't want me, but now I see I never stopped wanting it. I've been alone for so long. I don't want to be alone anymore."

Her heart jumped into her throat. "Really? You want a family? Even though. . ."

"Even though bad things happen? They could have, with Sergeant Waldo. Or Harry or Tripp. But they didn't die. I know that sounds ridiculous, but it was amazing to me that people I cared about didn't die. I know life isn't certain, Emily. Our pasts have taught us that over and over again. But maybe we both had it wrong. You spent years bracing for further pain while I ran from it. Yet you're on a new path now. I want to be too. Maybe I should embrace the blessings of each moment God gives us on this earth and be thankful He hasn't given up on us."

"That sounds like a good plan. If you're sure you're ready to stand still for a while."

"I think it's what God wants for me. From me. It makes sense to me now in a way I never recognized before. Dr. Munn didn't adopt me, but he did give me a legacy. Helping vulnerable young ones. And I'd like to do for those young'uns in that orphanage what he did for me, treat their ailments and show them they aren't forgotten in the world."

Oh! "You're going to start a practice in San Francisco?"

"I'm no longer needed here, and doctors are in demand pretty much anywhere. Almost as much as cooks."

She couldn't help but smile.

"If some other doctor is helping those young'uns, well, that's wonderful. I'll find another orphan asylum where I can offer my services. Much as I hate to say it, there will be plenty of asylums. Those children need care. And books."

"Definitely books."

"We'll do our best to help make their lives easier."

She didn't miss him including her in his statement. "We will, will we?"

His smile turned shy. "It's time I settled down. Lived in a home. Will you go with me, Emily? You and Harry, if he doesn't mind too much? You'll marry me?"

It was not the sort of proposal she'd read about in books, with moonlight and violins and rings on satin cushions. On the cliff overlooking Humboldt Bay, with the sound of lapping waves and tinges of salt and pine in the air, with a chill nipping her nose, Boyd looked down at her, his dark eyes wide and imploring, full of hope, desire, and love.

It was better than the proposals in books. It was real—his warm hands enveloping hers, his hair more ruffled with each gust of wind, his body shielding her from the brunt of the wind—and it was hers. All hers, to cherish forever.

"I will, Boyd."

His serious expression vanished, replaced by his adorable lopsided grin. "Say it again."

"Yes, Boyd."

His hands went around her waist. "Yes?"

Goodness. She'd said it twice. She couldn't help but tease him. "If you're sure you won't miss the army."

"Salt pork and beans? Hardly," he teased. "God gave me a lot of things through that work. Adventures and fun, but the best gift He gave me was you. So say it once more for me, please, my beautiful Emily. Will you?"

"Yes!"

He whirled her in a dizzying circle, leaving her breathless. But she couldn't breathe at all when he set her down and bent to kiss her. Quite thoroughly too.

Mercy. She was gasping for air when he stopped. But she wouldn't mind another kiss, either—

Oh my stars. People were laughing and clapping. She peeked to the right. A handful of soldiers had stopped whatever they'd been doing to watch them, and they weren't the only ones. Harry, ball in hand, stood beside a wide-eyed Colonel Buchanan. Emily's face grew hot.

Boyd's hands fell but not altogether away. One rested at the small of her back in a gesture that felt possessive and cherishing. It bolstered Emily's confidence as the colonel strode closer. How harsh would his reprimand be?

The colonel shook his head. "And here I've been scratching my head, trying to figure out how to settle the competition between you two."

"The competition may have been a tie, sir, but I consider myself the winner here," Boyd said. "Miss Sweet's agreed to be my wife."

Harry whooped. "Really?"

"Yes, really. We'll go to San Francisco together, if that's all right with you."

"I suppose it is." Harry's toothy smile confirmed the fact. "And

I don't think you should compete against each other anymore. You work better together, anyhow."

"We do, don't we?" Emily looked into Boyd's smiling face.

The colonel shooed everyone away. "Let's give them a minute to make their plans, men."

Emily imagined the home she'd share with Boyd. A place to be themselves. A place to belong.

And she couldn't help but laugh when she heard one of the soldiers sigh as he walked away. "It's gonna be a lot quieter around here from now on."

Historical Note

Three historical figures appear in this story. One is the fort commander, Captain Brevet Lieutenant Colonel Robert Buchanan. In 1854 the inspector general of the army, Colonel Joseph Mansfield, visited Fort Humboldt and noted, "Colonel Buchanan gave a handsome battalion drill."

The second figure, of course, is Ulysses S. Grant, eighteenth president of the United States, who served as quartermaster at Fort Humboldt from 1853 to 1854. He was not particularly happy there, longing to return to his wife and children in Missouri. He later admitted his issues with "intemperance" factored into his decision to resign.

Seth Kinman is the third true-life figure, hired to bring game to Fort Humboldt. Interestingly, Grant was not the only president he ever met. The hunter was later well known for crafting unique chairs from bearskin and elk horn, which he gave to Presidents Buchanan, Lincoln, Johnson, and Hayes. Kinman claimed a particular closeness with Abraham Lincoln, but he was known to exaggerate.

While these men were all together at this brief point in history in Humboldt, the events, actions, and dialogue in this story are entirely fictional, as is the temporary assignment I gave to the real fort doctor, Assistant Surgeon Simpson. I invented the other characters and circumstances, including the presence of a fort cook. One true fact, however, is that Kinman's favorite song was "Arkansas Traveler," and he played it over and over on a fiddle he crafted from the jawbone of his favorite mule, Dave.

Susanne Dietze began writing love stories in high school, casting her friends in the starring roles. Today, she's an award-winning, RWA RITA®-nominated author who's seen her work on the ECPA, Amazon, and Publisher's Weekly Bestseller Lists for Inspirational Fiction. Married to a pastor and the mom of two, Susanne lives in California and enjoys fancy-schmancy tea parties, genealogy, the beach, and curling up on the couch with a costume drama. To learn more, visit her website, www.susannedietze.com, and sign up for her newsletter: http://eepurl.com/bRldfv

SAVE THE LAST WORD FOR ME

by Lorna Seilstad

Beareth all things, believeth all things,
hopeth all things, endureth all things.

1 CORINTHIANS 13:7

Chapter One

Kansas
September 1864

The stench inside the stagecoach was unbearable. Adelina Dante pressed her rose-scented handkerchief to her nose and inhaled deeply. Why didn't the male passengers appear to understand the importance of regular bathing?

The stagecoach came to a jarring halt. The driver jumped down and yanked open the door. "All you men need to get out. We need to walk the horses through this part. Too many ruts crossing the creek."

Adelina moved toward the door.

"Not you, miss." The driver held up his hand. "You can stay inside."

"No, I'd like to stretch my legs, but I believe Sergeant Waxler may need to remain here."

"Oh yeah. Sorry, Waxler, I forgot about your infirmity." The driver glanced at the pale-faced amputee returning from Virginia still wearing his woolen blue uniform. "You take it easy, son." He handed Adelina down. "Let me know when you want to go back up, miss. It's hotter than an iron on scorching coals today."

Adelina shook out the skirt of her gray traveling dress. On this, her second day riding in the stagecoach, she could think of nothing better than moving freely. "Thank you," she said, "but I'll be fine."

"Suit yourself." He nodded and moved back to his team.

Even though it wasn't the least bit ladylike, Adelina pressed her hands to her lower back and stretched as the other five passengers made their way off the coach. She moved her head to the right, then to the left, and felt the kinks in her muscles ease.

"It's mighty pretty." Brother Durant, an elderly traveling preacher her mother had asked to serve as Adelina's escort, climbed down and moved next to her. He nodded his bald head toward the trees lining the creek.

She followed the direction of his gaze and took in the foliage now sporting the ambers, reds, and golds of fall. "It is beautiful."

They fell in step behind the stagecoach with the others, and after several minutes, Brother Durant cleared his throat. "So, if you don't mind me asking, why are you headed to Fort Riley? Got a fella there?"

Adelina laughed. "Didn't my mother tell you? The officers' wives at the camp advertised for a teacher for the fort's subscription school, and I accepted the position."

"Subscription school?"

"Yes." Adelina hiked up her skirt to step over a rut. "The parents will each pay a dollar per month per child to make up my salary. I'll also be staying with one of the families, so my room and board will be provided. Of course, I'd never turn away a child whose parents couldn't afford to pay."

He scratched his head. "I reckon there's presently about twenty children there—twenty-five at most. That's not much of a salary."

She forced a smile. "I don't really have a choice."

"I suppose you don't. Your mother said your father was in the Seventh Kansas Volunteer Cavalry Regiment, one of Jennison's Jayhawkers."

"Yes, he was killed on reconnaissance." She swallowed. "I'll be sending most of what I make home to my mother, but I love teaching, and I love new challenges."

"I'll guarantee some of those officers' kids will be challenges, for sure."

"Thank you for serving as my escort. It put my mother at ease to know I wasn't traveling alone all the way from Lawrence."

"My pleasure." He touched the brim of his hat. "I go where the Lord calls me."

"I guess I do too." Adelina smiled at Brother Durant, withdrew a fan from her reticule, and waved it in front of her face. The air was stifling, but it did nothing to snuff out the excitement building within her. It wouldn't be long now. They'd change horses in an hour or so and would make Fort Riley before noon. Would the children be there to greet her? She certainly hoped so. Then, her new work would begin.

ᔆ

Sitting astride his mount, Colonel Isaac Scott looked across the parade yard at the ragtag group of new recruits attempting to line up in company formation and sighed. What on earth was he supposed to do with this sorry lot of volunteers if a real emergency arose?

General Curtis had left him in charge of Fort Riley yesterday when he took a brigade on a campaign on the Overland Station route. A dispatch had earlier informed them that the Indians controlled the country from a point of seventy-five miles east of Fort Kearney to the forks of the Platte River. Curtis's troops were to join Major General Blunt's already en route.

Since Isaac's injury made him unfit for battlefield command, he'd been relegated to managing the day-to-day operation of the fort and commanding this remnant of volunteers. Naturally, General Curtis had taken the best soldiers with him. Some of the men that remained might be able to tell him when to plant wheat in the spring, but they were sorely lacking in military prowess. In fact, he noted that most of the members of the Fort Riley Glee Club now stood armed before him. He sighed. Well, if any Indian unrest occurred near the fort, maybe they could calm them with a lullaby.

He watched the men stumble into formation. If they had this much trouble falling in, what would they be like when it came to drills? And worse, how would they defend the fort or handle a skirmish? He'd have to meet with his few remaining officers and discuss the situation. Improvements must happen immediately. They needed to believe in themselves, and they needed to believe in him as their leader.

He adjusted the string holding the eye patch in place over the socket of his left eye and nudged his mount forward to inspect the troops. While he longed to be out on the campaign with General Curtis, that wasn't going to happen. He'd been ordered to serve here, and today, it was imperative for them all that he garner the respect of his troops as the temporary fort commander.

The stagecoach slowed, and Adelina lifted the leather curtain on the window to determine the reason. The rest of the passengers, including Brother Durant, had gotten off in Junction City awhile ago. The driver halted the team and announced they'd reached Fort Riley. When he opened the door, she accepted his hand and quickly stepped down onto the block of wood he'd provided. She read the sign on the door of the wood-framed building. "Sutler of Fort Riley."

The driver motioned to the door. "You go on inside the post exchange, miss, while I get your trunks down. It'll be awhile 'cause I have to see to the horses first."

She glanced around. No one seemed to be awaiting her arrival. Was she in the right place? She could see the cluster of buildings in the distance, lined up in neat, orderly rows. Clearly, they were outside Fort Riley, but where were the ladies who'd hired her? She desperately wanted to make a good first impression.

She opened the door to the sutler's store, praying she'd find a sweet lady inside. Instead, a man dressed in a striped vest worn over a checkered shirt looked up. "Good morning, miss. May I help you?"

She drew in a steadying breath. "Hello. I'm the new schoolteacher for the fort. I was contacted by the officers' wives. I was hoping one of them would be here when I got off the stage."

He chuckled. "Miss, we never know when the stage is going to pull in. I just sent my boy out on an errand. When he gets back, I'll send him over to Mrs. Major Adams and he can let her know you're here."

"If you point me in the direction of her home, I can walk." She gave him a reassuring smile. "It would be pleasant to stretch after the long ride."

The man rubbed his bearded chin. "I reckon that would be all right. Here, let me draw you a map."

A map? How far did she just offer to walk? She listened as the sutler drew a large rectangle in the center of the paper and explained there were six sets of officers' quarters, three on the north and three on the south. They faced one another across the parade field. He drew several smaller rectangles as he spoke and pointed to one. "This here is where Mrs. Major Adams lives. You can't miss her. She's shaped like a teakettle and spouts off just as much."

She stifled a smile.

He added a series of longer rectangles. "These here, on the east and west sides, are enlisted barracks. Three sets on each side. The post hospital is over to the east, and the stables and other outbuildings are to the south and west."

Adelina's mind spun. She didn't want to admit that she had no idea which way was north at the moment. In fact, beyond up and down and left and right, she had little use for any other directions. At least she could follow a map.

He handed her the paper. "Head on down the road and you'll be right as rain. It's about a half-mile walk."

"Thank you." She flashed him a warm smile. "I appreciate your help."

"It's my pleasure, miss. You're certainly the prettiest customer I've had all day. Once you're settled, have Mrs. Major Adams send someone for your trunks." He hooked his thumbs in the straps of his apron. "If you have any problems, come on back and we'll get you sorted out."

"I'm sure I'll be fine, but thank you again." She gave the door a gentle nudge until it opened. After checking on her trunks, she made her way to the dirt road leading into the fort. The path she needed to travel was relatively flat, so even the climbing temperatures didn't cause her undo concern. She noticed a church sitting away from the road and guessed it was the fort's chapel.

As she neared the buildings, soldiers stood at one end of the long field. What had the sutler called it? A parade field? These men were not parading in any way.

She walked along the edge of the field, careful not to intrude on the soldiers' area, but as she neared, heads turned in her direction. "Catch that ray of sunshine!" one soldier called out.

She whirled and stopped. Were his comments directed toward her? A man on a horse, whom she guessed was the commanding officer, now loomed over one of the men. If she remembered correctly, the large, yellow-gold shoulder straps on his dark uniform signified his rank as an officer. She couldn't tell from where she stood, but she imagined he had to be at least a captain to be in command of this many men. From the shiny buttons on his coat to the saber at his side, nothing seemed out of place—except for the black eye patch covering one eye.

"Private!" The officer roared. "Eyes to the front."

The young man's head snapped around, but the colonel flicked a glance in her direction.

"No soldier under my command will speak to a lady in such a manner at any time. Is that understood?"

"Yes, sir. It won't happen again, sir."

"To make sure it doesn't, perhaps a night of Buck and Gag will remind you?"

What was Buck and Gag? It sounded horrible. No matter what it was, she couldn't let this young man get punished on her account. Yes, what he'd done was inappropriate, but no real harm was done.

Before she could stop herself, she was marching across the field. "Sir," she called, "may I speak to you?"

The officer wheeled his horse around in her direction. The shock on his face was immediately replaced with anger.

"Miss, you need to leave the parade field immediately." He spoke with the same authority he'd used with his men.

She stopped in front of his horse. "Please, Captain, I don't want the young man to suffer on my account. No offense was taken."

A chuckle rippled through the ranks, and the officer glared first at her, then at his men. They fell silent.

A pimple-faced boy, no more than sixteen, stepped up beside her and whispered, "Colonel, miss, not captain."

The colonel in the saddle looked at the young man beside her.

"Corporal Taylor, escort the lady to my office—and guard her there until I return."

The corporal swallowed hard. "Uh, this way, miss."

"But the private—"

Corporal Taylor took her arm. "Colonel Scott is mad as a hornet, so if you want to spare the private any further punishment, you best do as the colonel says."

As he led her off the field, she glanced at the officers' quarters on the edge of the parade field to which she'd been heading. Several women had emerged and now congregated on their front porches, heads shaking in judgment. One woman—who, yes, was shaped like a teakettle—glowered at her.

Her breath caught. Mrs. Major Adams. So much for a good first impression.

Chapter Two

The boards creaked beneath Adelina's feet until she and the corporal stopped in front of a door. The young man opened it. "This is Colonel Scott's office, miss. I'm sure he'd want you to make yourself at home. If you need anything, I'll be standing guard outside."

She entered, and the door shut behind her. Something turned in the lock, and her stomach clenched. He'd locked her in. Was she now a prisoner?

Wrapping her arms around her torso, she fought the tears pricking her eyes. What if the colonel sent her home before she even started?

She glanced around the room and found the office sparse. A desk sat front and center with a chair behind it and another smaller one in front of it. A large map covered one wall, and she stepped closer to survey the terrain of the surrounding region. Stick pins with tiny paper flags dotted various locations. There seemed to be no pattern to them.

On the officer's desk sat a neat stack of papers in the right-hand corner. On the left, a stack of books stood like soldiers between two makeshift brick bookends. Among the titles were *Cavalry Tactics*, *Colonel Mann's Infantry and Cavalry Accoutrements*, and *Essays on the Theory and Practice of the Art of War*. There was also a thick volume of William Shakespeare's *Henry VI*. She picked up the tome and ran her hand along the embossed worn leather. She admired the colonel for reading her favorite author, but even this addressed war—the War of the Roses. Did the man think of nothing other than war?

She slid the book back in place. Could she use his fixation on war to her advantage when he returned? He was a soldier, so she needed to approach the situation logically and mount a good defense both for herself and for the young soldier. Perhaps she should suggest they got off on the wrong foot and they simply needed to start over. But would the commanding officer see that as retreating from a fight? Retreating, she had to admit, wasn't her usual manner of dealing with any given situation. She tended to speak before thinking. Before the war, her mother had constantly reprimanded her for a lack of acceptable decorum in social situations. "Ladies," her mother had often told her, "do not express opinions, no matter how well intentioned or well informed they might be." But how could she defend herself and the young soldier without expressing her opinion?

Despite her repeated prayers for a meek and quiet spirit, her speech got her in trouble much more often than it should. She offered up a prayer for wisdom to know what to say when Colonel Scott arrived. She needed that quiet spirit and words that would not irritate or anger him further.

Drawing in a deep breath, she returned to her surveillance of his desk in hopes she could glean something from its contents that would aid her in their upcoming discussion. The inkwell, pen, and blotter in the center all appeared to be well used and was probably military issued. Only the empty plate sitting on the left side of the desk seemed out of place. Apparently, the commanding officer ate his meals alone.

Nothing helpful.

She sat down in his chair and tried to imagine commanding a fort. She was in charge of a classroom, but what would it be like to be in charge of hundreds of men? But he was only a colonel. Hadn't she heard on the stage that General Curtis was in charge of Fort Riley at present? What if Colonel Scott sent her to the general?

Her stomach twisted, and her mouth turned dry. She stood and walked to the potbelly stove in the corner. Since it was probably nearly eighty-five degrees on this September morning, there was little need for a fire. Still, it held an enamel coffeepot. She lifted it, and the remaining tepid contents sloshed against the sides. She was thirsty, and there were two cups on hooks. Did she dare pour herself a cup? The corporal had said to make herself comfortable, hadn't he?

She took one of the tin cups from the hook, examined it for cleanliness, and poured the last of the pot's contents into it. The strong brew could use some milk and sugar, but she would make do without. She'd gotten used to doing without a lot of things in the last year.

Male voices outside the office alerted her. She heard the metallic click of a key being inserted into the lock, and then the door opened. The colonel entered, his gaze immediately falling to the cup in her hand. He frowned, and his dark brows scrunched.

Without a word, he stepped forward, removed the cup from her hands, and set it on the stove. Apparently, he didn't want her to forget for a minute that this wasn't a social occasion.

He motioned toward the empty chair in front of his desk. "Please have a seat." He rounded the desk, removed his navy kepi, and took his place. "I have a lot of questions, starting with who are you and what are you doing at my fort?"

"*Your* fort? I was under the impression this fort belongs the American people." She locked eyes with him and held his gaze, inwardly cringing. *This is not helping your case. Keep your mouth shut and just sit down.* She forced a smile and looked downward. "I apologize. I spoke without thinking."

"You seem to do that a lot."

Her gaze snapped back to his face. Did she detect a note of amusement in his deep voice?

She studied him. It was impossible to see his lips beneath the thick, dark mustache, and the eye patch only seemed to draw more attention to his uncovered deep-set eye. It was a startling gray blue, like the feathers of a pigeon.

A dark brow arched. "Your name, miss?"

"I am Miss Adelina Dante. I'm to be the new schoolmistress."

His eye widened. "At Junction City?"

"No, sir. Here—at Fort Riley." She sat up straighter. "I was hired by the officers' wives to teach the fort's children."

"Why didn't I know about this? I already have enough inept people inside this fort." He turned toward the door. "Corporal! Get me Mrs. Major Adams."

⟳

Isaac watched the parade of ladies file into his office until the tiny space was cramped. Miss Dante remained seated, fidgeting with a loose thread on her traveling dress.

"Mrs. Adams, this young woman says she was hired by you ladies to teach the children. Is that true?"

"Well, yes, it is, but—"

"Don't you think you should have sought my permission before making such a decision about fort matters?"

The rotund lady laughed and rolled her eyes. "As you know, my husband is currently with General Curtis, who is actually fighting the Indian aggression. My husband knew of this plan and, as one of the general's aides-de-camp, shared it with the general. We arranged to hire Miss Dante long before you were temporarily placed in charge during the absence of the general and his senior officers."

The way the woman emphasized certain words like "actually fighting," "temporarily," and "senior officers" irked him. He outranked all of the general's aides and was more than qualified to take command. However, Mrs. Adams wanted to remind him he was only in his position because he was unable to serve on the field.

The military had no official recognition of wives or families. Unofficially, a natural pecking order among the women had formed relating to the rank that the husband held. If competent Mrs. General Curtis hadn't gone to stay with her sister, he'd be dealing with her on this schoolteacher issue. Instead, the unofficially highest-ranking woman at the fort was power-hungry Mrs. Major Adams.

She was also probably right about the school. General Curtis had most likely approved this long before Isaac took over. He couldn't imagine what the general would do if a lady had questioned his orders in front of the men on the parade field. She might find herself in the brig.

Mrs. Adams sucked in a deep breath. "But I can assure you, if we'd have known Miss Dante was unable to adhere to the strict military rules required in a fort, we would have never extended our offer to her."

The other ladies murmured agreement, but one—Mrs. Captain Hanson—nudged her way to the front, a rosy-cheeked baby in her arms. "Shame on you, Alice. How could this young lady possibly understand even a fraction of the military rules we wives have learned? Not a one of us knew those things right away. We had to learn them."

"She should have known better than to march onto the parade field," Mrs. Adams huffed.

"Yes, ma'am, I should have." Miss Dante stood and faced the ladies. "And I freely admit I need to study the rules governing fort life. What propelled me forward was concern for the private being disciplined due to my sudden presence in the area. I hope you can all agree that compassion is one attribute you want your children to possess."

Isaac fought back a grin. Turning the tables on Mrs. Adams wasn't a tactic he'd expected. It was an impressive way for the school-mistress to spin things in her favor.

"But our children do not need to learn compassion from a reck-less young lady. If they are to flourish here, they need to learn order and discipline." Mrs. Adams glanced around, awaiting the expected nods from her fellow officers' wives. "We should send her back on the next stage."

Miss Dante's face paled. Was the young lady going to faint in his office? Clearly, this position meant a great deal to her.

"Ladies." Isaac stood and spoke loudly enough to get their atten-tion. "Perhaps you are being a bit rash. Miss Dante admits she was in error and is willing to learn the fort's regulations." He couldn't believe he was saying this, but there was a steel about Miss Dante that had reluctantly garnered his respect. "What are the plans for this school? How was Miss Dante to be paid?"

Mrs. Adams crossed her arms over her ample bosom. "Miss Dante was to teach in the education room attached to the chapel. This was to be a subscription school. She was to be paid one dollar per month by the parents of each student."

"If they're able," Miss Dante added. "I'd never turn away anyone who wants to learn."

"And where was she to be housed?"

"I offered to have her stay with me." Mrs. Hanson bounced the baby on her hip. "It's mighty lonely with my Lewis off on campaign. The children will bunk with me, and she can have a room to herself instead of my dollar a month."

Isaac nodded. The wives all stared at him as if he were a judge ready to pronounce a death sentence. He looked from them to Miss Dante. "Ladies, you hired Miss Dante, so her future is ultimately in your hands. However, I received notice that the stage won't be returning for at least two weeks. I recommend you let Miss Dante show you what she can do during that time period." He turned to Miss Dante. "And to make sure you don't march onto any parade fields, I'll be assigning Corporal Taylor to be your personal escort."

Miss Dante scowled. "Escort, or someone to mind me?"

"Either works for me, but if you want to stay, for the time being, he'll be by your side." He turned to the ladies. "Agreed?"

They nodded and mumbled words of assent. They slowly left the room without introducing themselves to the new schoolteacher. Only Mrs. Hanson hung back. "I'll wait for you outside, Miss Dante, and take you to my place so you can get settled in."

Isaac called in Corporal Taylor and gave him his orders, which included escorting Miss Dante to and from school and anywhere else she needed to go in the fort until further notice. The blond-haired corporal saluted and was dismissed.

Miss Dante, still miffed at the intrusion, set her jaw. "Am I dismissed as well?"

"Not yet." He stepped close to her so he could keep his voice low in case any of the ladies lingered outside. "I am in charge of protecting the lives of everyone in this fort, including yours, and the people in the surrounding area. If you *ever* undermine my authority again, I will personally make sure you are taken from this fort and deposited in Junction City to fend for yourself. Do I make myself clear?"

She tipped up her chin. "Yes, sir. Abundantly."

"You're dismissed."

"Yes, sir." She gave him a mock salute, whirled, and marched from his office.

Why had he dismissed her like she was one of his soldiers? He had no choice but to make his position clear about his command decisions, but she couldn't possibly understand the weight of responsibility he carried. Still, he needed to remember Miss Dante was no soldier. Could she handle the regulations and solitude of fort life? Would the ladies welcome her after her less than impressive introduction? Only time would tell.

He shook his head. Miss Dante wasn't his concern except for the distraction she'd serve for his men. Private McMasters wouldn't be the only man to notice her. Those hazel eyes he'd just stared into—a mix of green and brown swirled with gold—could distract nearly any man.

He needed to focus on the job he'd been given, so he'd keep Miss Dante at arm's length even if she was the prettiest thing that had stepped into this fort in a long, long time.

Chapter Three

The freckled face of a six-year-old boy stared up at Adelina, studying her.

"You're pretty," he said with a grin that revealed a missing front tooth.

"Miss Dante, meet my Eddie. He'll be in your class." Mrs. Hanson shifted the baby she was carrying from her right hip to her left. She kissed the baby's mass of blond curls. "And this is Rose. We had a son born between Eddie and Rose, but he passed two years ago from the fever." Her voice broke as she spoke.

"I'm so sorry, Mrs. Hanson."

"Thank you." The kind woman shook her head. "If we're going to be living in the same house, you'd best start calling me by my given name. I'm Jessica, or better yet, Jessie."

"Please call me Adelina."

"I like that. It suits you. Hang your hat on the empty peg by the door, and then let me show you your room."

The heat of the day grew heavier as Adelina followed Jessie upstairs. "The children will be sharing my room on the right. Yours was Eddie's, and it's on the left. I hope you like blue."

Inside the room, Adelina's gaze immediately took in the narrow bed's cobalt-blue quilt. The needlework was so fine it looked like a china plate. There was also a washstand and wardrobe in the room. A hobbyhorse sat in one corner.

"Sorry about that," Jessie said. "I couldn't get it moved downstairs on my own. Maybe your corporal can help."

"My corporal?" Adelina asked.

"Well, he's assigned to you, and from the look on that boy's face, he'd do about anything you asked of him."

Adelina ran her hand over the hand-carved horse head. "I'll ask him to move it if you like. Where does it go?"

"We'll put it in the dining room for now. I don't expect to be doing much entertaining while Lewis is away." The baby began to fuss despite Jessie's attempts to soothe her. "Why don't you wash the travel dust from your face and lie down for a bit while I tend to Rose? Then we'll see about getting your trunks delivered."

"Do you think I might visit the schoolroom as well?"

Jessie laughed. "I'm glad to see you're still eager to start. Yes, we'll head over to the chapel too. Now, get a little much-deserved rest."

After Jessie departed, Adelina took the woman's advice. She washed her face and lay down on top of the quilt.

She had a lot of work to do before classes started, but maybe she'd close her eyes for a few minutes. . . .

Isaac waited for the last of the fort's current commanding officers to settle in chairs around the conference table in a room connected to the general's office. Major James McGreggor, paymaster, sat to his right, and Captain Dunlop of Company H, Fifteenth Regiment, on his left.

"Gentlemen," Isaac began, "I have serious concerns about the readiness of these troops if they are called on to defend the fort or any of our neighbors."

Captain Dunlop scowled. "It's not our fault. The general took all the good soldiers with him. I don't have a decent shot left in my infantry."

"We have a few who are adequate cavalrymen, but the lack of horses would be a real problem if we're needed." Major Henning looked at James McClure, his first lieutenant.

McClure, who also served as quartermaster, leaned back in his chair. "The campaign has left us at a real deficit. I put another advertisement in the Junction City newspaper for horses and got three, but they're not broke yet."

"Men, failure is not an option." Isaac leaned forward. "At any time, we could be needed. We must rise above our limitations be it men, horses, artillery, or ammunition."

"Ammunition? Are we low on that too?" Dunlop asked.

"The general took the bulk of our supplies with him on the campaign. More should arrive soon." Isaac looked at each of the men. "No more excuses. Train the men under your command. Drill. Drill. Drill. Get these recruits prepared to defend this fort and the surrounding settlements. Until they are up to snuff, confine them to barracks."

McClure cocked his head to the side. "Sir, that won't be popular."

"I'm running a fort, McClure. I'm not running for president." Isaac unrolled a map on the table. "Indian skirmishes are on the rise. Before General Curtis left on his campaign, a wagon train from Santa Fe to Leavenworth was attacked at Cimarron Springs. Ten men were killed, and all the stock was captured. The wagon train was left abandoned."

"But that's the reason for the campaign, right?"

"That and the attack by two hundred Indians on the Seventh Iowa Cavalry en route from Saline to Fort Ellsworth. Four soldiers were killed." He tapped his pen on the papers in front of him. "Men, are you aware that in the last six weeks, three thousand horses and mules have been captured by the Indians? Collectively, the various bands have over four thousand warriors. While General Curtis's troops may be off protecting settlers along the trail route, there is no way for his men to be everywhere. There are fifty settler families living virtually unprotected northwest of Fort Riley, and I intend to keep those families safe." He pushed his chair back and stood. He waited for the others to stand at attention. "Gentlemen, get your men ready. We can't afford any distractions."

"Yes, sir," they said in unison.

"Dismissed."

When they'd all departed, he sank back into his chair and prayed for wisdom to lead his men in this difficult time.

For a moment Adelina forgot where she was when she awoke. She took in the room and the blue quilt on which she was lying and remembered she was in Jessie's home at Fort Riley. But how long had she slept?

She hurried downstairs and found Jessie in the parlor, mending a man's shirt. Baby Rose was lying on her stomach on a blanket on the floor, and Eddie was playing with blocks in the corner.

Adelina pressed a hand to her growling stomach. "How long did I sleep, Jessie?"

"Only about an hour. I figured you needed the rest after your travels and this morning's excitement." Adelina motioned to the side with her needle. "I left you a tray on the dining room table. Why don't you get it and come on in here? We can talk while you eat."

Adelina did as Jessie told her and set the tray down on a small oak table in the parlor. The tray held a slice of bread with butter and jam, a wedge of cheese, and stewed peaches. Although the tea in the pot had grown cold, Adelina found everything delicious and thanked Jessie profusely.

"Nonsense. Room and board is part of your pay, remember?" Jessie set down her sewing. "I had Corporal Taylor arrange for your trunks to be delivered. He reckoned the heavy one was filled with books, so he took it to the schoolroom. I hope that's satisfactory."

"Yes, that's perfect."

"Now that you're awake, I'll have him take the other trunk up to your room; then he'll take you to visit the chapel. I'd go along, but it's time to put Rose down for a nap."

"I'll be fine. I don't want to inconvenience you."

"Adelina, having you here is a breath of fresh air for me. You can't be more than five years younger than me, and I sorely need some friends my own age. As you may have noticed, most of the officers' wives are older, and we're not supposed to interact much with the wives of the enlisted men. How old are you?"

"Twenty-one. And you?"

"Twenty-six. I married Lewis when I was nineteen." She picked up a fussing Rose. "Why isn't a pretty girl like you married?"

"I was engaged, but my fiancé was killed in the Battle of Wilson's Creek. He was in the First Kansas Infantry."

"My condolences. I'm sure that was horrible for you."

"It was hard, but it was almost three years ago. I cared a great deal for Caleb, but I don't know if I ever truly loved him. I'd grown up with him, and everyone simply assumed we would eventually marry—including the two of us. If I do marry in the future, I want to be more than fond of the man." Adelina dropped her gaze to the floor. "But I'm not looking for love, and I hope you don't think me callous or crass."

"No, Adelina, you're refreshingly honest." Jessie placed a hand on her arm. "And take it from a married woman, you do want to be more than fond of a man if you're going to spend the rest of your life with him. Just remember, you don't have to be looking for love in order for it to find you."

Adelina chuckled. "What I need to find right now is the schoolroom."

With that, she slipped her hat from the hook by the door and tied the ribbons beneath her chin. Corporal Taylor, who was sitting on the front steps, stood when the door opened.

"Good afternoon, Miss Dante. Mrs. Captain Hanson said you'd want your trunk upstairs in your room after you woke up. Can I take it up now?"

"I think it would be better to take it up after visiting the chapel's schoolroom since Mrs. Hanson is ready to put the baby down."

He nodded. "Then the chapel is this way, ma'am."

As they walked, the corporal pointed out the various buildings. Flanking the parade field on both sides were the six double officers' houses. Six barracks, large two-story structures, sat at each end of the field, and he said the long stables sat beyond the far end.

"Where do the enlisted families live?"

"On Suds Row."

She cocked her head to the side. "Excuse me?"

"Suds Row is where the army's washerwomen live—enlisted families too, miss." He switched the rifle he carried from one shoulder to the other. "The large building over there is the hospital. Sometimes we have dances there on the top floor if there aren't many patients. As you know, that other building is where the officers do all their meeting and planning."

"This place is like a little city."

"Yes, miss. Besides the sutler's store where you came in, there's a billiards house, ordinance building, post office, and mess house."

"But why is it called a fort? There are no walls."

He shrugged. "It's actually more like a garrison, but it's called Fort Riley."

They approached the chapel with its smooth, limestone walls, slate roof, and an arched doorway bearing a cross over the door. "Welcome to St. Mary's, Miss Dante." He opened the door and held it for her.

The chaplain came out of his office in the back at the sound of their entrance. "Hello, Corporal, miss. Are congratulations in order? How soon would you like to wed?"

Adelina looked at Corporal Taylor, whose boyish face had turned crimson. "Uh, no, sir. This is Miss Dante, the new schoolteacher."

"Ah, I see. I beg your pardon." The middle-aged man smiled warmly, his blue eyes sparkling in the sunlight streaming through the windows. "Miss Dante, it's a pleasure to meet you. I'm Charles Reynolds, post chaplain, and I should have known you were coming. News of your arrival has spread through the fort like a Kansas wildfire." He motioned toward a door at the front of the sanctuary. "Come, come. Let me show you your classroom."

Excitement buzzed through Adelina as she stepped inside the small room adjacent to the chapel. A chalkboard lined the far wall, and a desk sat before it. There was a small potbelly stove in one corner, and a large crock for drinking water on a little table in another corner. There were no traditional school desks, but benches and long, narrow tables had been built to accommodate students. The floor, to her delight, was brick, not wood or dirt.

"Before the conflict began, my predecessor taught the youngsters for a while. Early in the conflict, this building was used as an ordnance store when Fort Riley served as a confinement facility for Confederate prisoners." The chaplain ran a finger across the corner of one of the tables. "I'm afraid the room will need a good cleaning. The crate in the corner contains slates for the children to use."

Corporal Taylor opened another door, which led to the outside. "This will make it easier for the children to come and go during the day. The outhouse isn't far either." His gaze snapped to Adelina. "I'm sorry, miss, for bring up such a thing in front of a lady."

"No need to apologize, Corporal Taylor. The children will need to use the facility." She turned to the chaplain. "So where can I find something with which to begin cleaning? I'd like to get started right away."

The chaplain grinned. "I like your eagerness. I'll fetch the supplies." He departed and returned a few minutes later with a bucket of water, a scrub brush, and rags.

"Thank you. If you don't mind, I think I'll begin." Adelina pushed up her sleeves and dunked the brush into the cold, soapy water.

"Chaplain, would you be available to help me bring in Miss Dante's trunk of books?"

"Certainly. I know just where it is."

The men departed, and Adelina set to scrubbing every inch of the room. When the children arrived tomorrow, she wanted everything in perfect order.

Chaplain Reynolds and Corporal Taylor lugged the trunk into the room and dropped it with a thud. "If you need anything else, Miss Dante, please don't hesitate to ask. My wife and I live in the house next door. We have two daughters who'll be coming to your school. They're very excited. When are you planning to begin? Next week?"

"Tomorrow."

The chaplain laid a hand on her shoulder. "My dear, you'll have to stay up half the night to be ready in time."

"Perhaps, but it will be worth it. I only have two weeks to make a good impression. You probably heard, but I didn't start off on a good foot."

The chaplain smiled. "What's done is done, and I can see you're dedicated to these children. I'll see to it the word gets passed around tonight that school begins in the morning."

"And I'll help any way that I can." Corporal Taylor opened the trunk. "I want these young'uns to have as much learning as they can before winter sets in. They're real lucky to have a teacher and a school."

"They are indeed blessed. On that point, I think I'll go see if my wife and daughters want to lend a hand as well."

After the chaplain had gone, Adelina turned to the corporal. "I've already scrubbed the desk, so you can set the books on there."

"All of them?"

"For now." She began to wipe one of the window sashes. "Set the McGuffey's Readers in a pile of their own."

"What color are those?"

"They're tan with dark red binding. I only have one set, so the children will have to share for now." She whirled and saw him pulling out all the books with red binding, but mixed in with McGuffey's were other texts. Couldn't he tell those didn't belong? All the titles were on the covers, unless—

She set down her rag and walked over to the desk. "Corporal Taylor, please don't be offended, but can you read?"

"No, miss. I never got the chance to learn. I can figure out a little, though." He thumbed through one of the volumes. "That's better than some of the boys."

She picked up a reader and pressed it against the bodice of her dress. Her pulse quickened. Had God sent her here to teach the children or to teach the soldiers? Maybe she was here to do both or at least to educate Corporal Taylor along with the children.

She drew in a deep breath. "Do you want to learn?"

"Yes, miss, but I'm no young'un."

"What if I offered to teach you outside of school? You're already assigned to watch me. Why couldn't we use the time to teach you your letters?"

A grin split his face. "You'd do that?"

"Absolutely."

"But my ma said book learning wasn't for me."

"I believe book learning is for everyone. It's my job to find the right way to teach you, and it's your job to learn." She set the book she was holding back on the pile. "We'll start tomorrow after the regular day. All right?"

"If you think you can spare the time, I'd be honored."

"It is I who's honored." She returned to the window where she'd been cleaning. "Corporal Taylor, come over here and look out this window."

She stepped out of the way so he could peer out. "I want you to think about something. Reading is like opening a window into a whole new world. Once that window is opened, no one can ever close it to you."

"Those are pretty words, Miss Dante."

"More importantly, they're true." She smiled at the young man. "And if we didn't have so much to do this afternoon, we'd start opening that window right now."

Chapter Four

Isaac stepped out of his office and drew in a deep breath. A cool breeze had blown in just before sunset. He hoped tomorrow would be cooler. The hot weather was brutal on the men during their repeated drills. He hated making them endure the situation, but keeping them alive was more important than momentary suffering.

Given that he'd confined them to their barracks if they weren't serving on guard duty, he headed toward the soldiers' quarters to make sure all was settled. He wouldn't keep the confinement up long, but they needed to understand how serious he was about their performance improving posthaste.

He reached the barracks and could hear music coming from the second floor. Apparently, the glee club members still had enough energy at the end of the day to sing. He was about to go to his own quarters when he spotted a lamp on in the chapel classroom. While it wasn't unusual to see the chaplain's office lit at night, it was unusual to see a lamp lit in the classroom. He rolled his eyes. Had the reckless Miss Dante left a lamp burning when she'd gone home?

He cut across the grass and hurried to the chapel. He saw a figure standing outside the door, but in the dusk it was hard to recognize the uniformed man. Great. One of the soldiers had broken curfew in order to seek Miss Dante's attention already. He feared the school-teacher might cause him more grief than she was worth.

Drawing closer, he called out to the soldier, knowing better than to startle any man holding a weapon.

"It's me, Corporal Taylor, sir," the soldier announced.

Isaac walked up to the young man. "Why are you still here, soldier?"

"My orders were to see Miss Dante to and from school, sir, and she's still inside."

"Have you had dinner?"

"No, sir, but neither has she." He motioned with his head toward the window. "Miss Dante is determined to begin class tomorrow."

"Tomorrow? Why didn't she give herself a few days to settle in?"

Corporal Taylor shrugged. "She said she only has two weeks to prove herself, sir."

Isaac stiffened. He hadn't meant for the two-week trial period to put undue stress on the young woman. "I'll see Miss Dante back to Mrs. Captain Hanson's quarters, Corporal. You're dismissed. Maybe tonight's cook will have something set aside for you."

"I sure hope so, but if not, I'll live." He started to walk away and turned. "She's a fine lady, sir. She reminds me of my older sister—strong, determined, and kind. Thank you for assigning me to keep an eye on her."

"It's better than drills?"

The corporal smiled broadly. "Yes, sir."

Isaac had considered rotating men watching Miss Dante, but he'd clearly found the right man for the job. He waited for the corporal to leave before knocking on the classroom door.

"Come in, Corporal Taylor." She kept writing on the chalkboard. "I promise I'm almost done."

Isaac didn't want to startle Miss Dante, so he waited. He looked around the small space. He'd been in this classroom a few times, but it had never looked so welcoming. A soapy clean scent lingered in the air, and the books on her desk were neatly wedged between matching bronze bookends she must have brought with her. A ledger lay open in the middle of the desk, probably ready for her to list students' names in the morning. There were additional books set on the flat surface of the potbelly stove.

Her cursive handwriting on the board was beautiful with lovely loops and flourishes. He hated to interrupt her, but it would be dark soon.

The wall clock ticked off the minutes and struck seven thirty. He cleared his throat, and she turned at last.

"Colonel!" She clasped the chalk to her chest. "I thought you were—"

"The corporal. I know." He took a seat on one of the long benches. "I dismissed him for dinner."

"Oh." Her faced paled. "I got so busy I forgot about eating. I apologize."

"I'm sure Mrs. Hanson has dinner ready for you. May I escort you home?"

She bit her lip. Was she seriously thinking of turning him down? Most likely, she wanted to tell him she could see herself back to the Hansons' quarters and didn't need an escort. Then, she seemed to reconsider, forced a smile, and set down the chalk. "Just let me gather my things."

It took her only a few moments to put on her bonnet and collect three textbooks from her desk.

He held the door for her then returned to blow out the lamp. Fireflies danced in the bushes as they fell in step on the road. He was glad the long, early fall day provided enough light to see the road.

She shifted the books from her right arm to her left.

"Here," he said, "let me carry those."

"I can manage."

He gently tugged them from her grasp. "What kind of an officer and a gentleman would I look like if I let you carry those home? Where is home by the way, Miss Dante? I mean, besides the Hansons' here at the fort."

"I'm from Lawrence. You?"

"Ohio." He slowed his step so she didn't have to work to keep up with his strides. "Is the rest of your family there?"

"My mother and older sister live there. My father was killed on reconnaissance. He was one of Jennison's Jayhawkers, along with my brother-in-law, who was also killed on the mission."

"So, your father was in the cavalry?"

"Yes, he was an excellent rider." He saw her swipe a finger beneath her eye. "You're a long way from home, Colonel. Do you have family in Ohio?"

"My parents have both passed, but I have two younger brothers. Both were serving the Union, but I've not heard from either for more than six months."

"Cavalry? Like you?"

"No, infantry. They joined the Forty-Second Ohio under Colonel James Garfield. Their term of service should be over soon."

"And yours isn't?" She seemed to look at the eye patch then averted her gaze.

"You mean since I was injured." He drew in a deep breath. "I'm a West Point graduate, a commissioned officer. I guess the US Army doesn't let us go as long as we have two legs to walk on and two arms

246

that can hold a gun. I won't be serving in the field, but I still have some skills of value. Besides, war is all I know."

"What do you like about it? Is it some sort of game to you?"

He gave a wry snort. "I didn't say I liked it, Miss Dante. I understand battlefield tactics and how to win on the field, but every skirmish, every battle, costs lives and ruins others'. I know there are a few in command that enjoy the thrill of the fight, but not me. It's never a game to me."

She was quiet as they approached the officers' housing units. She stopped at the door and turned to him. "What will you do when the conflict is over?"

"Before my injury, I thought I knew. Now, I'm not so sure. I'm leaving it in God's hands." He touched the brim of his hat. "Good night, Miss Dante. I pray your first day is successful. Please let me know if you require anything else."

After donning a thin cotton gown, Adelina knelt beside the bed in what had been Eddie's room. The hobbyhorse gave her a hard stare as if to say, *"This is not your bedroom. Where's my boy?"* Tomorrow, she needed to get Corporal Taylor to take the toy to the dining room.

Adelina clasped her hands on top of the quilt and pressed her forehead against them. Tonight's prayer would be a long one. She asked God to bless her students with excitement to learn and a desire to stretch and grow. She prayed to be filled with understanding for each student's needs. She asked for wisdom to know when to discipline and when to show mercy. She prayed to be blessed with leadership, guidance, patience, and energy. "And above all, Lord, I ask Thee to help me show Thy love to the precious souls in my care."

She started to end her prayer but thought of something else. "Lord, I pray that Thee will help me find a way to teach the illiterate soldiers how to read and write without upsetting the colonel. If this is Thy will, please show me the path Thou has planned."

After saying amen, she crawled into bed and rolled onto her side. Her stomach felt as if she'd swallowed the fireflies she'd seen in the bushes. Try as she might, sleep refused to come. She flopped onto her back and stared at the ceiling. Her thoughts drifted to Colonel Scott. She couldn't quite peg the man. He'd seemed so unreasonable at first, but tonight, he'd been almost solicitous.

"It's never a game to me," he'd said. He did seem quite serious, but he'd said this in reference to fighting. Was the mantle of leadership a heavy burden for him? And where were his brothers? It would be terribly difficult not to know what had happened to them.

Without getting out of bed to kneel again, she said a prayer on the colonel's behalf and added a request for herself that she not do anything to irritate the man. It wasn't going to be easy. Colonel Scott was used to having the last say about everything in his command. But she was used to having the last word.

Chapter Five

The blasts of the high-pitched bugle roused Adelina from her dreams just after dawn. The air in her room was crisp, and she made quick work of dressing, choosing a serviceable dotted, cotton, gray day dress embellished with white lace around the handkerchief sleeves and collar. She didn't want to wear a colorful dress for fear one of the ladies would think her showy, and she didn't want to wear a dark dress for fear the children would think her overly stringent. In truth, she only had a handful of dresses, so both the mothers and the children would eventually see them all.

Her fingers trembled as she fastened the row of pearl buttons down the front. When she was done, she drew her hair into a bun and secured it with pins. A glance in the oval mirror hanging on a nail told her what she already knew. Despite her best efforts for a perfectly smooth, parted-in-the-middle fashion, tiny curls formed at the nape of her neck and around her face. She disliked how they made her look even younger.

She grabbed her books, hurried downstairs, and found Jessie setting out a breakfast of warm corn bread, poached eggs, and fried potatoes.

"I figured you'd be anxious to get to the schoolroom early, so I got your breakfast ready first thing." She pointed to a chair. "Have a seat and eat up before it gets cold."

Adelina sat down and checked the tiny watch clipped by a chain to her belt. It was only seven, and school didn't start until nine. She wanted to arrive early, but perhaps she could persuade Corporal Taylor to let her observe the drills on the parade field before they departed for the chapel. It felt odd to know less about military life than her pupils.

Jessie brought a pail in and set in on the table. "Here's your lunch. Since it's your first day, I included a cookie with your cheese and bread."

"Thank you, Jessie, but you don't have to wait on me. Breakfast and dinner are more than enough."

"Enough for what?" Jessie laughed. "I won't have you fainting away while you're teaching my boy. And don't worry, I cook for Colonel Scott too, so I have plenty of provisions."

"You cook for him? But he doesn't eat here."

"Well, it wouldn't look proper for him to eat here with my Lewis out on campaign, would it?" Jessie sat down at the table and served herself a piece of corn bread. She smeared it with butter and took a bite. "A private comes to pick up the colonel's breakfast, lunch, and dinner plates. I suppose he eats in his office. He provides extra food supplies, and I make the meals. It sure helps me out."

"What does the fort's cook have to say about that?"

She chuckled. "Adelina, there is no official cook. The men take turns doing the task. Sometimes they get good food, and other times, they're lucky if even the beans aren't burnt to a crisp. And don't get me started on their hardtack."

"You're an exceptional cook, so I don't blame the colonel one bit for hiring you." Adelina finished off her potatoes and coffee. She blotted her lips with a napkin, pushed back from the table, and stood. "Will you do me a favor? Will you pray for me today? I've taught before but never in a school where there are no records from previous years. I'm starting from scratch."

Jessie held out the lunch pail. "I'm sure you'll have no trouble, but I'll be happy to pray for you."

The morning had a bit of chill to it, so Adelina retrieved her shawl and her books before going out the door. Corporal Taylor was waiting for her.

"Good morning, Miss Dante. I figured you'd want an early start."

"I do, but would it be all right if we went to watch the drills on the field first? I promise I'll stay on the side."

The corporal removed his hat and ran his hand over his oily hair. "I suppose it wouldn't hurt if I'm with ya."

Since Jessie's home was on the "B" side of the officers' quarters, it didn't face the parade field. They rounded the corner, and Adelina saw the troops had broken off into smaller groups. "Why aren't they all working together?"

"Reveille and roll call are over, and the flag has been raised. The men've had their breakfast, and now each company has their own drills to practice depending on if they're infantry, artillery, or cavalry."

She peered at the horses at the far end of the field. "Is that Colonel Scott?"

"It is. That's one of the new horses. I heard they were having trouble breaking it."

"So he's doing it? Isn't breaking a horse dangerous?"

Corporal Taylor grinned. "He's not breaking it for riding. He's breaking it to the sound of gunfire. A cavalry horse isn't much good if it can't handle noise."

She shielded her eyes from the morning sun to get a better look. "I see he's in the middle, but why are those other two riders riding next to him?"

"Those two horses are seasoned cavalry horses. The colonel's horse will be calmer because they're walking beside it."

She saw the colonel take something from his pocket and put it in the horse's ears. "What's he doing now?"

"We put wads of cotton in the horse's ears to help block the loud sounds." He paused. "The colonel always puts some in his own ears too. He says he already lost an eye, and he doesn't need to lose his hearing too."

The horse trio began to make their way down the field side by side. Adelina caught the glint off a pistol's gun barrel in the hands of a soldier standing opposite the riders. She grabbed the corporal's arm. "Is that soldier going to shoot at them?"

"No, miss." He chuckled. "He'll fire in the air."

She released her hold and watched the rider on the right raise his hand in the air. Then, after a few seconds, he dropped his arm to his side, and the standing soldier fired the gun. She jumped at the sound but didn't take her eyes off Colonel Scott and his buckskin mount. The horse's head lifted, and he threatened to bolt, but the colonel held him. The three horses continued down the field. The soldier with the pistol fired two more times on cue, and each time, the horse's reaction seemed to improve. Finally, the trio made their way to the soldier with the gun.

The soldier held the gun out for the horse to smell the sulfur-laced scent of burnt gunpowder wafting from the barrel.

The corporal shifted his stance. "That helps the horse learn he doesn't need to be afraid of the smell."

The colonel caressed the horse's neck, and she could imagine him praising the animal with words much kinder than the ones he'd used with her.

"Seen enough?" Corporal Taylor motioned toward the road. "We'd better go before the colonel sees us lingering."

Since she had no desire to get the young man in trouble or for the colonel to catch her watching him, she agreed to depart, but her thoughts remained on the scene she'd observed. What the colonel had done with the horse was not entirely different than what she did with some of her students. If she had a shy or frightened student, she often sat them between two confident students she believed would help them. She would then praise every courageous act by the shy child.

Courage, she'd always believed, was caught, not taught.

Perhaps that was true of both children and horses.

Adelina stood on the stoop of the classroom's door and rang the brass school bell she'd brought in her trunk. The children stopped their games and turned toward her, their faces filled with excitement. This morning, several mothers had come as well and were grouped together beneath an oak tree.

She waited for all to quiet. "Good morning, scholars. Would you please line up in two lines with the youngest up front and the oldest in the back? Girls on the right and boys on the left."

A dark-haired little girl with her thumb in her mouth tugged on Adelina's skirt. "I'm this many." She held up five fingers. "Where do I go?"

Adelina took the girl's hand. "I think you'll be in the front, sweetheart."

"Rufus," one mother called out, "you're younger than Cyrus."

"But I's taller."

She marched over and switched the two boys then glanced at Adelina. "My apologies, Miss Dante."

Adelina smiled at the now organized lines. She led the girls in first, directing the youngest children to sit on the front benches and the oldest in the back. Three children could fit on each bench. After the boys too had found their places, the mothers filed in and stood in the back.

She stepped up to the board and pointed to her name. "My name is Miss Dante, and now that you know my name, it's important that I know yours. When it's your turn, you'll come up and give me your name and age. If your mother is here, she can accompany you. Then you can say your goodbyes so she can go home to her chores."

The process went remarkably well. Besides Rufus and Cyrus, she had boys named Abraham, Chauncey, Francis, Elias, Stephen, and even one named Orlando. There were more girls than boys, and she'd be hard pressed to recall all of them, but the little girl with the thumb in her mouth was Lindy. The oldest girls, the daughters of the chaplain, were Faith and Charity. At least that was easy to recall. It shouldn't take long for her to put faces with the names of the others. Noticeably absent, however, were the daughters of Mrs. Major Adams.

Most of the mothers who'd come gave her a dollar when their child was called to the front. She was careful to mark a check in the column beside their names. One mother apologized for forgetting her dollar but promised to send it tomorrow. Even when every name had been recorded in the ledger, one mother remained in the back of the room, reluctant to leave her little boy.

"Elias, I think you forgot to hug your mom goodbye." Adelina pointed toward the lingering mother. "She'll need to carry your hug with her all day, so make it a good one."

Elias, who if she remembered correctly was seven, gave his

mother a generous hug and then practically pushed her toward the door.

Adelina fought back a chuckle but was glad to see the mother go. It was time to get down to business.

"All right, scholars, let's start the day with the Lord's Prayer, and then I want to learn more about each of you."

Chapter Six

"Miss Dante?"

Adelina looked up from the student she was working with and spotted Rufus with his hand in the air.

"Yes, Rufus."

"When is it time for nooning?"

The term *nooning*, referring to the noon hour children were dismissed to eat and play outdoors, always made her smile. She checked her watch and was shocked to see it was five minutes past twelve.

She stood. "I'm glad you asked, Rufus. Your stomach must know the time. Scholars, you may take your lunch pails and baskets outside. When you're done eating, you may play nicely with one another. I will ring the school bell when it's time to come in."

She watched them exit the schoolroom and followed them to the door. She looked out at her students as they found places to sit on the logs or the stoop. The chaplain's daughters took the five youngest children under their wings. They gathered them in a circle and helped them open their lunch pails. If she returned later, she expected the girls would be teaching them a game like Graces. She imagined the girls had the ribbon-bedecked rings and the catching wands necessary for the game in their house next door to the chapel.

Adelina's heart warmed. Their morning activities had begun with the children drawing pictures of what they wanted her to know about them on their slates. The older children, of course, used the precious paper. Then she'd called them each up to discuss their drawings and read for her, if they could. About half of the students were woefully behind where they should be for their age, but she was certain she could catch them up.

She sat down at her desk and opened her lunch pail. The cookie Jessie had packed was accompanied by a note reminding Adelina that God had brought her to Fort Riley for a reason. She tucked the note into her desk drawer. Yes, God had brought her here for a reason—at least twenty-two reasons who were outside playing right now.

The afternoon flew by as quickly as the morning, and she soon found herself saying goodbye to her new scholars as they left. She went back to her desk and pulled out a piece of paper. Now that she had a better idea of what each child's abilities and needs were, she was eager to make lesson plans.

"Miss Dante?"

She looked to find Corporal Taylor standing at the door. "Hello, Corporal."

"I know this was your first day and all, but you said for me to come in after the children had gone to start my—uh—lessons."

"You're right. I did." How had she forgotten? She'd been thinking of the best way to teach the young man since their talk yesterday. "Please come in. We'll get started right now."

"But if you have lessons to plan, I understand. Like my ma said, I'm not much for book learning. Maybe I ain't worth your time."

"Of course you are, and I can work on lesson planning later." She picked up a slate. "But before I teach you to read, I need you to teach me something."

"Me?"

She nodded and handed him the slate. "You're in charge of helping me learn what I need to survive at the fort, right? I want you to teach me what the chevrons on the uniforms stand for. You can draw them on the slate and tell me what each means."

"If you're sure." He sat down on a bench and picked up the slate. "It feels strange teaching the teacher."

"But you have knowledge I need." She pulled up a chair in front of the table.

"If you say so." He showed her the sleeve of his uniform. "All noncommissioned officers wear chevrons on the right and left sleeves of their uniforms above the elbow. You can tell where they serve by the color. Blue is for infantry, red for artillery, ordinance is crimson, and cavalry—"

"Yellow." She smiled.

"Yes, miss." He drew a wide double *V* on the slate. "This is what a corporal wears." He twisted again so she could see his sleeve.

"Yours is yellow, so you're a corporal in the cavalry."

"But that's an easy one, miss." He added another V-shaped bar on top of the corporal's chevron. "A sergeant has three bars like this. If it was blue, what would it mean?"

She paused to think. "Blue means he'd be in ordnance?"

"No, Miss Dante. He'd be a sergeant in the infantry, but don't worry, you'll catch on soon." He drew a diamond above the sergeant's chevron. "Now, when you see this, you're dealing with a first sergeant." After erasing the diamond, he added an arch over the three-rowed chevron. "Have you seen this one?"

"I think so."

"I'm sure you have. It's what a sergeant major wears on his sleeves. There are a few more, but that's good enough for now."

"All right. Test me."

"How do I do that, miss?"

She set three additional slates on the table. "Draw one of the chevrons on each slate. When you point to the picture, I'll try to tell you who would be wearing it."

"That ought to work." He grinned and set to work.

He announced he was ready, and she studied the slates. She got two right and two wrong on their first time through. He mixed up the chevrons, over and over, until she soon had them all mastered. Then he verbally added the colors of each, until she had them down as well.

He started to erase the slates, but she stopped him. "How did you learn all this?"

The corporal shrugged. "You just learn the symbols and what they stand for."

"That's all reading is too." She took one of the slates. "This chevron is a symbol for corporal. When you see it, you think the man's rank is corporal, right?"

"Yes, miss."

She picked up a different slate, erased it, and drew the letter *T*. "This letter is a symbol too. It's the letter *T*. When you see it, you need to think it makes the sound of *T* as in table, tall, and Taylor."

"My name?" He looked from the chevron to her to the letter and back again. "That's all there is to reading? Knowing what the letters mean?"

"There's a bit more, but it's a great place to start. You've already proven you can read, because you can read these." She pointed to the chevrons. "And I bet you know a lot more. Now, you just have to do the same thing with learning your letters. Think you can do it?"

"Yes, miss, I surely do."

Excitement bloomed in Adelina's chest. Believing it was possible to learn was an important step for Corporal Taylor. She prayed he would be a quick study, because any day now, Colonel Scott might decide she no longer needed someone to mind her every move. If that happened, how could she possibly continue the corporal's lessons?

Chapter Seven

With Corporal Taylor's first lesson completed, Adelina packed up her books and followed him out of the schoolroom. She drew in a deep breath, basking in the sunshine. Why did the air even smell better after she'd had a good day teaching?

She heard the scratching sound of digging in the distance and turned to see two soldiers hefting dirt out of a large hole. A new latrine? Asking Corporal Taylor would most likely embarrass him.

"Aren't the men finished for the day yet?"

"No, miss. It's still early enough to complete their assigned jobs for the day. Woodcutting, cleaning, digging—uh—"

"I understand." Adelina shielded her eyes against the bright sun. "Corporal, I'd like to make a stop by the sutler's store if you don't mind. I'm in desperate need of chalk."

The corporal agreed. He began singing softly as they made the trek to the store.

"You have a wonderful voice." Adelina lifted her skirts to step over a muddy hole in the road.

"Thank you, miss." Corporal Taylor beamed in her direction. "Did you know we have a glee club here at the fort?"

"Truly? How delightful. Who's in charge?"

Corporal Taylor blushed. "That would be me, Miss Dante."

"When can I hear you sing? Do you perform often?"

"No, not a lot, but we were supposed to sing in Junction City tomorrow at a get-together where a politician named Mr. King is going to talk about reelecting President Lincoln."

"So it's a political rally?"

He nodded. "Since you're a lady and all, maybe you don't realize the election is only a couple months away, so this is a really important event."

"Because I'm a lady, I can't vote for President Lincoln, but I am certainly aware of the upcoming election, Corporal Taylor."

"Sorry." He swallowed. "My point is we won't be able to perform for this rally now, since the colonel assigned us to barracks. I only wish we could get word to them to let them know we won't be coming. Maybe the organizers can find some other group to sing."

She frowned, understanding the corporal's dilemma. "Can you send a missive? You could dictate it to me."

"A letter would arrive too late." He reached for the handle on the sutler's door and held the door open for her. "I'm sure Mr. King can speak whether we're there or not."

Adelina entered and approached the counter. The sutler turned and smiled at her. "Good afternoon, Miss Dante. Did you get yourself settled at the fort?"

"Yes, I did. Thank you for your directions."

"So, what can I get for you today?" the sutler asked.

She dug a list from her pocket. "I would like to purchase a spool of black thread and a needle, but what I really need is chalk for the children's slates."

"The thread and needle I can do, but I'm afraid I'm fresh out of chalk." He cocked his head to the side. "You need it badly?"

"Yes, I do."

"In that case, I'm sure they have some at the mercantile in Junction City. I'm headed that way to collect a shipment that just arrived. Would you like me to pick up the chalk for you? Or maybe you'd like to see the town for yourself? You're welcome to ride to town with me if you'd like. Having some company would be a nice change."

She started to refuse his travel offer but then glanced at her young escort. Didn't Corporal Taylor need to deliver a message in Junction City? This might solve both of their problems. "Would you have room for the corporal as well? After all, he's been ordered not to leave my side."

"Miss Dante"—Corporal Taylor tugged at the collar of his uniform and swallowed hard—"I don't know if the colonel meant for you to leave the fort."

"He didn't tell me I couldn't leave, did he?" She smiled first at the sutler and then at the young man. "Besides, this will allow you to deliver that message you wanted to send."

Corporal Taylor licked his lips. "Maybe we should let the colonel know."

Adelina straightened her hat. "I don't see a need for that. We should be back long before dark, right, Mr. Watson?"

"Yes, miss. It shouldn't take too long. Junction City is just a few miles away." He removed his apron and draped it on the hook. "I'll go hitch my team and we'll be off."

A short time later, Adelina allowed the two men to help her into the wagon. She tightened her hold on the seat's side. While the front of the wagon provided a rough ride, Adelina imagined that Corporal

Taylor's position in the back had to be even worse.

As they ambled over the rough, rutted roads, Mr. Watson told her about the area and about Junction City itself.

"Lots of folks come to church services at Fort Riley's chapel, so you may see some folks you meet today again on the weekend." He snapped the reins, and the horses picked up speed. "Of course, they'll only come if there haven't been any reports of Indians in the area."

"Are we in danger now?"

He chuckled. "Miss Dante, we're on the frontier. We're always in danger."

Her stomach tightened. She glanced around the area, tensing as they neared every grove of trees or rounded a bend. She turned to look at Corporal Taylor. He sat with his rifle at the ready.

Perhaps she'd accepted Mr. Watson's offer too hastily. But then again, Mr. Watson said he'd lived in this area for a long time, and he'd not have offered if he truly thought there'd be trouble.

They arrived in the city, and Mr. Watson dropped her and the corporal off at the general store, saying he'd return in half an hour to pick them up.

Adelina turned to Corporal Taylor. "You go deliver your message, and I'll purchase the chalk."

"I should stay with you."

"I'll be fine for a few minutes by myself. What can happen buying chalk?"

Isaac's stomach growled as he made his way to Mrs. Hanson's home. Most of the time, he had a private pick up his lunch or dinner and have it delivered to him in his office. This afternoon, however, he decided to pick up his dinner himself and see how the teacher's first day went.

He knocked on the door, removed his hat, and waited, shifting from foot to foot.

Mrs. Hanson swung the door wide. "Colonel, I didn't expect you to come yourself. Wait right here, and I'll collect your dinner."

"Thank you, ma'am."

She returned a few minutes later with a napkin-covered pie tin. "It's chicken and noodles tonight with a slice of peach pie."

"That sounds delicious." He cleared his throat. "How did Miss Dante's first day of school go?"

Mrs. Hanson shrugged. "I don't rightly know. She isn't home yet."

He frowned. "Is she still at the school? Shouldn't she be home by now?"

"I figured she was working late on lesson plans." She smiled at him. "The sun might be setting, but it's not dark yet. I'm sure she'll be here soon. I'll tell her you were asking after her if you like."

He shook his head. "No. That's not necessary. I simply wanted to know how the school was doing." He held up the pie pan and nodded. "Thank you for dinner."

He heard the door close behind him as he walked away. He glanced at the sun, hanging low in the sky like a heavy pumpkin. She didn't need to stay at the schoolroom this late. The chapel was already some distance from the other buildings. Even though Corporal Taylor was with her, Isaac would be much more comfortable if the young woman was in the Hansons' residence before nightfall. He'd drop off his dinner in his office and go escort her home himself.

His nerves grew taut when he discovered the empty schoolroom. He touched the lamp, and no heat emanated from its flue. Where had she gone? Had the Indians somehow snuck in and taken her?

He glanced around the room. There was no sign of a scuffle, but where else would she go? And where was Corporal Taylor?

When he checked with the chaplain, the man admitted he'd not seen her. He made his way to the sutler's but found no one at home.

He considered checking the hospital, but he knew that he'd get a message from someone if either of them were there. He didn't dare waste another minute. He jogged to the barracks to arrange a search party. He called for twenty volunteers to find the new schoolteacher and was surprised when eager hands shot up.

Still, guilt nudged him as he sent them off to suit up. The men were exhausted from today's rigorous drills. Was this search really necessary, or was he overreacting?

He shook his head. He couldn't afford to second-guess himself. If Miss Dante and the corporal were in trouble, they didn't have any time to lose.

✎

Adelina didn't mind the jostling when the sutler urged his team to pick up speed. He said he didn't want them out after dark. Adelina had to admit that she didn't want to be outside the fort when the sun set either.

Mr. King, the politician, was actually speaking for two nights and had asked Corporal Taylor to sing tonight since he couldn't attend the following night. What had seemed like a simple request had ended up taking much more time than they'd anticipated. Then, both she and Mr. Watson had gotten wrapped up in the speaker's lecture about President Lincoln. If Corporal Taylor hadn't insisted it was time to depart, they'd have left even later.

"I'll drive you to the officers' quarters, miss," the sutler said. "I wouldn't want you tripping on the road."

They halted at the sight of a group of men standing in their way. What was going on?

"Whoa." Mr. Watson drew his team to a halt in front of the men. "Evening, gentlemen. Is there a problem?"

The colonel stepped forward, his jaw set firmly and lips pressed to a thin line. "Not with you, Mr. Watson." He glanced around to the back of the wagon. "Corporal Taylor, get out here."

The young man scurried down and skidded to a stop in front of his commanding officer. He came to stiff attention.

"Where have you been, Corporal?"

"In Junction City, sir."

"Did you have permission to leave Fort Riley?"

"No, sir!"

Adelina leaned forward. "Colonel—"

Colonel Scott sent her a mica-hard glare, but it was the silent plea in the corporal's eyes that made her break off her protest.

"Corporal, report for extra guard duty tonight."

"Yes, sir." He saluted and jogged away.

The colonel ordered the other men back to their barracks. Adelina climbed down from the wagon, but he offered her no assistance.

She waited until the sutler had pulled away to speak. "I can explain."

"Explain what? How you put yourself and Corporal Taylor in danger by leaving the fort? Or how your thoughtlessness made me rouse my men from their rest to find you? Or maybe you can explain how you put Corporal Taylor in the middle of all this?"

"He followed your orders. He never left my side."

"Exactly." He crossed his arms over his chest. "He could follow the order to stay with you or follow the one to stay at the fort. Either way, you put him in a position to break an order. Now, he'll be the one to suffer for that, Miss Dante. He'll spend extra hours walking guard duty tonight, and he'll miss out on dinner and sleep. You will not. I hope you're satisfied."

"I didn't mean to get him in trouble."

"But you did." He shook his head. "I'm not sure you're made for military life, Miss Dante. What did you go to town for, anyway?"

Her mouth was as dry as the dust on the road, and her throat felt tight and raw. "The children needed chalk."

"Chalk. You risked your life for chalk." He heaved a sigh. "Go to your quarters, Miss Dante."

She bit back the tears that threatened to fall and started down the road. Colonel Scott made no attempt to walk with her. Instead, when she glanced over her shoulder, he remained fixed in the road like an immovable statue.

With each step, her anger surged. The colonel should have let her explain. Her students needed chalk, and if he'd let her speak, he would have seen it was natural to lose track of time. But he hadn't even let her speak.

It wasn't fair.

She caught sight of Corporal Taylor walking guard duty. That wasn't fair either. Didn't Colonel Scott believe in mercy? Nothing about military life seemed fair.

Maybe Colonel Scott was right and she didn't belong here. Still, she didn't have a choice. She had to find a way to make this work. Her mother and sister were counting on her, and she couldn't let them down.

Chapter Eight

Chairs screeched over the wooden floor as Isaac's few remaining officers drew them up to the meeting table. It had been a week since he'd first met with them, and he was anxious to get their opinions on how well the men were advancing in their skills.

He looked around the table and took a mental roll call. Everyone was present. "Reports?"

"I'd say the cavalry unit is nearly up to snuff, thanks to your help." Major Henning rubbed his muttonchop whiskers. "If you can lend a hand in the next few days, I think we'll have the new horses jumping by the end of the week."

Isaac leaned on his forearms. "I can, but no need to push the jumping. What we need is men who are bonded with the new horses and comfortable enough with them to take them into battle if necessary. Man and horse working as a team." He turned to his right where Captain Dunlop sat. "And your men?"

"The men weren't happy with the extra drills and the confinement to barracks, but they have improved considerably. We're going to have to keep up the extra drills for the rest of the week, but I think they got the message."

"Good." He looked at Captain Smithers. "Artillery?"

"I wouldn't say I have the brightest soldiers ever to grace God's green earth. Still, I'm getting them in shape slowly but surely. What they lack in skills, they make up for in determination."

Isaac smiled and nodded. "Gentlemen, I like what I'm hearing, so let your men know that I'll lift the order for confinement to barracks. As long as they continue to improve, their free time is again their own to do with as they please—within reason."

The officers laughed. They all knew that if the soldiers did as they pleased, many would end up unfit for duty on the following day, especially with pay being drawn on Friday.

"And no one is to leave the fort. Be extra strict about curfews too." Isaac told them. "I want the men rested and where we can find them if they are needed."

Captain Dunlop agreed. "Any reports from General Curtis, sir?"

"No, but I hope to get one soon." He looked around the room. "I received an unofficial report that a group of Comanches were moving through the area. I'll be sending out scouts today. Since our regular scouts are with General Curtis, any recommendations?"

Major Henning's brows scrunched. "LeGrege knows the area well. He can take Hillibrand with him. Together, I think they'd do a good job."

"Then send them to see me." Isaac drew in a long breath and shifted. His saber clinked against the leg of the table, breaking the silence of the quiet room. "I'm also concerned about the ladies in the camp."

His thoughts immediately turned to Miss Dante. After the Junction City incident, he'd expected her to settle, but she'd still caused a ruckus on two different occasions since then.

One hot afternoon, she'd set up a table near the parade ground to pass out cups of water to the soldiers. She hadn't seemed to realize how moon-eyed those young men were in her presence. Then, on a different day, she'd marched her students down the main road singing "Yankee Doodle" at the top of their lungs. Naturally, the men's attention was diverted, so he'd had to speak to her. She simply didn't seem to think before she acted.

He returned his attention to the officers at the table. "Until we know what's out there, it would be wise to keep the ladies here at the fort instead of having them make excursions into Junction City to shop. I can't order it, but—"

"The ladies are sensible, sir," Captain Dunlop said. "They'll do as you suggest."

"Yes." He sighed. "*Most* of them are."

But he could think of one who was neither sensible nor apt to do as he suggested.

～

Adelina smoothed the bodice on her pink gingham day dress and knocked on the door of Mrs. Adams's quarters. A girl wearing a mobcap answered the door.

"The missus isn't receiving yet." The girl, who had to be around the age of twelve or thirteen, had a thick Irish brogue and a splattering of freckles across her nose. Was she Mrs. Adams's servant? She should be in school.

"Would you please tell Mrs. Adams that Miss Dante, the schoolmistress, is here?"

"Aye, but I still don't think the missus will see you. What time do you start school?"

"At nine, so I was hoping to speak to her beforehand."

"All right. I'll give it a go." The girl closed the door and left Adelina standing on the stoop.

Adelina waited for several minutes and finally decided to leave. She heard the front door open behind her and stopped. When she turned, Mrs. Major Adams stood in the doorway of her home with her arms crossed over her ample chest.

"I thought you wanted to speak to me."

"I did, Mrs. Adams." Adelina's stomach knotted. "I noticed that your daughters have yet to attend classes."

"How perceptive of you."

"Have they been ill?"

The woman scowled. "Of course not. My daughters are the picture of health. They simply will not be attending *your* school until I'm certain I want my daughters to be influenced by you."

"I see. Is there anything I can do to persuade you? We've been holding classes for a week now, and I don't want them to miss out on their education."

"I am capable of instructing them at home. Their sewing has never been better."

Adelina bit back a smile. "Needlework is indeed an important skill, but I'd like to teach them about classical literature, cultures around the world, music appreciation, and nature."

"Needlework will suffice. No wife needs to know about cultures around the world." She reached for the door handle.

Adelina put her toe in front of the door to block it. "Mrs. Adams, I know you are a very intelligent lady, and I have no doubt your daughters are learning a great deal from you on many fronts, but please reconsider letting them learn alongside the other scholars. I'm sure they'd be an asset to the class."

Mrs. Adams hiked an eyebrow. "I'll think about it."

Adelina moved her boot. "Thank you. I can ask for nothing else."

Corporal Taylor was waiting for her at the bottom of the steps. "You did your best, Miss Dante. I wish she knew what a good teacher you are."

"That's kind of you to say, Corporal Taylor."

"It's only the truth." He gazed upward and smiled. "Look."

"What is it?" She followed his line of sight and spotted Mrs. Adams's two daughters, both in their early teens, in the window, their faces filled with sadness. They waved their fingers at her as if to apologize for their mother. She returned the gesture, her heart aching for the girls. They'd most likely already begged to attend school with their friends. No amount of needlework would keep them from feeling left out.

"What are you going to do now?" the corporal asked.

She sighed and turned toward the chapel. "Teach the students that God has placed in my care and pray that He changes Mrs. Adams's mind."

Adelina's heart remained heavy when she reached the schoolroom. Corporal Taylor took the water bucket and filled it and then started chopping wood for the stove. The school would need it this winter and maybe even later in the fall. It was hard to believe on this pleasant September day, but he was right. Weather in Kansas could turn without notice.

She swept the floor, wrote the recitation for the day on the board, and then went outside to ring the bell. As her scholars filed in, her spirits lifted. As hard as it had been to see the Adams's girls sad faces, she had twenty-two bright, eager faces now sitting before her.

Once the children had recited the Lord's Prayer and sat down, she picked up a stack of white paper intended for the older scholars.

"Today, we're going to start learning about plants and how all of nature displays the glory of God. Later in the week, we're going outside to look for flowers that we can press for our classroom collection, but we have other work to do first." She returned to the board. "This verse is by Henry Wadsworth Longfellow. He's a famous poet who believed a writer asks a reader not to like what he writes, but to listen to it. Poets express their feelings and ideas in words that make us think and remember, but most of all make us feel."

She pointed to the verse as she read the words on the board aloud.

> *"Kind hearts are gardens.*
> *Kind thoughts are roots.*
> *Kind words are flowers.*
> *Kind deeds are the fruits.*
> *Take care of your garden and keep out the weeds,*
> *Fill it with sunshine, kind words, and kind deeds."*

She leaned against her desk. "What does that make you think about?"

Pearl, a bright eight-year-old with braids, raised her hand. "Flowers and gardens."

"Yes. And how do flowers make you feel, Pearl?"

"I love flowers. They're so pretty. It's like they smile at me."

"That's a lovely way to describe them." Adelina stopped speaking when the door opened and Colonel Scott stepped in. He removed his kepi and motioned for her to go on.

"Can anyone else add something about flowers or what Longfellow is telling us?"

No one seemed willing to speak in front of the colonel, so she turned to him. "Colonel Scott, what do you think about the verse on the chalkboard?"

He seemed to take time to read it. "I think he wants us to think about kindness like we do about flowers." He met her eyes. "When we use kind words and do kind things, it's like we're planting beautiful flowers. But like any garden, you have to mind it to make sure it grows."

"Thank you, Colonel." She pulled her gaze from his. "I want each of you to think about how you can show kindness in the next few weeks and how you can take care of your garden of kindness." She began to pass out the paper. "Now, we're going to practice penmanship as you copy this verse today. If you've begun learning cursive manuscript, please use that instead of printing."

Eddie raised his hand. "Why don't I get paper?"

She squatted down beside him. "Because you haven't learned to write yet and I only have a little bit of paper."

"But I can draw flowers."

She smiled. "I bet you can. Why don't you get the slates and pass them out to everyone who doesn't have a piece of paper while I speak with Colonel Scott?"

She stood, and once Eddie scampered off, she walked to the door.

Colonel Scott cleared his throat. "Everything appears to be going well. I'd hate for you to have to go to town to get supplies again. Do you need paper? Ink?"

"I could certainly use some."

"And you still don't have a place for your books."

"No, but we'll get by." She turned so she could keep an eye on her students. "Were you checking on me, or did you need something else?"

"A little of both." He motioned for her to join him outside. Once they were on the stoop, he continued. "I didn't want the children to hear this, but there's a great deal of unrest in the area. I've sent out scouts, but for the time being I'm recommending that all the women stay within the fort and not go to Junction City."

"That sounds wise. The husbands wouldn't be happy if they

learned you didn't take care of their wives during their absence."

"I didn't come here to tell you that I want the wives to stay here. I came to tell *you* to remain in the fort." His voice was deep and serious. "And the children, of course."

"Of course." She gave him a weak smile. Did she see genuine concern in his eyes? Surely not. He was simply in charge of the fort's inhabitants. "Thank you for letting me know."

He nodded and donned his kepi. "Miss Dante, I know this is all new to you, but please be careful."

The tenderness she heard in his words warmed her. She doubted Colonel Scott had to use kindness for quite some time. Maybe she'd reminded him there was more to life than rules and war.

Chapter Nine

With a board on his shoulder and a knapsack containing brackets, nails, and a hammer, Isaac made his way to the chapel. It was late enough in the afternoon that Miss Dante should be at Mrs. Hanson's quarters, preparing for dinner.

Isaac could have assigned one of the men to build the shelf for the classroom, but he'd decided to do it himself. It would be a surprise for Miss Dante and her students when they arrived tomorrow.

He swung open the side door and marched inside.

"Colonel!" Miss Dante gasped. "Have the scouts returned? Is there a problem?"

"Not at all, and I haven't heard from the scouts yet." He looked around the room. "Where's Corporal Taylor?"

"He's been stacking wood all day and working hard. I didn't want him to miss his dinner. I promised not to go anywhere while he ate."

"How kind." The corners of his lips lifted at the reference. "I thought you'd be at Mrs. Hanson's by now."

She rested her pen in a holder and replaced the cork stopper on her ink bottle. "I was making lesson plans for tomorrow. If there isn't any problem, what brings you here?"

He nodded toward the board. "I came to build you—I mean the school—a shelf. It was going to be a surprise."

"Thank you very much, but I know you're a busy man. Surely you can ask one of the soldiers to do it."

"Miss Dante, you taught the children today about kindness in both words and deeds. Don't you think the lesson will stick even more when they learn Fort Riley's current commander made the shelf for all of your books?"

"I can't argue with that." She smiled and swept her arm toward the blank wall. "Please, sir, tend your garden."

He set down his knapsack while Miss Dante returned to her lesson plans. After removing his jacket and saber, he rolled up his sleeves. The shelf he planned was a simple design. Nothing fancy, but it would do until he could find time to build a decent bookcase.

He secured metal brackets to the board and looked up to find Miss Dante watching him. He flashed her a smile, and she quickly averted her gaze.

When the board was ready to mount, he held it in position on the wall in a space left of the chalkboard at the same height as the chalkboard's tray. "What do you think of this spot? If I put it this low, the smaller children should be able to reach the books."

She joined him. "I think that's perfect. Can I hold the shelf while you nail it in place?"

He frowned. Was it proper for a lady to do that kind of work? But if she didn't help him, how would he get it positioned correctly with Corporal Taylor off eating dinner?

"It might be too heavy."

She stepped beside him and took hold of the board, brushing

against his arm. "I'm stronger than I look."

"Of that, I have no doubt." He looked down at her. "Okay, I'm going to let go now."

She grunted under the weight but kept it in place. "Don't just stand there, sir. Get nailing."

He dropped to the floor beside her skirt and pounded nails into the top hole on the first bracket.

"Uh, I'll have to get closer to—uh—your skirts to put in the next nails."

"Just do it." Her voice was strained.

He scooted around her and gently moved her skirts to the side to drive in the nails on the center bracket. When he drove the nail into the last bracket, he leaned back. He was struck by the way Miss Dante's skirt draped her hips from behind and the way tiny dark curls formed at the nape of her neck. Only God could make perfect curls like that.

Why had he never noticed anything like skirts and curls before?

"Are you done?"

"Oh, yes, you can step away. That should hold it while I put in the nails in the bottom of each bracket."

Slowly, she released her grip and stepped back. He finished the task, stood, and brushed the dust from his trousers. He tested the shelf by pressing down on it. "That ought to work fine." He crossed the room, gathered the stack of books off the stove, and carried them to her. "I'll hold them while you put them where you like."

She took the volumes and arranged them in order by subject. First, she chose the books on literature, then, arithmetic and history. He held out a science book. She wasn't looking and clasped his hand when she reached for it. Her eyes widened. He pretended he didn't notice, but the connection had jolted him as well. He watched as she laid the final music and science tomes flat on the shelf to act as bookends.

Her eyes glistened. "This is wonderful. Thank you."

"My pleasure." He picked up his knapsack. "Have you had dinner?"

"No, as I said, I'm waiting for the corporal's return. I think Mrs. Hanson is used to my late arrivals by now."

"Let's go eat in my office. I'll have the soldier on duty get your plate from Mrs. Hanson." What was he asking? Men didn't invite single ladies to dinner, unchaperoned. Miss Dante would think him an absolute cad. He cleared his throat. "I want to discuss your other needs for the school besides paper and ink. I think I can find a way to help."

"Thank you for the offer, but I'm afraid I'll have to decline. I would hate for any of the wives to get the wrong idea. Mrs. Adams still won't let her girls come to school."

"I understand." He started to walk to the door and stopped. "Wait. I have an idea. I'll pick up the plate she made for me from my office, and we can dine together with Mrs. Hanson or at least with her present and discuss your needs. Under those circumstances, no one can suggest anything untoward."

She licked her lips and met his gaze. How quickly it seemed that she'd become accustomed to his unsightly eye patch. "I think I can agree to that arrangement."

"Good." Warmth spread over his chest. It had been a long time since he'd enjoyed the company of a lady, especially an intelligent one, even if was simply to discuss supplies.

Corporal Taylor banged the door open. "I'm sorry it took so long, Miss Dante. Tonight's cook ran short on grub and had to make some more." He stopped when he spotted the colonel and snapped to attention.

"At ease, Corporal." Isaac shoved his arms back into his double-breasted shell jacket and did up the brass buttons. "I wasn't here to check up on you. I was building a shelf for the school." He motioned with his head to the corner.

"It looks good, sir."

"You're relieved of duty for the night, Corporal. I'll see Miss Dante back. We still have school matters to discuss."

The corporal's eyes darted to Miss Dante, and she gave him an almost imperceptible nod. What was that all about? Were the two of them spending too much time together and sparking? That couldn't be. Corporal Taylor was a boy, and Miss Dante, well, she was certainly a lady.

But if there wasn't an attraction, something else was afoot, and as the commander of the fort, he'd have to find out what it was.

∽

Adelina hung her bonnet on the peg and turned to Jessie. "Colonel Scott is going to bring his dinner plate over here tonight, if that's all right with you."

Jessie quirked a brow.

"He wants to discuss the school."

"I bet he does." Jessie scooped up a fussing baby Rose. "Why don't you go freshen up, and I'll set the table?"

"I don't need to freshen up. This is a business meeting."

"Even so"—Jessie smoothed the side of Adelina's hair—"I think you'll want to look your best."

Adelina rolled her eyes but went upstairs. She washed the dust from her face and repinned her hair, which had been mussed by her bonnet. By the time she descended the stairs, Colonel Scott had arrived.

"I'll take that and warm it up for you." Jessie took the napkin-covered plate from his hand. "You two go on into the dining room."

Eddie was riding the hobbyhorse. Apparently, Jessie had gotten someone to carry it down to the first floor.

"Yee haw!" He used a stick to hit the back of the wooden horse.

Colonel Scott grabbed his wrist and held it gently. "Never strike a horse for fun. A good horseman knows how to get his horse to run without beating it."

"Yes, sir." Eddie seemed on the verge of tears. "I was just playing. I love horses."

"Maybe you'll be in the cavalry like your dad. Would you like to visit the horses in the barn with me after school tomorrow?"

"Can I, Momma?"

Jessie brought in the warmed plates. "If Colonel Scott has time."

"I'll make sure I do." He ruffled the boy's hair. "And maybe you can ride on one too."

"Eddie, it's time for you to get ready for bed. Go put your bed-clothes on. I'll be up in a minute to read to you."

"Yes, ma'am." He slid off the hobbyhorse and skipped from the room.

"You two sit down before your food gets cold again." Jessie gave Adelina a broad smile. "I'll be down later, but I'm going up to put these two down."

Colonel Scott held Adelina's chair. "Shall we?"

She took her seat and spread a napkin in her lap while he took his place.

"Would you mind if I said grace?" he asked.

"Please do."

His prayer was short and simple but not a traditional rote table grace. She liked that.

They began to eat the braised tongue, corn, and scalloped pota-toes in awkward silence. Should she begin the conversation or wait for him? The sauce on the tongue was delicious. She could comment on that.

He took a sip from his water glass. "So, tell me about Mrs. Adams.

Why isn't she sending her girls to school? Wasn't this her idea?"

Her stomach twisted. That was not where she wanted this evening's discussion to begin, but it was too late now. She forced a smile. "I spoke with her this morning. Apparently, she isn't yet ready to trust me."

"I can believe that." He gave her a charming crooked smile. "But she's being foolish. I don't think you'd do anything to hurt a child in any way."

"No, I wouldn't. Not intentionally, at least. I couldn't persuade her to reconsider." She gathered corn kernels on her fork. "I'm praying about the matter. I hope God can do what I cannot."

" 'Beareth all things, believeth all things, hopeth all things, endureth all things.' "

"First Corinthians?"

"Thirteen, yes. It's about charity, but I think it's what a teacher—and a soldier—must do every day." Colonel Scott met her gaze. "We must never give up hope, Miss Dante."

She looked at his face, the roguish eye patch covering his wound, and she fought the urge to touch it. Not only had he lost part of his sight, but it meant his military career was virtually over. Had he wanted to give up hope?

"Now." He speared a forkful of potatoes. "About the supplies. What do you need most?"

She exhaled. This was much safer ground. "Paper. I was going to go into Junction City and purchase some, but—"

"I told you not to." He ate the potatoes. "I can requisition paper and pencils for you, but I'll have a harder time getting ink and pens. I can find one bottle of ink for your use, but not enough for the class. Do you prefer black, blue, green, or purple?"

"You have access to that many colors?"

"We have a limited supply for map work." He dabbed his mouth with his napkin. "What else do you need?"

"Corporal Taylor has been working on building up the woodpile. A couple of rulers would be wonderful, and I'd love to have a map or a globe, but that's wishful thinking."

He laughed. "Not really. The military likes to make maps and charts. I think I have a copy of Bacon's map of the country that we're not using right now. We can put it up in the school. It shows the free states, the border states, and the seceded states. I can set a couple of men to making you some rulers."

"Why are you doing all this? You didn't even want a school here."

" 'Suspicion always haunts the guilty mind.' "

"I am not guilty." She sat up straighter. "And don't quote Shakespeare to me. Yes, I know *King Henry VI* too. I saw you had a copy in your office."

"So you were snooping around?" His voice held a teasing note. "For the record, I never said I didn't want a school at the fort." He leaned back in his chair. "I'm in favor of education. What I objected to was not knowing about the plans to begin a school. I don't like surprises, especially when I'm the one who's responsible for everyone's welfare."

"It's hard, isn't it? I mean to have to bear the weight of caring for the whole area."

He drew in a deep breath. "It is. I've been in command on the field enough that I'm used to the rigors of battle. I've lost men under my command, which is always difficult, but I've never been responsible for the lives of women and children." He pushed his empty plate toward the center of the table. "That was delicious. Do you cook?"

"Not like Mrs. Hanson."

"Always had your head in books, eh? Let me guess, you love the works of Jane Austen."

She stiffened. How had he guessed that? She kept her copy of

Pride and Prejudice with her upstairs, not in the classroom. "I do, but how did you know?"

"Lucky guess."

She raised her eyebrows. "Then would you care to guess what I'm currently reading?"

"*Sense and Sensibility?*"

She shook her head. "Mary Shelley's *Frankenstein.*"

"Are you serious?" He seemed to fight a roar of laughter.

"I am." She finished her last bite of potatoes. "The first half of the book seemed a little slow, but now that I'm beyond the middle, I can barely put it down. Did you know Shelley was only eighteen when she wrote the story?"

"Same age as you?"

"I'm twenty-one, I'll have you know."

"I can only imagine the dreams you've been having." He chuckled. "Maybe you shouldn't share this bit of information with Mrs. Adams."

She laughed. "Mrs. Adams might faint dead away."

A knock on the door startled them both. She went to the door and found a soldier waiting there.

The soldier tipped his hat. "Sorry for the intrusion, miss, but Colonel Scott said he was dining here. I have an important message for him."

"I'm here, private," the colonel said from the dining room. He stepped into the parlor. "What's the message?"

"One of the scouts has returned."

"One?" The colonel's face darkened. "Where's the other soldier?"

"He's dead, sir."

Chapter Ten

Adelina dashed her finger under her eye and caught the tear that threatened to fall. A man had died tonight. A man Colonel Scott had sent out in order to protect them all.

"I heard someone at the door. Did the colonel have to go already?" Jessie stepped into the parlor and put her hand on Adelina's arm. "Is everything all right? You look white as a sheet."

Adelina allowed Jessie to guide her to the settee where she sank onto the cushions. "One of the scouts was killed. The other just returned with the news."

Jessie pressed her hand to her mouth. "Oh dear. Do you know his name?"

"No, the soldier who came here to report didn't say." Her throat felt thick. Her heart not only ached for the man's family, but also for the colonel. "Do you think we're in danger?"

Jessie wrapped her arms around her middle. "The soldiers will make sure we're safe here, but I'd hate to be one of the settlers with all this unrest going on." She sat down in one of the parlor's chairs. "How did things go with your dinner?"

Adelina welcomed the change of subject. "Colonel Scott is being supportive of the school. He offered to get me ink, paper, pencils, rulers, and a map."

"That's very generous." Jessie picked up a shirt she was mending. "And how did he come to eat here tonight?"

Adelina told her about his morning visit, the lesson on kindness, the shelf he built, and his invitation. She avoided explaining the special warning he'd given Adelina about leaving the fort.

"And why do you think he's making such an effort?" She gave Adelina a knowing smile.

Adelina was puzzled. "For the children. He's also a strong believer in education."

"Is he now?" Jessie barely contained a grin.

"Jessie, we talked about the school, literature, and Mrs. Adams because she still isn't letting her daughters attend classes."

Jessie frowned. "Did he have any ideas of how to change her mind?"

"No, do you?"

Jessie set her mending aside. She stood, picked up a blanket from the floor, and began folding it. "I think it's time for you to join the quilting circle. On Saturday mornings we make quilts for Union soldiers. Some of the older girls watch the children so the mothers can work. Are you any good with a needle?"

"I'm fair, but I'm not one of the wives. Are you sure I'd be welcome?"

"I believe so. They need to get to know you like I do." She draped the blanket over the back of the chair. "I think it will be more difficult for Mrs. Adams to continue to remain aloof if everyone else is beginning to like you."

"Can I think about it?" Adelina stretched. "Right now, I have lessons to prepare."

Weariness tugged on every muscle in Isaac's body. The remaining scout had reported that there had been a skirmish between the peaceful Kaws and a band of Kiowas and Comanches. The Kaws were overpowered and fell back on the settlements, asking the settlers for rations and a party to go with them to search for the aggressors.

While the two scouts were on their return with the news, they had been attacked by the Kiowa and Comanche war party. Only LeGrege had escaped.

After doubling the guards around Fort Riley, Isaac called for Major Henning and told him to take a cavalry company out to the area at first light, along with a couple of pieces of artillery. Isaac hoped that their presence would help the settlers feel safer and keep any war parties at bay, but the truth was that the same war party could be anywhere.

He'd also asked the major to retrieve Hillibrand's remains for a proper burial.

Even though the hour was late, he picked up his pen and dipped it into the inkwell. Writing letters to the next of kin when a soldier was lost was never easy. Writing this one seemed even harder. He had been the one to send Hillibrand on this mission. How did he tell this young man's mother her son would never come home?

He could have put off writing the letter, but doing it tonight was his way to honor the fallen soldier. By the time he signed the missive, his eye patch was irritating his skin from the long day. He folded the paper and sealed it. Tomorrow, he'd find out where to post it.

Once he'd tucked the letter into his top drawer, he pushed back from his desk and stood. He wanted to make one last check of the fort before he returned to his quarters. Crickets chirped and cicadas whirred in the chilly night air. The doubled guards remained on high alert, clearly understanding the danger. He walked around the officers' houses and noticed a lamp burning in Mrs. Hanson's dining room. Was Miss Dante still awake? Or had her reading of *Frankenstein* given her nightmares?

He released a heavy sigh. If only his nightmares could be based on fiction and vanish in the first rays of the sun.

Chapter Eleven

That's Major Henning."

Adelina looked at the man Corporal Taylor pointed out. He was heading a column of cavalrymen, and they'd taken two large pieces of artillery with them. She'd never before seen a red beard of that magnitude on a man. She hoped he didn't sunburn on the mission. Sunburn, however, might be the least of his concerns.

Adelina squinted in the morning sun. "Why are they taking the cannons?"

"I think Colonel Scott knows what he's doing. It's more for show, and those cavalry soldiers could end up grateful for the artillery support."

"Isn't that a lot of gun power?"

"The first is a three-inch ordnance rifle," the corporal said. "The second is a twelve-pound mountain Howitzer. It's easy to move on rugged terrains."

The wistfulness in his voice surprised her. "Do you wish you were going too, Corporal?"

He shrugged and grinned. "Naw, then I'd miss my lessons with you. By the way, I've been telling some of the fellows about you teaching me to read, and they want to know if you'll teach them too."

"Really?"

The two of them left the side of the road and began to make their way toward the chapel.

Corporal Taylor readjusted his weapon on his shoulder. "There's so many of us soldiers who joined up young. Some of us didn't get much schoolin'."

"I understand." Adelina glanced toward the remaining men on the parade field. "How could they come for lessons? Aren't the men confined to barracks when not on duty?"

"The colonel lifted that order. He said the men were doing better on their drills."

They paused at the door to the schoolroom. "I want to help. You know that, but let me speak with the chaplain before we make any plans. All right?"

"Yes, miss."

Adelina went inside and busied herself with preparing for the day, but her thoughts kept returning to the soldiers who wanted to learn to read. How could she work this so that she was appropriately chaperoned? Most were so young they would have scarcely been out of school if they hadn't joined up, but she didn't want any rumors spreading.

Corporal Taylor entered and retrieved the water bucket. Going to the well and filling the bucket had become one of his morning tasks. Adelina had to admit that she'd grown used to having the young soldier accompany her. He had, in fact, been helpful on many fronts, and she now considered him a friend or even a younger brother of sorts.

After the children had filed in and roll had been taken, she told her scholars that today was the day they were going outdoors to look for flowers.

"But before we go out, let's talk about how flowers grow." She drew a line on the chalkboard and a seed beneath it. "This seed holds the beginning of a new plant. It's in the ground, and when the seed gets wet, roots begin to grow from the seed." She added roots to the seed. "The roots feed the new plant with water and food from the soil. The roots dig down into the soil, and the plant emerges. A stem comes through the soil, and leaves grow." She added each part of the plant to the drawing.

She looked around to see if her students seemed to be grasping the concepts; then she drew a large sun in the corner. "Plants have a special way to turn sunlight into food to help them grow. After the plant grows, a flower begins to bloom. What have you seen landing on flowers?"

She called on Chauncey. "Bees."

"Yes, absolutely. Anything else? Stephen."

"Butterflies?"

"Oh, that's a great answer too. Bees and butterflies are attracted to the bright colors and sweet smells. So, scholars, what three things do flowers need in order to grow? Lindy?"

The girl had to remove her thumb from her mouth to answer. "Water, sunshine, and. . .uh. . .dirt."

"Well done, Lindy." She folded her hands in front of her. "The autumn flowers we have right now are different from those that grow in the spring. Today we'll be collecting flowers and identifying them. Then we'll press them in these large books." She pointed to the books on the shelf.

"Miss Dante, where did the shelf come from?" Cyrus asked.

"Colonel Scott made it." Adelina removed two of the heaviest volumes and set them on her desk. When she turned back to the class, one of the younger girls in the front raised her hand. "Yes, Sarah?"

"Was it because you're sweet like a flower?"

The class tittered, and Adelina smiled. She doubted the colonel would use the word *sweet* to describe her.

She walked over to stand before Sarah. "Remember the poem we read about gardens of kindness. It was an act of kindness for our whole classroom. I'll need everyone's help to think of a way to thank him, all right? But now, we have flowers to find." She crossed the room and put her hand on the door latch. "Be sure to stay near the fort while you're collecting, wear your shawls and jackets, and watch out for plants that protect themselves with thorns. When you find a flower, bring it to me, and we'll catalog it."

She let the children go with an additional admonishment to not wander too far. The first flowers to be returned were delicate purple bellflowers, sweet-scented asters, and the bloom of a bull thistle. It wasn't long before someone brought an orange-and-yellow Indian blanket flower with its jagged edges and a handful of purple clover. Soon yellow sunflowers, black-eyed Susans, and sneezeweed littered her shawl where the blooms had been placed.

Although they had plenty of specimens, she'd let the children explore a bit longer. They dotted the fields before her with the older children naturally helping the younger ones. Sarah returned and handed her a bouquet of goldenrod, and Adelina sneezed.

"Miss Dante! Miss Dante!" Faith, the chaplain's daughter, ran to Adelina. "I can't find Lindy!"

Adelina's pulse quickened. "When did you last see her?"

"She wanted to get one of those tall lavender flowers beyond the chapel, but I told her it was too far to go. Then I turned around, and now I can't find her anywhere. She's so little. It's all my fault."

"It's not your fault." Adelina cupped her hands to her mouth and called for Lindy but heard no answer. Fear knifed through her. What if the girl was lost? Or worse, since she might have ventured beyond the fort, what if she'd been taken by the Comanches or Kiowas?

Corporal Taylor joined Adelina. "What's wrong?"

"Lindy is missing." She turned to Faith. "I want you to go ring my school bell. Get everyone inside the classroom. Send your sister for your father. The children can practice their recitation until I return." Then she turned to the corporal. "Will you let Colonel Scott know what's going on? I'm sure I can find her, but I think he'd want to know."

"Maybe I should look, and you go tell the colonel?"

"If Lindy is lost and frightened, she might not come to a man." She touched his arm. "Please, just go. I don't want to delay any longer."

With that, she ran toward the thicket of tall, spherical flowers in the distance.

Isaac spotted motion at the far end of the parade field. He stopped his work training the men and their mounts and rode his buckskin mare to meet the soldier. He recognized Corporal Taylor before he'd gotten to the young soldier. Was something wrong at the school? Isaac's stomach clenched.

The corporal propped his hands on his knees in an effort to get his breath.

"Report," Isaac barked.

"One of the children wandered off at the school." His chest heaved. "They think she went beyond the chapel and left the fort area."

"Did Miss Dante go after her?"

"She did."

Isaac whirled his horse toward the road and took off at a full gallop. His heart thundered against his ribs. Had the child simply wandered off, or had she been taken? And what was Miss Dante thinking, going after the girl on her own?

He reined in his mare when he reached the classroom door and vaulted off. He flung open the door and saw the chaplain standing in front of the class. The chaplain motioned Isaac to step back outside, and he joined him there.

"How long have they been gone?"

"Charity came and got me about ten minutes ago. Miss Dante was headed toward those pink flowers on the hill beyond the chapel, but we haven't seen her or little Lindy yet."

"I'll find them."

"No need." The chaplain's face broke into a wide smile. "Look."

Isaac turned to see Miss Dante holding the hand of a little girl with a tearstained face. The girl held a handful of purple blossoms.

With a whoosh, relief flooded over him.

"All is well." Miss Dante led Lindy toward the men. "She got lost, but she came to me when she heard my voice, just like one of the shepherd's lost sheep."

"Praise the Lord." The chaplain wrapped Lindy in a hug. "I'm glad you're safe, little lamb."

Isaac crossed his arms over his chest. "Chaplain, would you please take the child inside? I'd like to speak to Miss Dante."

"Of course." He took Lindy's hand. "The other children will be delighted to know you're safe."

Once the door had closed behind the chaplain, Isaac slowly turned to Miss Dante. "I ought to tan your hide."

"Excuse me?" Miss Dante stepped down from the stoop and

moved away from the windows where the children could see their conversation.

He followed her until she was backed against the only tree in the yard. Didn't she realize the danger she'd been in? "What were you thinking, taking off like that?"

"I was thinking that Lindy might be scared, lost, or hurt, and I was correct. She was scared and lost. Thankfully, she wasn't hurt."

"And what if she'd been taken by Indians? They'd have been thrilled to get you too. It was foolhardy to go after her." He took off his kepi and wacked it against his hand in exasperation.

She flinched.

"You're too impetuous for fort life." He jabbed a finger at her. "You should have waited for me and not rushed in."

She stared at him, wide eyed. "Would you have waited?"

"I'm a soldier. It's my job to rush in."

"And it's my job to care for these children." Her back stiffened. She held her hands up, palms outward toward him. "I was not being impetuous. I made sure the other children were taken care of, and I sent Corporal Taylor to find you. I know you feel responsible for all of us, but not everything is in your control."

His chest heaved, and he fought to regain some hold on himself. Miss Dante was right. He'd have gone after the child too, so why had he reacted so poorly? There was only one answer. Miss Dante simply made him crazy.

For the first time, he noticed a scratch on her cheek. "Are you hurt anywhere else?"

"I'm not hurt."

He reached up and gently traced the scratch.

Adelina inhaled. "Oh, that's from when I walked into a branch."

He let his hand fall. For several moments, silence hung between them like a fog. At last, he cleared his throat. "I apologize for my anger, and for the record, I'd never tan your hide nor anyone else's."

She smiled. "That's good to hear."

He pinched the bridge of his nose. "I was upset because I care. I want you to be safe."

"I know that." She laid a hand on his arm. "That's why I sent for you. If anything had gone wrong, I knew you'd move heaven and earth to find Lindy."

"And you."

"Yes." The corners of her lips lifted slightly. "You care about every person at Fort Riley."

He looked into her honey-glazed brown eyes. Her face was scratched and her hair was mussed, but she'd never looked more lovely. The truth hit him hard. He wouldn't be this upset if anyone else on the fort had taken off on their own. It was because it was her.

He replaced his kepi and gave her a tight-lipped smile. "Yes, I care about everyone."

Chapter Twelve

The noxious smell of horse droppings made Adelina's nose wrinkle. Since Jessie was busy preparing dinner, she'd asked Adelina to take Eddie to the stables to meet Colonel Scott. Adelina had agreed and had rearranged her evening lessons with Corporal Taylor.

Adelina hiked her skirts, and with her eyes focused on her shoes, stepped carefully around the recently deposited pile.

Eddie laughed at her. "Miss Dante, it won't hurt you."

"I know that, Eddie, but I still don't want to step in it."

Having cleared the horse droppings, she looked up to see Colonel Scott grinning. "Bravo, Miss Dante."

She smiled. "Mrs. Hanson asked me to bring Eddie down for the visit you promised him. Did you forget?"

"No, I've been looking forward to it. Would you care to join us?"

Eddie frowned, his lower lip protruding. "She's a girl."

"She's a lady, and ladies ride horses too, only they use a sidesaddle." Colonel Scott looked at her. "Do you ride?"

"It's been a long time, but yes, I know how. Do you have a sidesaddle?"

"Sorry, we don't, and I wouldn't want you on any of these horses anyway." She frowned, and he hurried to continue. "Don't get riled up. Most of our horses are too green, and they sure haven't carried anyone on a sidesaddle. They're being trained for war, not for carrying a lady rider."

Eddie toed the dirt. "Can we please go see the horses?"

"I think Master Hanson is eager to begin." Adelina grinned and laid a hand on Eddie's shoulder.

Eddie gave her a sideways glance. "Who's Master Hanson?"

"You are." Colonel Scott ruffled Eddie's hair and motioned the boy toward the walkway with rows of horse stalls on each side.

"Your surname is Hanson, but your Christian name is Edward, right?" Adelina fell in step with the colonel and the boy. "And your friends and family call you Eddie."

He looked up at Adelina. "What do your friends call you?"

"Adelina."

"Can I call you that?" Eddie asked.

"When we're not in school, you may call me Miss Adelina if your mom agrees."

"Can the colonel call you that?" Before he received an answer, he turned toward Colonel Scott. "What's your name?"

"Isaac." He stopped in front of one of the stalls and met Adelina's gaze. "And yes, Miss Dante can call me that when we aren't with any soldiers."

"What should I call you?" Eddie asked.

"Colonel." He lifted Eddie up high enough to see in the stall. The boy scratched the center of the horse's head. They visited two more horses, a mahogany mare and an energetic paint, before Colonel Scott introduced them to a silvery gelding. "And since we've been talking about names, this beauty is Marengo. That was the name of Napoleon's horse. Would you like to take him for a ride, Eddie?"

"Me? Is it all right with Napoleon?"

Adelina and the colonel exchanged amused glances but managed to not laugh aloud.

"Napoleon lived a long time ago in France." Adelina patted the horse's neck. "This isn't the same horse. He just has the same name. He seems very sweet."

"Which is great for children, not much for war horses." Colonel Taylor dropped a halter over the horse's head and led him out of the stall.

Adelina watched as Colonel Scott—Isaac—first showed Eddie how to brush and curry the horse. Together, they saddled Marengo. He let Eddie lead the horse out of the stables and into an open area. Isaac then added a long lead rope and hoisted Eddie into the saddle. Once the stirrups had been adjusted, Isaac wrapped the reins around the saddle horn.

Thinking of him as Isaac still felt odd to her, but he had told Eddie she should call him by his Christian name. Social mores said that extending him the same courtesy would be equivalent to giving him permission to court her. Were such social rules different in a fort? Somehow, she didn't think so.

Isaac attached a long lunge rope to the bridle and walked about six feet away. "Okay, Eddie, sit up nice and tall. When you're ready, give him a little kick." The horse started to move, and Isaac's rope kept Marengo turning in a circle. "Push your heels down in the stirrups. Good."

He continued to tell Eddie things to try such as lifting first his right and then his left arm in the air or holding both arms out like the letter *T*. "Those exercises help you learn about having a good seat in the saddle. Now, do you know how to stop a horse?"

"Whoa!" Eddie yelled, and Marengo came to an immediate halt. Isaac drew close. "Well done. I think you'll make a great cavalry-man someday, just like your pa." He swung the boy off the horse and signaled a private to come take Marengo. "He'll take off Marengo's saddle and give him a good rubdown before he gives Marengo his dinner. And speaking of dinner, we'd better get going or your mother will blame me for you being late to yours."

Eddie's eyes grew wide. "Aren't you going to eat at my house again?"

"No, not tonight." He glanced at Adelina. "I have some work to do in my office."

Her heart squeezed. He'd had a difficult two days, and he didn't need to be alone, but there was more. She couldn't explain it, but somehow the events of the day had bonded them in some way. He'd made her the shelf, he'd offered supplies, he'd given of his time, and he'd rushed to aid her in the search for Lindy. He'd also been upset that she'd put herself in danger. Then this afternoon he'd taken the time to let Eddie ride a horse. There was more to Colonel Scott than war. A lot more.

She recalled the tender way he touched the scratch on her cheek. Her heart said that if she asked him to dine with them tonight, it would be more significant than sharing food around a table. It would be opening a door to friendship and maybe even more. Did she want that?

She looked at his face, the eye patch covering one eye and the other warm and tender. Her pulse quickened, and she drew in a deep breath. "You're welcome to join us—Isaac."

The skin around his eyes crinkled. "I'd like that, Miss Dante."

She bit her lip. "Please, call me Adelina."

Chapter Thirteen

Isaac had forgotten how good hot, fresh food could taste. He had to pace himself not to devour Mrs. Hanson's red beans and rice. He'd never had them this good in the mess hall, and Eddie had hinted at a pie for dessert.

Sitting around the table with a group of people, which tonight included Mrs. Hanson, Eddie, baby Rose, and Adelina, also seemed foreign to him. He couldn't remember dining with a family since he'd left for West Point. Oh, there had been some dinner parties as social functions, but that wasn't the same as a family meal.

Mrs. Hanson announced that Rose had sat up for the first time earlier that day. Adelina beamed at mother and baby. Eddie, of course, had the most to say at the table as he told about his ride on a real horse. Mrs. Hanson thanked Isaac more than once, saying the boy truly missed his pa.

Adelina was uncharacteristically quiet. Did she regret inviting him tonight? Was she still upset over the way he'd handled the lost little girl situation? From their time in the stables, he'd thought they'd moved beyond that.

Once the pie had been served and the dishes washed, Adelina declared she had papers to grade. Although he too had some work to do, he was reluctant to leave and offered to help her.

She laughed. "I don't think you can correct penmanship, but maybe you could handle the arithmetic work." She handed him a pencil. "Check away."

They worked side by side at the table for half an hour before he said anything. "Do you do this every day?"

She flashed him a broad grin. "You have your war. I have mine."

"War?"

"Fighting the war against ignorance, one student at a time." She giggled. "And no one is allowed to secede." Her eyes widened, and her face grew serious. "I didn't mean any offense. I shouldn't make light of the war."

"No offense taken. We have to laugh, and the war won't last forever."

"How do you do it?" Her voice was soft, and there was light in her honey eyes. "How do you keep fighting?"

"You have to have something worth fighting for."

She cocked her head to the side. "So what are you fighting for?"

"Adelina, I'm fighting for a lot of things. I'm fighting for the Union, for the freedom of slaves, and now—"

"What now?"

"I'm fighting for the people I care about." He held her gaze until she finally looked down at her papers.

"Isaac, about those people—your soldiers." She fidgeted with her pencil. "Some of them have approached me about teaching them to read. How would you feel about that?"

He sat up straight in his chair. "Those men have more to worry about right now than learning to read."

"But what if it didn't interfere with their routine? After the war, they'll be going home to start over. They need an education."

"I understand what you're saying, but the soldiers are under my command." He kept his voice firm and matter of fact. "With all of the Indian unrest, I need them focused on their jobs. I have the last word on the subject, and at least for now, that word is no."

～

On Saturday morning Adelina dressed in an ivy-green day dress with billowy mutton sleeves. The lace around the collar looked like a big smile, and she hoped it put the wives in a friendly state of mind.

She tightened her belt and attached her watch chain. After one more check in the mirror, she grabbed her sewing basket and headed down the stairs to meet Jessie.

"Nervous?" Jessie set a plate of hotcakes in front of Adelina.

"A bit." How could she tell Jessie that her thoughts had been jumbled for days now, especially since Isaac had dined with them? She couldn't tell if the cobwebby nerves she felt today were because of the dinner, the discussion about teaching the soldiers to read, or because she was about to face Mrs. Major Adams. Her emotions might be turning like a Kansas twister, but she'd come to one conclusion. In a very short time, she'd come to think of Fort Riley as her home, and she wanted nothing more than to remain and do the work she believed God had put her here to do. She'd prayed for a long time about teaching the soldiers to read and woke feeling more determined than ever to teach them. Isaac might think he had the last word, but in truth the last word belonged to the Lord.

"I believe things will go well today." Jessie squeezed her shoulder then pointed to the plate. "Eat up. We don't want to be late."

When it came time to depart, Adelina carried Rose, and Jessie wrangled the sewing baskets. Eddie followed behind. They walked to the Curtis home where the quilting circle was to be held. Since all of the Curtis children had grown, Mrs. Curtis had offered one of their upstairs bedrooms to set up the quilting frame. Before she'd gone to visit her sister, she'd told the ladies to continue their Saturday work and, according to Jessie, had even gone so far as to ask her maid to prepare refreshments for the ladies.

One of Mrs. Adams's daughters met them at the door. "Good morning, Mrs. Hanson, Miss Dante. May I take the baby?" She looked at Eddie. "The rest of the children are in the dining room having cookies."

Adelina passed Rose to the young girl and watched Eddie scamper off. She took in the home's decor. A tatted scarf lay beneath candlesticks on the mantel. The brick fireplace looked much like the one in Jessie's home. Since this was the general's quarters, however, it was larger than those of the other officers. Adelina noticed special items like a pianoforte, pieces of art, and chairs with lovely needlepoint. How far had these pieces traveled? General Curtis had most likely been assigned in many different locations. She'd never considered how difficult it was to try to build a home as a military wife, and she found herself admiring this woman she'd never met.

Could she build a home in a frontier fort?

Only with the right man.

Jessie passed Adelina her sewing basket. "Let's go up and get a seat."

With each step, Adelina's chest tightened. While she'd survived the two-week trial period, there was nothing stopping these ladies from sending her away at any time. They'd hired her, and they could also be the ones to fire her. She wished she could convey how much their children now meant to her.

A couple of ladies had arrived before Adelina and Jessie. Both ladies seemed surprised to see Adelina but weren't unwelcoming. It took a few additional minutes for the room to fill with wives. Even though Adelina had come to know their names through their children, she was surprised to see how quickly she could identify each woman. They were all seated by the time Mrs. Adams appeared.

The only empty seat remaining was situated next to Adelina, but Mrs. Adams remained fixed in the doorway. Finally, Lindy's mother, Mrs. Lieutenant Gillis, offered to move.

Not a promising start.

"Miss Dante, it's nice of you to join us." Mrs. Gillis placed a hand on Adelina's arm. "And I'm so thankful for you finding my Lindy the other day."

"If she'd been supervising the children like she should have, your Lindy wouldn't have wandered off." Mrs. Adams threaded her needle.

The chaplain's wife frowned. "According to my Faith, she was the one who'd taken responsibility for Lindy on the outing. It sounded like Lindy saw a flower she wanted and simply got a bit confused in the process of retrieving it. What kind of flower was it?"

"A Rocky Mountain bee plant. The lavender blossoms are very showy." Adelina flashed a smile at the group. "I told the class that the Indians boiled the leaves and used it like spinach in stews."

"You're teaching them about Indians?" Mrs. Adams scowled.

"No, but we have been discussing plants of this area." She opened her sewing basket. "The children have been fascinated."

"Well, my Rufus has never had a hankering for learning like he does now. I actually had to tell him to put a book down and go out to play." Mrs. Captain Snape smiled at Adelina and began stitching on the quilt. "And I heard tell that Chauncey has been writing some poems. Isn't that right, Georgina?"

"It is." She licked the end of a piece of thread. "He said you've been teaching them about a garden of kindness from a poem by a man with three names."

Adelina smiled. "Yes, Henry Wadsworth Longfellow, and I'm glad he enjoyed it. The children have been working on finding ways to be kind. Your children are delightful. You should all be very proud of them. They've figured out special ways to be kind to one another, and I hope they are carrying the lesson home."

"So that's why my Abraham helped with the dishes last night." Mrs. Captain Allen snipped a thread. "I didn't think I'd ever hear him offer to do dishes."

"All right, ladies, enough. I will admit Miss Dante has been able to teach a lesson on kindness and inspire a few of the students to explore learning." Mrs. Adams leaned back in her chair. "But we have no idea how she maintains discipline or what she does when she's not teaching school. I've seen her walking home from the school with the colonel on more than one occasion."

"If you would send your girls to school, perhaps they could tell you how she maintains discipline." Jessie pointed across the quilt with the needle in her hand. "Mary, what's that verse about bearing false witness?"

"It's one of the Ten Commandments. Exodus chapter twenty, verse sixteen."

Jessie smiled and returned to her work. "Thanks for the reminder."

Adelina focused on making tiny stitches and refused to look up.

"What do you think, Miss Dante?" Mrs. Snape asked. "Is it too late for Alice's girls to begin coursework?"

Adelina lifted her head. "No, certainly not. They'd be more than welcome to join us at any time."

Mrs. Adams harrumphed. "Of course they'd be welcome. They're angels. Perhaps I'll send them on Monday. At least then I can keep a better eye on you."

Jessie started to speak, but Adelina kicked her under the quilt frame. She didn't want anyone to say something that could make Mrs. Adams change her mind.

Adelina would consider today another victory in her war on ignorance, and best of all, there had been no casualties.

Chapter Fourteen

Isaac tore open the missive that had come in the morning post. Sitting at his desk, he read it carefully. Major General Blunt's and General Curtis's Union troops had been called to rally at Jefferson City after the Confederate army's attempt to capture St. Louis.

A part of him envied the men on the field. General Curtis was a strong abolitionist, and Isaac admired the man's position. When Isaac had been on the battlefield, it had been easy to fight because he too believed in the cause.

He touched the ever-present eye patch. He might be unable to serve with General Curtis, but he was needed here, and it looked like his command of Fort Riley would continue for a while.

"Sir." A corporal stood at the door to his office. "Major Henning and his men have returned."

"Thank you, Corporal. See him in as soon as possible."

Isaac steepled his fingers and steeled himself for bad news. Had any soldiers been lost? At least the fort now had another company available if it was needed.

Less than fifteen minutes later, Major Henning strode into the office. He stood at attention until Isaac said, "At ease" and pointed to the chair.

"We never found the war party." Major Henning stroked his thick red beard. "Maybe we scared them off or perhaps they were always ahead of us, but the only thing we saw was a herd of buffalo. We brought a couple of bison back for meat."

"Then it wasn't a total waste of time." Isaac stood and went to his map. "Show me how far you went."

Major Henning joined him at the map and drew a finger around the area. "I think they're long gone."

"I hope you're right, but they could be lying low, waiting for the right time to strike another settlement." He clapped Major Henning on the back. "Go get some well-deserved rest and thank your men on my behalf."

Isaac returned to his seat and sighed. Were they safe? Should he let his guard down? It had been three weeks since they'd lost the scout, and they'd not heard reports of any additional violence. Life at the fort had returned to the day-to-day monotony. Even Adelina seemed to settle into fort life. Mrs. Adams had finally sent her girls to school, and everything seemed to be progressing well.

While he loved eating dinner at the Hansons' quarters with Adelina and the others, he'd decided to only dine there on Tuesdays, Thursdays, and Sundays so that no tongues wagged. Adelina's stories of the children's antics delighted him, and getting to know her beyond the classroom had been most enjoyable.

It had taken time to see past Adelina's impetuous nature, but he could now understand that her exuberance sometimes overtook her common sense. He also discovered so many other things about her that made those irritating moments fade. He found he appreciated her sweet sense of humor and her devotion to God and to others. The other night she said that she'd come to respect him as a man of honor and integrity. For the first time since he'd been injured, he'd begun to see a viable future for himself.

He refocused his attention on the situation before him. In the last week, with the immediate danger past, he had sensed the men letting their guards down. He didn't blame them, and now with the return of Major Henning and his men, the current unrest did appear to have eased. Still, he worried about the safety of the women and children, especially Adelina's. He'd keep the guards doubled despite the grumbling.

Disgruntled, he'd tell his officers, was better than dead.

Adelina looked at the group of soldiers squeezed on the benches in the schoolroom. Since Isaac hadn't wanted her to begin classes while the area was under a threat, she'd waited until Major Henning had returned to invite the illiterate soldiers to join her. She could see no reason now that her classes would cause any harm, but she'd speak to Isaac at dinner tomorrow evening. This introductory class would allow her to tell him how many were interested.

She glanced at Chaplain Reynolds. Last week, before the classes began, she asked him if he would be willing to assist her. Besides needing his help, she wanted to ensure no one could accuse her of being unchaperoned with the soldiers.

"Welcome, gentlemen." She smiled at the men. "I applaud your desire to learn." She started the lesson the same way she had with Corporal Taylor, by drawing the different chevrons on the board. Once she had them convinced learning to read was within their ability, it was much easier to introduce the letters. "Like the chevrons, the letters are symbols. You need to know what sound each letter represents. We're going to start with a few letters tonight, and before you leave, you'll be able to read some words."

She introduced the vowels and their sounds. She repeatedly mixed them up until they could say the sounds that went with each letter. Then she added a few consonants. Before long, they were able to sound out words like pin, pan, pat, pot, cat, cot, and can.

Their eyes lit up as they began to catch on, many for the first time. A soldier in the first row raised his hand. "So, is *t-a-n*, tan?"

"Absolutely, and *n-a-p* is nap." She wrote a list of words on the board using only the letters she'd introduced. Since the soldiers seemed to catch on so well, she added another column with additional consonants.

"That's all there is to it?" one soldier asked.

"There's more because the English language has some very odd rules, but you've all made an excellent start." She held up strips of paper, one for each of them, where she'd carefully written the letters they'd studied today. "Take these with you. Keep working on learning the sounds of each letter. If you forget a sound, ask one of your friends from this group or Corporal Taylor to help you. Next time, when we meet again on Friday, we'll add more letters."

Each man thanked her as they left, and she wanted to shout for joy. She'd opened a window to a whole new world for these men tonight. It might take awhile, but when the war was over, they could go home with a new skill that might help them get better jobs and provide for their families.

She was indeed blessed, and she'd sleep well tonight.

"I saw it with my own eyes!"

Isaac stared at Mrs. Adams. The woman had marched into his office and demanded he do something about Miss Dante. What she was saying couldn't be true, could it? He'd told Adelina he didn't want the soldiers being distracted by classes. Could she have gone against his wishes?

Mrs. Adams propped her fists on her hips. "Last night one of my girls forgot her shawl, so I went back to fetch it, and Miss Dante had a whole room full of men. It's entirely improper. What kind of example is that?"

Anger and hurt mixed with a sick feeling in the pit of his stomach. Adelina's example was the least of his concerns right now, but he feared he'd not be able to smooth things over for her this time. Adelina had handed Mrs. Adams all the ammunition she needed.

Mrs. Adams, however, wouldn't be the one to send Adelina away. This time, the job would fall to him. When they'd first met, he'd told Adelina that if she undermined his authority again, he'd immediately send her to Junction City to fend for herself.

That was a lot easier to say before his feelings for Adelina Dante had begun to take root. Now he understood how her passion for teaching drove her, how she was supporting her mother and sister, and how the hair at the nape of her neck curled. Why had she completely ignored his wishes regarding his men?

Never before had Colonel Scott the man and Colonel Scott the officer been so at odds.

"I want her gone," Mrs. Adams huffed. "The sooner the better."

"You'd have to address that with the other officers' wives." Isaac stood. "Perhaps after I speak with Miss Dante."

"It won't change my mind. We have to do what is best for this fort."

He sighed heavily, his throat thick. "I know."

Chapter Fifteen

"Charity, can you please take this note to your father?"

Adelina passed the girl the paper. She didn't know what else to do. Her head pounded and her side ached so fiercely she feared she might pass out. If she could just get back to the Hansons' quarters, she hoped some rest would help.

She hadn't been hungry last night nor this morning, but she'd kept the nausea at bay with sips of ginger tea. If the chills she felt were any indication, she was now running a fever too.

Once the chaplain arrived to take over the class, she'd leave, but not until her students were cared for. Although it was unfortunate, she'd have to cancel this afternoon's second reading class for the soldiers.

When Chaplain Reynolds entered from his office within the chapel, she managed to stand.

The chaplain came to her side. "Miss Dante, you don't look well. Perhaps we should get you to my home."

"No, please, I want to go to the Hansons'." She leaned heavily on the corner of the desk, her teeth clenched. She had to pull herself together. She didn't want to frighten the children. "Scholars, Chaplain Reynolds will be taking my place for the rest of the day. Please do as he says, and I'll be back tomorrow."

The schoolroom door suddenly opened, causing her to startle. She winced and bit her lip.

"Colonel, what a pleasant surprise." She forced a smile. "What can I do for you?"

His jaw was set in anger. "I need to speak with you—now."

She pressed a hand to her side and slowly made her way toward him. She followed him as they stepped outside onto the stoop. She grimaced, the movement sending jolts of pain through her.

His brow furled. "Adelina, what's wrong?"

The chaplain followed behind. "She wasn't feeling well, so she sent for me."

Warmth swept over her body, and her vision grayed. Her knees gave way.

The next thing she recalled was being held in Isaac's arms. "How long has she been like this? She's white as a ghost and feverish."

"I'm not sure. Why don't you take her to my quarters?" the chaplain said. "My Mary can tend to her."

Corporal Taylor raced up to them. "Sir, what's wrong with Miss Dante? I was fetching firewood."

A jab of pain made Adelina moan.

"Corporal, fetch the surgeon. Miss Dante will be at the chaplain's quarters." He pulled her more tightly to his chest and began the walk to the residence.

Each step made her wince in pain.

"Shhh." He pressed his lips to her hair. "It'll be all right."

The chaplain reached the front door before they did and called for his wife. The kind woman directed Isaac to follow her up the stairs to the first bedroom on the right.

Adelina heard Isaac's saber hitting each step with a clink as he climbed the stairs. He seemed so concerned; she wanted to assure him everything would be fine, but she simply couldn't make any words come out of her mouth.

The bedclothes had been turned back, and when he laid her down, the cool pillowcase touched her cheek. She shivered, and he took her hand.

Mary stepped forward. "Go downstairs now and wait for the surgeon, Colonel Scott."

"But—"

"Go." Mary Reynolds nudged him out of the way. "I'm going to make her more comfortable."

Adelina squeezed his hand. "Why were you angry?"

"It doesn't matter." He kissed the tips of her fingers and set her hand on the bed.

Then he was gone, and the pain seemed all the worse.

Isaac paced the Reynolds' parlor. Major Davis, the district's medical director, was known as an excellent doctor, but he'd been upstairs with Adelina for almost half an hour. The chaplain had returned to the schoolroom to dismiss the students. He'd said he felt his prayers were needed more than his teaching skills.

Corporal Taylor sat in the porch's sole chair. He should tell the young man he was dismissed, but he could tell the corporal had no intention of leaving any more than he had. Besides, they might need him to fetch supplies.

Chaplain Reynolds returned at the same time the doctor came into the parlor.

Dr. Davis rubbed the back of his neck. "Miss Dante is a very ill young woman. I believe she has appendicitis. I'll have to operate."

Isaac grabbed the back of a chair, his knees feeling watery. "Surgery? How do you want to move her to the hospital?"

"I don't." The doctor rolled up his sleeves. "We'll do the appendectomy on the dining table. Can you send the corporal for one of the hospital stewards and my surgical instruments?"

Isaac gulped. "Will she be all right?"

He laid his hand on Isaac's shoulder. "God is in control of that."

Chapter Sixteen

The parlor curtains had been drawn, and both the chaplain and Isaac had been sent to the front porch to await the outcome of the surgery. Corporal Taylor had gone to let Mrs. Hanson know what was going on.

Before the surgery, Isaac had been summoned to carry a blanket-wrapped Adelina down to the table while the surgeon washed his hands and the steward prepared the instruments. She'd whimpered in his arms, and it made his heart ache like never before. When he'd laid her on the table, she looked so frail that he'd had to fight the urge to scoop her up and whisk her away.

"Thank you," the surgeon had said. "You can go now."

He'd bent and brushed a kiss on her forehead.

Now on the porch, he leaned over the railing with his hands folded, begging God to save her.

"He hears you." The chaplain squeezed Isaac's shoulder. "And He's with you both. 'The Lord is nigh unto them that are of a broken heart.'" He paused. "Colonel, I know you are concerned about her, but I sense your heart is heavy. You're concerned about more than this surgery."

"I am." He sighed.

"When you came to the school today, you appeared to be upset or angry. May I ask why?"

Isaac straightened and turned to the chaplain. He hooked his thumbs in his belt. "Mrs. Adams had just informed me that Adel—Miss Dante—has been teaching the soldiers how to read."

"Yes, we've only had one class, but she's the most gifted teacher I've ever seen. You should have seen the looks on the faces of those men when they read their first words. I'll never forget it."

"We? You were there?"

"She asked me to help and to make sure she was chaperoned with the men. She didn't want anyone to disparage her reputation."

Isaac drew in a deep breath. "Did she tell you that I didn't want her to hold the classes right now? In fact, I'd told her no when she asked."

"I see." The chaplain sat down in the chair Corporal Taylor had vacated. "No, she didn't mention that, but she did say you didn't want her to hold classes until things calmed down. Do you think she misunderstood you?"

He shook his head. "I made my position clear. My reasoning was I wanted the men focused, so when she saw Major Henning return, she thought my concerns were no longer valid. She did what she wanted and disobeyed my order."

"So, you're in love with a woman who disobeyed your order. Only she isn't a soldier." The chaplain chuckled. "Can't assign her to extra guard duty, can you?"

"This isn't funny. She undermined my authority."

"With whom?" His brow creased. "Those men didn't have any

idea you'd forbidden her to teach them, and the truth is, no one was endangered. What she hurt was your pride."

"What if I'd needed the men?"

"You'd have signaled, and they'd have come to arms." Reynolds ran his hand through his hair. "I imagine she thought the danger had passed and would speak to you later. You've heard the adage 'It's easier to ask for forgiveness than permission.'"

"But how can I build a life with her if I can't trust her to do what I ask?"

The chaplain paused. "Colonel, do you honestly think you're the only military officer who has ever struggled with a relationship? It's hard to leave your saber at the door. You're a man of duty, and duty has always come first in the military world. Now, you're struggling with something else in your life that means just as much and probably even more. You love her. It's all right to admit it." Reynolds leaned forward and rested his elbows on his knees, hands clasped in front of him. "I think God has a great sense of humor, don't you?"

"Why?" Isaac scowled.

"Because He gave you, a man who can control all the men around you, a woman you'll never be able to control. If you're thinking of a future with her, and yes, I believe you should, you need to rethink your approach. You're a cavalry officer. If you had a filly with a rare, free spirit, would you want to break that spirit?"

"No. Bend it, but never break it."

"Exactly. The same is true with Miss Dante. In the same vein, you need to think of marriage like a team of horses. They can only move forward if they pull in the same direction."

"I'm not sure we could ever pull in the same direction." He swallowed hard.

"Only the two of you can make that decision, Colonel."

Silence hung between them for what seemed like forever. Finally, the doctor came out onto the porch. "The surgery is done. She did well, and as long as there's no infection, I think she'll recover. The steward and I carried her upstairs and got her into bed before the chloroform wore off."

"Can I see her?" Isaac asked.

"Tomorrow." He rolled down his sleeves. "Right now, Mrs. Reynolds is with her, and I gave her morphine, so she's sleeping. We were blessed to remove the appendix before it ruptured." The surgeon shook both the chaplain's and Isaac's hands. "God must have heard your prayers. Be sure to thank Him."

Adelina woke with a start. Where was she?

"Ma, she's awake."

Adelina recognized the young lady's voice but couldn't place it. She hurt everywhere. It even hurt to move her toes.

Then she remembered. She'd had surgery.

Adelina felt a cool hand on her brow and opened her eyes. "Mrs. Reynolds?"

"Yes, dear. My Faith was sitting with you this morning." She sat down beside her. "You gave us quite a scare, and I don't think Colonel Scott is used to being frightened."

"Is he here?"

"He's been by three times already this morning asking if you're awake yet." She patted Adelina's hand. "Are you in pain?"

Adelina nodded.

Mrs. Reynolds poured something into a cup and gave it to her. "Now, before that takes effect, I'll go see if the colonel has returned. It's probably improper for him to see you in your bedchamber, but I think we can make an exception for him just this once." She smoothed Adelina's hair and pulled the blankets up to her neck.

Adelina thought about the last time she'd seen him. His face had been stormy. Why?

Oh dear. The classes. A sinking feeling joined the pain in her stomach and her eyes filled with tears. He hadn't wanted her to begin the classes. Would he send her away? Is that why he'd been here so many times today?

She heard the clink of a saber hitting each step, and she knew he was racing up the stairs to her room.

He entered, chest heaving, and removed his kepi. He stood at the foot of her bed.

"I'm sorry," she croaked.

"Whatever for?" He hurried to the chair beside the bed.

"I know why you were angry. It was the classes for the soldiers, wasn't it? I didn't think—"

"Seems to be a recurring theme." He smiled and clasped her cool hand in his warm ones. "Shh. We can talk about that later. Yes, I was angry, but I've made a decision already. Adelina, I want to ask you something—"

She tried to stay awake, but it was as if a great sleep leviathan swallowed her and dragged her to its depths. What had Isaac said? What would she have answered?

It wasn't fair. She wanted to have the last word.

Chapter Seventeen

Adelina stared at her packed trunk in the bedroom of the Hansons' quarters, finding it hard to believe her time with Jessie had been so short.

"Ready?" Jessie asked from the doorway.

"As I'll ever be." Adelina pulled on long white gloves, and Jessie assisted her with the buttons. She descended the staircase carefully. After almost three weeks of convalescing, she still wasn't at full strength, but that wouldn't stop today from occurring.

An ambulance wagon was waiting in the yard. The lieutenant lifted first her, and then Jessie, into the open-air conveyance. It was said the ambulance wagon offered a much smoother ride, and she certainly hoped that was true. Before they departed, the lieutenant let down the canvas sides then made sure both ladies were well covered for the journey despite the pleasant October day.

His effort was hardly necessary. The ambulance wagon stopped only a short distance away in front of the smooth-walled limestone chapel.

"I could have walked," Adelina told Jessie.

"But Colonel Scott had the last word on this. He didn't want his bride-to-be fainting on her wedding day." Jessie took Adelina's hand. "You look beautiful. That rose-colored gown is perfect with its ecru lace flounces. I'm glad we haven't had a dance since you arrived, because no one has ever seen it."

"Is anyone here?"

Jessie peeked through the canvas. "A few."

Adelina smoothed her skirt. "Right now, I don't care if Isaac and I are the only ones on the planet."

"I think even Mrs. Adams might show her face." Jessie squeezed Adelina's hand. "Putting her in charge of the Ladies' Literacy League was a stroke of genius. Were you surprised when the colonel and the chaplain suggested it?"

"Yes. I knew the chaplain had spoken to her. He said I'd gone out of my way to make sure I was chaperoned by him when I was with the soldiers. Still, it was Isaac who said until she felt invested in making sure I succeeded, she'd continue to be a thorn in my flesh. Together, they came up with the Ladies' Literacy League."

"I haven't asked, but will you keep teaching?"

Adelina nodded. "Classes will resume in a few weeks. A married teacher is better than no teacher."

"Miss, it's time," the lieutenant said from outside.

He lifted Jessie down, followed by Adelina. She stopped and stared. Her students had formed two columns for her to walk through. Each of the children held a wildflower—purple asters, white clover, black-eyed Susans, and more.

Corporal Taylor stepped up and offered her his arm. "As far as I know, I'm still on duty to escort you, miss."

She smiled at the young man who led her between the rows of children. She took the flower each offered and, by the end, had a lovely bouquet to carry for her wedding day.

The lieutenant opened the door, and the children scurried to sit with their parents. Jessie began her walk down the aisle as matron of honor.

Adelina looked around and gasped. The chapel was full. Everyone from Mrs. Adams to the men she'd taught had crammed into the pews.

But in the front, looking roguishly handsome in dark hair and dress uniform, stood the man who'd captured her heart. Their gazes connected, and it seemed as if everything else fell away.

This was a man of honor, integrity, and discipline, but he was also a man of compassion, devotion, and faith. And he loved her.

She wanted to hike up her skirts and run to him, but she forced her steps to remain steady. When she reached the front, she took the hand of the man with whom she'd face the future, whatever it brought.

Chaplain Reynolds spoke to the congregation about the love between Ruth and Boaz. He spoke of Ruth's bravery and devotion and Boaz's sense of honor and duty. He said their story reminded him of Adelina and Isaac's.

Then, though she may have been wrong, the chaplain seemed to look at Isaac when he recited the words, "Charity 'beareth all things, believeth all things, hopeth all things, endureth all things.'" Had he put extra emphasis on "endureth"?

Later, when the chaplain directed her to repeat the vows where she promised to "love, honor, and obey," she could have sworn the chaplain winked at her.

"I now pronounce you man and wife." Chaplain Reynolds beamed. "Colonel, you may kiss your bride."

Isaac looked into her eyes, cupped her cheek, and kissed her so sweetly it left her breathless.

"I love you, Mrs. Scott."

"And I love you."

He chuckled, and this time he let her have the last word.

Lorna Seilstad brings history back to life using a generous dash of humor. She is a Carol Award finalist and the author of the Lake Manawa Summers series and the Gregory Sisters series. When she isn't eating chocolate, she's teaches women's Bible classes and is a 4-H leader in her home state of Iowa. She and her husband have three children. Learn more about Lorna at www.lornaseilstad.com.

Winning the Lady's Heart

by Janette Foreman

Chapter One

Fort Garland, Colorado
October 1879

Inviting Miss Annie Moreau to Fort Garland had been a terrible idea.

Captain Jefferson Gray had known it with every word he'd scrawled for Martin O'Neal in the letter the man had sent her. Their correspondence was fairly new—they'd only met once and had only exchanged a handful of letters. Miss Moreau and Private O'Neal had no business getting engaged. Common sense told Jefferson that. But Martin had stubbornly wanted to marry a woman who'd captivated him, so Jefferson had gone along with the plan and written the invitation. Blame it on the bond he shared with the man much closer than a brother.

But it had been a terrible idea. Especially now that poor Martin was dead, and his unsuspecting fiancée would arrive any minute.

Afternoon sunshine pierced through the overcast sky though it wasn't enough to warm the mid-October air in the high desert terrain of Colorado. Jefferson tugged his jacket closer around himself, thankful to have anything when so many people went without, then continued to pace at Fort Garland's front gate.

His steps were surely wearing a strip away in the patchy grass, but he couldn't bring himself to stand still. There hadn't been time to send Miss Moreau another letter to inform her of her intended's untimely death. She was due to arrive soon, and recent tensions with the surrounding Ute tribe made travel unsafe as it was. If Miss Moreau arrived safely, as Jefferson prayed she would, she wouldn't be allowed to leave anytime in the foreseeable future.

Of course, if everything went according to plan, she wouldn't need to leave at all.

Groaning, he removed his hat. Scratched at his hair. This had to be the most insane thing he'd ever done—giving up a dream he'd carried for years so he could settle for a life that left his soul wanting more. With someone he liked on the surface but really didn't know well enough to marry. He'd only met her through her correspondence with Martin, after all, as his friend had needed Jefferson's help reading and writing.

Closing his eyes, he returned his hat to his head. It hurt that his buddy was gone.

As Martin died, Jefferson hadn't even thought twice when he'd promised to keep Miss Moreau safe and provided for, and he intended to do just that.

The sound of horses brought his head up. A coach approached the gate, its driver looking every which way in nervous agitation. Must've been worried about encountering the Ute. Before the guards could reach him, he was already working on turning his horses around.

"Wait!" a female voice called out from inside the coach. The door popped open, and a lively woman bounded down the steps, leather hat box and large valise in hand, before the man could urge his horses away.

A gust of wind grabbed hold of her brimmed hat, so she dropped one bag to smash the hat to her head and watched the wagon skedaddle down the road. It gave Jefferson a moment to take her in. Petite with brown hair, just as she'd written. No taller than five foot two, he'd guess. And her energetic movements showed the zest for life Martin had described.

But when she turned, amusement shining in her coffee-colored eyes, his thoughts scattered. Annie Moreau wasn't exactly as Martin had described. She wasn't just "the prettiest thing this side of the Mississippi." She was the most stunning woman he'd ever seen.

Maybe keeping his promise to Martin and forgoing his own dreams wouldn't be hard after all.

"Well, at least I had my bags with me," she said to the guards. "That could've been disastrous. My whole life is in these."

She moved toward the fort's entrance, and the guards edged together. Jefferson cleared his throat. "It's all right, gentlemen. She's who I've been waiting for."

Blinking, she seemed to notice him for the first time behind the guards. "I beg your pardon?"

Jefferson withdrew his hat and stepped forward. "Miss Moreau?"

"Yes."

"My name is Captain Gray. I'm here to assist you." More than she knew. It would all make sense once he managed to eke out the words. "Follow me, please."

The guardsmen parted, and Miss Moreau stepped through the gate. Wordlessly, she joined Jefferson, and together, they made their way into the encampment.

"This is Fort Garland," he began, thinking introductions were in order. "We're a small but tight-knit group. Or, at least, we were small and tight knit, until recent conflicts with the Ute brought in more companies to join our ranks to offer extra support and protection."

"Do you mean because of last month's attack at the Indian Agency?" she asked.

His chest squeezed at the memory and the responsibility now left to him. "You heard about that, then?"

"Yes. It sounds like it was terrible."

He swallowed. "It was." And she had yet to hear the worst of it. "Miss Moreau—"

"How many companies were called in?"

"Thirteen."

"Oh! How many were there before?"

"Two. I'm one of two captains who command the original companies here. Unfortunately, we're unable to house the influx of men in our barracks, so many of them have had to pitch their tents. You may have seen their encampment just outside the fort when you rode in." She seemed interested in fort life, which was encouraging. He searched for something else cordial to say. Something to delay the hard conversation they needed to have until they were within the privacy of the commandants' quarters. "Let me be the first to welcome you to Fort Garland, Miss Moreau."

"Thank you." Her smile warmed him. "I look forward to knowing this place better."

"I hope you'll come to like it."

"What did you say your name was?"

Her voice was sweet. In fact, so was her entire demeanor. Hope began to bloom in his chest. He'd been nervous about giving up his dream in order to marry a nearly complete stranger, but perhaps she'd make a wonderful wifely companion after all. "Captain Jefferson Gray."

"Oh." She tilted her head. "Jefferson. That's an uncommon name, isn't it?"

"Yes, I suppose so." He couldn't help but grin, delighted at the ease of conversation. "My parents were quite political."

"My grandparents were too. They raised me after my mother passed away. My father was gone often, trapping beaver in the Rockies. My grandfather was a general, and my grandmother always praised the army. She influenced my love for the military too."

He knew her story from Martin's letters. But it was surprisingly charming to hear her tell it. "The military had a strong influence on my family too. I was raised in Mississippi along with my younger sister. My father was an army chaplain for most of his career, and my mother formed a local aid society to sew uniforms for soldiers during the war."

At this, he could've sworn Miss Moreau's friendly smile wavered. "Oh. . .the war?"

"Yes."

"In. . .in Mississippi, then?" She peeked up at him. She still smiled, but it was merely polite. All the zest had fled from her coffee gaze, replaced by something registering as unease.

In turn, hitting him with the truth. He hadn't anticipated this seemingly sweet woman with Northern roots to still harbor resistance toward someone of Southern origin, especially when she was merely toddling around in diapers while the war had been fought. But there it was.

Searching for a change in subject, Jefferson cleared his throat. In the end, it didn't matter what she believed politically. He still had a promise to uphold to Martin. Time to search for common ground.

"We're about to approach the parade ground. Surrounding it are the barracks and other living quarters." He motioned to the long, single-story adobe buildings encircling the parade ground. "And beyond them are more buildings that house other facilities, such as stables, workrooms, the theater, the mess hall, and the laundresses' quarters. We'll be hosting a party soon in the theater as a welcome to the new companies."

Miss Moreau stopped short at the sight of the parade ground, edged with bare cottonwoods, its flagpole rising from the center of the rectangular patch of yellowing grass. Soldiers swarmed it like bees in a hive, working through military drills. There were so many men that they nearly didn't fit on the grass, overcrowded as they were everywhere else in the fort these days.

As if to punctuate the bedlam, a nearby horse backed up suddenly, and Jefferson tugged Miss Moreau out of the way just in time.

"Sorry, Captain Gray." Tom Nan, the fort's farrier, shortened the horse's reins before offering a salute.

Jefferson saluted in return then escorted Miss Moreau along the path outlining the parade ground.

He cleared his throat. "I apologize. You'll have to excuse the chaos, ma'am."

"Well, I'm. . ." She brushed off her skirt and gave him that small, wobbly smile. "I'm sure you're doing your best with what resources you have."

Was she already losing faith in Fort Garland? He knew it wasn't much to offer, that the humble conditions here were nothing she would've been prepared for, given the city life she was used to in Denver. And finding out about Martin's death wasn't going to help. But hopefully he could make everything right once they were in the commandants' quarters and they could be awarded some level of privacy to discuss pressing matters.

"I'm supposed to meet someone," she said as they edged the crowd, "though I assume you know that, since you were expecting me."

Jefferson's heart panged. "Yes, Private O'Neal." A man who had become like a brother. Or what Jefferson assumed brothers to be like. He only had his sister, Caroline.

"Yes!" She reached for his arm but quickly dropped it, as if sensing her breach of propriety. "Do you know where he is? Or how I can find him?" Her cheeks pinked. "I confess, we've been corresponding, and I'm eager to see him. Is he out there right now?" She whirled to face the men drilling on the parade ground and seemed to eagerly search the sea of faces.

The commandants' quarters were only a few yards away now. "I fear I have a confession for you, Miss Moreau."

"What is it?"

He motioned to the building. "Let's talk in here."

Escorting her gently by the arm, he moved inside the long structure, coming upon a meeting room where Fort Garland officers conferred with one another and with those who visited the fort. Both he and his brother-in-law, Captain George McGuigan, had their own offices within their homes as well, but this worked as a common space. Thankfully, it was presently empty.

"Miss Moreau…"Jefferson let go of her and moved into the room. He glanced out a back window and drew the curtains closed, as if he could ensure their privacy even more. Folding his hands behind his back to keep from fidgeting, he finally faced Miss Moreau. "Those letters you've written back and forth with Private Martin—"

"Yes?"

"I've read them."

"You *what*?"

"Er, well—I *wrote* them."

"Excuse me?"

"Um, what I mean to say is. . ." Judging by the woman's raised brows, this explanation wasn't going according to plan. "I aided Martin in penning his letters to you. And in reading your replies."

A myriad of emotions whisked across Miss Moreau's gaze before her thin brows lowered. "You've read my letters to Martin?"

Apparently, he might as well have confiscated her diary and read it aloud to his entire company. "I can assure you it was kept strictly confidential. I was only present because he needed me to be."

"And you so graciously offered your services."

Did he detect a bite to her words? "Actually, ma'am, I never would have volunteered for anyone but Martin. As one of his closest friends, I felt it my duty to help him."

Her brow furrowed. "Why would he possibly need help?"

"Miss Moreau, when a man can't read or write, he needs assistance."

She stood bone straight, shock registering across her face as she blinked. "He can't read or write?"

"That's right, ma'am." He shifted. "And another thing—"

"Why would you help him lie to me about that?" she said barely above a whisper.

Hold up. Jefferson's head jerked back. "Lie to you?"

"Yes, you deceived me." Her stare grew indignant. "How dare you."

"Miss Moreau, everything we wrote was true. There was no deceiving. Martin was very fond of you."

"Well, you pretended as if he can read and write, and—wait. *Was?*" She stepped back, seemingly to let that word sift through her. "He's given up on me, then?" Some fight fell away from her stance. "Well, that's certainly news, isn't it? And after I traveled all the way from Denver to marry him? I was a few days late, as you know, due to a mudslide damaging the train track, but I never would have thought that could change his mind about me." Her eyes suddenly glistened with tears, even though it was obvious she tried to blink them away. "Is that why you met me at the gate instead of Martin—to break the news?"

Jefferson opened his mouth to answer, but she held up her hand.

"No, I beg your pardon, Captain Gray, but I shouldn't be asking all this of you. It's rude." And somehow, Jefferson got the feeling she didn't want to speak to him anymore anyway. "Can't I speak with Martin directly? Even for a moment. This is private information I should be hearing from him alone. Where is he?"

Jefferson cleared his thickening throat. "I would gladly allow you access to Martin, Miss Moreau, but unfortunately, I cannot do that. He was involved in the battle with the Ute—briefly, but long enough to sustain injuries. He didn't want to worry you, but just yesterday . . ." He paused. "Our surgeon did everything he could, but I'm so sorry to say that Martin passed away."

There was no easy way to receive news like that. It slammed into a person, ripped through the heart. And the next bit of information he'd prepared to deliver wouldn't come across any smoother.

For a moment, Miss Moreau didn't say anything. Then air whooshed from her lungs, and she hastened to the nearest chair, her hands shaking. She sat and threaded her fingers in and out of each other on her lap. "He's gone?" She looked at Jefferson but seemed to look past him. "Just like that?"

"I'm very sorry, ma'am. He was a good man."

She looked away, frowning. "What will I do now?"

"If I may. . ." Jefferson grabbed a second chair and placed it beside hers. "I know this is sudden—all of this—but I have a proposition for you. Ma'am, your Martin placed his full confidence in me many times throughout his life, the last being that I would inform you of his passing and ensure that you'd be taken care of when you arrived. I'm trying to do exactly that." He took her hand, careful to caress it like a bird and not clutch it like the edge of a cliff. "I'm an honorable man, Miss Moreau. And if you'll have me, I'll see that your needs are always provided for."

It meant staying at Fort Garland until the army moved him somewhere else. It meant caring for a woman who didn't approve of his family's history. It meant never pursuing the difficult life of a surveyor as he'd dreamed of doing when his enlistment period was up early next year. Uncharted land was no place for a woman.

But for Martin, Jefferson would do anything.

The coffee color of Miss Moreau's eyes seemed to darken in contrast to her paling skin. She dropped her gaze to the hand that still rested in Jefferson's before fumbling for words. "Captain, you seem like you were truly good friends with Martin, and I imagine it was difficult to share the news of his. . .passing. . .with me." She swallowed. "But I'm sure you can understand that I simply cannot accept your offer."

Jefferson blinked. She was turning him down?

"Given our different backgrounds, for example, and the fact that the only thing I know about you is that neither you nor Martin were entirely honest with me throughout this courtship—"

Before he could formulate a rebuttal, the clicking of heels sounded from behind one of the side doors. The door opened, and they both jumped to their feet.

His sister Caroline appeared, her smiling warming. "Good afternoon. I hope I'm not interrupting."

She sent Jefferson a quick look, questioning if the proposal had gone as planned. He shook his head. "No, we were done. Miss Annie Moreau, this is my sister, Caroline. She's married to Fort Garland's other captain, George McGuigan. I arranged for you to stay with them for the duration of your visit, if that pleases you."

"Oh, thank you. That is very kind." She managed a bright enough smile, which he had to admit must have taken courage. "Nice to meet you, Mrs. McGuigan. I very much appreciate your hospitality."

"Of course." Caroline stepped back, ushering her guest through the door. "I'll show you to your room so you can settle in."

"Thank you both. For all your help." Miss Moreau sent Jefferson an apologetic look over her shoulder as she disappeared.

Of course, his sister also shot him an apologetic look—one that said they'd talk about it later. Then she shut the door and left Jefferson alone in the meeting room to somehow come to terms with what had just happened. He'd been rejected. It surprised him, and it stung a bit too. But mostly, he wished for Martin to come back.

Chapter Two

After a whirlwind supper at the McGuigans' table, surrounded by a passel of kids and Captain Gray's sister and her husband, Annie excused herself to retire early. Exhaustion had nearly overtaken her before she nestled into Grandmother's quilt for the night, which she'd carried in her valise during the journey. And in fact, she didn't wake again for twelve hours.

What woke her was the sudden call of a bugle, playing a lively number that had her jumping out of bed, heart pounding. Was it an alarm announcing danger?

She rushed from her room. The children were already gathering in the kitchen, and a couple of the girls giggled at her.

Caroline looked up, and a smile lit her face. "Good morning. Don't mind that reveille call—it's simply waking the soldiers for the day. You're welcome to join us outside in a few minutes when they raise the flag for the day. Did you sleep well?"

Annie couldn't conceal a sheepish smile. "Yes, I did indeed." And it was surprising how much clearer things seemed in the daylight after a full night's rest. She had ridden too long on the train and in that coach from the station to the fort. Each jostle had rattled her nerves all the more. And it hadn't helped that the driver had a penchant for spouting off his fears of driving through such dangerous territory. In the end, she'd tried to keep a cheery disposition, but seeing the rustic conditions of Fort Garland—when she'd been told it was practically a palace—had pushed her over the edge. Why, they didn't even have enough room for all the companies to sleep indoors during the winter.

And Martin. Discovering his lack of honesty and dealing with his demise had completely unraveled her resolve, her patience, her manners, and her dreams. Everything dear Grandmother had wanted for her, all the things she'd wanted for herself, were obliterated when Captain Gray broke the news.

All she wanted was to marry for love, to a man of honor, as Grandmother had done. She'd thought she'd found that in Martin, but apparently she hadn't. And to be someone's obligation, as she would have been for Captain Gray. . . She already knew what that was like—she didn't want to live that way in marriage.

So, after watching the soldiers raise the flag on the flagpole, she retreated to her room and neatly folded her quilt before returning it to her bag. She would be going home to Denver.

Annie wandered out to Caroline's kitchen, the sound of children's chatter leading the way.

"Forgive us," Caroline said. "We've finished our breakfast already and are getting ready to walk to the school." She wrangled her four kids toward the door leading out into the meeting room where Annie had met with Captain Gray yesterday.

"Oh, that's perfectly fine." Annie was accustomed to eating alone these days.

"You'll find grits on the stove," Caroline called over her shoulder. "Thank you."

Annie watched the family go before spooning grits into a bowl and taking a seat at the table. Once she'd finished, she would locate the post headquarters and make arrangements for a coach to pick her up and—

And what? Take her back to Denver? With Grandmother's death, she had no other connections there. Even if she could find a job, she doubted she could afford a place to live. At least not right away. She had been a member of a small church congregation, but most of the members were Grandmother's age and couldn't be financially responsible for another person in their homes. Not that Annie wanted to take advantage of their hospitality anyway, however short lived.

But surely once she reached Denver there would be something she could do about her situation. Right?

She finished her grits, washed her bowl and spoon, and then headed for the door. Outside, the early morning air chilled her skin. Air puffed from her lungs, and she pulled her shawl closer around herself, probably not much warmer than the threadbare uniforms some of the soldiers around her wore.

The enlisted men bustled by, some with arms full of various supplies, such as split wood or bags of potatoes, while others made a beeline toward one building or another as if on a mission.

Each soldier she passed sent her a nod, an interested look, and a friendly smile. Considering how she'd already found the presence of other women sorely lacking, she didn't know whether to be flattered or uncomfortable with the men's gazes fixed upon her.

She was beginning to wonder about herself too. She had thought she could do anything with Martin by her side; but now that he was gone, she could see what she was made of, and she didn't like what she'd found.

Annie whirled toward the front gate in hopes of asking the guards how to locate headquarters—but her steps faltered, as well as her woolgathering, as she slammed into the solid plane of a soldier's back.

"Whoa!" he said, turning.

"I'm so sorry!" She jumped back and straightened her hat. "I meant no harm. I wasn't watching where I—" Then she looked up into his eyes and recognized the deep blue pools staring back. "Captain Gray!"

"Miss Moreau." The captain, his dark hair hidden beneath his hat, offered her a small but polite smile—which only served to make her want to sink into the earth for all eternity. "Where are you headed so early in the morning?"

She rubbed a spot on her arm. "I'm on my way to call for a coach."

"A coach?"

"Yes, I. . .thought I'd go home to Denver. Since Martin is gone."

Concern knit his brow. "If you'll allow me to be so bold, are you sure you'll be all right in Denver?"

She shrugged. "Of course."

"Because you told Martin in your second to last letter that your beloved grandmother had passed. I'm sorry about your loss, by the way. And you said that her son, your uncle, had been willed the house and that he didn't like you and wouldn't let you stay."

Annie gritted her jaw. Of course he knew about her situation back home. "It's not just that he doesn't like me. It's that he doesn't accept my kind." Those with a prodigal for a father and a Native woman for a mother. Grandmother had been the only one to accept Annie as she was. Even Grandfather kept a cool distance.

But her words didn't seem to deter the captain. He took a step toward her. "I wouldn't want something terrible to become of you back in Denver."

She shook her head, clenched her hands at her sides. It wasn't fair. Even with the captain, a complete stranger to her, she couldn't shrug off her past, her present hardships, and pretend like they didn't exist. Because he'd violated her trust by reading her letters. Martin had violated that trust too.

Giving him the best look of confidence she had, Annie squared her shoulders and lifted her chin. "I have prospects," she said. "Besides, I don't mean to be disrespectful, but why should it bother you? It shouldn't concern you what becomes of a complete stranger after she leaves the fort."

He frowned. "I made a promise to watch out for you."

"Your promise to Martin?"

"Yes, and I intend to keep it."

"Is that why you proposed to me? Out of pity?" Exactly as she'd feared.

"Yes. I mean no, not out of pity." He closed his eyes as if to regroup.

The instant the words were out of Annie's mouth, she regretted the forcefulness of them. She never spoke in such a manner, especially not to someone she'd only met yesterday. But this man pretended to know her, and it unnerved her. He *didn't* know her. Not really. There was so much more about her that couldn't be confined to the page.

A notion that goaded her guilt. If Jefferson Gray didn't know her well, then Martin hadn't either. And considering she had never even heard of the captain until yesterday, she obviously didn't know a whole lot about Martin either. Not nearly as much as she'd thought.

Shaking her head, she attempted to refocus her thoughts on the day's plans. "Could you simply direct me to the post headquarters, please?"

"Headquarters would be the meeting room where we met

yesterday. As I mentioned, we're a small operation here at Fort Garland."

"Well, can you at least point me in the direction of whoever is in charge?"

"That'd be me, ma'am."

She raised a brow. "I beg your pardon, Captain, but you're a. . . captain. Where are your superior officers?"

"Fort Union, Fort Leavenworth, and Washington, DC. Each farther out of state than the last."

She grappled for another solution. "What about Captain McGuigan? Surely he could help me—"

"Let me save you the effort, Miss Moreau. You won't be able to get back to Denver anytime soon."

"What? Why?"

"Because with recent dangerous activity in the area, no one is leaving the fort unless they absolutely have to. Not until things calm down."

Stuck here? Annie worked to mask her shock. In the process, all she managed to do was bring a wave of tears to her eyes.

Great. Crying in front of an army captain. Ducking her head, she backed up. "I'm sorry. I must still be tired from my trip."

"I can imagine this is a lot to take in."

She peeked up at the captain. Her tears had embarrassed her—had made her absolutely certain she wasn't cut out for military life—and yet, the understanding that she saw in Captain Gray's eyes surprised her. Reminding her that she had indeed been through a great deal of wearisome activity in the past few weeks. Knowing someone saw her situation and didn't begrudge her her tears warmed her heart.

Maybe she could bear to stay at the fort a little longer—until she figured out what to do next.

Chapter Three

A knock sounded on the McGuigans' door. Annie looked up from drying the bowl she'd just washed.

"That must be Jefferson." Caroline left her side and headed for the door.

It was dinnertime, and the children had already been sent to the table—though their giggles were still as exuberant as ever. Annie had planned to tell Caroline she'd be going home as soon as a coach was summoned, but since she'd received Captain Gray's explanation, she'd forgone the announcement and had simply attempted to fall into the daily McGuigan routines. If she was unable to leave the fort, the least she could do was be a helpful guest to those troubled with hosting her.

The children, William, Jack, Minnie, and Sarah, had plenty of energy, but they were also dear little ones, all under the age of seven. And Caroline—she was quickly becoming the sweetest woman Annie had ever met. Warm and responsible, hardworking and gentle,

Caroline McGuigan showcased a beautiful strength that Annie hoped to emulate one day.

"Afternoon," Captain Gray said to his sister, stepping just inside so she could shut the door behind him. "Something smells good."

"Thank you. It's merely potato soup," she answered.

"Well, as much as I'm thankful for Private Benson's cooking, I'm always amazed at what you can accomplish with a simple potato."

"Maybe you should be the fort's cook, dear," Captain McGuigan said with a wink as he entered the room. He gave his brother-in-law a firm handshake before lowering himself into a chair at the dinner table. The man seemed like the kind who was quick to spout off what was on his mind—filtered or not—though Annie had only seen him a handful of times since her arrival yesterday.

Captain Gray met Annie's gaze, and he sent a polite smile. "Miss Moreau."

She nodded in return and replaced her towel on the edge of the sink. "Good afternoon, Captain."

He turned and busied himself with the children, asking them about their studies and what they were currently doing for fun during these chilly days that would soon turn wintry. Annie helped Caroline bring the prepared food to the table—ham-and-potato soup, biscuits, and beans. Then they all sat, Annie between Minnie and Caroline, and bowed their heads to pray for the meal.

As Caroline dished everyone's bowl, Captain McGuigan folded his hands behind his neck and grinned. "Jefferson, you're really missing out."

The captain dipped his spoon into his soup. "What are you talking about?"

"I'm talking about being married, my friend."

Captain Gray nearly choked on his spoonful. He lowered it to the bowl and brought his napkin to his chin. "George, I must say you have a penchant for bringing up the strangest dining topics."

"All I'm saying is if you had a wife like mine, you'd have home-cooked meals like this every day of the week."

"George!"

"Well, I never could have a wife like yours, sir, because there is no one quite like Caroline." Jefferson offered his sister a goofy grin, and she returned it, along with another ladleful of soup, before glaring at her husband. "Besides, what need would I have for a wife when I live next door to the best cook in the States? I can come over anytime I please."

"Maybe we should start charging you an entrance fee."

"George, enough." Caroline shot him a look that advised him to drop the conversation. "There's no reason to bring up marriage during supper."

"Why not?"

She closed her eyes a minute as if refocusing. That seemed to make her husband understand.

He sat up a little, clearing his throat. "I'm sorry, brother. When I mentioned a wife, I wasn't thinking of Liza."

Annie's gaze flicked to Jefferson's. His features grew tight as he shook his head. "No, of course not. Don't worry about it, George. Really."

Silence fell over the table. Annie turned her focus to Caroline, who was exchanging more silent conversation with her husband across the table as she sat down. Annie felt her palms beginning to sweat. She glanced around for topic inspiration and spied a little framed map on the side table between her and the wall. She raised her brows. That certainly looked familiar.

"I didn't realize you had one of Martin's sketches," she said, facing the others.

Caroline's spoon paused on its way to her mouth. "I beg your pardon?"

"That little map rendering there, on the side table. Of the San Luis Valley, I believe. Martin sent me a small version of that same sketch in one of his letters—to show me what Fort Garland's landscape looked like." Annie smiled even as the faces around her grew more perplexed. "I love this piece. I think it's beautiful."

Suddenly, a deep chuckle started in Captain McGuigan's chest. "That map's not by Private O'Neal."

Caroline hushed her husband. "George."

Annie frowned, unease growing in her gut. "Really? It looks just like it."

George was undeterred by his wife's gentle warning, his chuckle growing. "I've actually seen the poor fellow draw, and he couldn't put the tail on the hind end of a horse if he tried. Let alone something nice like that."

Couldn't draw? Narrowing her eyes, Annie pushed back from the table. She stood and took determined steps to reach the map. If Martin hadn't drawn this, then who had? Because it certainly looked like the same sketch. She spotted the name just as Captain McGuigan spoke.

"Must be one more thing the captain did for his buddy."

"George, please," Caroline said again.

"J.G." had been scratched into the bottom corner of the map in pencil. Of course it'd been drawn by him. She should have known.

Ducking her gaze, Annie retreated from the sketch and headed for the door. "I'll be right back. I'm stepping outside for a minute."

Outside in the stillness, she looked to the arid landscape surrounding the fort, and all she could imagine was Captain Gray seeing the same scenery with an artistic eye, capturing it on paper with zest and precision. Talent that should be recognized, not wasted on her in a letter.

Ultimately, she knew it shouldn't bother her that he'd drawn the picture instead of Martin. A picture was a picture, and it didn't make or break a relationship.

But it was something she had thought came from Martin's hand. So in the end, it meant that yet one more thing she thought she'd known about her fiancé had slipped away, causing him to feel even more like a stranger.

The door opened behind her, and she closed her eyes and stifled a groan. Couldn't she live with her humiliation in peace for just a moment? "Look, Caroline, I—"

She turned. And though he had the same color of eyes as his sister, the broad-shouldered man definitely wasn't Caroline.

Annie's cheeks began to burn, and she turned away. Lovely. This trip to Fort Garland had simply become one embarrassment after another. She couldn't bear to meet Captain Gray's stare.

He cleared his throat and moved alongside her. But thankfully, he remained silent for several minutes, allowing Annie's anxious heart rate to slow its rhythm.

Finally, his quiet exhale broke the stillness. "I should have told you I drew the map. In the letter."

Tears prodded the corners of her eyes, so she focused on toeing a spot in the sparse snow that had fallen that afternoon. She'd been so certain of everything before she arrived. Now she didn't know what to believe. "You should have told me a great many things, Captain."

At first, he didn't respond. Snowflakes began falling around them, landing on her shoulders and the widest part of her billowing gown. She was getting cold, and she knew she should go inside, but to face everyone just now—

"Martin was a proud man." Captain Gray's voice was quiet yet unwavering. "He didn't want you to know he couldn't read or write until he could tell you in person."

"Seems careless," she muttered before she could stop herself.

"What if I had been someone who was bothered by that sort of thing? My coming to the fort would have hurt both of us. And it would have wasted everyone's time." Oh, the irony. That last part had happened regardless. "Besides that, he should have known I wasn't the kind of person who would look down on him for that. It's not all that uncommon, is it? Many people are illiterate. I wish he'd had faith in me. To care for him no matter his knowledge of the English alphabet."

"To be honest, I'd hoped for that too."

"Oh?"

"I encouraged him to tell you right away." The captain's blue eyes snagged her gaze before she had a chance to avoid them. "But he wouldn't budge on his stance, and I didn't feel right about undermining him and writing you about it anyway. You can try your best to change the current, but unfortunately, you can't bend the Mississippi."

Annie's heart skipped. "Martin used to say that." But when Captain Gray didn't reply, the truth caused her heart to fall another notch. "Oh. *You're* the one who says that, aren't you? You put it in his letters."

His brows lowered, his gaze burrowing into hers as if he really wanted her to understand. "Martin wanted me to dress up his language. Just a little. Not change the meaning of anything, but make it flow smoother. His spoken English wasn't strong either—at least not in the way we Americans understand it. He carried a lot of Ireland over with him, and that made him difficult to understand at times."

"Yes, I remember. I met him once." And she'd figured his structured though simply worded letters were a result of his intense effort to learn the American dialect.

She frowned. Come to think of it, he hadn't spoken much when they'd met. Instead, he had let her talk, had let her pour out her heart about her dreams and passions. She'd taken him for a good listener.

Had he only been hiding his accent?

"In any case"—the captain broke into her thoughts—"Martin didn't want his speech to influence you when you were just starting a correspondence."

A scoff escaped her lips. "That doesn't make it right," she muttered under her breath.

"Beg your pardon?"

"I've simply heard about all I can handle, Captain Gray." Pulling herself up to her full height, which still only reached his shoulders, she raised her chin. "You may feel honorable in the ways you kept your friend's wishes, but they've made me feel quite foolish."

His head jerked back. "Foolish?"

"Yes. It's incredibly apparent that I knew nothing about this man I was so close to marrying."

She shivered as a gust of wind drove snowflakes onto her face and neck. Ducking her chin, she turned for the door.

"On the contrary, Miss Moreau," he said, "you knew quite a bit about Martin. He may have shielded certain parts of his life, but everyone does that at first, when they want to impress a pretty woman. I admit, it was a hasty engagement, sooner than you both probably would have liked, but your circumstances required it. And you should never doubt that he cared for you very much."

Though some of his words pricked her conscience, she still couldn't keep the weighted truth from her heart. Martin O'Neal had been a stranger in so many ways. It was too easy to suspect there had been other lies as well. Lies the captain had helped him tell. "I wish I could believe that, Captain. Please excuse me. I'll be retiring for the night."

Giving him a little nod, she fought to keep her tears at bay before entering the commandants' quarters alone.

Chapter Four

"Thank you for allowing me to wear your gown." Annie smoothed her gloved hands over the yards of pink fabric that billowed from her cinched waist. "I most certainly didn't bring anything like this in my valise. I would have been hopelessly underdressed."

Caroline laughed. "It's nothing. I'm just thankful I have one to share." Seemingly without realizing it, she placed a hand on her abdomen with a glow in her eyes that could only mean one thing.

The sweet woman had disclosed the secret to Annie just that afternoon. When she'd offered her gown to Annie to wear to tonight's party, Annie had been quick to reject the offer. After all, it wasn't right to borrow an officer's wife's only gown simply because Annie didn't have one of her own. She simply couldn't. But when Caroline finally revealed that she was in the family way and that she'd already sewn a new dress for the event since the pink gown was impossible to let out, Annie had run out of reasons to refuse.

And truthfully, she did want to look her best tonight.

After talking with Captain Gray last night, she had retired early and had stared at the ceiling for hours under Grandmother's quilt. The thought that kept crossing her mind was how she would possibly survive once she returned home.

She was left with very slim options. She could possibly make a living sewing, but she'd never find a place to rent. And as Captain Gray had pointed out yesterday, Grandmother's home had been willed to her son Titus when Grandfather had died. Of course, Uncle Titus had allowed Grandmother to continue living there until her death, but he had made it quite clear to Annie that once Grandmother was gone, Annie would need to move out as well.

In all honesty, she really needed to marry someone here. The fort would keep her safe and fed, and there was a small group of women who could be her friends. They would become her family. But first, she needed to find a man whom she could trust. And after learning that men couldn't be so easily trusted, like Martin and Captain Gray, she realized she needed help if she wanted to marry soon.

"Caroline?"

The woman looked up from her post at the vanity mirror, where she tied the ends of a ribbon she'd woven into her knotted hair. "Yes?"

"I—I want to ask you something. Would you introduce me around tonight?"

"Of course! Why, it's not very often we have new people at the fort. I'm sure all the ladies will be so excited to meet you."

Annie's gaze wavered to the wall. "Well, and the soldiers. I'd hoped you could introduce me to some soldiers too."

When her gaze returned to Caroline, the woman paused in her actions and looked at her. Annie's cheeks burned beneath the scrutiny. Then Caroline snapped to life and continued with the ribbon ends. "Of course. I can do that."

"I realize this isn't an ideal situation," Annie added, her voice growing hoarse. "It's a little unorthodox to ask you to help me meet soldiers when I turned down your brother only two days ago. And when I'd just lost my fiancé." She cleared her throat, praying for the right words. "I feel caught. It is important to me to marry someone kind and good, someone I can trust and who truly values me. . .but I don't have much time. I need someone's help to make a swift match so I can get to know him before I absolutely must marry—and you're the only friend I have."

She was thankful when Caroline smiled. "I understand. You don't have to worry about it. I don't know a lot of the enlisted men myself, but I do know a few. I'll do what I can to help you find a husband."

Later, snow's bitter chill nipped at Annie's cheeks as she clasped Minnie's hand and they made their way into the night. With Captain McGuigan and Caroline leading the way, Annie and the children wove through the enlisted men dotting the parade ground, all making their way toward the theater, where the party was to be held.

"I'm so excited," Minnie said, looking up at Annie with rosy apple cheeks and bright blue eyes. Her blond braid bobbed as she walked. "This is my first time getting to come to a party. Usually Mama keeps us home, or we stay with another family's children until the party is over."

Annie squeezed the girl's hand. "It is exciting, isn't it?" For a multitude of reasons.

Music met them at the door of the theater. The crowd pressed together in the small entrance, everyone eager to enjoy a good time after months of hardship. All the benches had been cleared from the floor and stored on top of the stage to offer more room for dancing and mingling. Annie smiled as someone took their coats.

She moved into the crowd, scanning the men clustered together, with a hopeful lift in her heart. Maybe this was her chance to finally find someone to share her life with. She turned to Caroline to say so but found her missing.

She glanced around, locating her back at the door, tugging off the coats and hats of her little ones, matching pairs of mittens that her children had discarded on the floor.

Well, no matter. Annie could help Caroline get the children settled before starting the introductions. She went back to the entrance.

"Here," she said, reaching her hand out to her friend. "Let me take those clothes so you have your hands free."

"Thank you." Caroline dropped a bundle of winter clothing in Annie's arms. "The coats are being hung along that far wall. Put the children's coats with mine, if you please."

Annie opened her mouth to state her agreement but stopped when Caroline whirled away to snag Jack, who'd located the refreshment table. She smoothed the boy's hair where his winter hat had ruffed it up.

It took Annie a few minutes to locate Caroline's coat among the sea of others. But when she did, she went about hanging up the other ones on the nail beneath Caroline's, taking special care to stow the mittens, hats, and scarves inside the children's coat sleeves. All the while, her gaze continued to flit over the crowd. Which men would be interested in meeting her? And of those men, which one would capture her heart?

She desperately prayed someone would.

From the coats, Annie spun toward Caroline, who had hoisted her littlest child into her arms while Minnie tugged on the folds of her gown. It appeared as if the eldest two had found a corner with someone else's children and were already busy with a game of jacks.

Caroline motioned with her head to a trio of women congregated near one wall, seeming to indicate that the two of them should meet up there, so Annie obliged.

"Ladies," Caroline greeted the others. "This is Miss Annie

Moreau. She's a civilian, staying with us for a few weeks."

Each woman nodded her greeting. "Nice to meet you," one said. "I'm Sheryl O'Toole. I'm a laundress here. It's not often we have guests at the fort."

Annie laughed softly. "That's what Caroline said too. Glad to meet all of you."

Mrs. O'Toole stepped closer. "So, Miss Moreau—"

Her words were swallowed up as Caroline's youngest let out a piercing cry. Caroline hurried to soothe the baby, rocking her close.

"I apologize for the outburst. She's teething right now." Caroline murmured something softly to the little one before placing a kiss on her forehead.

"Mama." Minnie tugged Caroline's skirts harder. "I'm hungry."

"Yes, we'll go find you a morsel in just a moment." Caroline placed her hand on the girl's blond head before turning back to the group. "Miss Moreau is looking to meet a gentleman while she's here. Unfortunately, one of our casualties from the incident with the Ute was Annie's intended, and she was already en route to the fort when he passed away."

"Mama—"

"Oh, that's terrible," said one of the women, cuddling a sleeping baby on her shoulder.

A spurt of childhood laughter echoed overtop the crowd, and suddenly one of the McGuigan boys who'd been playing jacks raced around his mother, tailed closely by another boy.

"Give that back!" the second boy yelled.

"Charles!" One of the women reached out to grab him, while Caroline did the same with William.

"What is going on here?" Caroline demanded. "We're in a public place, not a barn or an empty field. This behavior is much too wild."

"He took my ball!" The boy named Charles lunged for it, but his mother held him fast. "Make him give it back!"

As both mothers worked to solve the problem with their sons, Annie's gaze wandered toward a group of soldiers. She hated being distracted from the women and their families. It felt so counter to her personality, to focus so much attention on men when she had the opportunity to develop female friends. But she knew that, until her matrimonial future was secured, she couldn't take the time to get to know the women. And surely time wasn't on her side. No telling when she'd outstay her welcome.

"Annie," Caroline said, snagging her attention. She clasped William's arm as he tried to dart away. "Let me introduce you around."

"Mama, please!" The young girl jumped beside her, a fist full of skirt. "I'm so hungry."

"In a minute, love. I need to discuss appropriate behavior with your brother. Annie, are you ready?"

William writhed as his mother gathered him against her. "It's all right. Maybe another time." Annie offered a knowing smile. "You have your hands full right now."

Caroline nodded. Excusing herself, she carted her son outside.

Annie glanced around for Captain McGuigan, but he was far off, discussing something that seemed of great importance, according to his facial expressions. Something that no doubt kept his rapt attention and didn't allow him to notice the disarray of his own children.

And something that would no doubt distract him from answering any questions about his men that Annie might have.

Hope waning, she turned back to the women.

"I hope it doesn't appear off putting, considering my former fiancé's recent passing, but finding myself a husband really is of immediate importance." She looked from each concerned face to the next. "Can any of you direct me toward a good Christian man who might be of interest?"

To her disappointment, Annie was met with a trio of blank stares.

"I apologize, but I really don't know many of the men," one of the women finally ventured. "I'm pretty new myself."

"My husband doesn't like it if I talk to the other men," the second woman said, her voice low.

"I could point out one or two who are cordial when they come in to have their clothes laundered," Mrs. O'Toole stated with a helpless shrug, "but beyond their shirt sizes, I don't know much about them. I spend all my time washing and drying clothes. I never see the men otherwise."

Annie tried not to let her shoulders sag. "Oh." Just as she'd feared. "Well, I do appreciate your concern anyway." She'd just have to start the hard way by meeting them herself.

Mrs. O'Toole spoke up again. "If you really want to know anything important about the men, then you should really speak with one of the captains. Both are very kind, from what I've seen of them. Maybe they could help you."

"Or one of the other officers of lower rank," the woman with the sleeping baby said.

Unease settled in Annie's stomach, but she mustered a smile. "Thank you for the advice."

Politely excusing herself, she stepped back a few paces before turning to disappear into the crowd. She wasn't about to ask an officer she'd never met for marriage advice any more than she planned to ask Captain Gray. After finding out he'd helped Martin hide secrets from her, she wasn't certain the man could be trusted. Not on the subject of relationships, anyway. Besides, what did he know of marriage?

"Well, if it isn't our little Denver refugee."

Finding herself in a far corner of the theater, Annie turned toward the voice. A tall man with dishwater hair and a gold tooth approached her.

"Hey there, missy," he said. "Just wanted to meet ya."

A little forward, perhaps, but he seemed nice enough at first glance. "Good evening, sir. How did you know I'm from Denver?"

"People talk in a small community. I'm Private Rusty Schmidt, by the way. What's your name?"

"Miss Annie Moreau." She nodded. "It's nice to meet you, Private Schmidt."

"Eh, call me Rusty." He shrugged, taking a step closer. "*Private* is too stuffy." Shrugging again, he leaned a hand on the table behind Annie, pulling his person just a little too close for comfort. "I just use it to impress the ladies, you know?"

"Ah. Yes, well, I see." Annie cleared her throat and glanced away. Was Caroline back yet?

"You have the prettiest eyes. You know that?" Rusty grinned, his tooth gleaming. " 'Course ya do. Every pretty gal knows she's pretty. That's what spoils them. Though you seem nice enough."

Annie narrowed her eyes. "I think I'm going to continue mingling. Have a nice night, sir."

She turned away, but Private Schmidt caught her wrist. That's when she noticed a couple of other intimidating men nearing them.

"Can't be leaving just yet, Miss Moreau," Private Schmidt said. "I've waited two days to meet ya. Ain't very nice of you to leave like that. And just when my friends are getting here too."

One of the other men eyed her gown like he wanted to touch it. "Too bad ol' Martin can't be here. Guess one man's misfortune's another man's luck. Isn't that so, Rusty?"

Her back stiffened. "Private, kindly remove your hand from my wrist."

Challenge filled the soldier's eyes as he chuckled. "Or what?"

"Or you'll answer to me."

At the deep, commanding voice, the men snapped to attention, smiles sliding from their faces. Private Schmidt let go of her, and she scooted away from the table. A sting lingered on her wrist as she hung back near Captain Gray.

"Do I even need to ask what was happening here?"

"No, Captain—"

"That was a rhetorical question, private." Captain Gray sent Schmidt an icy glare to rival the depths of December. "How dare you touch a lady that way. I'm ashamed to call you a member of my company." He stepped close. "How does a couple of nights in the jailhouse sound? Weather's getting awfully cold. Should be a punishment you won't soon forget."

The captain arranged for a lieutenant and a couple of guards to escort the men out of the party without drawing too much attention to themselves. Finally, he turned to her.

"Are you all right?"

She rubbed her wrist, remembering the man's tightened grip around it. "I am now. Thank you."

"You'll have to be careful around those three—though I doubt you'll have to worry once I'm through with them." The captain shook his head, shooting a glare toward the door that spoke of a history of trouble. "If I know those three, I predict it won't be long before they're discharged from the army. Poor excuses for soldiers—and men too."

"Thank you for saving me."

He looked at her for a moment with warm eyes—*really* looked at her, like he hadn't yet before. "What were you doing, talking to the likes of them, anyway?"

"Private Schmidt approached me and started up a conversation. I didn't feel any reason to be alarmed at first. I just wanted to meet the men who make up Fort Garland." Absently, she touched her wrist. "Obviously, I'm off to a smashing start."

Captain Gray turned his gaze to the floor as if in thought. It seemed as if he wanted to say more, but then the warmth he'd displayed faded away to politeness.

"If you want to meet the men of Fort Garland, you'll want to meet the upstanding ones. The ones who'll show you the truly good things we have to offer, of which there are many. Like any community, you'll have your bad apples, but if you focus your attention on those in the crowd here"—he motioned to a group of young men—"those who are less rowdy and aren't fond of their drink, you'll meet some upstanding soldiers." He pointed. "Like Briggs, Van der Berg, or Peyton." He cleared his throat. "But honestly, you should make friends with the womenfolk. The soldiers' wives. They'll be the best company for you to keep."

Yes, they were. But it wouldn't do her much good to make friends with them if she was forced to leave soon. Annie nodded and smiled just the same. "Thank you. I'll consider that."

She certainly had a lot to consider about her future in the coming days.

Chapter Five

It shouldn't be possible for one woman to look that stunning. All it did was turn a solidly built man to pudding and muddle his thoughts to the point of madness.

At the desk in his personal office, Jefferson stared at the comprehensive monthly report he'd built for September and would soon send to his commanding officers. Stared at it but didn't see it. Hardly noticed the fire going in the hearth beside him either, despite the declining temperatures outside.

All he saw was Annie dancing through his mind in her pink gown, her cheeks flushed with color and her dark hair tied up off her neck.

He pushed his fingers through his hair and shook his head. Sure, he'd tried his best to ignore her as she mingled with others at the party. He'd worked hard to listen to the stories his buddies were sharing, but the truth of the matter was that he couldn't focus. Not with Annie Moreau so near and yet also so unattainable.

Not that he wanted to attain her. He'd simply been overwhelmed last night with all that had happened recently—the Ute attack, the new companies of men to organize, his promise to Martin and his grief over losing him. Annie had arrived at the party looking amazing and enjoying herself, and it'd caught him off guard. Grabbed his easily distracted mind and wouldn't let go.

Surely that was the only reason for watching her all night. Or, at least, that's what he needed to tell himself. Because she had firmly set up boundaries between them the moment he'd proposed. She didn't trust him, and he couldn't spend his life in agony wondering if she ever would.

He turned his gaze back to his report, noting the long section detailing the fort's involvement in combating the massacre at the Indian Agency and then the battle with the Ute that followed. Such a shame to see so many lives lost. Only a few were from Fort Garland, Martin being one of them—and he wasn't even meant to be in the battle—since he'd only been acting as a messenger for the fort.

Jefferson exhaled. Thinking of Martin made him think of his promise. How would he ensure that Annie was taken care of if she wouldn't marry him? Especially if she left the fort or he won an appointment with the Department of the Interior to interview as one of their surveyors for their new Geological Survey, a program intended to finally map out all the US uncharted locations west of the one hundredth meridian. He was just waiting for a reply before requesting leave from his superiors—and telling his family about his plans.

He would have to devise another way to help her.

Just then, the sound of a knock at his door snagged his attention.

Leaving his desk, he crossed the floor and opened the door, finding Annie lingering there, her hands gripped in front of her. The uncertain look in her eyes made his muscles rigid. "Miss Moreau?

Are you all right?"

"Yes, yes. I'm all right." Her gaze flitted away for a millisecond then returned to him. She smiled, though he thought it wavered, raising his suspicions that something was indeed wrong.

"Come. Have a seat." Leaving his door ajar, Jefferson offered the chair across from his desk and she took it.

She looked around the office. Today her hair had returned to its normal braid coiled at the base of her neck, and the fetching pink gown had been replaced by brown gingham. Everything had returned to its everyday appearance, and yet Annie looked just as beautiful as she had last night.

He shook the thought from his head. "You're certain you're all right?"

"Yes, quite. I—" Fumbling for words, she lowered her gaze to the nailbed she cleaned. "I have a question for you. A rather embarrassing one."

If the possibility of danger hadn't perked his ears, this notion certainly did. An embarrassing notion? What could she possibly mean by that?

She took her sweet time in continuing. "I have decided that my prospects back home are too bleak. I'd like to stay here and find another soldier to marry."

Her words, though said in her sweet, polite way, singed inside his chest like the red-hot end of a fire poker. He ran his finger along the edge of his desk, rubbing away a line of dust. "I see."

Annie's eyes shuddered closed and she stood. "I'm sorry. I don't have the right to be asking this of you. Please, forget I said anything."

She made a beeline for the door, but Jefferson's curiosity got the better of him before she reached it. "What do you mean? Asking what of me?"

Her footsteps slowed, and she swiveled toward him. It looked almost painful for her to be asking whatever it was.

"I—I want to marry a good man. Quickly. But as you know from the party, I might have difficulty deciphering who that would be in a short amount of time."

At the mention of his men's behavior last night, Jefferson's blood started boiling again. Just the thought of them circling her, pressuring her. What they'd planned to do with her if they hadn't been caught, only Jefferson's imagination could guess, and it made him shiver.

She made a small gesture toward the door. "I asked Caroline if she'd help me find someone, but she doesn't know many of the men, and besides that, she's so busy with her children and of course hasn't been feeling well lately—"

Jefferson frowned. "Why hasn't she been feeling well lately?"

Annie swallowed. "I only mean that she's willing to help me find someone, but hasn't truly been able." She took a step toward him, her petite shoulders squaring. "So, as I mentioned, I have no right to ask this of you, considering I already proved on my first day what a monster I can be." Her faced reddened, but to her credit she didn't look away. "But I can't return home. I don't know what would happen to me. Instead, if you could recommend someone I could marry, that would help me tremendously."

Jefferson glanced away to hide the dismay that undoubtedly crossed his unchecked features. She was right—that certainly was an embarrassing thing to ask of a man whose proposal she'd rejected only days ago. Either that, or entirely too audacious. How could he possibly recommend someone else for her to marry?

"I'm surprised you'd trust me for that kind of help," he said offhandedly but regretted it when she winced.

"I realize you're the last person who would want to help me," she ventured. "And believe me, I wouldn't dream of drawing you into this process if I thought there was someone else who could help. But you've seen my heart on the page. You know who would suit me better than anyone. And even more, you know everyone here. You've seen many of them in all types of situations. You know who is good, who is honorable, who is quick to listen and slow to act. You know who loves God and who doesn't." She paused as if to collect her thoughts. "I need that guidance. I now see from last night that it isn't safe for me to roam the fort unattended and unattached for much longer."

Guilt prodded him as he fisted his hand and released it. Annie was right on all counts. He did know her better than anyone else here—maybe anyone else left in her life—and was uniquely able to match her with an honorable man worth her time. But *should* he help her in that way? What if it only served to make him bitter?

Then again, perhaps it was an answer to prayer.

His gaze rose to meet hers. If she was happily married to someone who suited her well, then she'd be safe and taken care of. It would mean Jefferson had fulfilled his promise to Martin and had honored Annie's wishes at the same time. And maybe then the bruise stubbornly covering his heart could fade away.

"All right," he said with a sigh. "I'll help you."

A cautious grin broke across her face, and she clasped her hands together. "Are you sure? Oh, thank you, Captain. I appreciate this so much."

"You're welcome." He returned her smile, warming at the thought of her being happy for the first time since arriving at Fort Garland. It wouldn't be easy to give her away to someone else, but he could muster the courage to do it. He was a soldier, after all. He'd experienced much harder things than this.

Right?

Chapter Six

"All right, who did you mention to me at the party? The men you thought I should meet?"

It was the next day, and Jefferson sat beside Annie in the commandants' quarters' common meeting room, a sheet of paper and a pencil sprawled on the desk between them. They were beginning their first meeting hashing out the details of Annie's plan to find a husband, and it was already less fun than Jefferson had envisioned. She'd stated immediately that she wanted his help in holding interviews to find a suitable partner. He couldn't think of much else he'd rather *not* do. The good Lord had created him to be an adventurer, not a matchmaker.

But if it would help her be safe and provided for. . .

"Christopher Briggs, Levi Van der Berg, or Carl Peyton."

"Then let's start with them."

Jefferson eyed her as he picked up the pencil. "I thought instead we'd start by making a list of what you're looking for."

She paused a moment then nodded. "That sounds like a good idea. All right, what sort of things do you want to know?" She folded her hands in her lap and waited.

He gestured with his pencil as he grappled for words. "Let's talk about qualities, personalities first. What are you looking for in a husband?"

Annie breathed in and twisted her fingers in her lap. "I suppose I want the usual things. A man who is kind. Compassionate. Loving."

"Certainly." He scribbled the words on the paper. "What else? Anything specific that'll help me pick someone out of the crowd?"

She blinked. "Specific, how? Like, eye color?"

His brows rose. "Do you have specifications on eye color, Miss Moreau?"

"No." Her cheeks reddened. Sitting under his questioning apparently made her nervous. "However, I would like them to be soft eyes. Intent on me, showing me he's a good listener."

Jefferson imagined lining up his men to examine each of their pupils in search of softness. He cleared his throat. "Right then. Good listener." He jotted down the quality.

"Also a relentless nature."

Jefferson looked up from his page. "Relentless? How so? Isn't that a negative thing?"

"I suppose it depends on how you look at it. I see relentless as unwilling to give up. Our Lord is relentless in His pursuit for us, is He not? I want a man who pursues me like that. Who doesn't give up when love becomes difficult."

Nodding, Jefferson wrote down *relentless.* "Makes sense when you explain it that way—except that being relentless could have its downsides too."

"Such as. . . ?"

"Stubbornness. Selfishness. Greed. You name it."

"Well, no one is perfect, Captain. But I imagine you can keep your eye out for someone who struggles in those areas."

"Values. Let's move on to values. What's important to you?"

"Honesty." The word practically sprang from her mouth. And dug into Jefferson's chest.

He eyed her above his poised pencil, and she returned his gaze with fervor. *Relentless* fervor—maintaining the wall that surrounded her heart when it came to him.

He returned to his list. "Honesty."

They worked on a list of values for a few minutes before moving on to family and planning what questions to ask each man.

"I want to know about his relationship with his family," she said. "If he even has family. It's not vital for the marriage to work, but I do hope that my future husband has a good relationship with his parents and siblings. I'd love to join a family again."

He sensed the loss in her voice, so he set his pencil down and looked at her. "You were raised by your grandparents. But you never explained in your letters what happened to your parents."

"My father's still alive, as far as I know. I don't actually know where he is anymore. He lost interest in me when my mother died."

"I'm sorry. Can I ask what happened to your mother?"

"Fell through the ice." Tears suddenly filled her down-turned eyes. "It was winter, and the three of us were out checking traps. My father was complaining because I couldn't keep up. He said I was making their work take three times longer than it should. I was having difficulty carrying my pack—it was loaded down with extra supplies for the winter catch, and I wasn't used to that much weight. My mother offered to take some of my load and put it with the supplies in her own pack." She sniffed and wiped at a runaway tear. "Anyway, we were crossing a river, and my father said Mother was being too soft on me, that I needed to earn my keep. That's when she fell through the ice."

Jefferson frowned. "How old were you when that happened?"

"Ten." She shrugged, seeming to attempt deflecting the hurt. "Then my father couldn't take care of me anymore, so he sent me to live with his parents. Grandmother liked me and tried to care for me, but Grandfather was always distant. I think he saw me as no different than if I were a child begging on the street corner."

His frown deepened. Some honorable soldier this old general was—couldn't even accept his own granddaughter into his life. "Was it because of who your parents were? Did he disapprove of your father's occupation?"

"From what I can gather, my father was more reckless than my grandfather would have liked. And he never liked that my mother was Native. Neither of them did." She looked up into Jefferson's eyes then but seemed to look through them. "One time, I told my teacher at school about my mother. My grandmother was furious when she found out." She frowned. "As much as I loved my grandmother for taking me in, being my only family, it bothered me how much she didn't care for my mother. I was told to never share my heritage with anyone."

Jefferson sat a little straighter. "That's terrible."

Annie raised her eyes. "It's just the way my grandparents were. Very proud."

"That doesn't give them the right to take away your pride too. Your sense of identity and belonging. Everyone deserves a chance to be proud of who they are."

She let out a shuddered sigh. "And for that, I deeply apologize for how I treated you on the day we met."

The abrupt change in her words caught him off guard. "Beg your pardon?"

"I said I wouldn't marry you, given that you're Southern. And that's far from the truth. I was so shocked by the situation that I let my staunch breeding talk for me, but I realize now how incredibly closed minded and foolish I sounded. I'm very sorry." Her eyes glistened under lowered brows. "I know what it's like to be disregarded for the world I was born into and not for who I am as a person. Can you ever forgive me?"

"Of course." It wasn't hard to forgive a woman who spoke with such contrition. In fact, the more he got to know her, the more he though it wouldn't be hard to forgive Annie in general. He was glimpsing her true heart, something mere written correspondence could never really reveal. And it was getting harder and harder to deny how special she was—and how much he would miss not having her in his life.

∾

In the central office of the commandants' quarters, Annie wrung her hands in her lap, second-guessing her choices for the thousandth time that afternoon. Meanwhile, Captain Gray looked as relaxed as could be, wiggling his pencil between his fingertips until it appeared to be made of rubber.

She looked away from him and focused on the door leading to the McGuigans' residence, where all her belongings lay. Maybe she didn't need a husband. She could sew, after all. If she went back to the city, she could make a living. She could find housing somewhere. Surely there had to be at least one location in the whole of Denver that would provide her with shelter. Then she could put this whole interview-process nonsense behind her.

But no. It was too late to back out now. She couldn't even feign illness and hide away until tomorrow or the next day. Mr. Van der Berg had told Captain Gray he wasn't interested in a wife, but the next person he asked, Mr. Peyton, was eager and would be arriving at any moment. And besides that, it was only selfishness and fear that inspired her thoughts of returning to Denver, and weakness like that would never serve her well, regardless of what her future held.

Rather, this was a time for strength. For marching into the unknown with courage.

There was a knock, and then the front door opened. A man peeked his head in, and Annie's courage went scampering for cover beneath the captain's desk.

"Ah, Private Peyton." The captain stood, so Annie followed suit. "Please, come in."

Mr. Peyton entered, hat in hand, and tentatively approached the chair across the desk from the captain and Annie. He sent her a shy yet excited smile, and Annie's stomach knotted.

"Thank you for meeting with us." Sitting down, Captain Gray pulled out his pad of paper and crossed his ankle over his knee to act as a firm surface on which to write. "I'm sure my unorthodox request of your presence in this interview came as quite a surprise."

"It—it was a bit surprising. But not unwelcomed." Again, Mr. Peyton sent Annie a smile. "Can't say I haven't noticed you around, miss. Was hopin' I'd get a chance to meet you."

"Well, here's your big chance," the captain answered before Annie could even open her mouth to reply. "Let's start with the basics, shall we? State your full name."

"Carl Peyton, sir."

"Middle name, please?"

"No middle name. Guess Mama didn't see fit to give me one." He shot Annie another grin, his gaze growing steadier and more confident with each pass. If only it were the same for her nerves.

"Where were you born?"

"Peoria, Illinois."

"And did you always want to be a soldier?"

"Sir?"

"A soldier. Did you always want to join the army?"

"Well, I don't rightly know, I guess—"

"It's not a difficult question, private. Did you have long-standing plans to join the military, or did you have other pursuits in mind first?"

Annie cleared her throat. "Captain, with all due respect, you're making me just as nervous as you're likely making Mr. Peyton. Shall we keep the questions more directed toward relationships?"

Captain Gray's gaze met hers and narrowed a bit in disagreement. But to his credit, he pursed his lips and searched his list of questions for something more applicable.

"Have you ever had a lady friend, a fiancée, or been married in the past?"

"No, this would be the first one." He eyed her, and her stomach knotted further. What was wrong with her? This was an interview in which to find a husband, so of course he would be eager to gain her interests. His smile shouldn't unsettle her as if she weren't prepared for a suitor.

Though perhaps she wasn't as ready as she thought.

This was ridiculous. She needed to get her fear under control and stand up for herself. "Captain?"

She spoke up, cutting Captain Gray off midquestion. He frowned, as if she'd interrupted a most important mission. "Yes?"

"I think I'll take it from here and ask the questions. If you don't mind." She was, after all, the one looking to get married, not him.

After holding her hand out to him for a few seconds, she smiled when he finally handed over the notebook full of questions they'd worked through together earlier.

"Thank you." Squaring her shoulders, she gave Mr. Peyton a smile and dropped her gaze to the list.

The handwriting there caught her by surprise. *Martin.* Except, no, it wasn't Martin's script. It was Jefferson Gray's, and it had been the entire time. The handwriting she had come to adore, that she dared say had somehow aided in helping her to fall for Martin in the first place. Which was a pudding-headed notion. Who fell in love because of the way someone crossed their t's and swirled the tails of their y's?

And the way he worded things. Were they Martin's phrasing or Jefferson's? Because she'd fallen for that part of their letters too.

"Miss Moreau?" the captain prompted. "The interview?"

"Yes." She sprang to life, hoping she didn't appear flustered. "Um, here, let's try this question. What do you like to do for fun?"

A brow rose. "Fun, ma'am?"

"Yes, when you're not working, what do you like to do?" She waited, but he seemed to really need to search for an answer. "Reading, for example? Or perhaps whittling?"

"I play poker some nights."

Poker? She knew nothing of the game, since it'd been outlawed in Grandmother's home. It was hardly the answer she'd been expecting, and they couldn't possibly find common ground there. Blinking, she managed to nod, praying she didn't look surprised. "Oh, I see. Well, all right. Um. . ." She skimmed the questions in her hands. "What are your feelings toward our current president's policies?"

A blank stare met her. Mr. Peyton glanced at Captain Gray.

"Our commander-in-chief, President Rutherford B. Hayes," the captain prompted slowly. "What are your thoughts concerning his policies? As a voting citizen, of course, not as a soldier in uniform. You may speak freely."

Mr. Peyton wrinkled his nose. "You mean. . .what do I think of him?"

Captain Gray paused. "Yes," he finally said, slowly, as if he too realized that there was no shot at getting the private to understand the intricacies of the actual question.

"Sure, I like him. As good as the next man, right? Swell chap. Simply swell."

Annie pursed her lips. Grandfather would roll over in his grave if he knew she was interviewing a potential husband who had absolutely zero political interest or knowledge.

But he wasn't here anymore, and she might not get to be choosy. She attempted a tight-lipped smile. "Well, politics aren't everything. Surely there are other things we have in common."

"If nothin' else, Miss Moreau," the man said, sending her another grin, "I hafta say you've got the prettiest eyes I've ever seen. Like looking into a mudhole or somethin'. Don't need much in common if I could just stare at you all the time."

Annie swallowed. "That's, um. . .kind of you to say, Mr. Peyton." She glanced at Captain Gray, who'd suddenly found his cuticles quite riveting.

She stifled a sigh and browsed the list again. There had to be some question on here that would spark some interest between them. Some commonality. *Ah, here.* Maybe this one would do the trick.

"Do you consider yourself to be a Christian, Mr. Peyton?"

He shrugged. "Sure."

Wariness billowed up in her gut. " 'Sure'?"

"I guess so, ma'am." Chuckling, he repositioned in his seat, seeming to think he was doing an excellent job in this interview. "I mean, don't we all consider ourselves Christians?"

"Considering yourself to be one and actually carrying it out are two entirely different things." Captain Gray's dry tone echoed the sentiments deep in Annie's heart—confirming once and for all that this interview wasn't going anywhere productive.

"The captain is correct." Annie placed the notebook on the desk facedown. "I apologize for taking your time, Mr. Peyton, but I don't think we'd be well suited in a marriage."

The grin faded from the private's face. "What?"

"This interview is over, I'm afraid. Thank you for stopping in and offering your time."

"That's it?" Mr. Peyton frowned. "Was it something I said?"

"In a manner of speaking, yes," the captain said. "Simply that the answers you gave weren't the ones Miss Moreau was looking for."

"I can say something else."

The captain chuckled. "That won't be necessary. But the good news is that you got out of morning chores in order to do this interview, so there's that positive note to end on." He stood. "I'll see you to the door, private."

The man didn't look happy about it, but he followed the captain to the door and left without so much as a backward glance or parting word.

After Captain Gray closed the door behind Mr. Peyton, he walked back to his desk, his bootfalls the only sound filling the space between them—and the tangled mess of Annie's mind. Sighing as he took a seat, he reached for the notebook and pulled it back to his lap.

"I'm sorry that didn't work out." He closed the notebook before shutting it and the pencil in a drawer.

Annie pursed her lips in disappointment and dropped her gaze. "Me too."

They only had two prospects so far, and the first one had been an obvious no. She didn't know what would happen with the next interview. All she knew for certain was he might very well be her only chance. What if he were no better than Mr. Peyton?

Chapter Seven

A knock on Jefferson's door brought him to his feet. That would be Annie. They'd agreed to discuss over dinner the questions they had asked Private Peyton and what they could possibly do to have a better chance of finding Annie a decent husband. There was still Private Briggs to consider, but just to be safe, he should think again. Perhaps there was a man in his company he had overlooked. Tonight's conversation could spark inspiration for their search.

The floorboards creaked as he made his way to the door. He glanced in the mirror hanging on the wall and nodded his approval—the slight curls at the ends of his hair tamed somewhat, after he'd washed and groomed. He'd even shaved the short stubble that he'd let gather over the past week. Yes, the whiskers kept him warm in the winter months. But Caroline had always insisted he looked better without a beard, so. . .

Jefferson reached for the doorknob and cringed. What was he doing, washing his hair and shaving his chin? He wasn't Annie

Moreau's potential suitor.

Now feeling a bit sheepish for his polished appearance, he pulled open the door. When he caught sight of Annie standing there, her dark hair pulled up and her hands gripping the handles of a pot of soup, his heartbeat did a little *rat-a-tat* number in his chest. What did this gal think she was doing, getting all gussied up for a simple conversation over soup?

He looked down at his own nice white shirt buttoned to the collar and tucked in at the waist of his pressed pants. He could probably ask the same of himself.

"Come in." He stepped out of the way. "That smells great. Thank you for bringing it."

"It's no problem." She smiled at him as she passed, and he had to force himself to examine the polish on his shoes so his gaze wouldn't linger on her.

Jefferson closed the door and followed her into the kitchen where his small table stood against the wall beneath a window. He'd cracked the window a little because in his nervous haste to prepare for Annie's visit he had let the fire burn too long, overheating the small room. Not to mention his nerves could use a brief shot of frigid temps.

Seeing her today interviewing another man to marry had set him on edge. He'd wanted to throw the private from the room after the first question and insist that Annie marry him instead. It was ludicrous, really. He didn't love her. Couldn't love her. Impossible for him to have known her long enough for that. He'd been in love once before, but this felt different than anything he'd had with Liza.

Different in a way he didn't want to examine, but still.

So how did he explain his jealousy?

She placed the pot on a wooden trivet on the table then pulled off the lid to reveal a steaming batch of stew. His mouth began to water, and he excused himself to grab two bowls from the cabinet. "That looks delicious, Miss Moreau."

"Oh, it was just something I whipped up." She looked around. "I like your home. I should have told you that the other day when I was here, but circumstances had me too nervous to say much."

He cleared his throat to keep his thoughts grounded on the moment at hand and not scampering off to think about how this home could use a woman's touch. "Thank you." He held each bowl up as she ladled the stew. Then he placed them on either side of the table and waited for her to sit before he took a seat too.

"All right, let's review what we know so far." Annie opened her napkin and placed it across her lap.

"Sure."

"Mr. Peyton was a decent enough man—on the surface," she said. "But as we both can see, he isn't what I have in mind."

Closing her eyes, she seemed to wrestle with something before squaring her shoulders and dipping her spoon into her stew. "I'm attempting to stay positive. We have a second interview to prepare for. Mr. Briggs may very well be the perfect one." She smiled, but it wobbled at the edges, and a sense of protection and duty washed over him. Blame it on his occupation.

"I apologize about that. I'd hoped Private Peyton would've been a better match." And he truly meant it. Jefferson wanted nothing more than to give his blessing to a marriage that would make Annie happy and well provided for in all aspects of her life. "Let's look at what we learned from our interview and see how we can improve for the next."

"All right, I have one suggestion." She shifted so her forearms leaned on the table. "I've been thinking about this, and I've decided I should be the one doing all the interviewing."

Jefferson blinked. That was her first concern?

"I believe I'll have a better feel for what questions to ask." She shrugged. "It would feel more personal coming from me."

Narrowing his eyes, he leaned in too. "Then what am I even doing there?"

"You've provided the suitors' names, so you're acting as a mutual party. Plus it's only natural and safer to have a chaperone along."

A chaperone? Jefferson lifted a brow. Nope. He hadn't signed up for that. It was hard enough to have to choose other men for her to interview. But then to act as chaperone to them? She likely meant in places beyond the interview too if this second suitor made it that far—and Jefferson wasn't exactly keen on the idea of following the two of them around like a forlorn puppy with nowhere else to go.

But he kept his mouth shut about that. She didn't need to hear about his inner struggle of watching her be courted by someone else.

"Well, that's fine if you'd like to do the interviewing," he said, "but only under one condition."

"Which is. . . ?"

"I get a say in what questions you ask."

Annie shot him a look. "Captain, I'm perfectly capable of coming up with my own questions."

"I'm sure you're correct, but as an outside observer who is familiar with both parties, I have a distinct advantage. And it's Jefferson, if you don't mind." He'd long grown tired of his title separating them.

"What advantage would that be. . .Jefferson?"

"I can create questions that truly poke at the heart. It's similar to how an outside critic can point out what a painting is missing when the artist is too close to his work to see it on his own."

"You're saying I'm too close to my own flaws and interests that I can't make an informed decision?"

"Well, perhaps, given our short time frame. Or at least your suitor might be too close to his own flaws and interests. And for the record, my military question was a good one."

"Oh, really?"

"Yes."

"It seemed completely out of place to me."

"Trust me, it wasn't. It would have shown you immediately where his ambitions lie. An important aspect in a man, if I do say so myself." He took a spoonful of stew, delighted at the sudden kaleidoscope of flavors cascading over his tongue.

"What do you mean by 'ambitions'?"

"Ambitions in life. Does he have a plan, or is he floating from whim to whim? That sort of thing."

"And where do your ambitions lie, Jefferson Gray, if they are so important to you?"

His brows lowered, as did his spoon. "Miss Moreau, that's really not relevant to this conversation."

"You might as well call me Annie," she said, shrugging. "And you said ambitions are an important aspect in a man, so I'm simply trying to understand why it's so important to you."

"Look, I'm just trying to make sure you find a man who is driven."

She scrunched her nose. "But not too driven."

"Is there such a thing? Partially driven?"

"There is, when you have other responsibilities, like being a father and a husband. It's not just about careers or chasing dreams at that point."

He exhaled. This wasn't heading down the path he wanted, and it was prodding a little closer to home than he cared to admit. "All I'm saying is that I need to oversee the questions."

She shook her head. "I really don't think that's necessary."

"Just let me help you in this, all right?"

"Why does it matter to you so much to tell me what to ask?"

"Because I promised Martin I'd take care of you. And I'm not telling you everything you need to ask. I'm just saying there's information I need to know to set my mind at ease."

Annie was quiet a moment as if she were studying him. As if his motivations for meddling with her life were suddenly becoming clear. "You don't need to have control over every situation," she finally said, her voice barely above a whisper. Firm, yet with a hint of compassion. "I may not have done a great job getting to know Martin, but I'm wiser now. And I don't have the luxury of time to play coquettish games. I'm up against a very real deadline here. I must find a man to marry before I'm asked to leave this fort, which I imagine will be soon, and I'd like some time to get to know him first, even if it's just a few weeks. I understand the consequences, and I'm being very serious and thorough in my search."

He rolled his mug on the edge of its base. Out of his periphery, he spotted her hand as she placed it on the table beside him. For the electricity it sent through his nerves, she might as well have grabbed his hand.

"You can trust me to conduct a solid interview," she whispered. "Your promise to Martin will be upheld." He raised his gaze to meet hers, and a knowing but tender look lay behind her brown eyes. "I need your help in securing a husband, but this is a part of the process that I can—and should—do myself."

Even now, he wanted to resist. He wanted to say that trust was a mutual thing, and that it hurt when he remembered she didn't trust him in return. How were they to work together if she disregarded his help?

But did he honestly think he could do a better job interviewing suitors than the woman who would be doing the marrying?

Or was he just scared that she might actually find someone worthy of her? Someone who wasn't him.

That would be a good thing. Jefferson had to remind himself of that. On an hourly basis, apparently. Because after all, he couldn't have her himself. And he was really beginning to realize how much that disappointed him.

Chapter Eight

If Annie smoothed out the front of her dress one more time, she wouldn't have further need of an iron. Sitting at the common desk with the notebook of questions in hand, she waited for the top of the hour, when Mr. Briggs would appear for his scheduled interview.

Jefferson sat beside her, tapping a pencil on his knee. Besides the muted sound of his writing instrument brushing his trousers, the only noise was the incessant ticking of the clock hanging on the wall above the front door.

Lord, please help me. Closing her eyes, she tamped down her rising worry the best she could with spiritual platitudes. She knew God loved her, but the truth of her situation remained. Mr. Briggs might be just as incompatible with her as Mr. Peyton. Or he might be merely so-so, and then she may be destined for a marriage that was acceptable but not truly thriving. One that gave her shelter and food but not the joy of her husband's rapt attention and interest.

Must she settle for a marriage that would simply *do*—and not hold out for one that made her feel wanted and needed? If Martin had lived, their marriage would have unfortunately been that way. It still bothered her that he hadn't trusted her enough to share his true self, and she knew in her heart that her hurt would have followed them a long time.

And it still hurt that Jefferson had been involved. Pity, since the captain was turning out to be someone she would have longed to know better.

She breathed in then released a long, shaky sigh. "I sure hope this man is good."

The words billowed from her mouth like steam from a kettle— before she could stop them and keep her thoughts to herself. She'd just spent last night at Jefferson's dinner table trying to convince him that she had this interview process handled. And on the outside, she tried her best to look the part of confidence. But the truth was, inside she was a total mess.

"He seems like a decent enough man in the field." Jefferson set his pencil on the desk. "But as we both can see from the previous interview, I don't know everything there is to know about each of my men." He pursed his lips and shot her a guilty look. "It's a wake-up call for me as a captain. I don't know my men as well as I should, as their leader. My thoughts have been too preoccupied elsewhere, and I've let my job suffer for it."

Annie's brows dipped. "Where have your thoughts been?"

He blinked a moment, as if he'd been caught off guard or had realized he'd said too much. He shook his head. "It's not important."

She sensed he wasn't telling her something, and her stomach began to knot. "Were your thoughts on Martin and me?"

He met her gaze, hesitating. "Yes. . .and no." He searched her eyes as if grappling for the right words—or gauging how much he should disclose. "I'm planning to leave the army when my enlistment is up early next year."

Forehead wrinkling upward, Annie knew her surprise was written all over her face, and she couldn't conceal it. "You don't enjoy the army?"

He didn't speak at first. "That's a complicated question." He offered her a sad smile. "I did enjoy it for several years. But I keep thinking there's more for me to do, that this portion of my life has been fulfilled and needs to be put behind me."

"But what else would you do?"

The captain glanced at the door leading to the McGuigans' then leaned closer to her. "I'll tell you of my plans, but please don't mention them to anyone."

"Is there something wrong?"

"No, I just haven't told my sister and brother-in-law yet. And I don't want them to find out from someone other than me. You know, prying ears and all."

Annie's eyes widened. "Do you think there are prying ears?"

He shot another look at Caroline's door. "In a house full of children, it's quite possible."

"Oh." She let out a sigh of relief, which turned to soft laughter. She had imagined a soldier standing at the front door with his ear pressed against it, not one of the McGuigan children in their own home. "I promise I won't say a word. What are your plans?"

"I'm hoping to become a surveyor for the Department of the Interior."

Her brows shot up. "A surveyor? You mean, someone who collects data for city and county maps?"

"Well, yes, there are those. But this job would entail uncharted locations, mainly in the upper Rockies, Utah, and similar locations. The map in my sister's dining room? I'd love to help someone create maps like that with data I collect. I've always enjoyed art. Drawing and such. But my father insisted there was no future in it. No pride in starving while trying to sell my work. Rather, he said a job working for my country would bring me that sense of pride for which I longed." He met her gaze. "Well, surveying is almost the best of both worlds. I get to use my love for art to do a worthwhile job for my country. The Department of the Interior has a new program called the US Geological Survey. It just began this summer, and they're looking for surveyors to collect information about the uncharted areas west of the one hundredth meridian. There is a lot to do, and they need a lot of men."

Memories she wished she could forget barraged her mind. Her father and his furs. The constant arguing and uncertainty her mother had endured. The way her father's career had ruined their family even before Mother had died. His life in the uncharted world had ultimately been too hard on them all.

"That's great," she mustered, but only because it was polite to say so, and because she had no right coming down on his decision when it was fully his to make. Just because she could never endure such an unpredictable, dangerous life didn't mean Jefferson Gray couldn't face it.

But it did mean he'd be leaving Fort Garland—leaving the military for good. And it surprised her how much she would miss him.

His mouth rose in a slow, appreciative smile. "Thank you. I've been thinking of it for a long time."

Unease moved through her. "Were you thinking of becoming a surveyor even before asking me to marry you?" Had he planned to hide that secret from her too, until it was too late for her to back out?

"No. I mean, yes, but I was going to give up that endeavor."

Instead of receding, her unease grew. "You were going to give up being a surveyor for me?"

He didn't answer for a moment—only searched her gaze with

a million thoughts seeming to pass through his mind. "I knew how much being a military wife meant to you."

Of course. From her letters to Martin. He'd known of her excitement to marry a man in uniform, a man with an honorable career. But Jefferson's level of sacrifice—to give up all his plans so she could have the one she'd envisioned—would have only served to cause tension between them eventually. He'd feel bitter toward her for holding him back, just as her father had felt toward her. It would have caused them to quarrel, or worse. She couldn't do that to either of them, nor to any future children they would have.

"Well, I'm. . .I'm happy for you," she said. "I hope you get the life you've always wanted."

Jefferson offered her a quiet smile. But something sad still hung behind it, as if things were left unfinished. The look touched a crevice in her heart that sang of possibility. Of *what if.*

What would it be like to marry Jefferson Gray?

The door handle jiggled, and Annie dragged her stare away from Jefferson. At fifteen minutes until the top of the hour, the creaking hinges announced Private Briggs's punctual arrival.

"Captain Gray?" The man at the door nearly had to duck his head, his frame was so tall.

"Ah, Private Briggs." Jefferson stood to round the desk and meet the man at the door. Annie sat frozen in her chair, unable to think past the news Jefferson had just shared.

Her potential suitor saluted the captain then removed his hat, stepped inside, and turned his gaze upon her. He smiled, his hazel eyes shining under cropped light brown hair, and suddenly Annie saw her future sketched before her as if it had been charted on a map.

Chapter Nine

The sun was setting below the mountains. The colors had been lowered for the day, and a supper of salted ham and potatoes had been eaten, and now there was a snatch of free time before taps signaled lights out.

Pressing his back into the rough bark of a nearby tree, Jefferson watched as Private Briggs walked Annie to the commandants' quarters after a stroll around the fort.

"I had a good time tonight, Miss Moreau," the private said, reaching for Annie's hand. With a vast difference in height, the young fop smiled way down at her—before suddenly dropping his grin and shooting a glance at Jefferson.

With effort, Jefferson dragged his stare away to the field beyond the fort, where the moon lit the tall grasses that poked from the snow and bowed in submission to the breeze.

"I did too, Mr. Briggs."

"Shall I call on you tomorrow?"

"Yes, that would be acceptable."

Jefferson steeled his face against showing the averse reaction he felt to the connection forming at the commandants' quarters' door. Yesterday's interview with Private Christopher Briggs had gone well enough that Annie had allowed him to begin courting her. And just as Jefferson had expected, he had become the couple's chaperone.

Even if trailing Annie and Private Briggs had been a bit on the torturous side, at least he'd known she was safe. And happy. The young man had made her laugh more than once.

A sweet laugh it was too.

Hopefully, Annie was finding what she was looking for.

Just as she'd wished for him.

Yesterday's conversation in his office had swirled around him all day. He'd risked so much by telling her about his plans to become a surveyor, and yet, Annie had simply supported his decision. It made him wish he believed that charting the West was an endeavor that women could endure. Made him entertain the idea of asking her to marry him, to take her with him into his new career.

But thankfully, his sense had won out. Because if Liza hadn't been able to stick it out, then no one could.

He glanced again at Private Briggs, who'd said something that made Annie blush above a shy smile and a fetching blue dress.

A woman like Annie deserved her dreams—and they revolved around becoming a military wife. Something she would find here.

∽◯

Dear Miss Moreau,
You looked so lovely yesterday in your blue dress and white shawl. I couldn't take my eyes off you. I just wanted

you to know that you make every day at Fort Garland bright and I hope you stay.

Sincerely,
Your admirer

The short note had been pushed into the crack of the window in Annie's bedroom. She'd almost missed it, due to her sheer curtains being closed all night. But once the sun rose, she had drawn the curtains to look into the field behind the quarters and had discovered the corner of the note poking between the closed window and the sill.

Annie read through the note a few times. The handwriting was poor but at least legible enough for her to read. And, ultimately, it didn't matter what a man's penmanship looked like, as long as he was a good man.

Something twinged inside her, so she folded the note and placed it in the drawer of her bedside table for safekeeping. The sentiments in the note seemed a bit forward for someone she'd just met. But in truth, Private Briggs had spent quite a bit of time speaking in low tones and glancing at Jefferson yesterday during their walk. Perhaps he'd felt unable to express himself to her with such an imposing spectator behind them.

She recognized reveille on the bugle and made her way outdoors, following Caroline and the children. Captain McGuigan was already on the parade ground near the flagpole, as was Jefferson and several other officers.

Yesterday she'd attempted to find Private Briggs in the mass of soldiers, but even with his height, she hadn't been successful. Today wouldn't be easier. With fifteen companies squeezed onto grounds meant for two, there were simply too many faces to scan—even with each man standing at attention.

"Psst."

Annie frowned. Where had that come from? She turned toward the soldiers nearest her, and a couple of them had their eyes on her. One wiggled his brows. Eyes widening, she hastened to move to a different area of the grounds.

Being a single woman in a fort full of men certainly had its downside.

It was several hours before she finally met up with Private Briggs. During morning chores, she found him chopping wood near the fort's outer perimeter. Lest she get him in trouble for talking during work, she made her time with him quick.

"Good morning, private," she said with a smile, hanging back as he swung his ax.

He looked up and returned the smile. "Good morning, Miss Moreau. Nice to see you." He pulled his log halves off the splitting stump and tossed them into a growing pile.

"I won't keep you, but I just wanted to thank you for the note."

"What note?"

"The one you sent me this morning. It was considerate of you to send me something."

He steadied a new log on the stump before looking at her quizzically. "I beg your pardon, Miss Moreau, but I didn't send you anything."

She frowned. "You didn't?"

"No, I—"

"Annie, there you are." Caroline appeared around the side of a building, her smile quickly fading when she noticed Private Briggs. "Oh, good morning. Sorry, I didn't see you there."

"You were looking for me, Caroline?"

"Yes, I'm about to make those flaky biscuits. You know, the ones you asked me not to make without you next time because you wanted to see how they were done."

"Oh, all right, thank you." She glanced at Private Briggs, who nodded a farewell before swinging his ax. "I'll see you later, then," she said, following Caroline back toward the commandants' quarters.

But as she walked, she glanced behind her at the man chopping wood. Had he been merely shy about having written her a note and so he denied it in public? Or had he been telling the truth?

She faced the front again, focusing on Caroline as the woman told her a funny story involving her children. Surely, Private Briggs had just been embarrassed by his forward behavior. Otherwise, someone else had sent her that note, and she had no idea who would do such a thing.

"I love a good turkey dinner." Private Briggs held his arm against his torso, nestling her hand close as she grasped his forearm. Evening light accented his features as he smiled, guiding her around the walkway surrounding the parade ground. "Of course, I haven't had something like that since I joined the army."

Annie noted the flecks of green and amber in his eyes. "Food is fairly limited out here, isn't it?"

"It's not so bad, depending on the time of year. We have local suppliers as well as a few out of state, and we see a lot of beef, bacon, and ham, as well as rice, beans, and dried vegetables. That sort of thing. What is your favorite? If you could have anything to eat right now, what would it be?"

Memories swirled around her at the question. It'd been two weeks since Private Briggs's successful interview, and even though they'd spent every evening walking the fort grounds and getting to know each other, there were still new things to discuss. And many of them brought up memories she hadn't thought of in a long time.

"There was a dessert my grandmother used to make. Apple pie with dolloped whipped cream." Her insides warmed at the thought of the dessert coming out of the oven and being placed directly onto the table for after the evening meal. "My grandmother has passed, and I'd give anything to taste her pie again."

Private Briggs patted her hand. "That's a wonderful memory. What other fond recollections do you have of your grandmother?"

Communicating with this man was a totally different experience than when she'd written Martin over their short courtship. They'd jumped straight into conversing about their aspirations and their dreams. Even now, she had no idea what Martin's favorite food had been, or how he had liked his tea, or if he'd ever seen the ocean. Missing information like that made her question if she had known him at all—which, in turn, made knowing those things about Private Briggs all the more thrilling.

"I remember climbing a tree because I was trying to reach a butterfly. I loved them as a child. But then I fell from a branch and skinned my knee. I thought my grandmother would be furious at me for ripping a hole in my new stockings—she was a tough general's wife, you understand. But when she found me, she took me to the study and held me on her lap in front of the fireplace, humming old hymns to soothe me."

"My mother used to sing hymns to me too," Private Briggs said. "It's a special legacy to pass down to your children."

Tears suddenly burned the back of Annie's eyes, and she blinked them back before they could show themselves. "I'll never forget how Grandmother showed me mercy that day when what I deserved was justice."

"If I may, you don't give yourself enough credit, Miss Moreau." The private's voice turned low as he repositioned her hand, tucking her in closer to his side. "She saw in you what I'm beginning to see too. You're a well-intentioned, beautiful soul. And a child who tears her stocking deserves love, not punishment."

Annie's cheeks burned, and she bit her grin back from growing. "You're too flattering, Private Briggs."

"I, for one, am grateful for a chance to get to know you."

Annie looked up into his face. The amber in his eyes seemed to deepen above his soft smile and clean-shaven chin. They were nice eyes, a window into a heart that she believed was genuine.

A loud clang of metal made her jump. She whirled to find Jefferson outside the nearest building, the laundresses' workplace, kneeling to retrieve a bucket that had fallen from a stack beside the door.

Private Briggs exhaled. "It'll be nice when we can speak in private," he whispered in her ear. "I'm enjoying getting to know you."

"Me too," she replied. And she was—wasn't she? Although his personality was a tad on the bland side, he wasn't a hard man to get to know. And he listened closely to the things she said. That kind of thing did wonders for a woman's heart.

Warmth enveloped her hand as he moved it into his. "Well, ma'am, I—"

The lonesome sound of taps suddenly burst forth behind them. They turned, finding the bugler on the parade ground, announcing it was dusk—and thus, time to get in the barracks and extinguish the lights.

"I'd better go," Private Briggs whispered. "See you tomorrow, Miss Moreau." He scooted toward his barracks, protocol expecting him to be in his bunk before the brief yet haunting song ended.

Annie watched him go. How had they misjudged the time? Usually, he had plenty of time to say good night before leaving her at the McGuigans' and turning in for the night. She slipped Grandfather's old pocket watch from the pocket of her gown to check the time.

"Hmm." She frowned. The bugler had played a whole seven

minutes earlier than usual.

Then she spotted Jefferson nearby, observing the men caught unawares scampering to their beds. He stood calmly, arms behind his back, as if he'd been expecting the bugle call.

And knowing him, he probably had.

Taking the walkway, she rounded the parade ground. He looked up as she reached him and the final note of taps dissipated into the air.

"Why, Miss Moreau. You're out past curfew."

"I'll thank you not to interfere with my courtship, Captain."

His brows rose. "Excuse me, but I have no idea what you're talking about."

She held up her watch. "You had your bugler play early on purpose, didn't you?"

He shrugged. "The time of dusk changes each day."

"Certainly, but not seven minutes earlier from one night to the next."

"I'm simply commanding an orderly fort," he said. But the smug grin playing on his lips as he rocked back on his heels said otherwise.

She scrutinized him. "Indeed. Well, in either case, I'm asking you to leave my relationship with Private Briggs be."

His grin fell away to produce a more serious stare. "Knowing someone's favorite food isn't going to give you a solid foundation on which to build a marriage."

"We're taking it slow. There's plenty of time to learn everything else."

"No, there's not. Every day you remain unmarried is another day you are vulnerable to the rest of the soldiers."

"Then why are you trying to sabotage my efforts?"

"I'm not."

"The falling bucket? The early bugle call? It's as if you don't want me to get to know Private Briggs."

"I assure you that keeping you from getting to know Private Briggs is the furthest thing from my mind."

She narrowed her eyes, but he didn't squirm or change his story. Perhaps she had read too much into his actions. But maybe not. She bid him a quick good night before heading toward the McGuigans'. What might make him act that way?

"It'll be nice when we can speak in private."

Jefferson stifled a harrumph. Of course a young man with a new lady friend would think such a thing. He probably didn't care so much about *speaking* in private as he did about doing other things. Things that made Jefferson want to punch a hole in a wall and push Private Briggs through it.

"Sounding the bugle a few minutes early, aren't we?"

Jefferson turned, the frown sliding off his face. George sauntered toward him from the direction of the commandants' quarters. The twinkle in his brother-in-law's eyes proved he knew more of what was going on than Jefferson cared to admit even to himself.

So maybe Briggs and Annie were moving along at a steadier pace than he liked. Maybe she seemed happy connecting with the private, and that was bothering Jefferson more than he thought it would. Just because he had to oversee the courtship didn't mean he had to like it.

In truth, kicking over a bucket and sounding the bugle were about all he could do to slow the process at this point. He couldn't reverse what the interview had set in motion between them, and he shouldn't want to anyway. Lord willing, he'd win an interview to be a surveyor and would leave soon for that. And she needed a permanent and reliable place to live. It was best this way.

George reached his side as Jefferson watched Annie disappear indoors. "It's understandable, brother." He clapped Jefferson's shoulder while offering a knowing sigh. "I know I couldn't do it."

"Do what?"

"Watch the gal I fancy fall for some other man. Especially a private."

Jefferson cleared his throat. "Well, feelings have little to do with this arrangement." He started forward. "Come on. We'd better get inside for the night."

"Also, I wanted to give you this." George reached into the breast pocket of his jacket and pulled out an envelope worn with travel. "It was sitting on the desk in the office, so I figured you hadn't seen it yet. Must have been dropped off when no one was around."

Jefferson looked at the envelope, reading *The Department of the Interior* across the sender's line. Coughing a bit to conceal his unease, he tucked the letter away in his pocket to read later. "Thank you. I'm surprised any mail made it here, due to travel being ill advised." From the postmarked date, the letter had taken much longer to reach him than necessary.

Thankfully, his brother-in-law didn't ask about the letter's sender, or anything else for that matter. Jefferson made a quick getaway into his quarters and shut the door behind him. He tore into the envelope before he could lose his nerve and read through the short letter. Then he exhaled and read it a second time.

They had liked what they'd seen in his proposal and his letters of recommendation and wanted him to come to their office in January to interview for a surveying position.

Which wasn't long from now, as it was already the beginning of November.

Surprisingly, excitement at the announcement of an interview didn't come over him nearly as fast or as strong as he'd expected it to. Perhaps it was muffled by the responsibilities he currently shouldered and knew he must take care of first.

His enlistment period ended in January, after a monthlong business trip to Fort Leavenworth, Kansas, would take him away in the middle of December. So, ultimately, he realized he didn't have a lot of time to explain all of this to his family. Nor much time to get Annie married and taken care of.

Suddenly he felt pretty sheepish for kicking over a bucket and calling an early lights-out.

There was a lot to get done over the next several weeks, and Jefferson had a feeling he'd need to muster all the courage he had.

Chapter Ten

"If you'd like, you may call me Christopher."

Private Briggs's tone was feather soft, as if he didn't want their chaperone to overhear. Not that Annie could blame him. They'd been courting for nearly four weeks now, and still the captain stood within earshot of their every conversation.

Even so, after a month, she still wasn't sure she was ready to become so familiar with Private Briggs. Odd, since she'd been ready to call Jefferson by his first name in a matter of days. Why was this situation different? "All right," she replied, matching his volume. "That sounds agreeable." She would make it so.

"May I call you Annie?"

Annie couldn't help but flick her gaze toward Jefferson. Evening light fell across his coat, showing off his broad shoulders and chest. Arms behind his back, he lifted his chin as if he didn't hear, but she knew he had. And somehow, a piece of her heart wanted to know how he felt.

She refocused on Christopher. He'd asked her a question, and she'd better answer swiftly, lest he worry about her conviction.

"I'd like that," she said. She allowed him to kiss her hand before excusing herself to go inside the commandants' quarters. Once the door had closed, she moved to the window and watched Christopher leave. He suddenly paused and turned back, and Annie shifted her view through the curtains, noting Jefferson coming toward the private, saying something with an all-too-serious expression on his face.

A sigh escaped her lips. "Will that man ever learn not to interfere?"

"Oh, I'm sure he only wants the best for you."

Annie jumped and whirled around. "Oh Caroline! I didn't see you there."

"I was on my way to take muffins to the Clarkes." Smiling, Caroline motioned to her covered basket before joining Annie at the window.

"Oh, did they have their baby?"

"Yes, and all are doing well, from what I understand." Caroline peeked out. "So, which interfering man are we spying on?"

"Your brother. I fear he's always offering advice and following Christopher and me at too short a distance—"

"Christopher, is it now?" Caroline wiggled her eyebrows. "Sounds like things are getting serious."

Annie hesitated. "I need to marry someone soon." She nearly touched Caroline's cheek with her own as she looked out. "And Private Briggs is a good man."

"A good man. . ." Caroline didn't hide the concerned frown clouding her features. "Pardon me, but that's not very convincing."

Annie sent her a wry smile. "I know. But he really is a good man, and I think he'd make a devoted husband and father. And I do need to get married here. As I've mentioned before, there's nothing waiting for me back home."

"What about my brother?"

Her heartbeat stumbled, but Annie schooled her features. "What about him?"

"Why don't you reconsider Jefferson's offer?"

Shaking her head, Annie turned away from the window. "I could never ask him—or anyone—to marry me out of duty. I'd rather throw myself on the mercy of my home church congregation and hope for the best."

Caroline turned from the window too. "But why?"

Annie's eyes filled with tears before she could hold them at bay. "I've spent my whole life being a burden to others. First my father, who only stayed in a marriage with my mother because I came along. And then my grandparents after my mother passed away. I thank the Lord that my grandmother did come to care for me, but I fear my grandfather never did." She took in a shaky breath. "So, please excuse me if I refuse to be a burden to my husband as well. At least Christopher came into this courtship willingly."

Crossing her arms, Caroline peered at her through sad eyes. "Duty doesn't equal disinterest. You can feel obligated to do something that also excites you."

"I don't think that's the captain's situation," Annie said, her tone resigned. "Besides, though he's an honorable person, I don't think we would suit."

She was fairly certain Jefferson hadn't told his family yet about leaving the army to become a surveyor, and she was trying not to become the secret's leak. Even if she and Jefferson were a perfect match in every other way, she couldn't follow him into uncharted areas and risk their marriage, not to mention both their lives, in the same way her parents had.

Thankfully, Caroline didn't press for more answers. After a moment, she simply nodded and drew her shawl up farther on her shoulders. "How about you join me in delivering these muffins? I could use the company."

And Annie could use the distraction. Conceding, she tugged her own shawl closer around herself and followed Caroline out into the cold.

⁓

Dear Miss Moreau,

Take this butterfly as a symbol of my love for you. For you, I'd catch all the butterflies in the world, just to see you smile. I wish I could give you an apple pie too. I know they're your favorite.

Your admirer

Though she'd tucked the note—and the folded paper butterfly—into her bedside table's drawer with the last one, its eerie message had been imprinted on Annie's thoughts. They continued to follow her throughout the day, even as she went about helping Caroline bring extra food and blankets to the companies camping just outside the fort's perimeter.

It was nearly time for morning chores, and soldiers moved in and out of tents pitched as their temporary living quarters. Some carried bundles while others huddled near campfires for warmth in the last few snatches of time they would have until hours later. Annie looked at their sparse uniforms, their only real protection from the cold, and frowned. It was barbaric, forcing them to live outdoors during winter without adequate clothing. Thankfully, Jefferson and Captain McGuigan had worked out an arrangement to get everyone an extra blanket; but even then, it felt like too little too late.

"Good morning, gentlemen," Caroline said, handing off the blankets in her arms. "A blanket for you, to show our appreciation for all you do to keep us prepared and ready should danger strike."

"Hey, you're the civilian lady," one said to Annie, peeking around Caroline.

"Ain't you from New York or some uppity place like that?" another asked.

"Denver."

"All right, boys," another said, sharpening the end of a stick with a knife. "No need to pester the women bringing us food and warmth."

"We wasn't pesterin'. Just havin' a little fun with the lady, that's all."

Annie looked at the man who'd stood up for her. He offered her a smile; normally, it would have done her heart good. But after this letter, knowing someone had been watching her with Christopher, she wasn't certain she could trust another man's kindness.

"Thank you, miss." A man's eyes twinkled as she handed him a biscuit, and her skin began to crawl. "You have pretty eyes."

She withdrew her hand and stuck it beneath her shawl. "You're welcome, sir." Then she hastened to catch up with Caroline.

On their way home, Caroline tipped her head to look at Annie. "Are you all right? You're acting strange today. Not yourself."

"I've received a couple of strange notes. I'm unsure what to make of them."

"Who are they from?"

"That's just it. I don't have any idea. They're signed, 'Your admirer.'"

"Could it be Private Briggs?"

"I asked him about the first one, but he denied having written it. I'm beginning to think they're from someone else."

"Have you told Jefferson about this? Should I tell George?"

"No, no. Of course not." Annie shook her head. "I honestly thought the first one was written by Christopher, and that he was too bashful to admit it. But this one doesn't sound like him. It sounds like it was written by someone who listened in on a conversation I had a couple of weeks ago."

"I don't like the sound of that," Caroline said. "I think we'd better tell the captains."

"Please don't." She touched Caroline's sleeve. She'd already lived here off the generosity of others for too long. She didn't need to further add to their burden. "I don't think this person means any harm. I think it's just a shy admirer who'll back away once I'm married to Christopher."

Caroline pursed her lips. "Has he said anything threatening?"

"No. He's only made me a paper butterfly and told me I make his world bright. That sort of thing. A little odd but not scary." Or at least, it shouldn't be.

Mouth firmly drawn in a line, Caroline stared at Annie for a long moment. Finally, she exhaled. "Fine. We'll have it your way and not tell anyone yet. But if he writes you again, we should tell someone. Just in case. You never know when it might be someone looking to cause you harm. Or harm to someone else."

"I understand. I'll let you know if I receive another note." But hopefully that wouldn't happen. The notes had been sent out a few weeks apart. So another shouldn't arrive anytime soon. And, Lord willing, she'd be engaged or married by the time another showed up.

Moonlight cast a shadow over his floor as Jefferson slowly opened the door between his living quarters and the central meeting room. The worn hinges groaned quietly, and Annie looked up from her seat at the common desk. He thought he'd heard someone out here.

He leaned against the doorframe, watching her. She wore her hair in a long braid and a thick wrapper over her simple dress. When she met his eyes, he lifted one corner of a closed-lipped smile. "What are you doing up?" he murmured. "It's nearly midnight."

"I should ask the same of you, Captain."

"I couldn't sleep."

A smile tugged at her mouth then. "Same here." She showed him the Bible in her lap. "Thought I'd do a little reading."

Jefferson chuckled and lifted his arm, previously hidden behind the door. Also in his hand was a Bible, worn and faded. The one he'd sought counsel from for years in the army, his parents having given it to him at the beginning of his journey as a soldier.

"Feel free to join me out here, if you'd like," she said. "I wasn't reading anything specific. More praying than anything."

His mind was too full for him to take a seat. Instead, he had an idea. "Here." He plucked Annie's shawl off the back of her chair and placed it over her shoulders. "Follow me."

He cupped her back between her shoulder blades, and the warmth of her against his hand caused his breath to catch.

They made their way outside, the bitter night air pricking his skin and stealing his breath. Or was it Annie in the winter light that captured the air in his lungs?

Around the side of the building, they leaned against the split rail fence and looked over the field. "Are you warm enough?" he asked.

"Yes, for now," she said through a soft laugh.

His eyes traced the shape of her profile, her plaited hair, and the curve of her neck. All he wanted to do was hold her hands as Briggs had been doing often these days, to experience her looking at him in the same way. What did the private have that he didn't?

But the question wasn't his to ask. Regardless of the answer, life had already dealt its hand. She had her eyes set on another, and

Jefferson shouldn't try to get in the way.

"So, why haven't you told your sister about the interview?"

He cringed. "I need to. If I'm honest, it's because I've lost my courage. I'm afraid of hurting her unnecessarily."

"Why would it hurt her? I'd think keeping it from her would hurt her more."

"You're probably right. But the job could be dangerous, so I didn't want to tell her until after the interview, in case I don't get the job."

She stared at the ground, drawing paths through the snow with her shoe. His heart sank a little. Seemed like she didn't like the danger of the job either. Another reason why they wouldn't suit. Another reason why women accustomed to a certain level of living didn't belong in uncharted territory.

"Before I joined the army I worked for a little land office," he said. "I was engaged to a woman named Liza, and I tried taking her with me on my adventures, surveying the land." He ran a finger over the fence's rough top rail. "But she wasn't ready for that kind of life. It caused her a lot of distress—whether it was following me out to the land, or staying home and waiting for me to return."

Annie scooted a little closer, her forearms resting on the fence, just like his. "What happened?"

"She broke our engagement. Or, rather, I did—after finding her with my boss at the land office." He frowned at the memory. "I suppose she liked the idea of adventure, so long as there actually wasn't any."

Annie turned toward him. "I'm so sorry."

"Thank you." He faced her too, leaning his side against the fence. "I should have known it about her. I didn't acknowledge the signs."

Winter light looked beautiful on Annie, contrasting her dark hair and eyes with the creaminess of her skin. He couldn't help himself. He reached out and brushed a tendril of hair from her cheek.

She shuddered at first when his thumb touched her skin, but as he lingered there, she sank against it and closed her eyes. *Oh Lord, help me.* His arms ached to pull her against him, for his fingers to trace the line of her shoulders, neck, and jaw. But he forced his hand to only cup her cheek—and only that for an instant before dropping his hand to his side.

He cleared his throat and turned back to the fence. "I've decided to go it alone this time. If I get the surveying job, I'll be going by myself. Harder to hurt people if I don't have anyone depending on me."

Annie was quiet a moment. "I don't know the full situation, but knowing what I do of you, I suspect it's not entirely your fault she wasn't satisfied with that life."

But it was probably *somewhat* his fault. He'd spent too much time focused on his dream, letting it overtake his every thought, his every whim, and ultimately, it'd left Liza wanting more from him in their relationship.

Would he do that to Annie too, if she became his wife and followed him into the wilderness?

"Thought I heard someone out here." From the corner of the building, George stared at them, dressed in an undershirt and trousers. "You two better get inside before you get in trouble with the commanding officer." He crossed his arms over his chest.

"Hey, I *am* the commanding officer."

"Then you should know better, shouldn't you?"

If Jefferson wasn't mistaken, he thought he saw a playful spark in his brother-in-law's eyes, hiding behind the authority in his tone. Jefferson would never hear the end of this one. "Yes, sir," he replied. "We'll be right along shortly."

George lifted his chin a bit. "See that you are." He disappeared inside the commandants' quarters, the door closing behind him.

In the sudden stillness, Jefferson met Annie's eyes—and she

giggled, breaking the silence. He chuckled too. "All right, let's go before we get in trouble."

And as they walked inside, he realized he needed to work harder to let go of Annie. There were too many ways he could hurt her if they got together. And if she had any trust in him at all, it would be much too fragile for him to mess up now.

Chapter Eleven

Miss Moreau,

I can't stop thinking about you. Ever since I saw you at the party, I've wanted you for myself. I hope you see how serious I am. The captain could never be for you what I can be. I'll see to it that you never need anyone else but me.

Your admirer

H er fingers trembled as she reread the note in her hands. The captain? Had this person been out after curfew too, watching her with Jefferson? There'd be no reason for someone to be outside at that hour, and especially no reason to be around the commandants' quarters, waiting for her to appear.

What if she'd been alone out there, defenseless?

The idea made her shudder. She shoved the note into the drawer of the bedside table and buried her face in her hands.

Only a day had passed between the last letter and this one, and this one seemed more urgent than the others. Was the man growing desperate? And what would a desperate man do to get what he wanted?

The bugle had already sounded reveille, so she rose and dressed and joined everyone outside. After watching the flag raising, she followed Caroline and the children to the kitchen, where Caroline fed them breakfast before they walked to school. Annie only stayed inside a few minutes to grab the notes from her bedside drawer. Once they were secured in a pocket in her gown, she headed back out into the bitter cold. If Caroline saw Annie for too long this morning, she'd know something was wrong. Annie had never been good at hiding her emotions. But this wasn't news she needed to share with a female friend.

She really should tell Jefferson.

A shiver ran over her, as it wasn't any warmer now than it'd been last night. Why would someone brave these frigid temperatures at midnight to deliver notes if they didn't have to? The thick adobe walls of the sleeping quarters didn't entirely keep out the cold, but it was better than being outside.

Unless the person was accustomed to sleeping outdoors in this kind of temperature.

Soldiers dotted the parade ground, preparing to head to breakfast. She scanned each face, especially watching those she knew were in the companies that had been camping outside these past couple of months. Could her disturbing admirer be one of them?

As she scanned the faces, one met her eyes. She gasped. A man she hadn't seen before, with muscular arms and a thin moustache. Was it him?

But when she looked away, she spotted another soldier watching her out of his periphery as he waited in line with the rest of his men. Clean shaven with a square jaw and a hooked nose.

Where was Jefferson?

After a little searching, she noticed him off to one side of his company. She would have to try to catch him before he joined his men at breakfast.

When the bugler announced the morning meal, all the men headed to the mess hall. Annie had paced so much, her path had packed the snow to ice, but she was thankful to see Jefferson hanging back, saying something to Captain McGuigan. She hastened onto the parade ground.

He turned to leave, so she called out to him. Both officers stopped and looked. When they spotted her, Captain McGuigan patted Jefferson's shoulder and turned his steps toward the mess hall.

Jefferson headed toward her. "Annie? Something the matter?"

His mind always went there first, it seemed. Probably a result of his officer training. And on most days, it would bother her that he constantly wanted to protect, to manage, to shield her. Today she was grateful for it.

"I need to speak with you briefly, if you have a minute," she said, her breath white in the chill.

"Of course. What can I do for you?"

Hesitation crept up on her. What if the secret writer was listening now? What would he do if he knew she'd told someone about his letters?

Jefferson frowned. "Let's talk in my office."

She nodded, relief washing over her. "Yes, certainly."

They trekked through the snow back to the commandants' quarters. "Am I keeping you from your men too long already?" she asked.

"No, George will keep an eye on them. I'd rather make sure you're all right. You look like something has happened."

The McGuigan children burst from the front door in a flurry. When they spotted Annie and Jefferson, they righted themselves and offered polite greetings before walking calmly toward the school-house. Annie suspected Caroline was drying dishes at the sink, and she prayed her friend hadn't noticed Annie walking with Jefferson just now. She didn't trust her friend to keep from eavesdropping.

Once they were inside Jefferson's office and the door was shut, Annie checked each window to ensure it was latched tight and the thin curtains closed.

"Annie, you need to tell me what's happening. Are you in some sort of trouble?"

Jefferson stood stone rigid, as if bracing himself for whatever she would say. She took a breath and started in before her courage waned.

"Someone has been writing me strange letters. And not just strange, but a little forward as well."

Jefferson's frown grew. "What kind of letters?"

"Love letters, of sorts. They're from an admirer, and they appear wedged in my window at night, but I don't know where they're coming from."

"Can I see them?"

"Yes." She pulled them from her pocket, grateful to hand them over and not have to carry them anymore.

Without a word, Jefferson read each one—right there, in the middle of the room. He didn't even make a move to sit down at the desk. He flipped from note to note, reading each multiple times with his brow low and tight.

"When did you start getting these?"

"Last month. The first two were sent weeks apart. But the last one came within a day of the second. And as you can see, it's more threatening than the first ones."

Silence stretched for a long moment. Too long, and her nerves got the better of her. "Do you know who they might be from? I can't imagine. There are so many men that show me interest throughout the week. But whoever he is, I think he's watching me even at night. Like last night, for instance. Otherwise you wouldn't have been mentioned in that note." If this had been any other situation, she may have blushed at the idea of someone thinking she and the captain had developed feelings for one another. But as it was, none of that mattered. "Perhaps he was on guard duty?" she ventured. "They're out all hours of the night. I have no other real suggestions."

"Does Private Briggs know about these?"

She shook her head. "Not really. I asked him if he wrote the first letter, back when it arrived, but he said no. I haven't told him about the other two."

Which surprised her a bit, now that she thought about it. As her potential future husband, shouldn't he have been one of the first people she'd wanted to tell?

"Are those privates from the party still in jail?" she asked.

"No, they were there for a few days. Haven't heard a negative word out of them since, but they could be trying to keep from getting noticed." Jefferson folded the notes. "I'll check with them about this."

"Oh, I don't know if you should." She held up her hands as if to stop him. "If we're wrong about them, I don't want to create enemies—for me or for you."

The captain scoffed. "I'm not afraid of them."

"Well, I am," she said, hands on hips. "What if the admirer does something to me for telling you?"

Jefferson met her stare. Then he set the notes on his desk and approached her, searching her eyes with his in earnest. "As far as it is in my power, I will never let anything happen to you." His hands slid onto her upper arms. "I'll put a guard at your window and give you an escort everywhere you go. I'll comb every square inch of this place until I find that good-for-nothing scoundrel and teach him how treat a lady."

Air parted from her lungs, and she closed her eyes, his words sweet balm over her weary heart. Could it really be that easy?

"Thank you," she whispered, her voice suddenly breaking. She blinked and looked away, surprised at the wave of emotion his promise conjured up within her. "Thank you."

The captain set his jaw, his shoulders firm. He cupped her face and grazed his thumbs over her skin for just an instant before holding her upper arms again. "Trust me, Annie Moreau. As long as I am here, you don't have to be afraid."

Chapter Twelve

We need to talk. The children are in bed, and George is home to watch them, so now's the time."

Nudging her way into his living quarters, Caroline shot Jefferson a look that warned him not to turn her down, that she'd find a way to speak with him in one fashion or another.

Trifling with his sister was usually not a good idea. Jefferson glanced at his wall clock as he shut the door behind her then untucked his shirt as it'd been before she knocked and he'd thought it might be anyone else calling. He should have known only his sister would show up at his quarters at ten o'clock at night, unless there was an emergency.

"All right. State your problem."

In the middle of his office, she faced him, hands on hips. "Why in the world are you helping Annie find a husband?"

He glared at her. "It's been a month. You're just now asking me this?"

"I tried to keep my opinions to myself. I really did. But the way the two of you are dancing around this issue is driving me mad. Positively mad."

"Martin wanted me to keep her safe. Finding her a good husband would do that."

Caroline crossed her arms and stepped closer to him. "Then why not simply marry her yourself?"

He exhaled long and deep. "Remember what happened when I tried that? She's not interested in marrying the likes of me." This wasn't exactly a conversation he wanted to have at the end of a long day—or ever, really. He'd been preoccupied with Annie's concerning letters, mulling over who could have written them. "She's quite interested in Private Briggs, and you know what? That suits me fine."

One of her brows lifted. "Oh, really?"

"Yes. She's found someone else, and you're just going to have to be all right with it."

He turned toward his desk and shuffled the top pages, information about surveying, to the bottom of the stack in case she got close enough to see.

"Did she say why she turned you down?"

"It's because I'm Southern."

A skeptical brow rose. "Because you're Southern?"

"Yes. Her grandfather was a Yankee general in the war."

"I don't believe that's it." Caroline shook her head. "That sounds like a bluff answer to me. As if she gave you the first answer she thought of rather than telling you the real reason why she wouldn't marry you."

"All right, and that real reason would be. . . ?"

Caroline narrowed her eyes, scrutinizing. "What did you tell her when you proposed?"

His frown deepened. "I don't know. That I promised Martin

she'd be taken care of. But that doesn't have anything to do with her rejection."

"Did you tell her you had feelings for her?"

"No, of course not. I hardly knew her."

"You knew her as well as Martin did."

"Well, Martin was a little too spontaneous."

"Regardless, you have feelings for her now, don't you?"

"Where is this coming from, Carrie?" And when would it end? This conversation wasn't heading anywhere he wanted it to go.

"I simply don't understand what you're doing. She's a nice person. God fearing. And you do have feelings for her, right?"

"I wouldn't know, as I haven't allowed myself the luxury of considering it."

"Jeff, I don't believe you."

Shaking his head, he moved to another part of the room, as if pacing could somehow calm his building frustration. "It wouldn't make a difference even if I did. She isn't interested in marrying me. We talked about this already."

"Jefferson, the *real* reason she turned you down isn't because of your roots. It's because no woman wants to be married out of pity."

"Pity?" Confused, he made a face. "Who said anything about pity?"

"You did. When you told her you were marrying her because of your promise to her deceased fiancé."

"That sounds like loyalty to me."

"No. Definitely pity. And obligation."

Jefferson stared at his sister, her arms crossed again, and weighed the words she'd said. There was no way his proposal sounded like pitied obligation rather than the honorable promise that it was. Because he'd never marry someone out of pity. In fact, he probably wouldn't even marry someone out of honor to a good friend, unless he—

Unless he could already imagine a future was possible with the woman he would wed. Otherwise, he would have taken care of her in a monetary way only.

The truth pounded into him. He'd actually planned on marrying her because he'd imagined their life together and liked what he'd seen—the potential for a warm and wonderful marriage. He liked *her*. More than the simple disappointment that he wouldn't see her again when he left. More than the ribbons of jealousy he felt when he watched her with Briggs day after day. His attraction to her ran so much deeper than that—and that was a bone-chilling realization he had no idea how to handle.

His sister's hand landed softly on his shoulder. "Would you just tell me why you won't ask her again?"

Jefferson rubbed his forehead. It was now or never, and he'd put it off long enough. "Because I have plans to leave the army, and she's adamant about marrying someone in it."

Caroline pursed her lips. She had a look of realization, but not the level of surprise he'd anticipated.

"Did you know already?"

"Not exactly, but when the Department of the Interior wrote you, George and I started wondering. It made sense, with your interest in mapping and your disinterest in talking about next year's plans with us."

"I see." He turned and headed for his dining table. "Nothing is set in stone with them yet. I have an interview mid-January for a position as a surveyor in the uncharted parts of the West." He shrugged, wishing he could deflect the guilt he felt—at keeping the secret so long, at having hurt his sister. It certainly hadn't been the honorable thing to do. "So, now you know. I should have told you a long time ago, but I was afraid of getting you worked up if it wasn't even an option."

His dining room chair creaked beneath his weight as he sat. He motioned for her to join him, and she did, sitting across from him where Annie had sat a few weeks ago.

"I'm deeply sorry for not telling you."

She offered him a wry smile and folded her hands on the table. "It's fine. Really. And actually, you aren't the only one keeping secrets around here."

His ears perked. "What do you mean?"

Her cheeks reddened. "I'm going to have another baby. Around May."

Jefferson grabbed her hands. "Really? That's wonderful news. I'm happy for you and George."

"I wanted to find the right time to tell you. And then that time never came, so here we are." Laughing softly, she shrugged. "Poorly communicating things we should have said a long time ago."

At that, his thoughts grew solemn. "Caroline, I can't take Annie with me into the West. After all that happened with Liza, I couldn't do it."

She nodded. "I understand."

"And I don't think she wants to go into dangerous territory anyway, given her conflicted history with her father, a fur trapper." He moved his hands back to his side of the table, absently smoothing a knot in the wood with his fingers. "And there are things I can't give her."

"Like her dream to marry a soldier?"

"Yes, that being a major one."

She tipped her head to one side. "But you can give her other things a woman needs. Things that are much more important than being wed to a soldier. Besides, she may have already turned you down once, but that was within ten minutes of meeting you. Any self-respecting woman would have done the same. Now that she's been here a while and has gotten to know you better, she might have a different answer for you." Her eyes shone. "People's dreams can change, you know."

Jefferson shot her a wry look. "Yes, indeed. But I don't think that's going to work in my case. I really hurt her when she found out how I'd helped Martin write her letters." He frowned. "You can't build a relationship without trust. That's one thing I know for sure." And there wasn't enough he could do in the world to earn that trust from Annie, enough for her to become his wife.

Chapter Thirteen

T his is our first evening alone." Christopher reached for Annie's hand and smiled. "I thought it would never come."

"Alone?" Annie couldn't help but ask the question as she glanced behind them on their walk about the parade ground, Jefferson's second lieutenant she'd never met trailing them at a distance. "I don't think we're alone."

"But it isn't my captain, which makes it feel much more private," he whispered. "Lieutenant Wall isn't my direct superior, and he isn't following us nearly as close."

"True." Which unnerved her a bit. Since she'd told Jefferson about the notes, he'd been on constant duty, looking for the culprit. He'd added new precautions each day this week—the escort to take her places, for example, and the guard outside her window. He'd personally continued his watch over her during her evening walks with Christopher until tonight, when he thought he had a lead on someone and decided to pursue it immediately.

He had brought in the three men who'd bothered her at the party, but after thorough questioning, he said he was fairly certain they weren't involved in the note writing. They'd learned their lesson after swift punishment following the party.

As comforting as it was to have them crossed off the list, there was still an entire fort of men who could be guilty. Notes like these could have been delivered by either a stranger or someone she knew. With thirteen extra companies mixing with the two original to the fort, there was no shortage of suspects.

Annie glanced over her shoulder at the lieutenant again, who strolled with his arms behind his back in a leisurely manner as if he were simply biding his time until taps freed him. "Christopher, I've been receiving some really strange—"

"Notes. Yes, I know." Christopher furrowed his brow. "Captain Gray told me."

"Oh. Well, I don't know what to do about it. I'm at my wit's end." When he didn't answer, she watched his features, unsure how to read them. "Don't they concern you?"

Christopher grimaced as if weighing his thoughts. "They do if they get worse. But I think the captain is overreacting about them right now. They're just notes."

She felt herself pulling away from him slightly. Was he waiting for something bad to happen to her first before taking the notes seriously? "Captain Gray wants to be proactive."

"And that's fine, to an extent. But he's treating everyone like a suspect. Doesn't he trust any of us?"

She looked away. Jefferson did have a habit of trying to command every situation. "Perhaps it's his military training."

"Or perhaps he's sweet on you."

Annie gasped and pulled her arm away. "How dare you suggest he's only pursuing this harasser because he has feelings for me. I would hope it's because I'm a human being who, as such, deserves to have peace of mind."

"No, of course." He waved the thought away. "You're right. I apologize. Something should be done, and I'm at as much a loss as you, unless we can catch him in the act. Have you tried writing him back to tell him you're not interested?"

She blinked. "Honestly, I hadn't thought of it. But I have a feeling he isn't going to give up so easily."

"Why not?"

"Because he's been writing to me for a month, and I've never written him in return. I've continued being courted by you. He has no reason, whoever he is, to believe I'd be interested in his advances. Yet he still writes me."

A twig snapped nearby. Or perhaps it was a crunch of snow. She turned to look over their surroundings, the outbuildings surrounded by snow and the open fields beyond.

"Did you hear that?"

"Hear what?"

Her gaze combed the area, but nothing seemed amiss. "I thought I heard something."

"Well, we're not the only people out and about tonight. Surely you heard one of them. Or perhaps it was the lieutenant." Christopher offered her his arm again, smiling as if the matter were settled. "Come close, and I'm sure everything will be fine."

But would it really?

Thankfully Jefferson was watching out for anyone suspicious. But what was Christopher doing to help? Shouldn't he, as her soon-to-be intended, care more about her well-being than a friend did?

"I was thinking something like popcorn, if we can find some. Or little doves cut from paper." Annie touched the end of her pencil to her lips as she surveyed her list. "Or anything festive like that. What do you think?"

Caroline looked up from the dishes she was washing. "I think that's a great idea for your Christmas party. How many guests do you plan to invite?"

"I'm not sure yet. I thought perhaps the officers and their wives, and Christopher's friends from his platoon." She scribbled a few ideas down from her seat at the dining table, grateful for the feeling of excitement starting to grow in her gut. With the worry over her secret admirer plaguing her these past weeks, it was nice to have something productive to put her mind to.

"It was courteous of you to have the event before Jefferson leaves."

Even though it was a Christmas party, she'd decided to hold it at the beginning of December so that Jefferson could attend before going on his monthlong business trip.

And before he left the army for good.

Annie lifted her chin in order to ignore the sadness. The fort wouldn't be the same without him in command. But there was nothing she could do to change his mind. "I thought it could double as a send-off for him. To wish him well and show him how much he's meant to his company. I'm also hoping it'll encourage Christopher to ask me to marry him, either at the event or just before it, so we can celebrate." Annie's cheeks flushed. "That's terribly presumptuous of me, isn't it?"

Caroline smiled, but it waned a little beneath a resigned gaze. "Well, as you said, you don't have a lot of time to wait. And we both know Private Briggs has taken his sweet time in proposing."

Annie returned her gaze to the paper. "Yes. You're right." It had been nearly six weeks. What was keeping him?

A knock on the door interrupted her thoughts. She rose to

answer it, finding Lieutenant Wall, her escort, standing there, hat in hand. Jefferson had given him orders to stand outside the commandants' quarters several hours out of the day in case she might need assistance.

"Beg your pardon, ma'am, but Private Briggs is here to see you."

Annie frowned. "He is?" She glanced at the wall clock beside the door. "But it's chores time."

"He said it would only take a minute."

"Very well." She grabbed her shawl, bid Caroline goodbye, and then followed the lieutenant outside.

Sure enough, Christopher stood under the awning, fresh snow falling in thick flakes around him.

"Christopher? What is it?" She approached him, thankful when the lieutenant hung back.

"I wanted to talk to you as soon as I could," he said, "and I have a free moment before drill begins." He motioned for her to follow him around to the side of the commandants' quarters, out of earshot and out of the breeze.

Snowflakes fell on his shoulders and turned the top of his hat white. "What is it?" she asked.

"I just can't continue like this, Annie," he said, his brows low in concern. "The way you and I are, doing the same thing every day and not really progressing in our relationship."

"Well, we can switch things around somehow." She searched her thoughts for an idea. "Perhaps one evening the McGuigans would allow you to spend time with me around their fireplace, or—"

"It's more than that," he interrupted. He fisted one hand and rubbed his thumb over his fingers. "I don't think this is going to work between us."

She blinked, his words filtering through her. "What?"

"I don't think—"

"No, of course it will." She touched his forearm. "Why would you say that?"

"Because unlike many of the men here," he said, his voice scratchy, "I'd rather be unmarried my whole life than be with someone who doesn't love me. Or with someone I just can't find deep enough affection for."

Truth faced her in that moment. She did like Christopher, but if it could truly ever be romantic love, she just didn't know. And apparently, the feeling was mutual, and he'd seen through her attempts. She exhaled. "I know exactly how you feel."

Ultimately, that's what she wanted too. To be with someone who shared a romantic love with her. But she couldn't wait for one, and now her only option was gone.

Christopher smiled, slow and sad. "I think if you opened your eyes, you'd realize you can already have that."

Her brows pinched together. "What do you mean?"

"I think you know." He motioned over his shoulder in the direction of the parade ground. There, a bugler readied himself to sound off the drill call, and Jefferson stood beside him, observing those moving about the fort around him.

Her heart fluttered without consent, and she forced herself to turn her attention back to Christopher.

"I've seen you two together," he said, "and I know it's not something we have, you and me."

Her shoulders sank. If only he knew the truth, that she didn't have anything special with Jefferson Gray. Not really. No matter how much her feelings for him grew, she knew in the end that she was merely an obligation for him. And any delicate friendship they'd built would be shattered if they married.

Christopher walked her back to the commandants' quarters then bid her farewell.

As he joined others gathering on the parade ground, and the bugler sounded the call, she allowed her gaze to rest on the captain, pristine in his uniform coat and trousers.

Their dreams stood between them. What kind of a future could that possibly build? Someone would have to give, and knowing Jefferson, he wouldn't allow it to be her.

But how could she live with herself if she knew he'd chosen the military life out of duty to her?

Something brushed against her foot, and when she looked down, she realized it was Whiskers, the McGuigans' cat. He scrounged around from time to time, catching mice in the barn and occasionally wanting to come in out of the cold. She opened the door and let the cat in ahead of her. Knowing where his food and water were kept, he sprinted across the common meeting room and pawed at the McGuigans' door.

"Anxious, aren't we?" Annie said, unable to keep from smiling at the cat on a mission. She let him inside and followed.

"You're back quickly," Caroline said, her hands buried in a dishcloth.

Annie shrugged, hoping to appear nonchalant. "Drill was starting."

"What did he have to say?"

She hesitated. How did she explain this to Caroline when it was so new to herself, when she had no idea what the next step in her plan should be? "Well. . ."

"There's something on Whiskers's neck." Caroline, obviously unaware of Annie's misery, set her towel down and made her way over to the cat. She gathered him up. "It's a piece of red string—and something is tied to it." She gasped. "A note!"

Annie's heart plummeted. "No. Really?"

Caroline pulled off the note and handed it to Annie. "It's

addressed to you," she said, grimacing.

That's what Annie had been afraid of. Had her secret admirer found a creative way to send her another note that bypassed all the surveillance?

Slowly, she unfolded the small slip of paper.

Miss Moreau,

I can't stop thinking about you. You are the sunshine in my life, and I know without a doubt I just can't live without you. If you'd have me, then wear this simple string around your wrist and stand outside the parade ground tomorrow morning during reveille. Then I'll know I can have you for my own.

Please consider me, Miss Moreau. I can even make it easy for you to choose me instead of anyone else. I'd do anything for you.

Your admirer

"What does it say?" Caroline asked.

Exhaling, Annie handed over the note, unable to speak. The admirer was only getting more daring, and now she had no husband prospects to keep her from being vulnerable. Going home still wasn't an option. The walls were closing in on all sides, and she grappled over what to do next.

Chapter Fourteen

"Private Briggs?" Jefferson stuck Annie's latest note into his pocket and strode toward the barracks, where Briggs was going in for the night. "A quick word."

The man left his task and joined Jefferson at the side of the barracks. "Yes, Captain." He stood at attention, and Jefferson waved the formality away.

"At ease. We need to discuss what's happened between you and Miss Moreau."

The private's mouth firmed into a line, but he didn't speak.

"What's going on? She told me you ended your courtship today."

"It wasn't going anywhere, sir. She wasn't truly interested, and honestly, neither was I. It simply never built into anything. I'm sorry that doesn't meet your expectations, sir."

Jefferson sighed and rubbed the bridge of his nose. "Well, she may be in danger. And I was counting on you to keep her safe."

"Permission to speak freely, sir?"

"Permission granted."

"Forgive me, but why is it my duty? I'm a soldier, like every-one else here. I enlisted to serve my country, not marry a damsel in distress."

"Because you're the only unmarried man here that I trust with her hand." Jefferson paced a few steps before coming back. Time was running out. "At least consider it, private. She has no one to go home to, and if she stays here, she needs to get married. I fear that whoever is writing her might become dangerous if word gets out that she doesn't have a suitor anymore." He pulled out the note and shook it a little before stuffing it back into his pocket. "He's written her again. More forcefully this time." And the notion that he hadn't a clue who wrote the notes was killing him.

"You really care about her, don't you, sir?"

He did. More than he would've ever thought possible in the short time he'd known her. But how could he explain that, and the complications that came with his situation, to his subordinate?

Jefferson swallowed, as if it would also bury his emotions. "Just keep her safe. Please? Will you do that for me?"

Private Briggs stared at him, as if a war between two opposing wills now battled in his mind.

"Sir?" he finally said, seeming to walk the tightrope between respect for his officer and speaking his mind. "I shouldn't be the one to marry her. We wouldn't be happy. But if you want my honest opinion, here it is. If you're so concerned with her well-being, then you should ask her yourself."

Jefferson looked away and fisted his hands at his sides. "Well, I don't want your honest opinion, Private Briggs. That'll be all. Good night."

They saluted each other, and Jefferson watched the private disappear inside his barracks. The weight on his chest doubled as he turned and walked away.

∞

The band played a sweet song in the back corner of the McGuigans' sitting room while officers and their wives sampled small cakes Annie had baked in the kitchen that day while the snow fell outside.

As the others laughed and joked with each other, enjoying the food and the chance to forget the worries surrounding the fort, Annie managed a smile and tried to focus on positive things. Like her growing friendship with these people, and the joy of the evening.

She'd try not to focus on the fact that she'd soon be heading back to Denver without a future.

Oh, in the days following Christopher's rejection, she'd prayed for help. She'd tried not to give up hope and had asked God for a soldier to show interest in her, but so far, there was nothing—and she needed to accept the fact that God's answer was no.

"Annie." Jefferson's hand landed gently on her shoulder as she sat in a wingback and listened to some of the lieutenants share stories.

She looked up and smiled at him. "Captain."

"I have something for you," he said, his tone hushed.

"Me too, for you." She got up from her chair and followed him away from the group until she could break off and retrieve the present from her room.

She hadn't gone out of her way to plan a gift for Jefferson—it just happened. A piece of her longed for their friendship to last beyond this time together at the fort, and she hoped a memento would at least remind him of her, if nothing else.

When she returned to the sitting room, she found him leaning a shoulder on the door separating the living quarters from the common meeting room. When they made eye contact, he pushed open the door and stepped through it. She hastened to follow.

The music and the din of the guests muffled as she closed the door behind her. Jefferson, his uniform pressed and his face shaved, looked every part the honorable captain he was, and tonight, there was a smoldering look in his eyes that nearly buckled her knees.

"You look beautiful tonight, Annie." His voice came soft and low, gliding over her like a warm spring.

She felt her cheeks heat beneath his gaze. "I made you something." She handed the gift to him. "For your trip."

He accepted it and also reached into his breast pocket before pulling out his own gift, small and wrapped in brown paper like hers. "I have yours here, though I didn't make it."

She smiled, letting him place his tiny gift in her hand, his fingers brushing hers. "You first," she whispered, uncertain what had stolen her voice.

He ran his hand over the brown paper, pausing before pulling back the ribbon and wrapping. His grin widened when he pulled out the scarf she had knitted from yarn she had brought from Denver.

"How'd you know I didn't have one? My old one has been chewed through by varmints, and I just haven't asked Caroline to make me another." A twinkle in his eye danced above a dimple in his cheek. "Now I won't have to. Thank you, Annie."

Somehow her name on his lips sent jitters straight to her toes. "You're welcome. It's cold in the West this time of year, so I hear."

He laughed softly. "Now, open yours."

She unfolded the ribbon and paper, noting something hard yet delicate beneath it. Pulling back the paper, she caught her breath at the sight of an ornate silver hair comb the size of her palm.

"Jefferson." Annie searched for words, her stare glued to the comb in her hand. "I—I can't believe... It's much too—"

"It was my mother's. I've held on to it a long time, and I thought you should have it."

Shaking her head, she stepped up to him. "I couldn't accept this. It's too extravagant to give to me."

"No, Annie, you put this comb to shame." He put his hands around hers, capturing the comb in her palm as if it were a butterfly. "You're worth a thousand of these combs and so much more besides."

Her heart pounded in her ears, his warm fingers against hers, and words so sweet coming from his lips. Lips she'd admired and longed for.

No, she couldn't think that way. He wasn't meant to be hers.

"Jefferson—"

"Annie, wait. Before you say anything, I need to ask you something." Swallowing, he searched her gaze. "Will you be my wife? I know I've asked you before, but I hope by now your opinion of me has changed and that you'll be willing to enter into a marriage with me."

Thoughts swirled around her, like she was caught in a cyclone. His words echoed in her ears, and her mouth ran dry.

With a gentle touch, he removed the comb from her hand and placed it in her hair; then he more fully captured her hands in his and took one knee. "Please, Annie?"

She wanted to. She wanted to so much. But there was so much to consider. "What of your plans to interview for the Department of the Interior?"

Brief hesitation billowed between them. "I might not get the position," he said. "Or I don't even have to take the interview. We could just stay here and do our work at the fort."

A burn began behind her eyes. "And is this proposal prompted by Private Briggs's refusal of me?"

He didn't speak. The hope in his eyes turned to anguish, and Annie knew the truth. The burn in her eyes gave forth to tears, and her heart turned to ashes.

"Please," he said, though a bit of his warmth had faded into desperation. "You deserve a devoted husband, and that's what I'll be to my dying day. We can work out the details later, but either way, you'll be safe and provided for. You won't have to go back to Denver. You'll never have to want for anything, including my attention." He rubbed her hands with his thumbs. "Please. I can give you a good life."

His words, all good. All noble. But they left a hollow place inside her that ached for more. Because this life would be provision at his expense.

"Jefferson, I have spent my whole life as a burden to someone else."

"Don't think of it that way."

What other way could she think of it? She could see in his eyes that his dreams hadn't changed, that he was setting them aside for her in haste and would soon come to regret it.

He was a good man, and she knew in her heart that she held deep affection for him. Maybe even loved him. Was it selfish to marry a man she loved if she knew he could never come to love her in the same way?

Yet what other choice did she have?

She gripped his hands, encouraging him to stand. "I will," she said, managing a smile. "Yes, I will marry you."

"Wonderful." He kissed her cheek before gently tugging her into a hug. But was there hesitation in his actions?

The McGuigans' door opened behind them. "Oh!" Caroline said, her feet skidding to a halt. "Sorry, I—"

"It's all right." Jefferson unwrapped Annie and took her hand. "You should be the first to know. We're now engaged."

Releasing a shriek, Caroline clapped her hands together before throwing her arms around her brother and then Annie. "I'm so happy! It's about time, you two." Laughing, she pulled on Jefferson's lapels. "Come on, let's tell everyone."

They moved toward the door, but as they neared it, Annie's palms began to sweat. She needed a minute. As they disappeared inside, she saw her escape, so she whirled toward the front door and pushed her way through, out into the snow.

Chapter Fifteen

Darkness swept over the horizon, the bugle having played taps an hour ago, sending the enlisted men to their bunks. Annie ducked her chin as a gust pushed snow up into her face. Though she shivered, she folded her arms and continued walking. Until her thoughts, her heartbeat, could settle, she needed time by herself to pray.

Had she made the right choice in choosing Jefferson? Shouldn't an engagement be joyous instead of laced with uncertainty?

As she reached the far corner of Jefferson's end of the commandants' quarters, she braced herself for a possible crosswind that could greet her between buildings.

Suddenly, two hands shot from around the building and grabbed her, yanking her off the path and pressing her against the plane of a man's chest. Under the eaves, they were shrouded in shadows. One hand snaked around her middle, while the other capped her mouth to keep her screams at bay.

"Don't say anything." The voice slithered into her ear. "Just my luck, finding you here in the dark. Shouldn't you be around a warm fireplace with your officer friends?" He chuckled, and his grip tightened. "I was disappointed when you didn't wear the red string around your wrist. Don't you want to be with me? I heard your courtship to Briggs is over."

Her eyes widened. The secret admirer. He stood in the flesh behind her, gripping her so close she nearly couldn't breathe.

"Well, you won't be single long. Not with curves like that. And I intend to have you before anyone else can." His voice grew close again—and vaguely familiar. "We'll make our escape tonight. You and me, into that field. Sounds grand, doesn't it? We'll catch a train and be long gone into Kansas before anyone suspects you're gone."

He began to tug her toward the field. Their snowy tracks would be visible for now, but would they get lost in the dried stalks and all the horse and cattle tracks that already marred the snow in the field?

She dug in her heels, snow wetting the stockings above her boots, but he pulled her along as if she weighed no more than a rag doll.

A rumbling laugh rolled from her assailant. "No use runnin', ma'am. You're helpless against me."

Helpless. Like she'd been when Mother had carried her pack for her. When Mother had fallen through the ice. When Grandfather only saw her as another mouth to feed, no matter how much she tried to earn his love.

Helpless, like when Martin died. When her search for a husband resulted in rejection. When she got herself engaged to a dear man who would ultimately resent her for holding him back.

She knew all too well the feeling of helplessness.

"You're worth a thousand of these combs and so much more besides."

Her eyes widened. The comb!

They reached the split rail fence. "You might as well stop fighting."

He gathered her up and ducked through the fence like he'd carried someone through a hole that size multiple times.

As he righted her on the other side, she steeled herself, lunged her hand into her hair, swiped the comb, and jabbed it over her head at what she hoped were his eyes.

Her comb met a target. He cried out, threw his head back—and let go just enough.

Annie wriggled away. A scream burst from her lungs as she dove for the fence. Slipping on her petticoats, she gripped the nearest rail for balance.

Hands yanked her back, and an angry growl filled her ears. "You little snake! I oughta—"

"Stop!"

Quick footfalls barreled through the snow. Guards were on their way. The man let go of her and started to run. She hurried for the fence as two uniformed soldiers ran past her into the field. Another man rounded the building ahead of her and had a comforting shape she immediately recognized.

"Annie!"

Jefferson's voice soothed over her as she slammed into his chest. His big arms enveloped her, saving her, and allowed her to finally breathe.

"When you didn't come back into the party, it took me awhile to find you," he said into her hair. "All the footprints in front of our quarters from the party guests. . . I started my search in the wrong direction—"

"It's all right," she murmured into his lapels, taking in his scent, his presence. "I should've known better than to go outside by myself." She exhaled a shaky breath. "For what it's worth, I think the danger is over."

"For you, anyway." Jefferson's voice came low and menacing. "For this fellow, however, it's just beginning." He tucked her into his arm and turned toward the walkway. "Let's get you inside."

As they reached the door to the commandants' quarters, the tussle behind them announced that the guards had caught their criminal. Annie looked over her shoulder and discovered Private Peyton strung up between the guards' strong arms. In the glow of moonlight, a jagged cut scraped across his face, from cheek to eyebrow.

She gasped, and Jefferson looked too. "Well, Carl Peyton." He turned, assuming his full height as the guards neared. "I guess everyone has their secrets. When we're through with you, yours is going to cost you dearly."

Private Peyton only glared at Annie as the guards carted him away toward the jailhouse.

She rested against Jefferson's side, and he put his arm around her again. "Your mother's comb," she said. "I used it to escape. I'm sorry, but I lost it out there—"

"Don't be sorry about that." He turned her to him and gently lifted her chin. "A comb is replaceable. You are not."

His words pinged in her heart, and she searched his stare for any hesitation—finding none.

Instead, his gaze lowered to her lips then back to her eyes as if asking her. Her heart stumbled, and she released a sigh, which must have been all the permission he needed. His lips landed on hers, needing her in a way she hungered for so desperately. She clung to his coat, and he pulled her closer; in that moment, she realized she never wanted to be anywhere else but here.

Epilogue

The middle of January brought a week of spring temperatures, enough to melt off the snow before turning chilly again. Annie lingered by the gate, pacing a stripe into the yellow grass as she waited for a coach to bring her some much-anticipated cargo.

Finally, a stagecoach came into view, coming from the direction of the train station. Her heart flipped as it neared and stopped, and the side door opened to reveal Jefferson returning from Fort Leavenworth.

Suitcase in hand, he thanked the driver then gave each guard a brief nod before setting his sights completely on her.

"You made it," she said as he reached her side.

"In one piece." He set his suitcase on the ground and pulled her into a hug. "I've missed you," he whispered.

"I've missed you too. Come on. Caroline has been checking the window every ten minutes today, watching for you."

"No doubt she wants to discuss wedding details," he said with a wink. "I should never have told her she could help."

Annie laughed. "You've been away for a month, so you have no reason to complain. I'm the one living with her."

"Good point." Eyes warming, he tugged her under his free arm as they walked. "But I'm not sure I want to see her yet. I think we need to have some time to talk first."

She nodded. "I do too. There's a lot I have to say."

"Me too." Jefferson turned to look at her. "I'm sorry I made you feel as if I were only offering you marriage because Martin made me promise to care for you."

She raised her gaze to meet his, the sorrowful expression there clenching her gut. "Was there another reason?"

"Yes." His hands cupped her face, and he stared at her as if he didn't care one bit that they stood in the middle of the fort where all could see his vulnerability. "Annie Moreau, I've bungled my way through our fragile relationship from the beginning, and it's no wonder you thought my intentions improperly motivated. But know this—while there are many ways to provide for a woman that don't include marriage, it would have killed me to do that for you."

Her heart trembled. "Because. . . ?"

"Because I fell in love with you as I wrote Martin's letters. I know it crossed a line, and I did my very best to smother my affection for you when you were engaged to him. So much, in fact, that even after he died, it took me a long time to allow my feelings to surface. I'm truly sorry."

He pressed a tender kiss to her forehead, and she closed her eyes. His words ran over her like a cool water current, soothing yet strong, shoring up the decision she'd made for their future while he was away. Now she was certain what she was about to tell him was the right thing to do.

"My love for you is real," he said against her skin. "And I don't care if we live here at Fort Garland, or in some uncharted location, or on the moon. The messiness of our goals and dreams—we'll figure them out. They don't have to come between us."

"I feel the same way. And I know which choice is right for us."

"The right choice *is* us," he said, passion lacing every word. "I'm not going to take the interview."

She met his firm stare, matching it with her own. "Oh yes you are."

"People's dreams can change, Annie, and you're my dream now."

"And you're mine. Don't you see? I have my soldier, whether we're here or on some ridge in the Rockies." She reached up and touched his face, his dark stubble grazing her fingertips. "I've realized something while you were gone. You're honorable, understanding. You're aware of my needs and try hard to meet them. And I long to do the same for you. I'm not letting you give up surveying for me, Jefferson Gray. Not this time."

"Annie—"

"It took me a long time to realize it, but you don't see me as a burden but as your partner. I know I can do anything, even come alongside you in the wilderness."

He moved his thumbs along her jaw. "Are you sure?"

Hope traced his words, and she realized that even through all her searching for a man who would love and protect her, this one had won her heart from the beginning—from the words he'd penned for Martin. "I've never been surer of anything. Except that I love and trust you with all that I am. No matter what we do or where we go, I'll spend the rest of my life proving it to you."

Jefferson grinned, so she lifted her face and kissed him with a fervency that she prayed showed she meant every last word.